C000145358

FACING THE SUN

SUN-BLESSED TRILOGY ✳ BOOK ONE

CAROL BETH ANDERSON

Facing the Sun by Carol Beth Anderson

Published by
Eliana Press
P.O. Box 2452
Cedar Park, TX 78630
www.carolbethanderson.com

Copyright © 2018 by Carol Beth Anderson
Excerpt from *Facing the Gray* by Carol Beth Anderson, Copyright © 2018 by Carol Beth
Anderson

All rights reserved. No portion of this book may be reproduced in any form without
permission from the publisher, except as permitted by U.S. copyright law. For
permissions contact:
beth@carolbethanderson.com

Cover by Mariah Sinclair
Edited by Sonnet Fitzgerald

Paperback ISBN: 978-1-949384-00-0

First Edition

BE AN INSIDER

Insiders get updates on Carol Beth Anderson's books, plus early cover and title reveals, notifications of sales, and more. Sign up at carolbethanderson.com!

To Leah Faye, who believed any situation was improved with generous servings of food.

And to Jason, who loved his mother so well.

CHARACTERS AND PLACES

The Malin (MAY-lin) Family
Jevva (JEV-uh), father
Mey, mother
Misty, daughter
Tavi (TAH-vee), short for Tavina (Tuh-VEE-nuh), daughter, all-blessed
Other children: Zakry, Jona, Tess, Seph, Ista (EE-stuh)

The Holmin Family
Shem, father
Jilla, mother (Jevva Malin's sister)
Narre (NARR-ee), daughter, touch-blessed
Other children: Elim (EE-lim), Gillun

The Almson Family
Hilda, mother
Sall (SAHL), son, mind-blessed
Other children: Lorn, Berroll (BEAR-ull), nickname Berr (BEAR)

The Minnalen (MINN-uh-len) Family
Runan (ROO-nahn), father

Reba, daughter, sight-blessed

At the Midwife House in Oren
Note: The surname "Kariana" indicates that a midwife is a sun-blessed Karian (KARR-ee-an) midwife who can give blessing breaths to babies born facing the sun. Practical midwives are not sun-blessed.
Ellea Kariana (ell-LAY-uh kar-ee-AH-nuh), Karian midwife
Pala (PALL-uh) Rinner, practical midwife
Nydine (ny-DEEN), meditation teacher

The Grays
Konner Burrell (Bew-RELL), ungifted banker
Ash, real name Jerash Sheaver (JARE-ash SHAY-ver), touch-blessed
Sella, sight-blessed
Aldin (ALL-din), stride-blessed
Camalyn (CAM-uh-lin) Hunt, speech-blessed

At the Meadow
Tullen (TUHL-lin), stride-blessed and hearing-blessed
Kley, Tullen's father
Jenevy (JEH-neh-vee), Tullen's friend

Other Characters
Briggün Nolin, nickname Brig, mayor of Oren
Brindi (BRIN-dee), barmaid in Benton, mind-blessed
Gerval (GER-vul), pub owner in Oren
Les Andisis (an-DIE-sis), safety officer, hearing-blessed
Meri (MARE-ee), healer
Mola Ronson, Cormina Councillor
Relin (RAY-lin) the Fierce, ancient hero
Remina Birge (Reh-MY-nuh BERJ), Cormina Councillor, hearing-blessed
Riami Sheaver (ree-AH-me SHAY-ver), Jerash's wife, speech-blessed
Tisra (TISS-ruh), maid
Zagada (zuh-GEY-duh), touch-blessed man

Religious Names and Terms

Sava (SAH-vuh), the giver of life, magic, and all that is good

Kari (KARR-ee), the First Midwife who tamed magic when she gave her newborn son Savala a breath of life and blessing

Savala (SAH-vuh-luh), Kari's son, touch-blessed, the First Shepherd and first recipient of tamed magic. The city of Savala is named after him.

Karite (KARR-ite), a sect of the Savani faith

Kovus, a place of punishment in the afterlife

Savani (suh-VAH-nee), the faith of those who worship Sava

Savanite (SAH-vuh-nite), one who worships Sava

Senniet (SENN-yet), a place of peace and joy in the afterlife

Places

Benton, a town in Cormina

Cormina (core-MY-nuh), a nation led by the Cormina Council

Kovus, a place of punishment in the afterlife

Oren, a town in Cormina

Savala (SAH-vuh-luh), the capital city of Cormina, named after the First Shepherd

Senniet (SENN-yet), a place of peace and joy in the afterlife

Tinawe (TINN-uh-way), a large city in Cormina

The Meadow, a closed community thirty miles from Oren

PROLOGUE

I REMEMBER that birth with more clarity than any other I attended. Even inconsequential details of that home, on that day, are written on my memory with indelible ink. Running, squealing children playing in front of the house as I arrived. The smell of freshly cut wood piled by the front door. Soot stains on the wall around the fireplace, the knot in the floorboard I felt through my shoe, the squeak of the front door as it was thrown open.

At first I didn't recognize the girl who answered my knock. We stared at one another for a long moment before I exclaimed, "Misty!"

She was twelve years old, and it seemed that overnight, she had become a young woman. But when she gave me that big smile of hers and said, "I think the baby is a girl," she again looked like the child I knew.

I returned Misty's smile then waved to her father, who had fetched me from the midwife house. Jevva took the gesture as permission to leave. He would go fishing during this birth as he did each time his wife was in labor. I think he could not bear to see her in pain. With her father gone, Misty brought me to the bedroom where her mother waited. She then returned to her siblings outside.

I entered Mey's room, and she opened her arms. Embracing her, I whispered, "Hello, strong mother." At that moment, a birth pain hit, and she held onto me, pressing her head into my chest and swaying. It was clear her labor was already advanced.

When the pain passed, Mey turned to me in tears. "I'm glad you're here," she told me. It is those four words that brought me into midwifery. I love babies, but I chose my profession because I love women. Mey's six older children had all been born into my hands, and she had long ago claimed a special spot in my heart.

Soon after I arrived, Mey began to talk through the pain, as she had done during every one of her labors. "Ohhh, my child, come," she said, her voice rhythmic, vowels extended. "You know what to do. You were made for this. Come, child, come." It makes me smile, even now—that sweet invitation, a cry of pain and love.

The morning passed in the timeless manner characteristic of labor. The pains continued to strengthen, and in between two of them, I asked Mey my favorite question for a laboring mother. "What is your hope for this child?"

She did not even have to think about the answer. "I hope my child is kind," she said, "and I hope my child is strong." She paused and added, "And I know I shouldn't hope for it, but I have always wanted one of my children to be born facing the sun."

I smiled. "Nearly every mother shares that desire," I said, palpating her abdomen to determine her child's position. "From what I can tell, this baby is facing your side. Likely it will turn to face the earth before emerging, and that is the easiest position—for you and for baby."

Mey glanced out the window toward her six other children, all of whom had been born without complication, face-down. I knew as soon as her child was born, Mey would be filled with such joy, she would forget she'd hoped for a sun-blessed babe.

The house became stuffier and warmer as the afternoon wore on, and at some point Mey began leaning out the window between her pains, her arms folded against the sill, the summer breeze cooling her skin. Even now I can picture her face, still so young, lit by a slight smile as the wind tangled her hair.

It was through this window that Mey heard two of her younger children bickering. She was breathing deeply through a difficult pain. As it diminished, she spoke in a voice so low, I had to get close to hear her. "Please tell them if they don't stop," she said, "they may not survive the afternoon." Suppressing a laugh, I repeated those exact words to them, and they ran off as quickly as their small legs could carry them.

Not long after that, Mey lifted her gown over her head, threw it on the bed, and continued to pace. Any modesty had faded away during hours of purposeful agony. And why should she be ashamed? Mey, pacing naked in her bedroom, was lovely. As every mother is.

I suspected Mey's sudden lack of reserve signaled a progression in her labor. Sure enough, when the next pain hit, the sounds coming from her mouth changed. Words had long ago become moans, and now moans became grunts, arising from deep within her. When the pain passed, I asked, "Time to push?"

"Yes," she said, her voice both determined and desperate.

"Good," I said. And when I smiled at her, her tired face found the strength to smile back.

On the next pain, Mey turned, putting both her hands on my shoulders, guiding me to my knees as she squatted in front of me. She held onto me as if I were the one tree still standing in a storm, and as she pushed, she roared.

But though Mey was ready, her child was not. It had been years since Mey had needed to push more than a few times to birth a child, but an hour passed, then another half hour, and still her baby did not emerge.

Mey's pushing continued with little progress. When I saw discouragement taking hold of her, I summoned my gift. Magic filled my hands, glowing with a golden light. I touched Mey's tense shoulders. In seconds, she was awash in peace, and she was ready for the next pain—or at least as ready as any expectant mother can be.

As I pulled my hands away and released my magic, there was a soft tap on the door. "Mama? Can I come in?"

Mey told me to open the door, and Misty entered. She did not talk to her mother. Instead, placing her hands on Mey's rounded abdomen, Misty spoke to the child inside. "I'm your sister. We're all so excited to meet you. I can't wait to hold you and teach you things. I'll always be there for you." And I believed her, believed she would do anything for the child that was coming.

Misty left, and I saw great peace on her mother's face. Yes, my magic had comforted Mey, but Misty's visit had helped her even more. Her oldest child had reminded Mey that her youngest child would be born into a family characterized by love.

Still the labor continued. I was as surprised as Mey when the gold and crimson light of sunset filled the sky. Her pains had begun before sunrise, and now I was lighting lanterns. Mey had by then been pushing for three hours.

She looked at the sky and said one word. "Beautiful." Then, as if the dying sun had renewed her strength, Mey pushed harder than she had in hours, and my hands at last guided the child's head out of its mother's body.

Mey's eyes, which had been glazed, burst to life again. Her teeth, which had ground together in effort, separated in a joyful smile.

But I could not speak. The head that had just emerged was still covered in its bag of waters. And Mey could not see that yet. Nor could she see the child's face, pressed against the sac that had been its home. Face-up. Facing the sun.

Mey examined my face, and her expression shifted from triumph to concern. "Is everything all right? Is the baby well?"

I gathered my wits and smiled. "Yes, all is well. On the next pain, you will hold your baby, and it will be born in its bag of waters."

With an expression of awe, Mey touched her child's head, covered in the smooth sac. I don't quite believe any of the old traditions about a baby born en caul. I didn't expect that Mey's child would be more fortunate than any other, or would be a strong swimmer. But such a birth seemed extra-miraculous, the infant reminding us of its mysterious first home, within a sac in its mother's womb.

When the next pain swelled, my hands guided the baby out of its mother, into the warm summer air. Mey watched in awe as I pulled the sac off the child's face and body. I then handed the slippery babe to its mother. Heedless of the dirty floor, of her nakedness, of the fluid puddling under her, of everything except the new creation she had just birthed, Mey brought her newest child to her chest. The room filled with the cries of mother and baby.

Mey exclaimed, "I have a daughter!" I laughed; I had not even thought to check, so focused had I been on removing the sac and on the child's position at birth.

I touched Mey's shoulder. "There is something else I want to tell you," I said. "Your daughter"—and my voice caught; this moment never got old—"your daughter was born facing the sun."

Mey froze for a moment. Then she was again crying, and she pulled me to her in an embrace, the baby, now quiet, between us. "She is sun-blessed?" Mey asked. "Truly?"

"En caul and sun-blessed. What a lovely birth. What a special child."

Mey was so focused on her new baby; she was barely aware of me as I cut the child's cord. Then I spoke. "You did your part beautifully today," I told her. "It's time for me to do mine."

She handed me her daughter and watched in wonder as I held the baby face-up on my forearm, head cradled in my hand. Light from a lantern fell on us, and the little one promptly squeezed her eyes shut. "Sun-blessed child," I said in a low voice, "in the name of Sava, who giveth the breath of life, I give thee the breath of blessing."

My mouth covered the infant's nose and mouth, and her tiny chest rose as my breath entered her lungs.

After she received her blessing breath, the baby's chest glowed with a strong, golden light that put the lantern to shame. The glow spread up her neck, up both cheeks, and then around her eyes, like a mask. "She is sight-blessed," I said, and Mey laughed with joy.

I opened my mouth to tell Mey what she might expect as her child grew, but the words stopped in my throat as I saw the glow on the baby's chest spreading again—this time down her legs and into her feet, all the way to the tips of her toes. "Stride-blessed as well," I said. Excitement filled the air between Mey and me. Twice-blessed!

And then I did not know where to look, because the golden light moved in all directions: down her arms, to her hands. Up the sides of her neck, to her ears. Up the front of her neck, then filling her lips, her nose. It was as if the glow were itself alive, breathing, spreading under the child's skin. As suddenly as it had started, the movement stopped, and I forgot to breathe as I lifted the babe, supporting her head, examining all sides of her. There was no part of her that was not glowing golden, from the bottoms of her feet to every strand of hair, which shone through its blackness.

My arms jolted when the newborn wailed again, and I handed her to her mother, who looked as if she didn't know whether to cry or sing or faint. Instinct took over, and Mey held the baby's mouth to her breast. The infant suckled greedily. As she ate, the glow faded, and she looked like any newborn eating her first meal.

Mey and I raised our heads to look in each other's eyes. She wet her lips with her tongue. "What . . . Why . . . ?" was all she could manage.

"I don't know," I said. "I don't know."

One question filled my mind: *Who is this child?*

-From *Midwife Memoirs* by Ellea Kariana

CHAPTER ONE

The autumn festival in Oren is the most popular festival of the year. We midwives host it, and we work for months, arranging the details of the feast, the games, and the children's music.

Yet I think we could skip all this, and the town would still gather. For at its heart the autumn festival is not about food, games, or songs. It is an exuberant, joyful celebration of magic. And I love it.

-From Small-Town Cormina: A Midwife's Reflections *by Ellea Kariana*

THE WOMAN'S voice rose in a haunting melody, her wordless music captivating the crowd. Though the singer's mouth shone with a golden glow, no one watched her face. Instead, every eye was focused on a small, green plant, peeking above the top of a large pot at the singer's feet.

As the song swelled, the sprout began to vibrate, a movement barely visible to those watching. A leaf emerged from the sprout. The plant continued to flourish, moving in harmony with the exquisite notes of the song. The stalk grew wider as it rose higher, and more leaves pushed themselves into the air, reaching toward the light of the autumn sun.

In time, the end of the thick vine wound itself around the waist of the singer, then up her back. As her song's last refrain saturated the air, the vine stopped growing above the woman's shoulder, and a large flower of vibrant pink and orange sprouted there.

The crowd broke their silence. Their cheers filled the street, and the singer laughed in delight, her mouth still glowing. The ovation continued, and the woman bowed as well as she could, considering the vine that still embraced her.

At last, the applause diminished. A dozen more notes left the singer's mouth, these dissonant and harsh. At the jarring tones, the vine dried up so completely that the woman easily snapped the portion around her waist. She stepped away, and once again, the crowd cheered.

Tavi Malin's palms stung from her enthusiastic clapping, but she continued to applaud until she was interrupted by a hand tugging at her arm. Her best friend Reba Minnalen guided her down the street.

Once they were away from the loud applause, Reba spoke. "I've heard that woman charges farmers such a high price, she only has to work a few weeks a year! She can cause an entire season's worth of growth in a single day. She's one of the wealthiest people in Tinawe."

"I believe it," Tavi responded. "Not many speech-blessed people can make plants grow. My mother would give anything for her to come to our garden! And her voice—it's beautiful!" She looked to the side of the road. "Let's stop here," she said. "I love Nem's smoke stories."

Unlike the singer, who was visiting from a large city, Nem was local to the town of Oren. He was touch-blessed, and his magic allowed him to mold smoke into whatever shape he wished. It wasn't a practical gift, but that didn't seem to bother Nem. Whenever he had the chance, he entertained anyone who would watch. He had built a fire at the edge of the street, and now he stood above it, telling a story while forming the smoke into airy, animated illustrations.

Tavi and Reba had missed the beginning of Nem's story, but they knew it well. It was the tale of Savala's life. It was appropriate, as the day's autumn festival was held in honor of Savala's birthday.

Because Savala had been the first to tame magic—with the help of his mother Kari, who had given him a breath of blessing at birth—his annual festival was a celebration of all things magical. On this day, many of the town's Blessed loved to show off their gifts, which were usually used for more mundane tasks (or, in Nem's case, not used much at all.)

As Nem told the story of Savala's awakening, Tavi watched it play out. Savala, created out of gray smoke, used one of his gifted hands to heal his foot, which had been pricked by a thorn.

Again, Tavi felt a pull on her arm. "This is for children," Reba said.

"There are adults here too!" Tavi protested.

"They're all parents."

Tavi looked around and saw that Reba was right. With a small sigh, she walked away with her friend. At twelve years old, perhaps she was meant to have outgrown her love of stories.

Reba pointed down the street. "Let's go watch Zagada!" she said, pulling her friend with her.

Zagada was touch-blessed, just as Nem was. Zagada's gift, however, was more practical. Exceptional strength filled his hands. He earned his living through construction, but he seemed to enjoy these street shows more than anything. He lifted a massive boulder over his head, pretending to struggle with it for the sake of the children in the audience.

Tavi watched Zagada's act every year, but she still gasped and jumped when he pretended he was about to throw the boulder into the crowd. Embarrassed, Tavi looked around. She was relieved to see that most of the other spectators had been startled too.

As she scanned the crowd, Tavi found a pair of eyes on her. She shifted her gaze away and whispered to Reba, "Mayor Nolin is standing over there." When Reba's head turned to find him, Tavi said, "Don't look at him! He's already staring at me; I don't want any more of his attention."

Reba frowned. "Why don't you like him?"

9

"He's the one who arranged for our house to get indoor plumbing —for free," Tavi said. "Remember?"

"And you don't like him because he gave your family a gift?"

"That's not it. I just don't trust him. I don't see why he would have done that for us. Misty says politicians never give anything away without wanting something in return." Seeing Reba's shrug, Tavi added, "Besides, his teeth are too straight and too white."

Laughing, Reba said, "I think his teeth are perfect!"

"I heard," Tavi said, "that there's a touch-blessed woman in Tinawe who uses her gift to straighten teeth and whiten them. I heard he visited her, and it was very painful, and very expensive."

Reba's eyes grew wide. "I didn't even know that was possible!" She ran her tongue over the front of her teeth.

"Don't even think about it!" Tavi said. "Your smile is perfect. Even if it weren't, you don't see me planning to move these down." She pointed at her top canines, which had both come in higher on her gums than they should have, crowded out by other teeth. "I think he looks like he's trying too hard to be handsome."

"Well," Reba said dreamily, her eyes finding the mayor, "it's working."

When Zagada's act ended, the crowd applauded. Mayor Briggun Nolin rushed to Zagada and put his arm around the young man. "Excuse me," the mayor called in a polished voice. "If I could have your attention for a few moments, please?"

The mayor's voice was audible over the crowd's murmurs, thanks to a touch-blessed woman who held her hand on his back. She had the gift of voice amplification, and she often accompanied the mayor at public events. If he wanted, he could whisper and still be heard by everyone. But it wasn't in Mayor Nolin's nature to whisper.

The crowd quieted, and the mayor continued, "What talent we have in Oren! Let's give Zagada another round of applause." He allowed them to clap for several seconds before holding out his hands to stop them. "I am also honored that one of our young Blessed is here today. I know we are all waiting for the awakening of our very own all-blessed resident, Tavina Malin!"

He gestured to Tavi, and every person in the crowd turned toward her. Then they began to clap. Tavi felt her stomach twist with dread and her face fill with the heat of a thousand suns. She tried to escape, but every direction was already filled by smiling faces and clapping hands. Faces looking at her, and hands clapping for her.

The crowd had Tavi hemmed in, but they shifted for Mayor Nolin. He made his way through them toward Tavi. She hadn't thought this moment could get any worse, but it did. The mayor approached her, put his hand on her shoulder, and steered her toward the makeshift performance area.

Walking with the mayor was the last thing Tavi desired, but she found herself doing it anyway. Her mortification grew with every step. Then they were both in front of the crowd—the mayor smiling, his white teeth glistening, his hand waving; and Tavi, her lips pressed together, eyes wide, arms folded, trying to hold back embarrassed tears.

Mayor Nolin was talking, but Tavi absorbed little of it. Something about the bright future of Oren and Tavi's place in it. She might have heard more if she hadn't been silently begging him to stop. *Please, please, let go of my shoulder and let me get away from here. Let me do something more enjoyable, like be with my friends or eat a snack or pluck feathers off chicken carcasses—anything but this.*

Her silent pleas went unheeded. At last the mayor's speech ended, and the crowd dispersed. Tavi escaped without another word.

Tavi soothed her humiliation by getting four cookies from the dessert table. As she ate them, Reba tried to console her.

"He was just trying to honor you," Reba said. "Just think—maybe a year from now you and I will be performing at the autumn festival." She sounded excited at the prospect.

Tavi shook her head. "I wouldn't want to. And who knows if our gifts will have awakened by then?"

Reba looked down at her figure, which had shifted in the previous year, the hard lines of childhood softening and swelling into a more womanly shape. "I don't think it will be too much longer for me." She glanced at Tavi's small form. "It'll take longer for you. But just imagine it! People will crowd around us like they did for Zagada, and we can share our magic with the world."

"We don't even know if we'll have anything worth sharing," Tavi said.

"Don't be ridiculous," Reba said. "Of course everyone will want to see you show off your gifts. And I have high hopes for my sight gift too. Maybe I'll be able to tame wild animals just by looking at them. I heard a story about a sight-blessed woman who could do that. Can you imagine? I could own stables full of horses I tamed!" She laughed.

Tavi's vision of the future wasn't so optimistic. Yes, they would both see their gifts awaken, but would they be powerful? Reba was sight-blessed, the most common gifting. There was a reason most sight-blessed individuals did not demonstrate their magic at the autumn festival. The gifts usually weren't all that impressive.

And what about me? Tavi thought. Maybe she would be different. Everyone seemed to think so. But no one, least of all Tavi, even knew what *all-blessed* meant. Perhaps she would have magic so diluted throughout her body that it was useless. Or possibly she would have unprecedented gifting, and everyone would expect her to do amazing things for them. Tavi wasn't sure which extreme scared her the most.

Tavi felt Reba's eyes on her, but didn't know how to respond. Misty approached them. Relieved, Tavi told her older sister, "I'm ready to go home."

"I'll walk with you," Misty said. She and Tavi said goodbye to Reba before beginning their walk home.

They strolled along the dirt streets of Oren and soon exited the town proper. The sisters had the road to themselves, and Tavi silently reflected on the mayor's actions and Reba's words. After a few minutes, Misty said, "I heard what happened."

"Word spreads quickly."

Misty touched a hand to her sister's tight shoulder. "You must have been embarrassed. Can you talk to me about it?"

Tavi told her sister about the scene the mayor had made. "Every person in that crowd was staring at me, like everyone always does," Tavi said. "I'm so sick of strangers wondering when my gifts will awaken. I think they're convinced that if they look at me long enough, I'll suddenly sprout breasts and shoot fire out of my eyes."

Misty laughed. "I'm sure that's not what they're thinking."

"Reba tried to help, but she didn't understand," Tavi said, telling Misty of Reba's hopes for their future magical development. "Everyone expects my gifts to be so impressive, but they have no way of knowing that."

Misty threw a sidelong glance her way. "Is everything all right with you and Reba?"

Tavi sighed. "She's . . . changing."

Misty raised her eyebrows. "Changing?"

"She's so much taller than me now, and she's getting curves." With her hands, Tavi outlined an impossible hourglass figure in the air—a shape that didn't in the least resemble her friend. "She talks about our gifts awakening all the time. She's not as fun as she was. She's . . . leaving me behind."

"You and Reba only have a few years to be children, and the rest of your lives to be old and responsible. You should both enjoy this while you can."

"Easy for you to say. By the time you were my age, I bet you already looked like a woman."

"A lot of good it did me." Misty ruefully looked at her full figure, then at her wrist. She was twenty-four and did not yet wear a wedding bracelet. "You will grow up. And Reba is right about one thing—with your gifts, you'll be able to do anything you want."

"You can't know that!" Tavi's voice was shrill. "I might end up with less impressive magic than anyone who's ever lived! I'll be filled to the brim with weak magic, in a body that looks like it belongs to a nine-year-old boy!"

Misty stopped walking, and Tavi followed suit. The dirt road was empty and quiet. "Tavi," Misty said. She took her sister's slender shoulders in her hands and looked into her eyes. "I do expect you to be someone very special when you awaken. But you are already very special now, and it has nothing to do with being all-blessed! You are one of the smartest people I know. Your heart is generous. And you didn't slap the mayor, so you must have some self-control too."

Tavi laughed and found herself enveloped in Misty's soft, strong arms. She melted into them, finding comfort from the sister who was more like a second mother. When she felt the familiar warmth in her body, she pulled back.

Holding her sister's hands, Tavi uttered a peaceful sigh as light shone from her skin, intensifying to a bright, golden glow, as if the sun itself lent her some of its brilliance. Her whole body shone as it had twelve years before when the midwife had first given her a breath of blessing. The glow held no power, not yet, but it was a delicious hint of what was waiting to awaken. Tavi looked at Misty, whose face held a familiar expression of awe and wistfulness.

Smiling, Tavi gazed down at the warm glow radiating even through her dress. Suddenly, her shoulders drooped, and the light shining from her whole body faded to nothingness.

"What's wrong?" Misty asked.

"Oh. I lost my focus. I was feeling so content, and then . . ." She shrugged. Misty waited, and Tavi continued. "Well, I looked down at my glowing chest, and I thought how much nicer that light would look if it were shining from two hills instead of one flat plain."

Misty burst into laughter, and she put her arm around her sister's shoulder as they continued down the road.

CHAPTER TWO

Anger can be a tool of justice
Or a weapon of vengeance.
Will you master your anger,
Or will it master you?

-From Proverbs of Savala

JERASH SAT at the back of the store, on the floor, leaning against a table leg. The door rattled as someone attempted to open it. He was losing business, and he did not care.

He held a small piece of clay, and his hands shone with golden light as he molded and remolded it, making miniature pots and cups and bowls, his fingers moving so quickly that they blurred together. Then he moved on to sculptures—a chicken, an ant, his wife's face.

Jerash looked at the face of clay in his palm. It looked so real; he had captured her perfect lips, and the way her eyes squinted when she smiled. He breathed her name. "Riami."

And then he cried. He buried his face in his hands, smashing the clay against his cheek, where it soaked up his tears. "Riami."

It had been four hours since he'd closed the store so he could go home and fetch a vase from the small workshop at the back of his house. A customer was buying its twin and wanted a matching set.

In minutes, Jerash had arrived at the workshop behind his house. He had been about to open the door when he'd seen movement in the window of their bedroom. Too much movement, and too much flesh.

His first inclination had been to look away; what he was seeing should be private. But that was his wife in there, and there should be nothing hidden between them, nothing at all. When had Riami started keeping secrets? And, oh Sava, who was she with?

Jerash later regretted not staying long enough to discern who the man was, but instead he had run, horrified, back to the street and all the way to the shop, where he had given his confused customer a convoluted lie about a broken vase. As soon as the customer had left, Jerash had locked the door, picked up a piece of clay, and sat on the rough floor, where he had been ever since.

He forced himself to stop weeping and to stop working the clay. He released his gift, and the glow in his hands faded. Jerash's tolerance for magic was high; he could work for a long time without resting. But he had been using his touch gift for hours, and his body was feeling drained. He needed energy to walk home. It was almost closing time. He needed to go to Riami.

The clock tower struck six. Jerash stood up and exited the shop. His eyes were already sore from tears, and the cold wind stung them further. He blinked several times, locked the door, and began to walk.

"I CAME HOME this afternoon for a vase," Jerash said. He had not planned this confrontation, and that was all he could think to say.

Riami was cutting potatoes, and her knife stopped as she looked up. "Oh?" she replied, and her voice was strained. "I didn't see you."

"I saw you," Jerash said. "Both of you."

Her face crumpled, and she began to cry. "I'm sorry."

His heart lifted. They could move past this; she was sorry, and he would find a way to forgive.

Her trembling voice continued in between sobs. "I can't help it, Jerash. I'm in love with him, and I can't change that."

Jerash stopped breathing. He only knew he was still alive because he could feel his heartbeat, not just in his chest, but in his head and his hands.

"You can't see him again," he croaked.

Riami cried harder, and he wondered how it was that she looked so lovely when she wept, her beautiful lips spread wide, her brown eyes glistening, and her black braid shaking with each sob. "I'm sorry," she wailed. "I can't change this. I'm so sorry."

Her last words were barely audible past the pounding in his head, and past his breathing, which was urgent and desperate. He had to change this; he had to do something.

Jerash grabbed Riami's shoulders and pushed her against the wall, and he kissed his wife.

But this was not Riami. Riami, whose speech-blessed mouth glowed as she spoke exquisite poetry to express her love. Riami, who interrupted kisses with laughter, unable to contain her pure joy in life, in Jerash.

This woman could not be Riami, for she was fighting him, her perfect hands pushing against his chest. He pulled his mouth away and watched as his hands moved to her neck. He would swear to himself afterward that his actions had surprised him as much as they had surprised Riami—and yet when he saw her neck held lightly in his hands, he did not move.

He kissed her again, but when her hands rose, trying to pry his fingers off her neck, he knew she did not want this, did not want him.

Jerash continued to kiss Riami, inhaling her breath deep into his own lungs, and then he felt her breath stop. He pulled his head back in confusion, and it took a moment for him to realize his fingers had tightened around her neck. He saw her scratching and pulling at his hands, his arms, but he could not feel the red gouges on his skin. Then her hands fell; her eyes were glassy, and her body was limp.

17

Still Jerash stayed there, his hands a vise around her neck, for long minutes. At last he loosened his hands and stepped away.

He stumbled backward as Riami's body slumped to the floor. "No," he said. "No. No. No." He crashed into the table.

Suddenly, the skin above his lungs felt as if it were on fire. He pulled his shirt off and looked down. The center of his chest glowed a dull gray, like a storm cloud in front of the sun. Jerash watched in horror as the gray light spread to both sides, and he cried out for the pain of it. He flung both arms wide as it spread down his biceps, his forearms.

Then his sun-blessed hands were burning with gray fire, and he realized he was once again sobbing, in confusion and grief and pain. The moment he had released Riami's neck, he had known he had damned himself to eternity in Kovus. Now, with magical heat searing his hands, it felt as if he were there already.

His chest felt the relief first, and Jerash again looked down, watching as his skin tone returned to normal, a bit at a time, until even his hands were again empty of light and fire.

He stood still for one full minute, trying to get enough air into his lungs. Then he put his shirt on and stuffed whatever he could into a sack—a change of clothes, bread and cheese and sausage, and, finally, Riami's wedding bracelet, pulled from her cool wrist.

Jerash fled into the gray wind.

CHAPTER THREE

When you visit a woman who has just become a mother for the first time, remember that what she needs most is not medical care. She needs your words of encouragement, your gentle touch, your belief in her. Your love.

In fact, these needs are not unique to new mothers. If you are fortunate enough to train sun-blessed students, give them the same care.

New mothers and gifted students are all strong, and they are all fragile.

-*From* Midwifery: A Manual for Practical and Karian Midwives *by Ellea Kariana*

"GOOD AFTERNOON, DREAMERS," Ellea Kariana greeted the small group gathered around the kitchen table in the midwife house. "I hope your week is going well."

Tavi smiled. She looked forward to her awakening, when Ellea would become one of her primary magic instructors. For now, Tavi enjoyed every minute she spent with the town's head midwife.

"I would like to introduce you to my newest apprentice," Ellea continued. "Pala Rinner is training to be a practical midwife, and she has also studied magical theology at Savala University. She will give your lecture today, and I know you will give her the attention and courtesy she deserves." Ellea pointedly looked at Reba, who rarely held back in expressing her opinions on their weekly lecture topics or on the people who taught them. "She should be here any minute," Ellea assured them as she left the kitchen.

As soon as Ellea left, Reba huffed. "A practical midwife?"

Next to her, Sall Almson protested. "Practical midwives are very important! They're often more skilled than Karian midwives. The only thing they can't do is give blessing breaths." Sall's mother had been a practical midwife for several years before leaving the profession.

"That's not the only thing they can't do," Reba argued. "They also can't do magic. How is she supposed to teach us anything about magic if she doesn't have any experience with it?"

From the doorway behind Reba, a woman's voice interjected. "I can teach you about magic because I have studied it for years—and I have just as much experience doing magic as you do. Now let's get started."

Pala was middle-aged, older than Tavi had expected. Her appearance matched her voice, sturdy and stern. She began her lecture. It was informative, accurate, and incredibly boring. Pala was reviewing information they all knew. She waxed on about magic's inherent goodness. Then she talked about Sava's divine sovereignty and his unwillingness to allow the Blessed to use their gifts in unacceptable ways.

The fourth student in the room, Narre Holmin, dozed off. Pala snapped her fingers next to Narre's ear and chuckled when the girl started. Maybe this stern instructor did have a sense of humor.

After half an hour of theological minutiae, Pala instructed them, "You will have ten minutes to discuss this question: Would Sava ever allow magic to be used in a way that results in someone's harm? Please stay on topic." She gathered her notes and left the room.

"I can't believe I fell asleep!" Narre whispered.

Tavi let out the laugh she'd been holding in since Narre's short nap had ended. "I can't believe the rest of us stayed awake!"

Sall spoke up, louder than the girls. "Sava, in his divine knowledge, may occasionally allow magic to be used to harm. He would, however, have a greater good in mind."

The three girls all stared at Sall, and he nodded his head thoughtfully. After a second, he looked toward the doorway, which he could see from his side of the table. "Close call; Pala was checking on us," he whispered.

Narre smirked at Sall. "Good thing we have you to protect us from the midwives' wrath."

"I'm quite sure Pala doesn't display wrath." Sall grinned. "She exhibits well-modulated indignation."

Tavi laughed. Sall spoke with the words of an adult and the high voice of a child. He was just a few months younger than her, but strangers always underestimated his age. Sall was short, with narrow shoulders and skinny limbs. Similar to her, come to think of it.

Thanks to Sall, I probably won't be the last to awaken in our group, Tavi thought. It didn't seem fair that the timing of one's awakening was tied so closely to physical development. If it were up to her, other qualities would prompt the awakening—perhaps emotional maturity, or proven responsibility. But wishing was useless. All she could do was wait. *Possibly forever,* she thought glumly.

Narre turned to Tavi. "We're coming to your house for dinner tomorrow!" she said.

"Oh, good!" Tavi brightened. "It's been a while!" Narre's mother and Tavi's father were siblings, and the two girls were the only young, sun-blessed members of their extended family. Narre was nearly a year younger than Tavi and was waiting for her touch gift to awaken. She and Tavi had felt drawn to each other as soon as they were old enough to realize how different they were from their siblings and cousins.

Although Narre was the youngest of their group, she was in a tight race with Reba to see whose gifts awakened first. Somehow Narre's changes bothered Tavi less than Reba's, and Tavi found herself rooting for her cousin. Ellea and the other midwives assured them that the timing of awakenings wasn't a competition—and, like every group of Dreamers that had come before them, they all knew it most definitely was.

"Mama wants me to bake some bread to bring over," Narre began with a grimace. Everyone knew Narre was a terrible cook. "I told her maybe if Sava gives me the gift of healing, he would also let me touch someone who was about to die, to help them die faster. That would hurt them, but it would also be kind, if they were in a lot of pain."

First Tavi was confused at the abrupt change of subject, but then she saw Pala watching from the doorway. Tavi gave Pala a big smile, then turned back to her cousin. "Narre, you're right!" she exclaimed. "Such wisdom from one so young!"

When she glanced behind her again and saw that the doorway was empty, Tavi whispered, "Don't you think you could just give that poor, dying person some of your baking? That would kill them even faster than magic."

The entire table broke into loud laughter, and when Pala marched back in, they were forced to suffer through ten more minutes of discourse on both theology and behavior before they were allowed to leave.

ELLEA KARIANA STOOD at the window in the sitting room of the midwife house, watching the four students walking down the road toward their homes. She rose and found Pala standing at the door, hands on her hips.

"Shall we check on our patient?" Ellea asked.

Pala nodded, and as they walked toward the mother's rooms at the back of the house she told Ellea, "Your 'Dreamers,' as you call them, need lessons in conduct! I'm quite sure that during discussion time, they were talking about everything but theology."

Ellea stopped walking and smiled, touching Pala's shoulder. The older midwife's hand glowed with a gentle, golden light as she offered calm to her irked apprentice. "I know your lecture was very informative. Thank you for speaking with them."

Pala stepped back from Ellea's touch, and her eyebrows drew together. "I have never heard of children being trained before their gifts awaken."

Ellea nodded. "True, most midwife houses offer no training until a student awakens. That was my experience when my touch gift first made itself known. It was difficult, however. Suddenly I was leaving my school friends after lunch to spend half of every day at the midwife house, training with older students I barely knew, who understood my magic better than I did! It was a disconcerting transition."

"I can see how that might be the case," Pala conceded.

They began walking again, and a moment later, they reached their patient's room. The woman had given birth the previous night, choosing to have her first child at the midwife house instead of at home. She smiled when the two midwives entered.

Ellea watched as Pala gave the young woman time-honored advice on breastfeeding and mothering. As her apprentice worked, Ellea's mind wandered back to the students who had just left.

The early training offered at the Oren midwife house was clearly effective. For over thirty years, Ellea had watched cohorts of Dreamers suffering through weekly lectures. Their disdain for the instruction was nearly universal, yet Ellea watched in delight as each group bonded in their confusion and excitement, and even in competition, as they waited for their gifts to awaken.

Ellea's eyes returned to Pala. The apprentice was speaking gently to the new mother, and her expression, so often stern, had softened. Ellea smiled. Some women only wanted a midwife with the surname "Kari-ana," which indicated she was gifted. Ellea had long believed that practical midwives could care for women just as well as gifted ones, and Pala was proving that to be true. Pala gave the mother a hug, and the two midwives left the room, closing the door behind them.

Pala picked up their conversation where it had left off. "I've never heard the term 'Dreamers,' " she said.

"It isn't an official term," Ellea told her. "I began calling them that years ago. These are children whose gifts are still asleep, children who dream every day of what their magical futures will hold. It's—well, I suppose it's a term of affection."

"Hmm." Pala raised an eyebrow and walked toward the stairs.

Ellea entered a storage room and began the daily task of sterilizing medical instruments in lime water. As she worked, she thought about Tavi. The girl was frightened of what her awakening might bring, yet impatient for it to happen. What Tavi did not know was that every night she was kept awake by anxiety and excitement, wondering about her future, Ellea experienced the same.

How will I even teach her? Ellea asked herself. She was a good teacher, perhaps one of the best. Yet Tavi's gifting was unprecedented, and Ellea did not know what to expect.

She gave herself the same answer as always. *We will learn together.* In recent years, Ellea had rarely visited with her pre-awakened classes, instead delegating their training to others. This cohort was different. Ellea still did not give many lectures, but she frequently found ways to spend time with their group. She expected Tavi's awakening to be overwhelming and bewildering to both of them. The trust the two of them were building would serve them well as they broke new ground together.

But for now, Ellea would attempt to model patience to her young Dreamer, and to never display her own restlessness as she waited for the girl's awakening. It would happen soon enough.

CHAPTER FOUR

I have now been healing others for three-quarters of my life. It feels entirely natural to me. Yet during my childhood, when my hands shone, I could not discern the purpose of it. Each time my hands filled with light, my heart filled with trepidation.

-From Savala's Collected Letters, Volume 2

THAT WINTER WAS as close to perfect as any season Tavi could remember.

There were only two big storms, and they were both just right—one day of blizzard, with blankets and fires and books instead of school; and a second day off while the roads were cleared, a day when Tavi and her older siblings acted like young children, competing to see who could build the best snow people.

The week-long, midwinter school break was unseasonably warm, the bright sun reflecting off melting icicles and slush. Tavi spent every day with Reba, Sall, and Narre. It was sublime. Sall was witty, Narre was playful, and Reba was full of the infectious laughter that had characterized her whole childhood.

The entire week overflowed with ordinary magic: sledding and sliding on hills that were too icy; tasting the hot, mulled cider Narre's mother made; and taking turns imitating Pala's dreadful "lecture voice."

The night before school resumed, the four friends built a bonfire behind Tavi's house. In its warmth, Tavi and Reba put on a concert using two simple wooden flutes Reba's father had purchased for them years earlier. They had been practicing together all week, laughing when it went wrong and delighting when their efforts resulted in beautiful music. After the performance, Sall and Narre cheered so loudly that Tavi's father came outside to make sure they were all right.

That week was enough to make Tavi wish they weren't sun-blessed, that instead they were four regular children who could grow into adulthood together, enjoying their beautiful, simple life.

Weeks passed, the days growing longer, and for the first time, Tavi didn't want winter to end. She was surprised to find tears in her eyes when the last of the snow disappeared from the shady spot beside their chicken coop. She dreaded the changes spring might bring—not in her surroundings, but in her friends.

On the first day of spring, the town of Oren celebrated the new year with a singalong at the parish hall. Tavi and her friends enjoyed their day off but complained that the holiday wasn't longer. The next day, however, Reba was absent from school. That afternoon, Tavi gathered Reba's textbooks and walked to her friend's house.

"Hello, Tavi." Reba opened the door and gave her friend a warm smile.

"We missed you at school today," Tavi said, holding up the books.

Reba took them and tossed them on a table near the door. "Come in; I want to show you something," she said, taking Tavi's hand and leading her upstairs. "I'm so glad you came; I need another eye on something. I've been wanting to redo my blue dress." She chattered nonstop as they climbed the stairs.

They arrived at Reba's bedroom. Her best dress was hanging on the back of the door. Reba continued her narrative, picking up two pieces of lace. "I love the design of this one, but I'm not sure cream goes well with the blue of the dress. The white works, but I'm afraid the lace itself is old-fashioned. What do you think?"

Tavi blinked, surprised to be given a chance to talk. Ignoring the lace, she said, "I just wanted to check on you since you were absent. I thought you might be sick, but you don't look sick."

"I'm not sick." Reba looked around as if expecting eavesdroppers in the empty house. She leaned forward and spoke softly. "My mother cycle started."

"Oh." The jealousy hit hard, catching Tavi off-guard. She forced a smile. "That's wonderful. Why did you stay home? Does it hurt?"

"I feel fine. When I realized what was happening this morning, I asked Father if I could have a day off school." At two years old, Reba had lost her mother to a lung disease, and she lived alone with her father. "When I told him why, he was so horrified, I think he would have said yes to anything."

Tavi couldn't help but giggle. When she stopped, she had nothing to say, and she took the lace from Reba, holding it up to the dress without really looking at it.

Reba broke the silence. "You know, it will happen to you soon! Well, maybe not soon, but . . . eventually."

"I know it will," Tavi said. "I'm really happy for you, Reba. I like the white lace. I'd better get home."

As Tavi walked, she couldn't shake the feeling she had just left the house of a stranger, rather than a friend.

Six weeks later, Tavi was pulled aside by an excited Narre, who confided that she, too, had started her cycle, two days before her twelfth birthday. Tavi tried to sound genuine when she told her cousin how happy she was for her.

Lunchtime at school became an irritating affair. The three girls and Sall sat under a tree each day as usual, to eat and talk. Now, however, Reba frequently leaned over to Narre to hold whispered conversations which ended in Narre blushing and both girls giggling.

After two weeks of this, Sall found another tree to sit under with his lunch, giving an excuse about a book he wanted to read. With Sall gone, the two girls (for Tavi could not think of them as *women* yet) no longer whispered. Instead, Reba initiated conversations about topics Tavi did not want to hear about—boys, dress patterns, gossip about other girls, and the impending awakenings of herself and Narre.

Tavi felt as useless as a hen who has stopped laying eggs. After two days, she joined Sall at his new lunch spot.

"Too much whispering for you, too?" Sall asked.

"They stopped that. Now they talk as if I'm not even there," Tavi said. "The topics are all either embarrassing or ridiculous."

"What is going on with them?" Sall asked. "They both seem so different."

Tavi shook her head. Sall had only brothers, and he seemed unaware of the girls changing before his eyes. "They're just determined to grow up," Tavi said.

The four of them still walked home together, but Reba and Narre's silly lunchtime conversations invariably intruded into their afternoon walks. At those times, Tavi and Sall slowed their steps, allowing the chatty girls to walk ahead.

Tavi supposed it was nice to walk with Sall, but it wasn't the same. She wanted things back to the way they'd always been. But every time she saw Narre laughing with Reba, jealousy inserted itself into Tavi's chest, a heavy ache she couldn't seem to banish.

One afternoon when Tavi and Sall had fallen several feet behind the other girls, Reba abruptly stopped. "Look!" she said. "That mama bird is feeding her babies!"

They all looked in the direction she was pointing. Sall squinted. "Where?" he asked.

"In that big oak tree! See?"

No one spoke, and then everyone did. "The oak tree across that field?" "How in the world can you see that?" And, finally, from Narre, "Your eyes are glowing! You're awakening!"

Then Narre and Reba were running up and down the road, Narre asking Reba to identify faraway objects, while Tavi and Sall stood several feet away, watching.

Tavi felt very small and very young. She turned to Sall. "They sure aren't acting like women now, are they?" He didn't seem to know how to respond.

During the following days, Reba talked of little other than her awakening, and Tavi avoided her. Narre didn't seem to know which of her friends to spend time with, and she made circuits between them.

Two weeks later, the four friends sat at school, writing essays. One of their classmates walked through the room, searching for someone who would loan her a pencil. Narre told the girl, "I'll break mine for you, but you'll have to sharpen it."

Tavi watched as Narre snapped the pencil in two, her hands glowing briefly. All sun-blessed children were used to experiencing a warm glow at times of contentment or relaxation. Narre seemed to take little notice of it as she handed one pencil half to her classmate.

"How did you do that?" Sall asked from behind Narre, tapping her shoulder.

"Do what?"

Sall pointed to Narre's desk. "Look at the pencil you broke."

Narre picked it up. It was broken so smoothly that the end looked as if it had been cut by a sharp saw. Her face took on a look of awe. She closed her eyes and took two slow, deep breaths, and when her hands glowed again, she opened her eyes and picked up her half-pencil. This time, she put almost no force into the motion of her hands.

Snap. She now had two small pencils in her hands, perfect halves.

Narre's touch-blessed hands could break things, easily and precisely.

Tavi sat two rows back and wiped a tear from her cheek.

Now that Reba and Narre were attending full training every afternoon at the midwife house, Tavi and Sall's weekly classes were held with a younger cohort of students. Tavi found it humiliating.

Several weeks passed. During training one day in late spring, Ellea brought her Dreamers upstairs to observe the awakened trainees practicing their gifts. Tavi was envious of them, but she was also enthralled.

One boy's bare feet glowed as he jumped all the way across the large room in a single bound, flipping in the air as he went. A mind-blessed girl asked a Dreamer to give her a word, and then the girl used that word in a perfect, complex poem, composed on the spot. And Tavi's mouth dropped open when she watched Narre's glowing hands break pieces off a rock, first large chunks and then smaller bits, until she held a smooth, heavy orb.

Tavi turned toward Sall to share her amazement with him, but the words didn't come out, because she was so surprised at what she saw. She wasn't looking at Sall's face; she was looking at his shoulder. She had to lift her chin to see his thin face and shaggy hair.

"Are you taller?" Tavi whispered. It was a silly question; he was clearly several inches taller, and she didn't know why she hadn't noticed it before.

"I keep having to buy new pants," Sall replied with an embarrassed grin.

On their way home, when Sall left Tavi to walk down the path to his house, she watched him. His shoulders were getting broader too.

How had she failed to notice? And how was it that Sall, who had always been the smallest boy in their class, was growing before she was? Tavi had always heard that girls matured faster than boys; her body seemed determined to disprove that idea. For months she had seen small changes in herself, but her body certainly wasn't in any hurry to develop.

Summer arrived, and Tavi celebrated her thirteenth birthday. It fell during their midsummer break from school, and her mother allowed her to invite Reba, Narre, and Sall to spend the day with her.

Reba's father's carriage arrived at Tavi's house half an hour before the appointed time, but Reba only got out of the carriage for long enough to tell Tavi that she couldn't stay due to a dress fitting. Tavi mumbled a senseless reply then turned and ran back into the house.

She barely made it to her room before she burst into tears. She indulged her grief, stoking it into anger and resolving to stop referring to Reba as her "best friend." Somehow, that decision made things worse instead of better.

Misty must have heard her, because she rushed in, asking, "Why are you crying on your birthday?" Tavi calmed herself long enough to tell her sister what had happened.

"I'll run to town, find Reba, and stab her stupid, gifted eyes with the dressmakers' pins!" Misty declared. But instead, she took a deep breath and held her sister close, letting her cry as long as she needed.

Tavi had barely dried her tears when Sall arrived. He gave Tavi an awkward hug and said "Happy birthday!" in a voice that could not possibly belong to him. It was deeper and a little scratchy. Sall didn't quite seem comfortable with it, as if he were trying on his father's voice and it didn't fit.

Tavi tried to ignore the seedling of panic growing in her chest. Her friendship with Reba was obviously over. And since Narre had awakened, Tavi's friendship with her cousin often felt awkward. Tavi was depending on Sall to keep her from feeling alone. What would she do if he awakened soon?

For a couple of weeks, things seemed fine. Tavi got used to Sall's lower voice. She convinced herself that perhaps his awakening would be delayed. It was always difficult to predict when a boy would awaken, anyway.

Then there was a subtle shift. Sall began sitting in the back of the room at school, instead of near Tavi. Most days he stayed at school late, and Tavi walked home alone. The route felt too long and too quiet.

Sall was also getting irritable. This wasn't a new thing; Tavi was used to her friend occasionally coming to school bleary-eyed and cross, unwilling to explain why. Now, however, it was more frequent. He stood and walked away in the middle of a story Tavi was telling, and he snapped at other students and even at the teacher. Tavi grew more and more annoyed.

At lunch one day, Sall was nowhere to be found. Tavi had to search for him for ten minutes before she found him sitting against a tree at the edge of the forest. He had his long, skinny legs pulled up to his chest, his arms around his knees. His face was down, and he was crying.

Tavi sat across from him and reached out to touch his knee. "What's wrong?"

Sall cried harder. Tavi sat helplessly, and after several minutes, Sall took a few slow breaths. He wiped his face then released his knees and folded his legs in front of him, resting his elbows on them. He began to speak.

"Jahn is terribly worried, all the time. I'm not sure why. Elison is convinced nobody likes her because she talks too much. Lian hates coming to school, hates it in a way I didn't know anyone hated school. Miss Abana's heart has recently been broken. Abren is so very lonely underneath her smiles. Korin—"

Tavi interrupted. "How do you know all this?"

Sall's eyes dropped to the dry soil between him and Tavi. "I see someone or hear them or feel them nearby, and I know."

Tavi swallowed hard. For the first time, it occurred to her that Sall was wearing a knit cap, had been wearing one every day, even inside. She told herself not to ask, but her rebellious voice spoke. "Did your gift awaken?"

Sall nodded.

"How long ago?"

"Nine days."

Tavi gasped. "Nine days? Why didn't you tell anyone?"

Sall's broadening shoulders began to shake again, as his tears returned. "I've been so overwhelmed," he gasped between sobs. "I hoped that my mind gift would be a simple increase of intelligence."

"As if you needed that!"

Sall managed a small laugh, and his crying slowed. "I don't even think this is a gift."

Tavi didn't know how to respond. She wondered if any magic was truly a gift; it seemed to be more trouble than it was worth. "I'm sorry," she managed.

"*I'm* sorry," Sall said. "I'm sorry that you are lonely, and jealous, and that you feel so much pressure."

Tavi froze.

"I know you hate the unfairness of it all," Sall continued. "You are so anxious for your awakening, but you're also deeply frightened—"

"Stop," Tavi croaked, louder than she intended. Sall looked up at her. She stood, desperately trying not to cry, because tears would prove the truth of all he had just said.

Tavi clenched her fists, turned around, and forced herself to walk rather than run as she returned to the school. She felt the sun lending heat to her dark hair, and she wished the winter had never ended.

CHAPTER FIVE

War turns men into heroes,
Women into widows,
And children into orphans.

-From Proverbs of Savala

"OUR FIRST NOMINEE is Konner Burrell. Please come forward."

Konner stepped onto a small platform. He faced a large, horseshoe-shaped table, inside of which was an oversized marble statue of Savala, the first Savani shepherd and the capital city's namesake. This was the Chamber, the meeting space for the Cormina Council, the center of national government.

Around the table were twenty-seven wood and leather chairs, twenty-six of which were occupied. The empty chair had, until recently, been occupied by a councillor from the city of Savala. She had resigned due to illness. Because annual elections were several months away, the rest of the council would choose her replacement. Konner had been nominated after discreetly letting his interest in the empty seat be known.

Konner's sonorous voice filled the room as he told the council of his rise from poverty to affluence. "I have found a measure of success as a bank president," he said. "Now I wish to attain true success through service."

When he was done speaking, he answered questions from the council, including the inquiry he was dreading. "Are you sun-blessed?"

Konner met the councillor's gaze. "I am not." A murmur filled the room, mostly coming from visitors in the balcony gallery.

After a few more questions, Konner was sent back to his seat. The process was repeated with the two other nominees, a touch-blessed man and a hearing-blessed woman, both moderately successful business owners.

Next the public was given the opportunity to speak. The first citizen spoke positively of all three nominees but concluded by saying, "Mr. Burrell seems nice, and I know he's smart. But I've been voting for two decades, and I've never voted for someone who doesn't have magic. Mr. Burrell sounds like a very good banker. He should stick with that."

All the speakers echoed her sentiment. In the citizens' minds, all of Konner's success could not overpower his great failure: his lack of magic. He listened to the ignorant words, and his jaw hurt from clenching his teeth.

After an hour of public comments, the matter was put to a vote. The touch-blessed man received eleven votes, and the remaining fifteen went to the woman with the hearing gift. Konner received none —not even from the councillor who had nominated him.

Konner forced himself to sit through the rest of the council meeting, despite his humiliation. They were discussing a bill regarding the expansion of rural plumbing lines. A middle-aged councillor's mouth glowed golden as she spoke, forming perfect sentences, full of intelligence and passion. The next speaker's hair shone with the light that emanated from his scalp as he crafted a well-formed argument that somehow managed to agree with everything his colleague had said.

Konner was disgusted. These councillors, each of them gifted, were profoundly weak. He had been determined to bring the council to a position of dominance and supremacy, just as he had done with himself. But the stupid, simple people of Cormina trusted only the Blessed to be their councillors, trusted only them to make good, fair decisions.

At last, the session wrapped up. Konner stood, and something in the gallery caught his eye. Most of the visitors were making their way toward the stairs. But a man and woman in practical, faded clothing stood at the gallery railing, watching the proceedings on the floor.

Konner could not look away from the stout woman and gray-headed man. His parents. He had not seen them in years—his decision, not theirs. Konner's father lifted his hand in a hesitant wave, and that movement jolted Konner out of his frozen state. He jerked his chin down, breaking eye contact, and rushed to an exit.

Konner entered the bathroom in the hallway and locked the door. He paced in the small space. His parents must have heard of his nomination. How did his father feel, seeing Konner rejected due to his lack of magic? Was the old man ashamed?

The story of his birth filled Konner's mind. His mother had told him the tale countless times throughout his childhood. She had gone into labor and sent her husband to fetch a midwife. Along the way, he had stopped in a tavern, where one too many refills had landed him on the floor, unconscious. Konner's mother had given birth by herself, and when her baby had emerged facing the sun, she had walked to the midwife house, bleeding and desperate, carrying her child. Yet it had been too late for a blessing breath. Konner was not gifted, and nothing could change that.

The day after Konner's birth, his father had returned home and learned the truth. Full of remorse, he had never taken another drink and had desperately tried to make up for his error. But Konner had responded to his father's every apologetic overture with disdain. No amount of parental solicitude could correct the damage done on that one night.

Konner hated them. He hated his father for leaving his mother on that night forty years earlier, and he hated his mother for not leaving his father every day since.

Splashing water on his face, Konner tried to think of anything but his parents. After a quarter hour in the bathroom, he was calm enough to exit. He walked halfway down the hallway, then stopped to take in the bas-relief carving of Relin the Fierce on the wall. Konner nearly laughed aloud at the irony of that artwork in this location.

As a youth, Konner had devoured every ancient epic he could find. Some of his favorite stories had been of Relin the Fierce, who had led the Corminian army, fighting for the fledgling nation's very existence. Relin had been one of the world's last true heroes.

In Relin's day, magic had been an erratic, though benevolent, force, entering the world whenever it wished. Then Kari and Savala had come along, and magic had been tamed, gifted to certain people at birth. Soon, political power was concentrated in the hands of the gifted. The Blessed.

The Blessed could not wage war using magic; they would encounter resistance. So they had used their gifts to create peace instead. Konner's world had not known war for centuries. Communities, too, were quite safe. With stride-blessed officers chasing down thieves, sight-blessed investigators who could easily see pertinent evidence, and mind-blessed detectives analyzing that evidence, most people thought twice before breaking the law.

Corminian society was a well-oiled door, swinging open and shut on hinges that never squeaked, always moving but going nowhere. They were missing the vicious vitality that only came with trials, conflict, and unimpeded competition. Humans, Konner believed, were meant to claw their way to power—and if those claws left gashes along the way, so be it. How could the citizens of Cormina look at this carving of Relin and not see what they'd lost?

Konner let out a long sigh and turned away from the carving. He buttoned his coat, put on his hat, and exited the council building into the clean, peaceful streets of Savala.

CHAPTER SIX

My travels go well, or as well as might be expected. I know Sava has called me to travel and share the gift he's given me with the world. But every day I wish you were with me, my dear. The road is longer when I walk it alone.

-From Savala's Collected Letters, Volume 1

TAVI STEPPED out of the schoolhouse, carrying her lunch bag. Her steps took her to the edge of the schoolyard where she began a brisk circuit around the grounds. She pulled an apple from her lunch and took a bite. It was sweet, but it settled like a rock in her knotted stomach.

Tavi's eyes found Reba, who now ate lunch with a group of older, sun-blessed friends. Tavi felt she barely knew Reba now. Her childhood best friend continued to grow into a strikingly beautiful young woman. Reba trained daily at the midwife house but still struggled to control her sight gift. She could not consistently activate it upon command, and when she did, it was weak, and she tired quickly. Despite her unremarkable ability, she mentioned her gifting at every turn.

Reba's father catered to her demands, yet appeared ignorant of the effect his indulgent parenting had on his only child. In Tavi's large family, there was little tolerance for self-centeredness, and Tavi's patience with Reba had waned, especially since her birthday. The occasional conversations they had were awkward, and they had stopped seeking each other out.

Watching Reba, Tavi's throat tightened, making it impossible to swallow the bread she was chewing. Over the years, she and Reba had made so many plans—to marry brothers, live next door to each other, and name their daughters after each other. Tavi knew those plans had been idealistic, but she didn't understand how Reba could leave their friendship behind with no regret.

On most days, Tavi told herself it didn't matter. But occasionally she admitted the truth—losing her best friend had left her adrift. Tavi kicked hard at the dry leaves at her feet, trying to distract herself from such thoughts.

She looked for Narre and Sall. They were sitting under a tree, eating their lunches. Tavi could not bring herself to eat with them. She was no more comfortable with Sall's gift now than she had been on the day he revealed it. His magic was strong, but he struggled to control it, and his gift activated far more often than he wished.

Tavi still felt great affection for her smart, witty friend, but she wanted to protect her emotions from his inadvertent magical eavesdropping. She would have sat with Narre, were it not for Sall's presence. At least she still saw her cousin outside of school when their families spent time together.

Tavi had heard Narre's training was going well. Besides her ability to break, she had discovered an ability to bind. Narre could bind fragments of the same substance, such as two pieces of wood, and she was working on binding disparate substances together, which required a great deal more strength and concentration.

Tavi wanted to talk to Narre about her cousin's impressive gifting, but she feared if they talked about magic, Narre would see her as an outsider, just as Reba did. Instead, Tavi heard updates from others. While she felt pride in her cousin, the envy she felt was greater, and it sat between them, unspoken.

So Tavi avoided her friends at lunchtime, choosing these solitary walks instead. She worked hard to keep a confident, content expression on her face, as if daily lunches alone were exactly what she wanted. In reality, she counted the minutes until class would start again.

Years later, Tavi would remember these walks, and she would grieve for that lonely, thirteen-year-old girl. Now, however, she didn't shed a tear. She didn't even talk to Misty about it. To talk about it would have been to face the question that simmered in her mind. Was something wrong with her that was driving her friends away? Tavi told herself this was the cost of being different. She told herself she was all right.

Relief filled Tavi when the bell rang again. She watched the gifted, awakened students streaming toward the school gates. They would spend the afternoon training at the midwife house. A hot ache filled Tavi's chest as she continued to her classroom.

After school, Tavi again walked alone. Her brother Seph and sister Ista, being older, stayed at school for an extra half hour of mathematics each day, and she didn't want to wait for them. Tavi arrived at home, greeted her mother and Misty, and walked to her room to put her bag down. The wooden flute Reba had given her caught her eye from its spot on top of her chest of drawers. Tavi hadn't played it in months. She picked it up and ran her fingers along its smooth sides. Instead of placing it back where it had been, she buried it under old dresses in a drawer.

Tavi left her bedroom and called, "Mama, I'm going to walk in the forest." When her mother acknowledged her, she exited and meandered through the trees behind their property.

These forest wanderings had become Tavi's after-school routine. She didn't feel as lonely among the trees; it was a place meant for solitude. Every day she made small discoveries: bird nests, colorful lichen, and clearings where she could sit and rest. The peace of the forest often led to her body lighting up with warm magic, and she loved those moments, though they made her yearn even more for her awakening.

A stream bubbled nearby, and Tavi followed the sound. She knelt to take a drink.

"Last time I drank from that stream, I was sick for three days."

The voice startled Tavi, and she snatched her cupped hand out of the water, splashing her skirt. She stood and spun around in one movement, seeking the source of the words. Her eyes found a boy who appeared a few years older than her. He had spoken in a strange way, his vowels subdued and his phrases bearing a slight singsong rhythm.

"Is that so?" was all Tavi could think to say. She continued to study the boy. He was tall and lanky, with a tanned face and a few days' worth of stubble around his mouth.

"It's true, I swear it." The boy smiled, which made him look younger.

Meeting this boy who leaned against a tree in his homespun wool shirt and patched pants, Tavi felt she could leave behind her parents' lessons on polite small talk. "Who are you?" she asked.

He made no move to shake her hand, keeping his position against the tree. "I'm Tullen," he replied.

"What's your last name?"

"I don't have one."

After staring in confusion for a few awkward seconds, Tavi asked, "Where did you come from?"

"I'm Tullen of the Meadow."

Tavi's eyes widened. She had heard many stories about Meadow Dwellers but knew most of them couldn't be true. The basics, however, were agreed upon: A community dwelled in a spacious, isolated meadow in the forest. They schooled their own children and grew, raised, and hunted their own food. Their interactions with people in nearby towns were minimal. But why would a Meadow Dweller be here? "That's twenty miles away!" Tavi blurted.

"More like thirty." Tullen smiled. "I run pretty fast."

Tavi narrowed her eyes at that statement. "What are you doing here?" she asked.

"Wait, wait, wait." Tullen stopped leaning against the tree and took a step toward Tavi. "You haven't told me your name yet."

Tavi had no idea what this Tullen of the Meadow intended, but she supposed if he wanted to hurt her, withholding her name wouldn't prevent that. "I'm Tavi . . . of the Town." Then she felt stupid, and her voice insisted on continuing at a higher pitch and a faster pace. "Well, we are part of the town of Oren, but our house is on the outskirts. In fact, if I was loud enough right now, my mother could probably hear me." There. Now if he had bad intentions, maybe he'd think twice.

Tullen dropped his chin in what struck Tavi as more of a small bow than a nod. "Well met, Tavi of the Town."

He said it with an amused smile, and she wondered if he was making fun of her. At least he didn't seem to want to attack her. "What are you doing here?" Tavi asked.

Tullen gestured to the tree where a bow was resting. "I was trying to hunt," Tullen said. Ah—now Tavi saw the arrow fletching peeking over his shoulder. He continued, "But lately every time I come to this part of the forest in the afternoon, my hunting is interrupted by the loudest steps I've ever heard! All the game gets frightened away. I thought it must be a giant stomping through the forest, so I tracked that giant. And instead I found you! After seeing you here for the last couple of weeks, I thought I should introduce myself and ask why you don't want me to catch any food for my community. Are you so determined that we should starve to death?"

Tavi felt her face grow warm. "Oh, I'm so sorry!" she said in horror. "If I'd had any idea—" and then Tullen's big grin registered with her, and she was even more embarrassed. "You know," she said, "you could have picked another part of the forest to hunt in. And perhaps I wasn't quiet; I wasn't even trying to be. But a giant? Really?"

"Huge, thumping steps!" Tullen insisted, demonstrating by lifting his knee high in the air and bringing his foot crashing into the dry leaves.

Tavi couldn't help a small laugh though she wanted to slap herself for it. Then something else Tullen had said came back to her. "Wait, did you say you've seen me here for the last couple of weeks? Were you watching me?"

That sheepish smile returned. "I've only glimpsed you a couple of times. I was going to leave you to your wanderings, and then I saw you trying to drink that water, which, as I mentioned, is not a good idea." Tullen held his hand to his stomach and grimaced.

"Well, thank you for that." Tavi narrowed her eyes. "But let's talk about you being thirty miles from home. Why? And how did you get here?"

"I like to explore different areas of the forest," Tullen said. "It keeps me interested. And I told you, I run fast."

A suspicion was growing in Tavi. "How long does it take you to run here?" she asked.

"On a good day, about one and a half hours." Tullen spoke matter-of-factly, but Tavi could see amusement tugging at the corner of his mouth. "I usually stay for a couple of days to make the trip worth it."

"You're stride-blessed."

Tullen nodded. "Yes. My feet are quick and quiet. But in the Meadow, we don't call it 'stride-blessed.'"

"What do you call it?" Tavi asked.

Now Tullen was more than sheepish; he looked downright embarrassed. "They say I have feet of gold." A laugh burst out of Tavi. But Tullen wasn't done. "And . . ." He paused. "Ears of gold too."

Tavi's amusement was smothered in surprise. "Ears of gold? You're hearing-blessed too?"

"I am," Tullen said.

All Tavi could manage was, "That's impressive." It was rare to meet someone who was twice-blessed. After a moment, she said, "I can see why you're a hunter. It's the perfect combination."

"I keep my people well fed."

Tavi didn't know what else to say, but she wanted to talk to this strange boy more, to hear about life in the Meadow. It was nice to meet someone who wasn't waiting for her to awaken. Without thinking, she blurted, "I bet you're hungry; would you like to come have a snack?" As soon as the words escaped her mouth, she wanted to take them back. What would he think, being asked to her house just after she'd met him?

But Tullen beamed. "I would!"

"Oh!" Tavi said, surprised. She gathered her wits and gestured south. "It's this way."

They entered through the kitchen door. Mey and Misty were working on dinner. Tavi introduced Tullen and told her sister and mother he was from the Meadow.

Mey accepted this information with raised eyebrows, but her only response was, "You must be starving. We'll get you and Tavi a nice snack."

Tavi smiled. She could have written this script; her mother believed any situation was improved with generous servings of food. Her mother placed bread, cheese, and fresh vegetables on the table. She and Misty sat down.

Tullen picked up one of the vegetables. "What's this?"

"It's a carrot," Tavi said.

"It's red!"

Mey laughed. "I like to experiment with hybrids; it's a hobby of mine."

Tavi said, "Don't let her deceive you; it's more than a little hobby. She sells produce from her garden, and everyone in town wants to buy her red carrots."

As they ate, Misty peppered Tullen with questions, which he answered in his good-natured manner. When the conversation slowed, Mey turned to Tullen. "I hope you will stay with us when you visit this part of the woods," she said. "The forest must get cold this time of year."

"Be forewarned, though," Tavi said with a smile. "My brother Jona snores so loudly, you'll think you're sharing the room with a hog."

"What a generous offer." He paused, looking between Tavi and Mey. "We do things differently in the Meadow. We do not have many interactions with outsiders. I appreciate the hospitality, but I must discuss your offer first with my parents, and possibly with the Meadow elders, before I can respond."

Tavi's eyes narrowed. "They allow you to spend days by yourself in the forest, but they don't trust you to choose if you can stay with someone who opens their home to you?"

Tullen's face was serious. "As I told you—things are different there."

Mey placed a calming hand on Tavi's shoulder and turned to Tullen. "We hope you can accept, but we understand if you cannot."

"I'll be going home this afternoon—in fact, I should get going,"

Tullen said. "I will talk to my parents, and I'll try to come back this way in a few days."

They said goodbye, and as soon as the door closed, Misty turned to her sister with raised eyebrows. "I can't believe you met a Meadow Dweller! He's handsome!"

Tavi's face twisted in distaste. "He's old!"

Misty looked confused. "He's just a boy."

"I bet he's sixteen years old! He's nearly an adult!"

Misty smirked. "You're right, he's positively ancient. I hope he doesn't drop dead before he can make it home."

Tavi laughed. "It's nice to make a new friend," she said. And when she saw the soft smiles on the faces of her mother and her sister, she wondered if they had noticed her loneliness, despite her efforts to hide it.

CHAPTER SEVEN

My trainees often ask me why there are restrictions on magic. Why are they prevented from using their gifts in ways Sava deems unacceptable? Wouldn't it be better for them to have full freedom and learn from the consequences of their choices?

I've asked Sava these questions many times. Not having discerned a response from him, it is difficult for me to answer my students. I wonder—is Sava protecting society from the Blessed or protecting the Blessed from themselves?

-From Training Sun-Blessed Students *by Ellea Kariana*

KONNER EXITED his bank and took a deep breath of the cool autumn air. After telling his driver he would be walking home, he proceeded along back streets, avoiding crowds.

In an alleyway, Konner nodded at a smiling young man walking toward him. Their sleeves brushed each other as they passed in the narrow alley. Out of habit, Konner patted the pocket that held his coin purse.

It took less than two seconds for him to spin around, grab the back of the man's dirty shirt, and throw him against the wall. Konner shoved his shoulder into the man's back, and the man squirmed, reaching his hands behind him. Konner raised his knee to reach a knife strapped to his calf. He pulled it out of its sheath and held the cool metal to the side of the man's throat. The man stopped struggling.

"Give me my money," Konner growled.

"I don't have it!"

A harsh laugh came out of Konner's mouth. He'd spent much of his first two decades of life as a ruffian who loved to fight, and those skills hadn't left him when he'd put on a suit and become a banker. Keeping his knife at the young man's throat, he used his other hand to grab one of the man's arms, wrenching it back. The man's other hand was free, and when he started to move it, Konner rotated the knife so its blade scraped the man's neck, nearly breaking the skin. The man froze. Konner brought his face close enough that the would-be thief's unkempt beard brushed Konner's cheek.

"I know you don't have the money." Konner spoke quietly. "You returned it to my pocket, though you did it with swiftness so unnatural, your hands were a blur. You used magic to attempt to deceive me, and doubtless you used it to steal from me as well. You and I both know that's impossible." Konner bent the thief's gloved hand backward at the wrist. When the man groaned, Konner spoke again.

"I'd like to offer you two options. The street just past these buildings is well-patrolled by safety officers each night." Konner's home was on that street, and he made large donations to the officers to ensure their presence. "Your first option is this: I will break both your arms, and then I will flag down an officer who will take you to jail. I will make arrangements for your stay to be a long one."

The man shook and whimpered. He reeked of sweat and fear. Konner smiled. "If you prefer, I will release your arms and put away my knife. You will remove your gloves and fold your hands in front of you, keeping them free of magic. We will walk the streets of this city, and you will tell me precisely how you used magic to commit a crime. After that, I will reevaluate your future. What say you, friend? Which option do you prefer?"

47

"The second option," the man gasped.

"Very well." Konner released his grip. When the man had pulled his gloves off and folded his hands in front of him, Konner unstrapped his knife sheath, slipped the knife back in it, and put it in the inside pocket of his coat. They exited the alley together. "What is your name?" Konner asked.

"Ash."

Konner's voice was cold, even as his steps remained smooth and casual. "You seem to be under the impression that if you are truthful, I may ruin you. You do not understand the situation. No matter who you are or what you have done, I can ruin you with as little energy as I expend in ordering breakfast. Your only hope at this point is to tell me the truth and pray that my efforts will be directed to your benefit rather than your harm. Your name."

The man looked up, seeming to consider the question. Finally, he spoke. "Jerash Sheaver."

"Jerash Sheaver," Konner said, "tell me how you obtained the ability to use magic to steal and deceive."

"I don't know."

Konner spun around to stand in front of the man, who skidded to an anxious stop. "I thought I was clear!" Konner stormed. "The truth, and every detail!"

A deep breath or two was required, but then Jerash began to talk. Konner led his companion along quiet, residential streets, and their steps slowed as Jerash retold every detail of the day he had killed his wife. He followed with the tale of the weeks he had spent traveling on foot to the city where they now walked, and of the months since, living on the streets.

When Jerash stopped talking, Konner asked, "Aren't you concerned someone will travel here and recognize you?"

"I expected to be caught soon after I fled," Jerash said. "I barely slept for the first week. I can only guess it took some time for them to discover her body. Now that a year has passed, and I am so far from home, I hope I am safe."

"I can see why you've changed your name, and I'm perfectly happy to call you Ash," Konner said. "Tell me, can this phenomenon you've described be replicated?"

"I—I don't know. I still don't even understand why my gift changed."

Konner stared at Ash. "You don't strike me as an imbecile. You must understand."

"At first I thought it was because my hands are gifted, and I used them . . . on her. But then I realized that could not be so."

"Because there have been hundreds of touch-blessed men and women who have committed murder through the years," Konner said.

Ash nodded. "And of course my gift was not active at the time. So perhaps it had something to do with the kiss. I—I breathed her last breath."

A smile of awe filled Konner's face. "It's beautiful. At birth, you were given breath that gave you magic. Through death, you were given breath that gave you power." He turned his head toward Ash, who nodded.

They stopped in another shadowed alleyway. Konner asked, "If I told you to use your gift to break a man's neck, to grab him so quickly he had no way of anticipating it, could you do it?"

In a moment, Ash's hand was grasping Konner's neck, not tight enough to prevent airflow, but with enough pressure to send fear coursing through the older man's veins. Konner forced his face to remain calm. Ash pulled his hand back.

"Perhaps with your history, a neck wasn't the best example?" Konner asked. Ash turned his head to the side, but not before Konner saw the fury in his eyes.

Konner turned his attention to Ash's hands, grasping them and examining the stormy, gray light they emitted. He raised his gaze to Ash, not trying to hide the wonder he felt. After a moment, Konner said, "Your face looks pained. How does it feel?"

Ash stared in the banker's eyes. "It feels like fire." He pulled his hands away and shook them, releasing his magic.

Konner said, "We will attempt to find ways to make the pain more bearable."

"What do you mean by 'we'?"

"We." Konner pointed at Ash, then at himself. "Perhaps I'm getting ahead of myself." He relaxed his face and stance, taking on the posture of a nonthreatening businessman. "You have one more choice to make. I will allow you to walk away, free and unharmed. You can live on the streets and use your gift to barely exist, as you have been doing."

"Where does the 'we' come in?" Ash asked—and Konner knew he had him.

"Your second option is the 'we' option." Konner stared into Ash's eyes. They were haunted. Weary. Desperate. "Ash," Konner said, his voice warm, "The first step will be to get you off the cold streets, to give you a home where you no longer need to fear discovery. You will live in a warm, comfortable guest suite at my home.

"But you need more than physical provision and safety. You need purpose. I see your passion. You may have lost sight of it, but it is dormant, not dead. So once you're full and warm, we will work together to explore your gift. We will discover how to share that gift with others. I know it's hard to envision the future right now, when you're cold and hungry. But, Ash, hear this. In the coming days, you and I will change this nation in ways you cannot even imagine."

Ash's eyes were wide and intense, his body taut. Konner knew that look; it was the same look a young woman had when she listened to her new lover speak. It was belief, and it was hope.

Konner asked, "What is your choice?"

"The second option," Ash said for the second time that evening.

"Very well." Konner, suddenly businesslike, strode back the direction they had come. Ash walked alongside him. They proceeded in silence, and Ash's eyes grew wide when they entered the front gate of Konner's large, stone home, the most opulent on a street full of luxury. Konner stopped and pressed a strong hand onto his guest's shoulder. "Jerash Sheaver, I require absolute trust. If that is ever broken, or if you ever again lay a threatening hand on me, you will learn the true meaning of regret. Is this understood?"

Ash swallowed. "Yes."

Konner strode to the door, knocked, and waited for a maid to answer it. "I will send a servant in to take you to your bath, and another to bring you food. Tomorrow, we begin."

THE NEXT AFTERNOON, a maid brought Ash into Konner's study, where the banker was sitting behind his desk. Konner pointed between two leather chairs on the other side of the desk. "Stand there," he commanded.

Ash stood in the indicated spot. Konner examined him. A barber had come that morning, and with his hair short and beard shaved Ash was an uncommonly handsome man. Konner had also sent his tailor that morning; when Ash's custom wardrobe was complete, he would be even more striking. People would follow this man.

"Have a seat," Konner said. Ash sat ramrod-straight. "I'm glad they've cleaned you up," Konner said. "I know my clothes aren't a perfect fit, but you'll have your own soon." He smiled and said, "No need to be nervous, Ash. We came to an understanding last night, and I want you to be as comfortable with that as I am. Please, relax."

Ash's shoulders dropped, and he nodded, looking his host in the eye. "Thank you, Mr. Burrell."

Konner's smile widened. "Please, call me Konner."

"Yes, sir—Konner."

"Let's get to work, shall we?" Konner opened a thin, leather-bound book. "I use bank ledgers as notebooks," he said. "They remind me that details are crucial to successful plans." He picked up a fountain pen. "I would like to talk about *gray magic*—unless you know a better term for it?"

"That term makes sense."

"You are the only living expert on gray magic."

A brief grin brightened Ash's face. "I'm not a well-informed expert."

"That will be remedied as quickly as we can manage. I would like to start by writing what you do know about gray magic, even if it's a short list."

Ash talked, frequently interrupted by Konner's questions. After twenty minutes, they had a list three pages long. It covered everything from the physical sensations associated with using gray magic, to a detailed description of the events preceding and during

Ash's gray awakening—another new term, but one that seemed to fit.

Next, they discussed the questions they must answer. To achieve a gray awakening, did both parties have to be gifted, as Ash and his wife were? Could an ungifted person receive a gray awakening? Or bestow one? When he had entered the questions in his ledger, Konner said, "Excellent. This is a good start."

"A good start for what, sir?"

"I told you yesterday," Konner said. "We will change the nation of Cormina, together."

Ash didn't respond, but his face reflected his questions. Konner leaned forward. "Ash, what do you think the world was like in the days before magic was tamed by Kari and Savala?"

Ash's eyebrows drew together. "I don't know a lot of details, but I remember learning that society was devastated by war," he said.

Konner grimaced. "That is the way they frame it in textbooks, isn't it?" Then he talked about the ancient epics—the heroes and villains and, yes, the wars. He highlighted the freedom of those ancient days, the brute strength of individuals, and the dramatic rise and fall of mighty societies.

Ash's eyes were wide, his breaths coming quickly. Konner smiled inwardly. He wasn't stupid; he'd known the day before that Ash had agreed to join him more for the food and lodging than anything else. But that was changing already. These legends were intoxicating, and an ember had been lit inside of Ash, a desire for power. With careful words, Konner could stoke that craving into a roaring flame.

Konner then stood and walked around the desk, sitting in the chair next to Ash. He leaned forward, his eyes boring into Ash's. "Magic is the greatest power available," he said, "and because magic is always good, we have driven ourselves into a rut of stagnation. The outcome of anything truly important is predestined by this terrible, magical goodness." Konner placed a hand on Ash's shoulder. His voice was warm. "On the day you received your gray awakening, everything changed. Do you see it?"

"I don't know."

Konner was patient. "With you—and others like you, for there will be more—everything will change. The power of magic will no longer be constrained by goodness, a hollow ideal that comes from a distant god, if he exists at all. You will be free to discover whether there are standards more important than goodness. You can explore strength and ambition and creativity.

"It is time to write our own epic. We will not attempt reform; it is too late for that. Instead, we will tear down and then rebuild our nation, so we can live in a world that once again welcomes those who value real, visceral humanity."

Ash was nearly breathless as he asked, "What do we do first?"

Konner smiled again. "We must discover how gray awakenings are achieved." He gestured to the ledger. "We will perform various tests to answer these questions. Each time we are successful, we will add a gray-blessed member to our team."

"I suppose the more powerful the person is, the more value they have for our cause?"

"We will seek people with exceptional giftings," Konner affirmed.

The younger man spoke slowly. "This may sound ridiculous, but years ago, I heard rumors of a girl. No one seems to know where she's from—some small town. They say she was born facing the sun, and her entire body glowed when she received her blessing breath. The story sounds like a myth, but if it was true . . ."

The very air in the room seemed to go still. At last, Konner spoke. "I have heard the same. I, too, assumed it was a baseless rumor. But if the story has spread to your hometown . . ." His jaw hardened, and his gaze met Ash's. "We will discover whether this girl exists," he said. "If she does, we will find her. Whatever it takes."

"Whatever it takes," Ash repeated. He smiled broadly, and in the wildness of that grin, Konner saw not a potter on the run, but an ancient hero from the legends of old.

CHAPTER EIGHT

Remember, magic should be fun.

-From Training Sun-Blessed Students *by Ellea Kariana*

THREE DAYS LATER, Tavi again strolled through the woods. She told herself that the strange Meadow boy probably hadn't come back that way yet, or perhaps he was hunting, and he most likely wouldn't come at all. Why would he want to befriend a thirteen-year-old girl?

Having convinced herself that she probably wouldn't see Tullen, Tavi tried to keep her walk leisurely and peaceful—but instead, knowing he could be waiting around any bend in the trail, she found herself stuck in nervous anticipation.

This is ridiculous, Tavi told herself. *If he's here, fine. If not, even better. I'll enjoy the forest alone, and then I'll go home and study. Maybe I should head home now.* She had nearly decided to do just that, when she heard a voice ahead calling, "Tavi of the Town, come see what I have found!" She smiled broadly, and then tried not to smile, resulting in an expression she was sure qualified as a grimace.

Tavi found Tullen standing at a tree, using a small knife to remove a misshapen growth from the trunk. She watched him for a moment before saying, "You know no one actually calls me 'Tavi of the Town,' right?"

Tullen was still focused on his task. "Of course," he assured her. "But it has quite a ring to it." He turned to her and winked.

After putting his knife away, Tullen pulled and twisted until the odd growth popped off the trunk. It was cream-colored, speckled with light brown splotches. "You're in for a real treat," he said. "This is antlerfruit. Observe these points protruding from it, like antlers. It's not a fruit at all; it's a fungus. But once I peel this hardened skin off the outside, you'll find the inner portion to be delicious."

When he had peeled it, he cut off a small piece and handed it to Tavi. It was spongy and moist, and she looked at it suspiciously. "I've seen these, but I've never been tempted to eat one."

Tullen grinned. "I know everything out here that's edible. Trust me on this; after your first bite, you'll be searching for antlerfruit daily."

Tavi took a small, cautious bite and chewed once. Immediately she spit it out and dropped the rest of the piece on the ground. "That's what you eat when you're out here? It's bitter!"

Tullen cut a bite for himself and put it in his mouth, savoring it. "That's what makes it so irresistible!" he exclaimed.

Tavi shook her head. "You know, we could get real food back at the house." She caught herself. "Of course, I know you probably can't stay there, but we could get a snack—"

Tullen interrupted, "They've given me permission to stay with your family. In fact, my mother is relieved I'll no longer be struggling to get enough sleep on the forest floor. I didn't realize until now that her biggest concern when I hunt is not that wolves will eat me, but that their howling will keep me awake at night!"

Tavi laughed. "You must not have mentioned Jona's snoring to her!"

They began to wander through the trees. Tullen said, "The hunting has been good today. I've caught several rabbits and squirrels."

"Where do you keep them before you head home?"

Tullen replied, "When I make a kill, I clean it. Then I place the meat and skin in large, ceramic pots I store in the river. The cold water keeps it from spoiling."

"How do you carry it home?" Tavi asked. "Doesn't it get heavy?"

"That's the beauty of my gift. When I run, my body feels almost weightless, as does anything I carry."

"That sounds amazing," Tavi said wistfully.

"At home, I often take my siblings on my back when I hunt," Tullen said. He gave her a mischievous smile then took a few steps so he was standing directly in front of her, facing away from her. He patted his back and said, "Let's go, Tavi of the Town."

She caught Tullen's enthusiasm, and almost before she knew what she was doing, Tavi had hopped onto his back. She grasped his shoulders, and he held her legs, her feet sticking out in front of him.

Tullen took two deep breaths . . . and then he ran.

In just a few seconds, trees were flying by in a blur. Tavi gasped, and then a sound emerged from her—half laugh, half squeal, and all joy. Tullen followed that by his own cry of, "Whoooooyaaaa!" His sun-blessed feet somehow knew how to effortlessly leap over roots and holes and when to slow so he could avoid branches and other obstacles blocking the path.

"This is glorious!" Tavi cried. Then she leaned closer to Tullen's ear to say in a low voice, "I'll try to be quieter so I don't scare away all your prey!"

Tullen's voice was loud and carefree. "No need. Tomorrow, we hunt. Today we fly." And his feet moved even faster, leading Tavi to squeeze her arms and legs tight, as her heartbeat quickened. Their laughs and screams filled the cool air of the forest.

It seemed Tullen could run forever without getting winded. When the initial thrill had passed, he spoke. "Tell me about your family."

"It's big," Tavi replied. "I have six siblings." Her fingers counted them off, tapping against Tullen's shoulders. "Misty is the oldest, and she helps Mama at home. Zakry is married and lives in town. Jona works at a nearby farm. My sister Tess is a monk outside Savala. Seph and Ista are still in school. Then there's me, the baby."

"That may be a large family in Oren," Tullen said, "but not in the Meadow. At last count, I had over one hundred siblings."

56

"What?" Tavi's head spun, her chin knocking against Tullen's ear. "Sorry about that—but over a hundred? How many wives does your father have?"

Tullen roared with laughter, jostling Tavi. He explained, "He has one wife. At the Meadow, all of those in the same generation are called brothers and sisters. All but three of them are actually my cousins." He turned his head to glance at Tavi. "What is your father's profession?"

"He's a Savani shepherd." Tavi realized she had no idea what the religion of the Meadow was, if any. "That mean's he's a member of the clergy. Do you . . . do you worship Sava?"

"Most of us do," Tullen said, "but not in quite the same ways you do. Our worship varies from person to person. We feel worship should come in many forms, just as people do."

Tavi nodded thoughtfully. "That sounds nice."

At last Tullen stopped, and Tavi jumped down. He retrieved his bow and supplies, and they walked to the house.

Tavi opened the back door and halted. At the kitchen table sat Narre and Sall, eating a snack of cheese and milk. "What are you doing here?" Tavi blurted.

"It's great to see you too, Tavi," Narre responded with a raised eyebrow.

Tavi's mother turned from her spot at the stove and said, "I saw Jilla in town yesterday, and I realized it had been ages since Narre had visited. We thought it would be a nice surprise for her to come have dinner tonight. I told Jilla that Narre could invite Sall and Reba too."

Narre interjected, "Reba . . . couldn't make it."

Tavi gave a little shrug. "That's fine." She felt that familiar ache and wanted to kick herself for it.

"Tavi, you're keeping Tullen from coming in," Mey admonished her daughter.

"Oh—yes." Tavi stepped inside and gestured toward Tullen. "Narre and Sall, this is Tullen. He's a Meadow Dweller. Have a seat, Tullen—and some cheese, if the antlerfruit didn't fill you up." She turned away to help with dinner preparations.

"You're from the Meadow?" Sall asked. "That's at least forty miles away, isn't it?"

"Just thirty, an easy run."

Tavi could hear the smile in Tullen's voice. She said, "He's twice-blessed. Stride and hearing."

"Twice-blessed, really?" Narre asked. "Of course, it takes more than two gifts to make an impression on Tavi!"

Behind Tullen, Tavi turned from her position at the stove, adamantly holding a finger to her lips. Tullen was the only person she knew who wasn't aware she was all-blessed, and she didn't want that to change. She caught both Sall's and Narre's eyes. Narre looked confused, but Sall threw Tavi a lifeline. "Tavi's read so many books on magic; there's not much that impresses her," he said. Tavi gave him a grateful nod before turning back to the stove.

"Goodness, I forgot to gather the eggs this morning!" Mey said. "Tavi, go get them for me, please."

Tavi picked up the egg basket from the countertop. "I'll come with you," Sall said, following her out the door. At the chicken coop, Tavi began to gather eggs. Sall stood quietly with his hands in his pockets and finally spoke. "I'm surprised you didn't tell Narre and me you'd made a friend from the Meadow," he said.

Tavi stretched to the furthest roost to get the last of the eggs, then reluctantly turned around. "Well, I don't see you very often anymore," she said.

A sound came out of Sall's throat; Tavi wasn't sure whether it was a cough or a laugh. He shook his head and said, "Perhaps that's because you've been avoiding both of us since our gifts awakened."

"No, I haven't." Seeing Sall's look of incredulity, Tavi admitted, "All right. I've avoided you." She looked in the basket of eggs, rather than meeting Sall's eyes. "But it's only because we don't have much in common anymore, since you awakened."

"Tavi!" Sall exclaimed. "Before our gifts awakened, we had endless subjects to discuss! Do you really believe my gift is the only thing I think about?" He quieted, and when Tavi finally looked at him, his eyes were waiting to meet hers. She did not look away as he said softly, "Tavi. We miss you."

Tears sprang to her eyes, and Tavi tried to blink them away. It was quiet for several moments, and then Sall spoke again. "I had almost no control over my gift during those first weeks. I'm still working on it, but it's much better. Have you noticed? My head hasn't glowed once since you got home." He gave a self-deprecating smile, but Tavi could hear the pride underneath his words.

"That's wonderful, Sall," she said. The silence returned, and Tavi again felt tears in her eyes. She might regret this later, but she had to speak. "When your gift first awakened, I hated that you knew those things about me," she said, her voice breaking. "I don't know how you didn't just run away from me when you saw how jealous I was of you and Narre and Reba."

When Tavi risked another look at Sall, he was giving her a sad smile. He said, "In the past, when I was angry, or critical, or spiteful toward others, I hated myself. I thought surely no one had so little control of themselves as I did." He laughed ruefully and continued. "When I began to see emotions in others, I was shocked—because I realized that every person around me has those same dark feelings I have. The most important thing I've learned is that even in the darkest part of my soul, I am not alone."

Tavi could only ask, "Really?"

Sall smiled. "Really! I've found it impossible to judge almost anyone, because I've realized how alike we all are."

"Almost anyone?" Tavi prompted.

Sall looked a little embarrassed, and he admitted, "I still judge Mayor Nolin. He's a stupid, power-hungry pig."

Tavi laughed out loud in shock, and Sall grinned. They walked back to the house, and he draped an arm around her shoulder, giving her a squeeze. "You're getting taller!" he said.

Tavi returned the gesture, her arm comfortably around her friend's waist. "Sall?" she said. "I've missed you too."

At dinner, Tavi felt ridiculous because her mouth insisted on breaking into a smile every time she glanced at Sall—her *friend*, Sall— but no one seemed to notice. After dinner, he walked home, and Tavi was delighted to hear that Narre would stay the night.

When Tullen had been settled in the boys' room, and everyone else was in bed, Tavi brought Narre outside, where they sat on the porch steps, a blanket wrapped around their shoulders against the summer breeze. They ate leftover bread from dinner and talked.

Eventually, Tavi gathered her courage and asked Narre to explain her gifts of breaking and binding. Narre looked surprised at the request, but her voice filled with joy as she told Tavi of all she was learning. Then she grasped her cousin's hand. "Ever since we were little girls, I've looked forward to sharing magic with you," she said. "I can't wait until we can experience it together."

Tavi's eyes filled with tears, but they were the happy sort. She squeezed Narre's hand in gratitude. When they went to bed, the stars shining bright in the midnight sky, Tavi fell asleep with a smile on her lips.

CHAPTER NINE

Be skeptical of your own thoughts,
Particularly your justifications.

-*From* Proverbs of Savala

KONNER WAS HALFWAY up the mountain road when he spied a wagon ahead. He kicked his horse's sides, and soon he was close enough to see the writing on the back of the wagon: CITY ICE.

He nodded in satisfaction, even as his stomach tightened with anxiety. He led his horse forward and drew up alongside the wagon.

Smiling widely, Konner greeted the driver. "Father!" he said. "I thought that might be you!"

Konner's father, surprised, pulled back on his horses' reins. "Hello! What are you doing this far from the city?" he asked.

"I'm visiting a potential client whose portfolio is substantial," Konner said. "I didn't want to leave the job to anyone else. I've allowed my horse to run quite a lot, however, and I think he would like a rest. Is there somewhere we could stop?"

His father nodded. "In another half mile or so, the road widens. You can rest there."

"I hope you'll stop with me," Konner said. "Surely your delivery can be delayed a few minutes?"

Konner's father, the poor sod, nodded, clearly delighted at his son's solicitude. After ignoring his parents for years, Konner had recently begun playing the part of the caring son, sharing simple dinners around the hearth of their tiny home. Konner had never seen his father so happy.

They soon reached the spot where the road widened. It boasted a sturdy wooden hitching post and a small bench. When Konner and his father had both tied their horses to the post, they sat on the bench, gazing ahead. Beyond the road, the ground dropped off into a sharp cliff.

Konner looked at the old man next to him. He was taller than Konner, but he did not have his son's natural strength. Konner wondered how his father carried the heavy ice blocks he delivered.

"Beautiful day," his father said.

Konner nodded. He no longer trusted his voice. He took a deep breath and, in one quick motion, Konner turned to his father, grabbed the man's shoulders, and pushed him backward off the bench. Konner landed on his father's body, and sturdy knees pinned old arms to the dirt.

Those thin arms were stronger than they looked, and Konner's father struggled to escape. His body twisted, and his legs kicked, but young determination beat aging desperation, as Konner had known it would.

"What are you doing?" Konner's father gasped.

Konner had considered this moment for weeks and had determined to stay silent. His objective was not to exact revenge, and he would not give himself or his father the satisfaction of listing his grievances. Instead, Konner continued to act, despite the struggling body underneath him.

His first step was crucial and strange. Konner had not so much as hugged his father in decades, yet now he brought his open mouth down to his father's. Their lips connected, and Konner breathed in deeply as his father cried out.

The next step would be tricky. Keeping his mouth firmly in place, and still pinning his father, Konner used one hand to pinch the man's nose. With his other hand, Konner pushed against his father's chin, forcing the old man's teeth closed, and then Konner pulled his own mouth away, moving his hand to cover his father's mouth before the man could take a breath.

The sensations were shocking to Konner; while he had planned every detail of this act, he had failed to consider how it would feel—the body writhing under him; arm muscles and bones compressed beneath his knees; dry lips, wet tongue, and hard teeth against his hand.

The struggle was intense, but quick. After his father stilled, Konner did not move for several minutes, wanting to be certain he had received the man's last breath. He leaned in close enough to smell the cheap tobacco his father used, and he spoke the words he'd wanted for years to say: "Go to Kovus, Father."

The irony of it didn't escape him; after the action he'd just taken, Konner was surely the one who would spend an eternity suffering. Yet as he stared in his father's sightless eyes, he found he didn't care. After the fateful council meeting weeks earlier, Konner's hatred for his father had grown. The man had robbed him of magic, and therefore of a seat on the council.

And then Konner had met Ash. They had agreed to work together to change Cormina, but first they had to learn how gray magic was created. The initial test would be simple: One person must kill another, neither of them gifted. At this stage they needed to keep their plans as private as possible, and Ash had suggested Konner participate in the first test.

Konner's first reaction had been confusion. "I'm not a murderer," he had said matter-of-factly.

A haunted look had entered Ash's eyes when he had replied, "Neither am I."

It was his first response—*That's not the type of man I am*—that had led Konner to reconsider Ash's proposition. He was the type of man to fight for necessary changes. He would do whatever it took. Or he had thought he would, until a place deep inside had insisted, *Well, anything but that.* This ultimate transgression, taking a life, felt different. It was too crass, too cruel.

But would a team ever follow Konner if they knew he was unwilling to push past his personal desires and sense of propriety— particularly when they would be required to kill if they were to gain gray magic? Konner determined he must take a life, but at least he would ensure it was not an innocent one.

So he had visited his parents' house. Over many weeks, he had built trust. His father had been more than happy to share with Konner all the tedious details of his job delivering ice.

And now Konner knelt, hands tight on his father's mouth and nose. It had not been as difficult has he had expected. Finally, he was confident it was over. He removed his hands, confirmed his father had no pulse, and stood.

There was no burning in his chest. He unbuttoned his shirt to be sure, but his skin looked normal. He had harbored serious doubts that a gray awakening could be obtained under these circumstances, yet his heart still fell when he saw proof of his persistent ordinariness.

This was no time to simmer in disappointment. Konner dragged his father's body across the road. One shove, and it tumbled down the cliff. Once he had buttoned his shirt, Konner untied his father's horses. The beasts would pull their full wagon to his father's customer further up the mountain, or they would return to the city. With any luck, the body would be found by animals before investigators came across it.

When his own horse was untied, Konner pulled himself into the saddle. He stopped near the edge of the cliff and gazed at his father's broken body below. Then he nudged his horse's sides, and they headed down the mountain.

CHAPTER TEN

When entering the profession of midwifery, you will not only assist at births. You will diagnose pregnancies and give comfort after miscarriages. You will offer one woman tips on how to make pregnancy more likely and advise the next woman on how to prevent it. If you are lucky, you will educate gifted young people. And when you are tired from all this, you will still be needed by someone. Always.

-*From* Midwifery: A Manual for Practical and Karian Midwives *by Ellea Kariana*

ELLEA KARIANA ENTERED the front door of the midwife house, walking slowly. The birth she had just attended had been long and difficult. Baby and mother were healthy, thanks be to Sava (and thanks be to Ellea's decades of experience.) But challenging births took so much out of her these days.

A hot bath beckoned, and Ellea was about to answer its call, when she heard a voice through the door of the kitchen. It was Pala, lecturing on the technicalities of ancient magical heresies. A soft chuckle rose from Ellea's chest, and she prayed that her Dreamers were managing not to live up to her pet name for them. Pala did not appreciate dreaming students.

Again, Ellea took a step toward the bathroom and the tub that awaited her, and again she halted. Ellea's recent schedule had been busier than usual with expectant mothers, new babies, and older students. She had not had even a short conversation with Tavi in months.

The tired midwife sighed. The bath would have to wait. She opened the door of the kitchen. "I'm sorry for interrupting," Ellea said when Pala paused her lecture, "but I have a task to complete, and I could use some help. May I please borrow Tavi?"

Pala looked irked, but she nodded. "You may."

Tavi smiled as she gathered her things and followed Ellea out of the room. "We have a large pile of sanitized rags and blankets, just waiting to be folded," Ellea explained as they walked. When they arrived at the storage room near the back of the house, Ellea showed Tavi how to wash her hands with lime water, to ensure they transferred no contamination to the clean cloths. The midwife then demonstrated how to properly fold both rags and blankets. They set to work, standing across from each other at a tall table.

"I appreciate your help," Ellea said. She let the silence stretch, hoping Tavi would break it. When it became evident that wouldn't happen, she prompted, "I'm sure you're ready for your gifts to awaken."

Naked frustration was written all over Tavi's face. "Yes! How much longer do you think it will be?"

"I wish I could tell you," Ellea said. "You're thirteen, and I would expect your mother cycle to start within the next year, though I can't make any promises."

"A year?" Tavi's pleading eyes found Ellea's face.

"Possibly much less! And once that begins, most young women awaken within days or weeks. Sometimes it takes many months, though no one knows why." Seeing Tavi's hopeless expression, Ellea assured her, "Tavi, your gifts *will* awaken. I promise."

With a sigh and a nod, Tavi continued to fold the cloths. Ellea said, "Tell me about the Meadow Dweller you've befriended."

Tavi perked up. "His name is Tullen, and he's sixteen. I met him a couple of months ago."

"Is it true he's gifted?"

"He's stride-blessed and hearing-blessed! But in the Meadow they say he has feet and ears of gold." A giggle burst out of the girl, and Ellea laughed too.

"If he lived here," Ellea pointed out, "he would train five days a week. I've never understood how gifted individuals in the Meadow can fully develop their magic when they get no training."

"They don't?" Tavi asked. When Ellea shook her head, the younger girl said, "I wonder why. I'll have to ask him."

"It would be interesting to hear his response," Ellea agreed. "I often don't understand their ways."

For several seconds the only sound was the rustle of cloth. Finally Tavi said, "Maybe they're more like us than we think."

"Perhaps," Ellea said.

They folded and chatted for another quarter hour, and then Ellea told Tavi she could head home early rather than rejoining the lecture. The girl gave a wide smile as she rushed toward the front door.

SEVERAL DAYS PASSED before Tullen came back to the forest. When Tavi found him, he spoke just two words: "Hunting time." Tavi grinned, took Tullen's quiver of arrows, and leapt onto his back.

In the previous weeks, Tavi had learned to ride quietly on her friend's back and to shift positions when it was time for him to nock, aim, and loose an arrow. Tullen had even taught her the basics of archery, but when she had jumped off his back one day to try it on a rabbit, she had made so much racket that the animal had hopped away. Tavi had decided she would leave the arrows to Tullen; her favorite part was the run, anyway.

Tullen adjusted Tavi, his bow, and his pack. He took his customary deep breaths to activate his stride and hearing gifts, and the hunt began. Their first run through the trees was short. Tullen stopped, and Tavi was still. He had heard an animal.

After a few seconds, they were off again. Tullen stopped twice to listen, and at last they slowed and ever so carefully approached a deer.

In seconds, it was over. Tullen's shot had been perfect. He and Tavi each let loose a cheer, and they approached the animal. Tavi turned her head when Tullen used his knife to end the deer's suffering.

Next Tullen would gut and skin his prize, then cut it in smaller pieces for transport and storage. Tavi was not at all interested in learning to field dress a deer, so she made herself as comfortable as she could, sitting against a large rock. Tullen gathered his tools and began his work.

Since her conversation with Ellea, Tavi had been waiting to ask Tullen about magic in the Meadow. She had continued to keep her own gifting secret, with the help of Sall, Narre, and her family. However, Tullen was always willing to talk about his gifts.

"When did your magic awaken?" Tavi asked, but before Tullen could answer, she continued, "Wait, wait—I bet you don't even call it 'awakening' in the Meadow, do you? I want to guess what your term is for it." She stared at Tullen until he raised his head from his work to meet her gaze. "Tullen," she said seriously, "When did your gold begin to glimmer?"

His laughter was immediate and loud, and she joined him, her straight face failing her. When the laughter died down, Tavi asked, "Really, what do you call it in the Meadow?"

Tullen responded dryly, "We call it 'awakening.' "

Tavi scowled. "I like my idea better! So, when did it happen for you?"

Tullen went back to his work. "I was almost fifteen."

Tavi nodded. That was somewhat late for boys, and it meant Tullen had only been practicing for a year and a half. "How are you so proficient already?" she asked.

"We don't have formal magical training in the Meadow," Tullen replied. "Mostly, I experiment to find out what does and doesn't work for me. There are adults in the community who share my gifts, and when I need help, I approach one of them."

"Why don't they train you like the midwives do here?" Tavi asked.

"Perhaps a better question is, why do the midwives train as they do?" Tullen replied. "I've heard Sall and Narre speak of their training, and much of it sounds pointless! Narre said she nearly always falls asleep during their long meditations, and Sall complains that many of the practical exercises are uselessly repetitive."

Tavi was immediately defensive. "Midwives have been working on their training program for generations!"

"Just enough time to develop dozens of meaningless traditions," Tullen retorted.

Tavi forced composure on herself; Tullen would wonder why this was so important to her. She reflected on her conversation with Ellea, and she was glad the midwife wasn't there to hear Tullen's words. Ellea would consider the Meadow Dweller terribly sacrilegious.

Tavi's thoughts were interrupted by Tullen's voice casually asking, "Are you looking forward to your gifts awakening?"

Tavi froze. She stared at Tullen's lowered head, at his hands cutting into the deer. She heard the scrape of the knife and the crinkle of dry leaves under his knees. Then she realized she wasn't breathing. Her inhale was more like a gasp, and she forced the words out. "How long have you known?"

Tullen looked up at her with a small smile. "I've known ever since you told me your name."

Her voice was soft, but she enunciated every word. "What do you mean?"

Tullen put down the knife, wiped his hands on a rag, and turned toward Tavi. He seemed to sense her turmoil, and his face was now serious. "I know people see Meadow Dwellers as isolated," he said, "and that is usually true. However, we have men and women who travel to Oren and elsewhere to buy and sell.

"Thirteen years ago, one of our farmers returned from Oren with news of a birth. He said a sun-blessed baby's entire body had glowed golden when she received her breath of blessing. I didn't hear the story from the farmer himself; I was too young. But the tale is repeated, even now. The tale of a baby named Tavina, who was called Tavi."

Halfway through Tullen's words, Tavi's head had begun to shake slowly. "I didn't think you knew."

Tullen's brows knit together. "Why did you want to keep it secret?"

"Because I've never had a friend who didn't know about me." Tavi swallowed past the lump in her throat. "I thought you wanted to be my friend because of who I am, not because of my gifts."

"But I do!" Tullen insisted. "Remember, I spoke to you before I knew who you were!"

"And within seconds, I revealed myself as the mythical all-blessed baby!" Tavi's voice was loud in her ears. "I wondered why you kept coming back, and now I know!"

"Tavi!" Tullen gave a frustrated laugh that displayed no real humor. "Why would I even care whether you are all-blessed, or barely blessed, or not blessed at all?"

Tavi found herself standing, and her voice was even louder. "Because that's all that anyone cares about! All my life that has been the first and last thing people think about when they hear my name. And I thought you were different!"

Tullen came to his feet too, and he stepped toward Tavi. His arms were folded, and she wasn't sure if he was confused, angry, or both. In a controlled voice, he said, "I am trying to understand you. Please answer me this: In Oren, are the Blessed treated differently? Are they seen as . . . special?"

Tavi's arms spread in exasperation. "Of course they are! Aren't they in the Meadow?"

"No!" Tullen's voice was full of incredulity. He took a deep breath and continued more calmly. "Why would I be treated with extra respect because of something that happened to me at birth?"

Tavi wanted to answer the question, but she could not.

"Do you want to know who is given extra respect in the Meadow?" Tullen asked. At Tavi's nod, he continued. "My mother is respected because she has been weaving fabric for a quarter-century, and she improves every year, even teaching her skill to others. My father is respected because he puts his entire soul into his tasks in the fields. He works harder than I ever will. I was never seen as special due to my gifts; however, I am gaining respect because I am learning to use those gifts in a way that benefits my community." He gestured toward the deer. "This deer will show my people I am working hard for them, and for that, I will be respected, but not for the speed of my running."

"That sounds . . . very nice," Tavi said.

Tullen's face and voice softened. "My reasons for being your friend have nothing to do with you occasionally turning into a glow bug," he said.

Tavi's mouth dropped. Several times, she had felt the glow beginning when she was particularly content with her new friend—but each time, she had forced her thoughts to something sad or stressful, attempting to shut down the reaction before it was noticeable. "Have you seen that happen?" she managed to ask.

Tullen laughed. "Of course I have! You're a lantern that insists on lighting up, even though you shutter it as quickly as you can!"

Tavi covered her cheeks with her hands, but this time she was warm with embarrassment, rather than with magic. Tullen said, "I'm your friend because I enjoy spending time with you. Nothing more, nothing less."

Tavi tried to stop it, but there was no preventing the sudden tears in her eyes, and they insisted on escaping down her cheeks. Then her shoulders were shaking with sobs, and her nose was running, and it was *awful* and *wonderful*, and she sat down again, her back against the rock, crying because her new friend didn't care that she was magical, but he did care about her.

Her face was in her hands, and she was crying too hard to hear Tullen approaching, but she did feel him sit next to her. He put his arm around her, and she lay her head on his shoulder and let the tears fall.

CHAPTER ELEVEN

In the smallest of towns, one woman often acts as both midwife and healer. I have always been glad Oren is large enough to have separate midwives and healers. I am unsure whether I could help a woman give birth one day and support a dying patient the next.

-*From* Small-Town Cormina: A Midwife's Reflections *by Ellea Kariana*

ASH SAT at a rustic table in a kitchen dimly lit by one lantern, waiting for the woman who would meet him there.

Soon after meeting Ash, Konner had instructed him to find a job in a healing house. The first clinic Ash had visited, three blocks from Konner's home, had jumped at the chance to hire a touch-blessed domestic whose hands could work at several times the normal speed.

Rolling bandages, chopping vegetables, and doing laundry hadn't been what Ash had expected when he'd agreed to partner with Konner. He despised the work, made even worse by the waterproof kidskin gloves he wore, under which his hands sweated all day. But the gloves prevented others from seeing his gray magic. When asked why he wore them, Ash said his gift had made his hands sensitive to light of all sorts.

Besides the tasks assigned to him by the healers, Ash had another responsibility, given to him by Konner. The healers' work with ill patients was often difficult, and Ash was to offer them friendship and emotional support. The response had been positive, thanks to Ash's natural charm. Ash had a reason for building these relationships. He was looking for a particular type of healer—and he was quite sure he had found her.

Unlike many of the healers, Meri was not sun-blessed. She worked with people who were dying, beyond the help of gifted hands. She was still called a healer, but in reality, she was a comforter, and it took its toll.

Ash had offered himself as a confidante to Meri, and she had begun to trust him. Today, Meri had arrived at the healing house after spending all day with a dying man. She had cried while describing the sick room, which for hours had been filled with the sounds of the patient's rattling breaths and his family's helpless weeping. The man had not yet succumbed to his illness when Meri had left.

Ash had listened to Meri and comforted her. He had then asked her to meet him in the kitchen late that night when the other healers were sleeping. She had seemed hesitant, but she had agreed. Now he waited for her.

At last, Meri arrived. Once she sat, Ash greeted her and smiled. "May I tell you a story?"

"Yes."

Ash began, "When I was a child, my grandfather lived with us, and I was close to him." He watched Meri, who was nodding with a kind expression on her face. "Unfortunately, he grew old, as I suppose we all will. I was only twelve when Grandfather became sick. When you described your patient today, it was as if you were describing my grandfather in his last days. His suffering was agonizing to witness."

Meri's eyes brimmed with tears as Ash continued to describe his grandfather's last days. For the next half hour, they discussed the injustice of difficult deaths, which so many people experienced, despite having lived lives full of goodness.

Ash's hand reached for Meri's, and she did not pull away. "I'm so glad to know someone else sees this the way I do," he said. He took a deep breath and watched her face carefully as he continued. "It seems the most merciful thing to do would be to end the patient's pain. If they could speak, wouldn't they choose to enter Senniet, to be eternally with Sava and those who have gone before them, rather than to continue suffering?"

Meri dropped her eyes, and Ash feared he had gone too far. However, when she looked up, she was nodding. "I have had that same thought," she admitted.

Ash spoke and answered questions, and above all he displayed understanding and mercy. By the time the clock struck one, the young healer across from Ash had unwittingly agreed to be part of Konner's plans.

THE NIGHT after his conversation with Meri, Ash arrived at the weekly meeting of the Sun Society. Months ago, at Konner's request, Ash had joined the Savala chapter of the group.

The Sun Society was an organization for the gifted. The membership rolls were long, but meetings were attended primarily by a few dozen dedicated members.

Ash entered through the front door of the Society Hall and sat at a table along with a few men and women he had befriended. This table, Ash had discovered, attracted sun-blessed individuals who were disillusioned with their gifts. The weekly ritual of complaining began.

"I tried to use my sight gift seven times yesterday, and it only worked four times," one woman complained.

"Were you attempting to look through the bedroom curtains of the man next door again?" another woman asked. Laughter broke out, and the original speaker did not deny the allegation, smiling mischievously. The conversation continued along these lines, with more members willing to share their stories as they consumed glasses of cheap wine.

Eventually, the meeting wound down. When the sight-blessed

woman who had first spoken rose to leave, Ash stood as well. He bade his friends goodnight and caught up with the woman outside.

Her name was Sella Ketter, and Ash had been watching her closely in recent weeks. His first impression had been her irreverent sense of humor, but Ash also perceived a depth in her. Sella was more disciplined than most members, drinking perhaps half a glass of wine at each meeting. She laughed and joked with the best of them, but occasionally she asked a question that made it clear she was thinking about the problems within magic, culture, and society. Sella's gifting was strong and impressive. She could look through all solid substances except metals.

Sella had never disclosed her profession in Society meetings, and her clothing and speech gave the impression she was nothing remarkable—perhaps a household servant. However, Konner had investigated Sella and learned that mining companies around Savala and beyond paid exorbitant hourly rates for her to use her gift to guide their digs. She lived like an ordinary person but had multiple bank accounts under different names, with enough money saved that, at twenty-eight, she could have retired in luxury had she so wished.

Ash approached Sella. "May I walk you home?" he asked.

She gave him a suggestive grin. "Only if you'll agree to stay once we get there."

His response was quick and firm. "That's not what I meant." Since Riami's death, Ash had felt ill when he thought of being with another woman. Holding Meri's hand the night before had been difficult enough.

Sella's feet stopped moving, and when Ash realized it and turned around, her eyes locked on his. "What is this about?" she demanded.

Ash was taken aback; his charm usually allowed him to control conversations, but Sella was reversing that. "I need to talk to you," he replied.

"In private?"

"Yes."

"Come on." Sella walked briskly, and Ash continued next to her, confused but quiet. She did not say a word as they walked several blocks, turning twice. They stopped before an apothecary, and Sella pulled out a key, opening the door of the dark store. She closed and locked it behind her, lit a lantern, and led Ash through the store, past shelves of labeled jars of all sizes and shapes, and into an office. She closed the door, and they sat in chairs across from a small desk. "Tell me why you need to talk to me, and don't dance around the truth," Sella said.

"Where are we?" Ash asked.

"My father's apothecary," Sella replied. She raised her eyebrows, waiting for him to speak.

Ash had planned for this conversation to be full of smiles and gentle deceptions, as his chat with Meri had been the previous night. His expectations were changing. He wasn't sure if it was possible to regain the upper hand, but he would try.

Instead of speaking, Ash pulled his gloves off. Sella's eyes widened as his hands glowed gray, and Ash fought to keep the pain off his face. On the desk next to them were several small bottles, and in half a second, Ash had taken one of the medicines, put it in his pocket, and folded his hands in front of him. He released his magic and stared at Sella. Her hand was extended as if to stop him from taking the bottle, but she had been far too slow.

Awe and fascination filled Sella's eyes. "What was that?" she asked.

Ash allowed himself a smile. "Gray magic."

"You used it to steal."

"Yes."

"Please tell me how."

Ash complied. As he described Riami's death at his hands, Sella looked interested, rather than disgusted. Ash continued, explaining his connections with a wealthy businessman and a young healer. He told her what would come next if she would agree to be part of it. He disclosed everything, save Konner's and Meri's identities and his own true name.

When Ash stopped talking, Sella leaned forward, her eyes blazing. "Tell me what to do and when to do it."

HOURS LATER, Ash and Sella waited under a tree across the street from a row of narrow, attached homes. The wind penetrated through their coats, but they stood straight and still, watching the second home from the left. The downstairs front window filled with lantern light, the symbol Ash and Meri had agreed upon. It meant that the healer was meeting with the family in the front room. Ash and Sella crossed the street, rounded the building to a dirty alley, and crept through a back door, left unlocked by Meri.

In the sick room, Sella took the man's last breath and smothered him with an efficiency that unsettled Ash. They left as quietly as they had arrived and strolled through the streets, arm in arm, a couple enjoying a walk through the cold city. Sella's skin retained its natural color the whole way.

Ash had explained the experimental nature of the evening's task, but as they entered the apothecary office twenty minutes after they had left the house, Sella's voice was filled with controlled anger. "We will try again," she said.

At Konner's house, he and Ash discussed the result of the test. It was impossible not to feel discouraged. They now knew those who were ungifted could not bestow gray awakenings at all, even if the attempted recipient was sun-blessed. They could not risk exposure by killing any more of Meri's patients who were not blessed.

The next night, Ash again had a midnight meeting with Meri. Tears in his eyes, he explained that while he was gratified to have relieved the old man's suffering, the act had left him far more troubled than he had expected. "I fear that if I do this regularly, I may go mad," he confessed. Ash then continued the story from two nights before, telling Meri of his grandfather's hearing-blessed ears. Could she lead him specifically to gifted patients whose suffering he could relieve in honor of his grandfather?

The young healer appeared surprised by the sudden change, but she agreed to it.

Meri only encountered sun-blessed patients on the edge of death occasionally. Weeks later when she finally brought news of one, Ash allowed Konner to perform the act of mercy. Konner remained unchanged afterward, and both men again felt their hopes dashed.

Ungifted people could not receive gray awakenings, even from the sun-blessed.

Five weeks later, on a cold winter night, Ash struggled to contain his elation when Meri approached him with the story of a suffering, sun-blessed man. Sella's patience had been waning, and Ash was not sure what his potential protégé would do if she were not given a gray awakening soon. After the three previous tests, all failures, Ash harbored a deep fear that even this test, replicating his experience with Riami closely, would fail. Yet anticipation overpowered his nerves, and he made the arrangements with both Meri and Sella.

Sella's actions the next night were just as quick and competent as they had been the first time. She and Ash exited through the alley behind the residence, and as they walked, her eyes remained unchanged—except that they narrowed in a furious glare. "I don't know what you're up to, but I will not continue killing for you," she said in a low voice.

"I don't know what could be wrong!" Ash insisted as they exited the alley and walked down the street. "The only thing that was different was that I was angry when I received my gray awakening—perhaps that's it. Perhaps you have to be angry, or you have to love the person. I don't know."

Sella stared at him, the muscles in her jaw tensing. "Or perhaps you lied about this whole thing, and you're just a freak who was born with different magic than the rest of us. Perhaps you get off on watching people die, but you're too cowardly to kill them yourself." She stopped, and Ash did as well. "I'm leaving," she said. "Don't follow me." She raised her hand in an obscene gesture, then pivoted and walked the other direction. Ash watched her, but he did not follow.

After she had taken several steps, Sella stopped, standing stock-still in the middle of the road. Ash strode to her, coming around to face her.

Sella gazed at Ash, her eyes surrounded by a mask of thunder-clouds, shining with the lightning of magic. Her brow was knit—that was the pain, he knew. But she was smiling. He guided her to the shadows between two homes. She directed her attention to a shuttered window in the building across from them.

In a low voice, strained with pain, Sella said, "There is an open box of jewelry in that room, and no one is there. The window is not latched. We could steal every bit of it if we wished." Ash knew Sella felt the terrible burn of gray magic, yet she released a quiet laugh of delight.

Ash activated his own gray magic and held out a glowing hand to the woman in front of him. She shook it firmly, and he smiled through his own pain.

"Welcome to the Grays," Ash said.

CHAPTER TWELVE

As you requested, I will tell you of the day my magic made itself known. However, it is a terribly unimpressive tale. I stepped on a thorn, pulled it out, and grasped the small wound with my right hand. My hand began to glow, and my foot healed.

-*From* Savala's Collected Letters, Volume 2

THAT WINTER WAS much colder than the last had been. Tullen only came twice, during short, warm spans. Tavi missed her friend, but she delighted at all the days school was cancelled. As often as possible on snow days, she, Narre, and Sall trudged through the cold streets toward each other's homes. When they found each other, they made their way to one of the girls' houses to huddle in front of the fire or play in the snow.

They often talked about the time they had spent together the previous winter. They all missed Reba. She had further distanced herself from all of them, even Narre. Still, they enjoyed the season, and when the bitter cold departed, they resignedly adjusted back to their normal schedules, uninterrupted by snow days.

With the arrival of spring, Tullen hunted in the area frequently again, staying with Tavi's family for two or three nights at a time. Tavi often hopped on his back so they could run through the forest, hunting or exploring. Occasionally on a weekend day, Sall and Narre came, and the four of them spent hours exploring and laughing. Those days were close to perfect.

Spring stepped aside gracefully, and Tavi welcomed the warmth of summer. Again, her birthday fell during the week-long midsummer break from school. Tullen, Sall, and Narre had planned a surprise party for her, complete with a decorated cake, and it was so delightful that Tavi barely thought about the fact that, at fourteen, her body still refused to welcome her to womanhood.

Summer was winding to a close, the afternoon heat letting up, when Tavi awoke one morning, visited the outhouse in the back yard, and immediately returned to the house to find Misty. Her sister listened to Tavi's whispered words, and then Tavi had to cover Misty's mouth to keep her from announcing the secret to the whole house.

Misty and Mey helped Tavi gather the supplies she needed and insisted on educating her with information that Tavi had known for years. Tavi then walked to Narre's house to share the good news with her cousin, whose response was an enthusiastic, "Finally!"

After school, Tavi was walking home when she heard running footsteps behind her. It was Sall and Narre. "Ellea let us go half an hour early today," Sall explained. When Tavi saw Narre's conspiratorial smile, she knew her cousin must have followed through on the plan they'd formed at lunch. Narre had agreed to have a short conversation with Ellea, explaining Tavi's situation and pleading with the midwife to end her training at the same time school ended so the friends could spend the whole afternoon together.

Tavi tried to sound surprised when she responded, "That's great!" There was a pause that felt too long, and she said, "Tullen came in yesterday; we can go find him."

At Tavi's house, they took the snacks offered by Mey before heading into the trees. Tullen soon found and joined the trio. In unspoken agreement, they headed toward their favorite clearing. Narre and Tavi lingered behind the boys, and Narre leaned toward her friend and whispered, "How are you feeling?"

Tavi replied quietly, "I feel normal. Is that normal?"

Narre laughed softly. "I think so! It took me a few months to feel any pain, and mine is usually mild, anyway."

Sall looked back at the girls with a questioning expression.

At the clearing, they sat in the grass and laid out the snacks Tavi's mother had provided. As they ate, Sall turned to Tullen and spoke to him, too softly for the girls to understand.

"Is that so?" Tullen asked loudly.

Tavi and Narre immediately responded. "What are you saying?" "Is what so?"

Tullen laughed. "Sall was just telling me about all the whispering you girls have been doing today."

Tavi's eyes widened. Narre smiled and said, "Sometimes young women need to talk privately." Tavi looked at her friend in warning, but Narre continued, "It has been a big day for Tavi, and I simply wanted to make sure she is handling it well."

Tavi felt her face burn in embarrassment. Even her ears were on fire. But it wasn't over.

"Did you finally start your cycle, Tavi?" Tullen asked.

Silence filled the clearing; it was as if even the birds were shocked.

Tavi felt her mouth drop open, and she turned to Narre in horror. She would literally die of mortification, right here in this beautiful clearing, and her gifts were not even going to awaken in time for her to enjoy them! When no one said anything, she covered her face with her hands, begging Sava to send a distraction like a bear or a lightning strike—straight onto Tullen or Narre.

"I can't believe you said that!" Narre admonished Tullen.

All right, so Sava wasn't going to answer Tavi's prayer. She peeked through her fingers at Narre's wide eyes and at Sall's face, which was just as bright red as her own. Tullen, on the other hand, was sitting casually, a look of mild confusion on his face.

"Did I say something I shouldn't have?" Tullen asked.

"This is so humiliating," Tavi moaned, and then she realized she had said it out loud, which just increased her consternation.

Narre was ready to defend her cousin. "Tullen!" she admonished. "It is highly inappropriate for a boy to ask a girl about such things."

Tullen's voice was matter-of-fact as he replied, "It's entirely appropriate in the Meadow. Sometimes I wonder what is wrong with the rest of Cormina!" Tavi took her hands off her face, and Tullen's eyes shifted to her. "You're really distressed, aren't you, Tavi?" he asked, clearly dismayed.

She nodded, and Narre continued to speak for her. "Of course she is!"

Sall chimed in, "This is very awkward." Tavi nodded again, in flustered agreement.

Tullen was still watching Tavi, and he looked upset—as he should, Tavi reflected. "I don't quite understand what's happening here, but please accept my apology," Tullen said. Tavi nodded, and he took that as permission to keep talking. "As we have discussed, I have over fifty sisters. We all live close, and we don't keep many secrets. When a Meadow girl starts her cycle, we celebrate! She is entering adulthood, or at least the first part of it. It's nothing to be ashamed of."

Narre's eyes narrowed in thought. "That makes a lot of sense," she said. "But it's still odd and not entirely natural."

Tavi nodded, and then her eyes met Sall's. He was looking at her with such compassion, and—oh, no, his head was gently glowing. Tavi widened her eyes in disbelief, and he responded with a rueful smile. "Sometimes I still can't help it," Sall said. "Are you all right?"

Tavi knew he could sense every emotion she was feeling, but she still appreciated the question. "I'm all right," she said. "Really."

"Good," Narre said. "Let's eat already." The tension was broken, and as they ate, their talk turned to mundane topics.

Tavi joined in the light conversation, broken by frequent laughter. She sighed happily, wishing she could trap her contentment in a jar, drinking from it whenever she wanted. Suddenly, she felt a familiar warmth all through her body. Tullen noticed first, winking and mouthing, "glow bug." She smiled and basked in the peace of her gift.

Tavi sniffed. What was that odor? She thought it was the sweet, musty smell of plants decomposing on the forest floor, but perhaps it was the raisins in the bread Mey had sent with them . . . or the sap on the surrounding trees . . . or was it smoke from her family's stove, way beyond the trees? Or was it all of those things? Yes, she thought it was.

The confusion of that conclusion—that her small nose was detecting all those odors at once—was suddenly overwhelmed by a dozen, a hundred, a thousand more sensations.

Tavi heard her mother and Misty talking about the dinner they were preparing. It sounded as if they were just around a bend in the trail, but she knew they were back home, half a mile away. Tavi's breaths were coming more quickly, and she drew her knees up to her chest, but when her feet flattened on the dirt, she felt a vibration through her shoes, and she somehow knew it was the movement of water flowing deep underground.

Tavi looked in panic at her friends, and her eyes caught a strange distortion in the air around Narre's head; she blinked and saw the same distortion around many areas of her friend's body—her armpits, the insides of her elbows, and her feet. Tavi shook her head hard, and when she looked at Tullen and Sall, she saw the same phenomenon around them.

Tearing her eyes from her friends, Tavi looked at the basket they had used to carry their food, and with just a glance, her mind was full of diagrams of how the basket was made, the process of weaving every piece of straw in and out, up and down, to make an intricate pattern.

Tavi was too stunned and overwhelmed to cry or even speak. Every thought, every nerve, was full to bursting. She was overpowered by it all—the smells, multiplying by the moment; the sounds of her family talking—not just her mother and Misty now, but her siblings too; the vibration of water rushing deep under her feet; the sight of strange, twisting air around her friends; the diagrams in her mind of the woven basket and Narre's shoe and the buttons on Tullen's shirt.

A small part of her mind realized all conversation had stopped, and her friends were staring at her with concern. Tavi reached out to Narre and grabbed her cousin's hand—but instead of the comfort of a friend's grip, her palm filled with even more sensations. She could feel the blood running through Narre's vessels, how it was pumping faster than perhaps was normal, but one finger was getting less circulation thanks to the tight ring on it.

Tavi let go of her friend, and she lay on the ground, on her side, curled into a ball. Her voice rose in a loud groan, a sound unlike any she had ever heard from herself.

In an instant, Tavi's friends were kneeling next to her, and they were all talking. The first words Tavi could understand were Sall's: "Take a deep breath, Tavi. A deep, slow breath." Tavi realized she was crying, but she did her best to do as Sall instructed, and her panic lessened.

Next, Narre's voice rose above the others. "You're all right, Tavi. We're here, and you're all right. Look at us." Tavi gazed at each of her friends, and she saw worry in their faces, but love too. Still she cried, but she kept her eyes on them.

Tullen's words broke through. "Tavi." His voice was close to her ear as he leaned in. "One at a time. Move every bit of focus to your hands. Only your hands, Tavi."

Tavi continued to watch her friends, kept taking deep breaths, but she took her mind off everything but her hands, which she found were being held by Narre and Sall. She was aware of blood urgently pulsing through her friends, under their warm skin, and she converged every thought on that feeling.

With her focus shifted to her hands, Tavi's mind no longer fixated on how the things around her were constructed. Gradually, the other sensations went away as well. Her feet had already lost most of their awareness of the water when she had lain on her side; now she could not feel it at all. The voices of her family faded to nothing. The smells dissipated, and the air around her friends appeared ordinary.

Tavi gazed at her hands; they were still alive with a golden glow, but her arms were normal, and the rest of her body had lost the telltale warmth of magic. Tavi found that she was now comforted by the sensation of blood rushing through her friends' hands, a pulse of life and love. Her eyes again on her friends' faces, she continued to breathe deeply. Finally, even her hands released their magic. Her body filled with peace, along with a deep weariness.

"Let's help you up." Tavi wasn't sure which of her friends said it,

CAROL BETH ANDERSON

but she allowed them to assist her into a seated position. Then they were all close to her, hands on her shoulders, her back, her head, quietly offering words of comfort.

When Tavi smiled, they all became silent, their faces full of relief and hope.

"I'm all right," Tavi whispered.

Narre cupped her friend's cheeks with her hands. "Tavi," she said, "I think you've awakened."

CHAPTER THIRTEEN

I love small towns. People take care of each other in a way I have rarely seen in large cities. I enjoy being able to walk anywhere I need to go, and I love the proximity of quiet areas where I can enjoy nature.

But there is one thing I miss about living in a large city, and I will disclose it even at the risk of sounding shallow. I miss the shops.

-From Small-Town Cormina: A Midwife's Reflections *by Ellea Kariana*

"Sella," Ash asked, "What do you see?"

Sella closed her eyes a split second longer than usual, and when they reopened, they were lit with a gray glow. She shivered, and a wild grin filled her face. Ash shook his head. It had been months since Sella's gray awakening, and he still couldn't understand why she thrilled in the pain of it.

Sella looked across the street. A moment later, she turned to the young man next to her and whispered, "The guard is patrolling the lobby! Go now!"

The third person in their party, Aldin Stannel, did not even take time to nod. Crouching low, he dashed across the cobblestone street, his shadow long in the dim light of the gas streetlamp. Once he reached the bank building, he crept along the side of it. He placed one foot on the gray brick and froze in place.

Though Ash couldn't hear it, he knew Aldin was taking quick breaths from his mouth, a whispered "huh-hoo" repeated five times. Ash glanced at Sella, who was glaring at Aldin.

"That kid has got to figure out a quicker way to activate his gift," Sella said.

Then Aldin's other foot was on the brick, and he was running straight up the wall, still crouched, a two-footed spider. In seconds, he reached the third floor and entered an open window.

"Report what you see," Ash instructed Sella.

"He's walking around the office."

"I thought he was going to grab the item and leave," Ash said.

"He was," Sella said. "I'm positively shocked at his lack of focus, aren't you?"

Ash laughed. Sella's disdain was justified. Six weeks earlier, Aldin had received a gray awakening and joined their group, and Ash often wondered if allowing that had been wise. The young man was only seventeen, but he had been on his own since fifteen, living on the streets and in cheap boarding houses, finding jobs where he could. He was young, and he acted even younger.

Every time Ash wanted to kick himself for bringing the immature young prankster into their midst, he thought about Aldin's gift. Ash had never heard of anyone who could walk up walls and across ceilings as if on flat ground. Aldin had a lot to learn about how to best use his magic, having only experienced a few months of training at a midwife house. His control was weak and unpredictable. But Ash and Konner wanted that level of raw talent in their group.

"Where is the guard now?" Ash asked.

Sella's eyes shifted downward, toward the lobby, and she did not answer.

"Sella?"

"I don't know. I'm looking." Then her gray-lit eyes widened, and her words came quickly. "The guard is climbing the stairs. He's nearly to the third floor. He must be checking the offices early."

Ash cursed. "Is Aldin almost done?"

"He's still roaming around the office. Stupid kid! He's kneeling in front of the desk chair. I don't know what he's doing. Wait, he's standing up—no, now he's lying on the couch."

Ash stared at the building, wishing it would give him its interior secrets as it did for Sella.

"The guard has unlocked the first office door," Sella said. "Aldin is in the last office—the fifth one. The guard is moving on to the second office now."

"What's Aldin doing?"

"He's still lying down. He's wiggling around on the couch, like he's trying to get comfortable. His magic isn't even active anymore."

Ash turned to her. "We need to decide how we're going to get out of here without being seen. If Aldin's caught, safety officers will swarm this place."

"The guard just finished with the third office." There was silence for half a minute. Sella whispered, "The guard's at the last door. Key in the lock—Aldin heard it; he's running to the window. But it'll take too long—oh, sweet Sava's knuckles, the guard used the wrong key. Aldin is on the windowsill; he must be activating his magic—the guard is trying again—"

"He did it!" Ash said, louder than he'd intended.

Aldin had indeed done it; he was sprinting down the side of the building. Ash shook his head; he'd never get used to seeing Aldin sideways like that, gravity bent to his will. The young wall-walker made it to the ground and didn't stop running until he'd reached the other side of the road.

Sella's gaze could have frozen a hot coal. "Someday your luck will run out, you twit."

Aldin gave her a rakish grin. "Grabbed this on the way out," he said, tossing her the item they'd come for.

Ash shook his head. He felt as if his heart would beat out of his chest; how could his young accomplice be smiling after all that?

THE NEXT MORNING, Ash walked into Konner's study. Konner wasn't there, but three of the seats were occupied. "Good morning," Ash said. "How did yesterday go, Camalyn?"

Camalyn Hunt, the newest member of the group, held up a hat. It was gorgeous, constructed of vibrant blue wool with peacock feathers. Ash looked at it appreciatively, ever the artist. "Tell me about the hat."

"It was priced at forty chips." Eyebrows around the room rose; at that price, the hat must have come from one of the finest shops. Camalyn's pink lips held a proud smile as she continued, "I had a delightful chat with the milliner, and he agreed to pay me twenty chips, three quads to take it."

Ash laughed and asked, "He paid you twenty and three to take it?"

Camalyn's grin widened. "I explained to him how much his business will improve when all the women of Savala see me wearing it, and I tell them where they can purchase their own."

Ash shook his head in disbelief. "That was very good."

Camalyn's father, a businessman, had taken out multiple loans at Konner's bank. The man had recently defaulted on all of them due to his own poor decisions. He had begged Konner for yet another loan, explaining that his gifted daughter Camalyn could not bear to live at a lower standard than she was accustomed to. His arguments had not swayed Konner, who knew when to cut his bank's losses. However, Konner had arranged a meeting with Camalyn, and his promises of influence and affluence had easily convinced her to become a Gray.

Camalyn was speech-blessed, and since experiencing her gray awakening, she had delighted in using her persuasive powers to manipulate willing shopkeepers. It didn't hurt that she was exceptionally pretty, and she knew it. She had become accustomed to getting her own way before her magic had even awakened. Now that her gift no longer resisted being used for questionable purposes, she was enraptured with her own success.

"Any issues with being detected?" Ash asked Camalyn.

She looked unsure. "I don't think so. The cosmetics make the glow around my mouth less noticeable. I keep my lips close together when I speak. I've also taken your advice, holding up a fan." Camalyn demonstrated, looking beguilingly over the top of her fan at Ash. With those eyes looking at them, the shopkeepers probably didn't even care if the gray glow was evident.

"Excellent," Ash said. "Sella and Aldin were busy yesterday too. Would the two of you like to show Camalyn what you retrieved last night?"

Sella handed a small canvas bag to Aldin. With a flourish, he pulled out a desktop name plate reading, "KONNER BURRELL, PRESIDENT."

Camalyn's mouth dropped open, and it widened into an incredulous smile. "You broke into his office?"

Aldin nodded proudly while Sella raised an eyebrow in annoyance. "He was nearly caught," she said. "He treated the office as his own personal lounge. We had agreed he would get in, take the name plate, and get out, but he was in there for a good five minutes. He barely made it out the window while the incompetent night guard was trying to unlock the office door."

"Well, I had to leave him some of these." Aldin pulled a jar out of his pocket. On the front was a handwritten label reading, "TWILL-BERRY PRESERVES."

Ash was confused. "You left jam in his office?"

Aldin's young face was filled with satisfaction as he announced, "I spread some on his chair!"

The other residents of the room widened their eyes. Sella said, "If you don't warn Konner before he sits in those, I'm pretty sure he'll kill you."

"It's too late!" Aldin said, laughing. "I'm sure he's already left for work."

"You're an idiot," Sella stated.

Aldin shrugged, and he still looked remarkably proud of himself.

Ash pointed to the name plate. "You'll probably want to make sure Konner doesn't see that."

"What's the point?" It was Sella speaking, her arms crossed. She was staring at Ash.

"Of what?" he asked.

"Of all this," Sella said. "Now, before you say we're practicing our gifts in ways that won't garner us a lot of attention, stop. I know all that. I've been here for six months now; we've added two new people; and you and Konner still haven't told me why we're here. I've stopped working. I'm living in this huge house. I'm given anything I need, and I know it's not from the kindness of Konner Burrell's heart. Tell us why."

Ash cleared his throat. "Well—"

He was interrupted by Camalyn. "I agree. When Konner brought me in, he told me we'd change the world together. Don't get me wrong; I'm loving all this, but a peacock feather hat doesn't change the world."

Ash looked at Aldin, waiting for him to join the cry for information. The young man looked uncertain, then asked, "Were there any scones left after breakfast?"

Sella and Camalyn groaned, and Ash shook his head, which was becoming his standard reaction to Aldin. When Ash looked up, the two women were still watching him expectantly.

This was a predicament. Even Ash knew few details of Konner's plans. But this wasn't the first time Sella and Camalyn had pushed him to tell them more. He was concerned that if they weren't soon satisfied, they would leave the group, taking their gray magic with them.

Ash opened his mouth. "Well—" he began.

At that moment, the door to the library opened. Konner Burrell stepped in, and Ash bit back a laugh when he saw Aldin shoving the nameplate underneath his seated form, then squirming. The brass edges couldn't be comfortable to sit on.

Konner joined Ash, standing in front of their seated compatriots. "Have a seat, Ash," he said. Ash complied, and the banker leaned back, half-sitting on the edge of his desk. He gazed at each of the four people in front of him. His mouth held a small smile. After several seconds, Konner spoke. "I have spent the past weeks and months watching you. You are all skillful. More importantly, you are all trustworthy. I stayed home this morning, because it is time to tell you what we're working toward."

Ash looked at Camalyn and Sella, who appeared just as surprised as he felt. Could Konner have heard them through the door? No, the door was thick, and they hadn't been speaking that loudly. Was the man that skilled of a strategist, that he had somehow predicted the exact time when his fledgling team would have reached a breaking point, the time when he could come in and be the hero, giving everyone what they wanted?

Konner continued, his voice solemn and thoughtful. "Every day, I look at the world around me," he intoned, "and I am grieved."

He spoke to the four of them the same way he had spoken to Ash a year earlier. Konner shared his disgust with the weakness and complacency of their culture. He harkened back to the time of the ancient epics when strong individuals and nations had ruled the world.

Ash felt the same internal stirring he had experienced during that first conversation, and he knew the others in the room felt it too. He could see it in their posture, leaning toward Konner, and in their eyes, locked on the banker's face.

The foundation established, Konner said, "I'm sure you've been wondering what's next. What can we do to change this?" Ash nodded, along with the others.

"The Cormina Council must be stopped," Konner said. "They have outlived their usefulness. They have become an agent of stagnation instead of progress. Their lifespan is limited. They will be replaced by something stronger." He paused. "We will be led by a powerful, determined, inspirational monarch."

Ash drew in a breath. A monarchy—like the kingdoms of old.

As if he had read Ash's mind, Konner continued, "It will be like the ancient days, the days when men and women of will and desire formed the world into what they wanted it to be!

"But it will also be modern, unlike anything history ever saw or dreamt, for in this room is something new and unstoppable—gray magic. Together, we will be a relentless force, leading society into a position of strength again. We are the Grays. And we will introduce a monarchy that will reshape our world."

The room was silent; Ash knew the others were contemplating the dream of ruling a nation, just as he was. Finally, Sella spoke up. But her voice did not hold its customary cynicism. She simply asked Konner, "Will you be the king?"

Konner gave a small laugh. "No," he said. Then his face was again sober, deliberate. "Ash will."

Ash couldn't get enough air. Magic filled his hands, fiery pain he tried to tamp down. He hadn't accidentally activated his gift in a long time, but this news was too much to take. He forced the gray storm to leave his hands and struggled to breathe deeply. Everyone in the room was watching him, and he felt he should say something, but he could not. He was relieved when Konner spoke instead.

"People want to be led by someone they can look up to," Konner said. "But they also want to feel they can relate to their ruler. Ash has the distinction of being the first recipient of gray magic. In time, that will be known publicly, and the people of Cormina will be unable to imagine a greater honor than to be ruled by such a man.

"But Ash also has a charm about him that will captivate people. Men will imagine sitting in a pub with him, and women will imagine lying in bed with him.

"If we are to be effective in changing the world, we must ensure the world wants to be changed. I am confident that most people of Cormina will willingly trade our incompetent council for King Ash . . . though we must come up with a better name than that for him." Konner smiled, and the others laughed—all except Ash. He was still trying to regulate the thoughts tumbling through his head. King?

Aldin spoke up. "When will this happen?"

"Be patient," Konner said, still smiling. "This will take time—years. We will take many intermediate steps in the meantime. To begin, Camalyn, how do you feel about becoming a member of the Cormina Council?"

Camalyn responded with widening eyes, and those perfect lips parted in surprise. In a few moments, she sputtered in response, "I don't know anything about politics."

"Don't worry about that," Konner said. "I will guide you."

"All right," Camalyn said uncertainly.

Konner narrowed his eyes. "I do have one more question for you."

Camalyn's voice was quiet. "Yes?"

Konner's smile, usually dignified and controlled, turned mischievous. "How do you feel about becoming a religious zealot?"

CHAPTER FOURTEEN

Occasionally an expectant mother will ask you whether there are ways she can encourage her baby to be born facing the sun. She may repeat ridiculous advice she has heard — to stand on her head; to place fragrant flowers in front of her pelvis (which is meant to encourage the child to turn in that direction); or, most frighteningly, to physically rotate the child from the outside.

It is our job to dissuade all such efforts. Adolescence is difficult for nearly all children; it becomes doubly so when a child must deal with a burgeoning magical gift. Sava should be the only one who determines which children are born facing the sun.

-*From* Midwifery: A Manual for Practical and Karian Midwives *by Ellea Kariana*

TAVI WALKED along the road toward school, her sister Ista on one side and her brother Seph on the other, just as she had done countless other days. On this morning, however, everything seemed peculiar.

Her head was unfocused and her whole body exhausted. When

Tavi's friends had brought her home after her awakening, she had gone straight to bed, leaving them to explain everything to her siblings and parents. She had slept through dinner, and then all night, and when she had woken the middle of the next morning, she had still been tired. Tullen had already gone home when Tavi had emerged from her room. She had spent the weekend doing little but sitting outside with Sall and Narre, but Tavi still felt spent.

This morning also felt different because Tavi was flat-out nervous to go to school. These were the same classmates she had known for years, yet she did not want to see them. She tried to convince herself that perhaps no one knew of her awakening, but surely that wasn't the case. Oren was small. Word traveled quickly, and the entire town had been waiting for the all-blessed girl's gifts to awaken. Tavi dreaded all the questions, and if everyone stared instead of questioning her, that might be even worse. She feared her classmates would want a demonstration, and she had no idea how to give them one, had she even wanted to.

Seph's voice intruded into her thoughts. "So you get to take half the day off school from now on."

"I'll still be learning, just at the midwife house instead of at school," Tavi said. It didn't matter; this was a variation on the same conversation they'd had all weekend. Seph was convinced that Tavi would live a life of ease now that her magical training was beginning. He would graduate in half a year; Tavi did not know why he was so fixated on her schedule change when his schooling would be over soon enough.

"I hope you have a great time at your training," Ista said. Tavi gave her an appreciative smile.

Despite her anxiety about school, Tavi was looking forward to seeing Narre and Sall. These daily walks to school often reminded Tavi of how different she was from the rest of her family, and she wanted to be around friends who had experience with magic.

The rest of the walk was silent until they entered the schoolyard. Seph and Ista both rushed to their friends. Tavi didn't see Narre or Sall yet, and she thought it would be best to avoid socializing in the yard. She walked toward the front doors, eyes straight ahead. Perhaps school would start without incident.

Tavi arrived at her classroom and sat at her desk. She rearranged her books and supplies though they were already organized. When she finished, she looked at the clock on the wall and saw that ten minutes remained before the start of class. Sitting quietly, Tavi became aware of rustles and whispers behind her. She took a deep breath, tried to ignore it, and failed. She risked a short glance over her shoulder.

The classroom doorway was filled with students of all ages, jostling to see in the room. Tavi turned toward the front of the class again, her face burning with embarrassment. Why had she worn her hair back today? Her ears were hot, and now everyone could see the evidence of her humiliation.

"Excuse me!" An insistent female voice broke through the murmurs, and Tavi released a breath. Thank Sava, Narre was here. "Don't you all have somewhere to be?" Narre asked. "You too! Get to class!"

Narre sat next to Tavi. "Everything's fine, the gawkers are gone," she said.

Tavi turned to her cousin. "Thank you."

The relief was short-lived; other students arrived, and each one who passed Tavi's desk looked at her. Tavi swore she could feel the eyes of those behind her too. As the morning continued, it didn't get much better. Tavi continually caught people staring at her—even her teacher. Lunch couldn't come soon enough.

When the midday bell rang, Tavi, Narre, and Sall agreed to take their lunches to the midwife house instead of eating in the schoolyard. Tavi felt enormous relief when they rounded the first bend in the road, and the school was no longer in sight.

At the midwife house, the three of them ate lunch under a tree. They chatted as they ate, and Narre and Sall both made fun of their classmates and teacher, mimicking the wide-eyed stares Tavi had received all morning. The ensuing laughter helped.

After a quick lunch, they walked into the midwife house and headed toward the stairs, which would lead them to the training rooms on the third floor. Before they could ascend, however, Ellea exited the kitchen. Her face broke into a huge smile.

"Tavi!" she exclaimed, rushing forward, and then her soft, strong arms were enveloping her newly awakened student. The enthusiastic welcome reminded Tavi that her awakening was worth celebrating. When Ellea released her, Tavi was surprised to see that the midwife's eyes were shining with tears. "I'm so glad you're joining us," Ellea said.

Upstairs, Sall and Narre showed Tavi the various rooms on the training floor. There was a classroom where Sall assured her Pala was not one of the lecturers (though Narre pointed out that some of the other teachers were almost as boring.) Next to that was a spacious room with no furniture. Small rugs were rolled up along the walls; this was the meditation room. The third room held wooden blocks, ladders, chairs, tables both short and tall, ropes, crates full of smaller items, and more. It was the practicum room where students worked on honing their gifts. Last, there was a library, small but crammed with several hundred books on magic.

Class wouldn't start for another fifteen minutes, so the three of them looked through book titles as they waited. After a short time, however, Ellea entered the library. The midwife approached Tavi with a friendly smile. "I have a meeting with every new student before they start training," Ellea explained. "It's a beautiful day—let's go outside."

Tavi wasn't sure what to make of this, but she followed Ellea downstairs and out the front door. They began a circuit of the grounds of the midwife house, Ellea smiling at other trainees as they arrived. She turned toward Tavi and addressed her. "We've waited a long time for this day."

A nervous laugh burst out of Tavi's mouth—"a long time" felt like a terrible understatement. "We have," she said.

"Students are often anxious about these meetings," Ellea said. "Please don't be. This is not a test, and you can't fail. I simply want to talk to you about your awakening and prepare you for a successful training."

Ellea reached out a hand and gently touched Tavi's forearm. The midwife's hand glowed, and Tavi felt peace wash over her. After a few moments, Ellea removed her hand and spoke again. "I would love to hear the story of your awakening."

Tavi looked around her, the trees reminding her of the clearing where her magic had awakened. A touch of panic from that day crept back in, and she wasn't sure she could put the experience into words. Ellea must have sensed her student's discomfort, because she smiled and said, "Don't worry about telling it perfectly. Just start at the beginning. What is the first thing you felt?"

Tavi talked, and the sentences formed themselves. She described her suddenly sharp sense of smell, the ensuing onslaught of other sensations, her friends' support, and her exhaustion afterward. Ellea was an excellent listener, inserting short comments or questions as needed and proving with her frequent smiles that she cared about every phrase her student spoke.

When Tavi finished, Ellea asked, "How have you felt since then?"

"Exhausted," Tavi said, and in speaking it, she couldn't hold back a small yawn. "Also, I'm not sure what's wrong with me. I haven't felt even a glimmer of magic since my awakening. And . . . well, I only bled for two days, and only a little. Is it possible to awaken and then . . . go back to sleep?"

Ellea smiled. "That question is more common than you might think," she said. "Regarding your mother cycle, it often starts small and doesn't regulate itself for months. That's perfectly normal. And when a sun-blessed individual has a dramatic awakening, as you did, it usually drains their energy and their magic. However, once you've awakened, it doesn't undo itself! You will soon recover and experience your gifts again."

Tavi nodded, relieved. "All right—thank you."

Ellea said, "This is a good time to talk about power, tolerance, and control. What do you know of these concepts?"

This would be easy; Tavi had been in the weekly training program for long enough to hear many lectures on the topic. "Power refers to how strong someone's gifts are," she began. At Ellea's encouraging nod, she continued. "Tolerance refers to how much magic someone can use before they need to take a break."

"Very good. And control?"

"Control refers to someone's ability to activate their magic when, and only when, they desire to do so."

"Excellent." Ellea was smiling. "You've been listening to the lectures! Every sun-blessed individual awakens with certain levels of power, tolerance, and control—and these levels vary widely from one person to the next, according to Sava's will.

"Through diligent training, you can further develop your power and tolerance, though the potential for improvement in those areas seems to be limited. However, with dedication and discipline, most students can improve their control significantly. That will be the focus of much of our training."

Tavi nodded. "My exhaustion—is that because my tolerance for magic is low?"

"That's a good question," Ellea replied. "My guess is your physical reaction is tied to your control, rather than your tolerance. Few people awaken with high levels of control. Your body was flooded with a tremendous amount of magic, and you were overwhelmed. I don't know of anyone who could have handled that, regardless of how much tolerance they have."

Tavi's eyes narrowed. "But Narre has always had a lot of control over her gifts."

"True," Ellea said. "Narre is in the minority; she has a great deal of natural control. Her diligence in training has allowed her to further increase it. She has more control now than many Blessed have after decades of training."

Seeing Tavi's nod of understanding, Ellea continued. "Let's talk about each of the gifts you displayed at your awakening." They discussed Tavi's gifted nose, ears, and feet, then moved on to her eyes. "You sounded confused about what you were seeing—the air around your friends that seemed to twist," Ellea said. "Do you know what that was?"

Tavi shook her head. "It was strange!"

"It's not one of the more common sight gifts," Ellea began, "but I have seen it in others. I believe you were seeing body heat. You saw distorted air around your friends' heads and under their arms. These are areas that are warmer than average."

Tavi's eyes widened. "That makes sense!" she said.

They talked about the other gifts Tavi had displayed, and then Ellea asked, "What about your mouth; did you notice any speech gifting?"

Tavi grimaced. "I couldn't say a word during the whole awakening. But my friends said my mouth was glowing like the rest of me."

"Likely we'll see a speech gift reveal itself in time," Ellea assured her.

They walked quietly for a couple of minutes, then stopped under a tree. Ellea placed her hand on Tavi's shoulder and spoke gently. "I'd like to talk about Tullen."

Tavi stiffened. "What about him?"

"You said he was there when you awakened."

"Yes, he helped me, along with Sall and Narre."

"I'm glad you weren't alone," Ellea said. "But, Tavi, I'm concerned about Tullen bringing Meadow influences into your training."

"Meadow influences?"

"As we discussed before your awakening, the Meadow doesn't train their Blessed."

Tavi shook her head. "I know you've heard that, but I asked Tullen. He's received training. It's just more informal."

"Informal," Ellea repeated. "That concerns me. The training we do here is based on many years of study. It lines up with our teachings about Sava. Its very formality protects the students."

"Protects us?"

"Throughout magical history," Ellea said, "heretics have attempted to take magic in directions Sava did not intend. Gifted men and women have tried to break through resistance. Entire groups of Blessed have banded together to gain power by combining their magic. It has never turned out well. Our training protects you from teachings that might lead you along dangerous paths."

Tavi didn't respond. She could ascribe plenty of qualities to Tullen, but *dangerous* was not one of them.

"I know you may not see it the way I do," Ellea said. "But will you please promise to be careful?"

Tavi nodded. "Of course."

Ellea's serious expression softened into a smile. She began to walk again, and Tavi went with her. "You handled your awakening beautifully," Ellea said.

"I panicked! I thought I was dying!"

Ellea laughed. "That is more common than you might think too, particularly when a twice-blessed individual awakens. I can't imagine how it must have felt to experience so many gifts at once! But you listened to your friends, and you calmed yourself. You did well. Do you have questions for me?"

Tavi took a moment to think. "I have so many questions, I wouldn't know where to begin," she admitted.

"That doesn't surprise me," Ellea said. "I can at least help you with knowing where to begin! We have found through the years that relaxation and meditation are crucial in developing control. Three times a week, we hold a mandatory, hour-long class teaching these skills. Today's class will begin soon. We'll go inside and get a pair of cotton pants for you so you can participate."

"Pants?" Tavi asked.

Ellea said with a small laugh, "Nydine, the volunteer who teaches the class, sometimes introduces the strangest exercises. I have pushed for years for all our young women to wear pants instead of skirts during training, but I continue to encounter opposition. For now, a pair of pants under your skirt will have to do."

When Tavi was attired in cotton drawstring pants under her skirt, she made her way to the meditation room. Nine other students were present, and eighteen eyes turned in Tavi's direction when she entered. She sighed and found a spot near Sall and Narre. Following their lead, she took off her shoes, then unrolled one of the small rugs and stood on it. Tavi was just starting to quietly update her friends on her meeting with Ellea when Nydine entered.

The young instructor's round face was all smiles as she took her place at the front of the class. She gave a little nod to Tavi, but thankfully she did not verbally acknowledge her new student. "Please stand straight, with your feet shoulder-width apart, toes facing forward," Nydine began. She then led the class through breathing exercises.

When they were in a good rhythm, Nydine walked through the room, guiding students to adjust their stances and their breaths. When she reached Tavi, Nydine showed her how to use her hand on her belly to ensure that she was breathing from deep in her gut. Tavi hadn't known how she would feel about these classes, but at the moment, she felt more at peace than she had in days.

After some time, Nydine asked them to lay on their backs, and she guided them to tighten and then release one muscle group at a time while continuing their deep, rhythmic breathing. Tavi's entire body felt deliciously relaxed. Nydine then encouraged the students to picture themselves walking along a peaceful path. She asked them to imagine what each of their senses felt.

Tavi feared the instructor's soothing voice would lull her into sleep, and she was relieved when they were told to move to their hands and knees. Nydine guided them in exercises involving lifting one or more limbs up into the air. Tavi was glad for her pants as she pointed one toe as high as she could.

It was at that moment the classroom door opened, and a loud voice broke in to their collective reverie.

"Well, well, this is certainly innovative training!" Tavi knew she had heard that voice before—male and filled with arrogant cheer. She couldn't place who it was, however, so she opened one eye and looked around. Weaving through the students, most of whom had set their knees back on the ground, was Mayor Briggun Nolin. Tavi gasped and closed her eyes, hoping against reason it would keep him from seeing her.

Nydine's voice became shrill and uncertain. "Mayor!" she said.

Mayor Nolin walked to the front of the room, and his voice filled the space. "What a pleasure it is to visit our town's best and brightest!" he said. "How about a brief break?"

Nydine said tightly, "Students, you may sit back on your heels." They complied, and as Tavi glanced around her, she saw that everyone else looked as confused as she felt. Apparently mayoral visits weren't common.

"I heard the good news this morning," Mayor Nolin said, "and I could not let the day pass without stopping by to offer my personal support and congratulations."

"I'm sorry," Nydine said, "I'm not sure what news you're referencing."

Mayor Nolin gave a hearty chuckle that sounded fake to Tavi and replied, "Why, Tavina's awakening, of course!"

The skin of Tavi's face, neck, and ears again filled with heat. Every eye in the room landed on her, and her relaxation fled. But the mayor wasn't done.

"Perhaps you'd like to step to the front and demonstrate your impressive gifts, Tavina?" he asked, those bright, straight teeth filling the room with their gleam.

Tavi was frozen in place, her mouth open but no air or words emanating from it. Nydine rescued her. "I'm afraid that won't be possible, Mayor Nolin."

He appeared taken aback, but he quickly recovered, beaming again. "Very well," he said. "Another day, perhaps!" He looked straight at Tavi. "Our entire town is gratified that you're part of it, Tavina," he said.

Then Mayor Nolin again walked back toward the door, and when he passed Tavi, he patted her head. She wasn't sure whether to laugh, cry, or find a bathroom where she could scrub her hair. Tavi did not turn around as she listened to the mayor's footsteps recede, and she let out a breath when the door closed again.

"Well," Nydine said, "that was unexpected." She gave Tavi a sympathetic look. "Return to your backs, please, class. Let's try to recapture our relaxed state."

For Tavi, that was a hopeless endeavor.

CHAPTER FIFTEEN

Occasionally something happens to remind me that magic itself was not fully tamed when Savala was born. Magic has always retained a certain wildness.

From Training Sun-Blessed Students *by Ellea Kariana*

OVER A WEEK HAD PASSED since Tavi's awakening, and she hadn't felt the slightest hint of magic since. Her classmates weren't staring anymore, at least not often, which she supposed was nice. But despite Ellea's assurances to the contrary, Tavi wondered if she might be the first-ever blessed person to have run out of magic right after her awakening. She was sure everyone around her was thinking the same.

Going to training in the afternoons with Sall and Narre was wonderful, but it would be so much better if Tavi weren't so helpless during practicum sessions. Every day she stood in the room, breathing deeply, watching others for inspiration, and focusing on rousing her reticent gifts. All the while, the surrounding students turned their magic on and off as easily as opening and closing window shutters. It was embarrassing. Nydine and Ellea encouraged Tavi to redouble her efforts in meditation class, but if she relaxed any more effectively, she'd be napping.

On this summer morning, Tavi sat in her school classroom, drowsy from the stuffy air. She knew she should focus on Miss Maybin's droning voice, but instead Tavi's gaze wandered the room. When her eyes met Reba's, Tavi tried to look away, but she wasn't fast enough to miss the smirk Reba gave her. Tavi hated those smirks.

Like Sall and Narre, Reba had a front-row seat to Tavi's attempted gift development. Only Reba seemed to relish the difficulties Tavi experienced. Tavi had hoped their old friendship would be rekindled once she had awakened. Clearly she'd been not only mistaken, but also embarrassingly idealistic. Reba didn't seem interested in having a pleasant relationship with any of her three former friends. Tavi wondered if that would ever change. She desperately wanted it to.

The odor of chalk tugged Tavi's attention to the front of the room. At the same second she thought, *I don't usually smell chalk from my desk,* she noticed her other gifts activating. It brought back an immediate, sharp memory of her awakening, and her heart responded by initiating a frenzied beat against her chest wall.

Tavi reached out a hand to Narre, who sat next to her. When her cousin saw Tavi's glowing skin, her eyes widened. Narre took the proffered hand, but it didn't help. Tavi was again pummeled by an overabundance of awareness—of teachers' voices throughout the school, Narre's blood pulsing and flowing, waves of body heat around every person in the room, vibrations from an underground stream, and diagrams in her head of how her desk was constructed.

Tavi's thrumming mind struggled to remember what had helped before. First she attempted to breathe more deeply and slowly. This wasn't easy; her breath wanted to keep up with her heart. But she tried. Then she looked in Narre's eyes, drawing in the comfort she found there. Last, Tavi remembered Tullen's advice to focus on one gift at a time. She attempted to turn every thought toward her feet.

Each person in the classroom was watching her now, as her body lit up the air around her, but Tavi closed her eyes, trying to ignore the others. Her feet—the magic needed to be in her feet only. She pictured the light throughout her body flowing into her feet, and imagination became reality as magic traveled up her arms and down her neck, torso, and legs, rushing toward the floor.

Tavi's gifts settled in her feet. In addition to the underground stream, she sensed the lesser vibration of a swarm of organisms moving purposefully below her. Ants.

With all the other sensations gone, Tavi relished what she was experiencing through her feet. She observed a setting and society underground that was just as real as her world above. Tavi smiled in awe, and drawing on some deep instinct, she sent a message to her magic: *More.*

At once she felt another vibration, stronger than the water and ants, like the floor itself was moving. Tavi tried to sense what this new feeling was, but a sound broke into her consciousness: screams. Tavi opened her eyes to see a room full of panicked students, and she realized in horror that the floor *was* moving, undulating like waves, the wood already splintering in places.

Pictures fell off the wall and desks hopped and danced, their contents spilling onto the living, rolling floor. The window glass cracked, and with a great crash, the slate blackboard fell, narrowly missing the teacher's feet.

Narre grabbed Tavi's shoulders and cried, "Is this you?" Tavi was confused, frozen, but after several seconds the words were absorbed into her mind and she knew the answer. She could feel her magic being sent into the building and the ground beneath. She nodded.

"Lift your feet!" Narre shouted. "Lift your feet!" Tavi tried, but it was as if she had grown roots; her feet refused to be moved. Then Sall was there, bending down, grabbing Tavi's ankles, and pulling. His action was ineffective; Tavi's feet were still on the floor, seemingly attached there, and now the wall was cracking loudly. The building would come down soon, Tavi was certain. Her eyes filled with tears as she and Sall both pulled with all their might.

Then Narre's eyes widened, and she raised her hands in front of her face. In an instant, they filled with an almost blinding light. "Move!" Narre cried, shoving Sall away. Her gifted hands grabbed her cousin's ankles, and her magic broke Tavi's connection to the ground.

Tavi's feet left the floor so quickly that Narre fell backward, sliding on wooden planks that were suddenly still.

Tavi's gift released all at once as soon as Narre's glowing hands gripped her feet. To Tavi it felt percussive, shocking, as if a clay jar of her magic had exploded, dispersing all its contents in an instant.

With the room still, the students' screams transformed into panicked questions and relieved sobs. Miss Maybin took control of the class, guiding everyone toward the door. Her eyes locked on her newly awakened pupil. "You stay here," she commanded. When Narre and Sall tried to remain with Tavi, Miss Maybin refused, ushering them out of the classroom with everyone else.

Tavi listened to the footsteps of her classmates and other students, rushing through the halls toward the exits. Sitting at her desk, she felt she should cry, but she couldn't. The damaged classroom filled her with horror, but even more, she felt terror at her own power and her lack of control over it. And underneath it all, she was aware of her position in the room—utterly alone.

After ten minutes, the door behind Tavi opened, and she looked back to see Miss Maybin entering, followed by the headmaster, Mr. Comani. He stopped just inside the room as if he feared coming closer. "Come, Tavi," he said, his voice level. "We will take you home."

The walk was silent, and when they arrived at her house, Tavi went straight to her room, ignoring her mother's questions. With the door to her bedroom closed, Tavi lay on her bed and waited. She shut her eyes, breathing deeply as Nydine had taught her to do, but instead of picturing herself on a quiet forest path or walking through the ocean's surf, Tavi relived those two terrible minutes over and over. It was a harrowing meditation, resulting in a growing knot of distress in her gut.

When her mother entered her room, Tavi was not in the least surprised to hear she would not be returning to school until it was deemed safe for her to do so. Mey tried to engage her in conversation, and then Misty attempted the same. Tavi simply lay on her side, facing the wall, giving one-word responses. "Fine." "Yes." "No." "Tomorrow." "Goodbye." At last they left her alone, and Tavi slept.

CHAPTER SIXTEEN

I treasure the letter you sent, but I must correct the words therein! You claim that I desired to leave. My dear, leaving you was the antithesis of my desire. I simply followed Sava's path. Obedience must be allowed to subdue desire.

-*From* Savala's Collected Letters, Volume 1

"Little bird ri-i-ise, Open your ey-ey-eyes. Little bird ri-i-ise, Open your ey-ey-eyes."

Tavi groaned. She flipped face down on her bed and put her pillow on top of her head, using her arms to press it against her ears. Still the words continued, louder now.

"Little bird ri-i-ise, Open your ey-ey-eyes." It was Tullen, and he was enthusiastically singing, but she couldn't tell what the tune was supposed to be. His singing voice was appalling.

"Stop," she groaned.

Tullen continued, and now he was accompanying himself with loud clapping. Clapping! "Little bird ri-i-ise, Open your ey-ey-eyes."

After a few more rounds of the asinine chorus, Tavi threw her pillow toward the door where Tullen stood. But because she was laying on her belly, her aim was terrible, and the pillow landed on Ista's empty bed. Tavi opened her eyes and squinted angrily against the bright sun streaming through the window.

The poorly thrown pillow didn't deter Tullen; he was even more cheerful. "Little bird RI-I-ISE," he sang, bellowing the last word for emphasis. "Open your ey-ey-eyes."

Tavi pushed herself up, placed both feet on the floor, and stood. As soon as she was upright, Tullen cut his song short in the middle of a phrase. He was grinning, and Tavi responded with the biggest frown she could manage.

"My mother has always sung that song to wake me," he explained.

"I'm sorry your mother is so awful."

Still smiling, Tullen replied, "She's not awful."

Tavi glared. "I'm sorry she raised you to be awful too."

"Get dressed. We're headed to the forest."

"No, we're not," Tavi replied.

"Your mother said you can weed the garden all morning or train with me in the forest," Tullen turned to leave, and called over his shoulder, "So get dressed." He closed the door.

What did Tullen mean by "train with me"? Certainly Ellea wouldn't approve—but Ellea wasn't there. She didn't need to know. If Tavi's parents had agreed, surely it would be fine.

Tavi yanked off her nightgown, then found the oldest, ugliest dress she owned and pulled it on. In a few minutes she was ready, her shoes on and her unbrushed hair tied into a messy knot at the back of her head.

"Nice dress," Tullen said when Tavi entered the kitchen.

She looked down, feeling a little self-conscious. The faded dress didn't quite fit anymore, now that she had a few curves. She stuck her tongue out at Tullen. "I want breakfast," she said.

He held up a basket, infuriatingly cheerful grin still in place. "Picnic breakfast today. Let's go."

Tavi released a dramatic sigh but didn't bother arguing. Following Tullen out the back door, she asked, "Where are my mother and Misty?"

"They left early." Tullen paused and glanced toward Tavi. "They're helping repair the school. Your father too."

"Oh." Tavi felt the knot in her gut returning.

The two of them didn't say a word as they walked through the forest, stopping at their favorite clearing. Tullen laid out a small table-cloth and placed the food on top—sausage, cheese, and cold biscuits. He opened a small bottle of milk, took a drink, and handed it to Tavi. She drank too. It wasn't as cold as she preferred, but it was fresh and filling.

"Tell me about yesterday," Tullen said.

Tavi sighed. She knew Tullen wouldn't rest until she gave him the details, so she told him everything she could remember. Her voice was steady and calm. When she finished, she raised her eyes to Tullen, prepared to see the same horror in him she felt toward herself. Instead, he was studying her, hands folded, his face full of compassion.

"That must have been terrifying for you," he said.

And that's what did it; the tears she hadn't shed the day before formed all at once. They streamed down her cheeks, accompanied by sobs she didn't even try to stifle. Tullen reached out a hand and placed it, warm and firm, on her knee. Tavi's own hands were on her face, catching her tears and covering her grief. She cried for a long time, but eventually her breathing slowed; her puffy eyes stopped producing tears; and she pulled her hands away from her face.

"All right, then?" Tullen asked softly. Tavi nodded, and he pulled his hand away. "I'm sorry," he said. At another nod from her, he continued, "Since you have some extra time on your hands, I've offered my services as your trainer, and your parents have graciously accepted."

"What do you mean, my trainer?" Tavi asked.

"On the days I'm here, I will help you learn to use and control your gifts."

"Don't you need to hunt?"

"Done," Tullen replied. "While you were still snoozing. Three fat rabbits."

Tavi continued to protest. "But I already go to training!"

With a skeptical look, Tullen asked, "How effective have the midwives' lessons been, really?"

"Well, I've only been going for a week!" Tavi retorted. "You didn't get any training in the Meadow; how are you supposed to help me?"

Tullen snapped, "Tavi, I've had plenty of training; it's just not done in strict classes like yours!" He paused, then continued with a more controlled tone. "We do things differently, and you must admit our Meadow ways have worked well for me. Maybe they'll work for you too."

She sighed. "I suppose it's worth a shot."

His good humor returned. "Excellent! While we clean up this food, why don't you tell me what you learned with the midwives last week?"

Tavi complied, explaining the routine of lectures, practicum sessions, and meditation.

Tullen put out a hand and stopped her. "Wait," he said, "you spend three hours a week learning to relax?" When she nodded, Tullen asked in disbelief, "Why?"

"Ellea and Nydine both say relaxation is the key to controlling magic," Tavi explained.

Tullen shook his head in frustration. "I agree that it is the key for some individuals. But what about the many others whose magic doesn't work that way? I've seen people discover many other keys to their magic. One person might need to feel connected to a greater purpose; another must be mentally alert. I know one person who can only activate his magic if he consistently exercises. What about those people?"

"Well . . . I don't know," Tavi admitted. "I suppose students can discover those types of things during practicum sessions."

"Or," Tullen said, "they may not discover those things at all, and they may end up causing an earthquake at their school." He looked at her pointedly, but with a small smile.

Tavi raised an eyebrow at him. He was treading on sensitive ground. He was right though. "Fair enough," she said. She stood and picked up the basket. "Teach me, oh great master of Meadow magic."

Tullen stood. "Master of Meadow Magic. I rather like that title. You should use it all the time."

With a sidelong glance, Tavi retorted, "Don't push your luck. What are we doing first?"

"First, we're—" Tullen stopped abruptly. His face took on a look of terror as he pointed over Tavi's shoulder and let out a full-throated scream.

Tavi gasped, turning to look behind her, but she saw nothing out of place. Tullen continued to scream while Tavi shouted, "What? What? What?" She was nearly as afraid as she had been the day before, her heart pounding and her head and hands tingling.

Tullen's screams stopped. He looked at Tavi. "Anything?" he asked.

She stared at him in confusion, her chest rising and falling with her rapid breaths.

"No magic?" Tullen asked. When Tavi didn't respond, he explained, "I screamed to frighten you. Some people find that fear is an excellent magical stimulus. Apparently it's not for you."

Tavi's face screwed up in disbelief, and she reached up and pushed Tullen in the chest. When he responded with an amused smile, she continued to push him. Tullen chuckled, stumbling backward, and he caught Tavi's wrists to prevent her from forcing him into a tree.

Now Tullen was laughing hard as Tavi tried to pull her hands away from his. Between laughs, he protested, "Stop! Tavi, you can't attack your trainer."

"I won't push you, just let go of me!" Tavi insisted. Tullen complied, and she responded with one more light push before she snatched her hands away. "Stop laughing!" Tavi said.

Tullen calmed himself but was still smiling when he said, "I'm sorry you were unprepared for that, but don't you see that was the only way to terrify you?"

"You're lucky my heart didn't stop!"

"I'm so relieved," Tullen said, laughing again. "Let's get started. Our first goal, as you may have guessed, is to find a consistent way for you to activate your gifts. Today will be full of experiments. We've already crossed both 'utter terror' and 'righteous anger' off the list of possible stimuli, so we've gotten a good start! Let's sit so you can calm down before we continue."

They sat, and Tullen asked, "What happened immediately before your magic awakened, and before it activated yesterday?"

"I don't know," Tavi said. "Both times I was just sitting there, and it happened."

"What were you thinking of?"

Tavi shook her head. "I don't know. If I'd known that was impor-tant, I would have paid attention—but I honestly don't know."

"Don't worry," Tullen replied. "We'll track it down."

After a couple of minutes of rest, Tullen stood and held out his hand. "We're going to run," he said, helping her up. When she moved as if to get on his back, he chuckled. "No, you're going to actually run, using your own two feet. I'd like to see if exercise will help stimulate your gifts."

Running didn't work, but they continued to experiment. They tried whatever they could think of, determined to find a way for Tavi to acti-vate her gifts. They sang a song together—and then Tavi sang alone, since she couldn't stop from laughing when Tullen tried to carry a tune. Next, Tavi held her breath until she was desperate for air. She walked barefoot along the forest floor and through a stream. She climbed a tree. They counted leaves, voices joining in rhythmic numbering. In a clearing, they lay on the grass, and Tavi told stories about the shapes she saw in the clouds. They even did some of the exercises from Tavi's meditation class, hoping she might more effec-tively relax when she was with only one other person.

Nothing worked. Tavi's magic still slept. She groaned in frustration. "I'm hungry," she said. "It must be nearly noon; let's go eat lunch. Misty pickled some cucumbers, and I could make a whole meal of them. They're perfectly salty and sour, and—oh!"

Tullen, who was examining a piece of antlerfruit and fumbling for his knife, turned around. He grinned when he saw the glow around Tavi. "Good," he said. "We're doing this differently this time. Breathe deeply now, and take my hands."

Tavi complied, taking deep breaths and grasping Tullen's

outstretched hands. She was tense but did not feel the outright panic she'd experienced at her awakening.

"Tell me what you are experiencing, Tavi," Tullen said. "Start at the top—your mind gift."

"The fabric of your shirt," she said, her voice strained. "I see exactly how it was woven. I can picture it on the loom, the pattern of horizontal threads weaving through the vertical ones. I could reproduce it though I have never made fabric."

Nodding, Tullen said, "Your eyes; what do they see?"

"I see the heat around you, under your arms and escaping from under your hat." She looked down. "And coming from our hands too."

"Any heat besides body heat?" Tullen asked. "Look around the forest."

Tavi looked, and her eyes widened in surprise. "There!" she said, pulling away one of her hands to point. "Where the sun is coming through the trees and shining on that rock. I see heat there too." She gave her hand back to Tullen.

"Your ears," he said.

"It's our neighbor," Tavi replied. "She is explaining to her husband her ideas for reorganizing the plants in their garden. She's very excited, and it's very boring." Tavi gave a little laugh. "What about your ears, Tullen? I want to hear about your awakening. What did you hear first?

"I heard my friends' voices first," Tullen said. "I thought they were close but—No, Tavi! Tell me what you're sensing. Your nose."

"I want to know what it was like for you," Tavi insisted.

"I was running," Tullen replied, "and I didn't even know how fast I was going. I looked—" He stopped and shook his head hard. "No. Later. Tell me what you're smelling."

Tavi sighed. "Loam," she said. "Scat. Leftover sausage from breakfast. Leaves. Sap. And . . ." She hesitated.

"And?" Tullen prompted.

"You and me," Tavi said. "We were running, and we both smell terrible."

Tullen laughed. "I'm not surprised," he said. "Let's keep going.

You're doing so well, Tavi. You're keeping it under control. Tell me about your mouth."

"I still don't know," Tavi said. "I can feel the magic there, but I can't tell what it does."

"That's all right," Tullen replied. "What about your hands?"

"Your blood is pumping," Tavi said. "It's slower than it was when this started."

"Excellent. Your feet."

"There isn't any running water beneath us," Tavi said. "But I sense ants again. It's beautiful. They move as if they are one animal, but there are thousands of them. They're like a great army marching in formation."

"That's amazing." Tullen squeezed her hands. "Now I want you to choose which gift you will hold onto. You'll let the others go."

"My mind," Tavi replied.

"Your mind," Tullen repeated. "This time, instead of sending all your other magic into your mind, I want you to release the magic from every area except that one. Let it go."

"How?" Tavi asked.

"I don't know," Tullen said. "Just try."

Tavi closed her eyes, her brow furrowed in concentration. There was no change. Tullen let her try for a minute or two, then suggested, "This may be a good time to use your relaxation exercises. Try to breathe the magic out."

Tavi inhaled, tightening every muscle she could. Her face contorted into a dramatic grimace, and she squeezed Tullen's hands. She then let out her breath in a *whoosh*. Her muscles relaxed, and all the glow seemed to be pushed out of her body, dispersing into the air. Tavi opened her eyes and found Tullen watching her with a small smile. "I tried to hold onto my mind gift," she said, "but it left with all the rest."

He squeezed her hands again before releasing them. "I know it didn't end quite how you planned," he said, "but you were outstanding. How do you feel?"

"A little tired," Tavi admitted, "but good. That was so much better than before."

"Let's sit for a few minutes before we go home," Tullen said.

Once they were seated, backs propped against trees, Tavi spoke. "I activated my magic, but I don't know how."

"You had just told me how hungry you were, and then you described your sister's pickles," Tullen said.

"So do I have to be hungry to use magic?" Tavi asked.

"I doubt it," Tullen said. "We need to look at what was underneath that hunger. I think it was desire. You were so focused on your desire for pickles." He laughed.

Tavi shook her head. "That makes no sense, though. In practicum, I want my gifts to activate; I couldn't desire it more, but they never do."

"I'm not sure why, but when someone's activation is tied to desire —as yours seems to be—they generally need to desire something besides magic. One of my sight-blessed friends back home thinks about how much she wants silk stockings, and *poof!* her eyes act as magnifying glasses. When you want your magic to activate, Tavi, try thinking of something you want—even if it's a pickle!"

"I can try it, but it seems so odd," Tavi said.

"Well, you are an odd girl," Tullen said, and Tavi stuck her tongue out at him. Then he gave her a serious look. "I have a question. You really don't know what your speech gift is?"

"No."

"You displayed it today. When you asked me to talk about my awakening, I felt compelled to answer. I had to focus my efforts to stop answering your question. I had no intention of talking about myself while your gifts were active, but when you asked a second time, I once again found myself responding."

"I forced you to answer me?" Tavi asked.

"No. Rather, you made me want to answer. I could refuse, but only with a strong act of will. And that was with you using it accidentally. I imagine if you were putting more power behind it, I might find it impossible to resist."

"That could be a useful gift," Tavi said.

"And a dangerous one," Tullen rejoined.

"Dangerous? I can't use it to do anything Sava deems unacceptable."

"That's true. But recall how you feel when Sall senses your emotions. He has good intentions, but sometimes it still feels like a violation. You don't want your friends to worry you'll coerce them with your words."

Tavi nodded. "I'll be careful." She grew thoughtful, then said, "I've been confused about what happened yesterday. I could have brought the whole school down on top of us. How is it that Sava allowed my gift to be used in that way?"

"I've been wondering the same. Was anyone hurt?"

"No."

He nodded. "I think your magic would have stopped itself even if Narre had not intervened. I can't imagine Sava allowing you to cause major destruction through your gift. Perhaps there was some higher purpose for the quake. Or perhaps it was neither good nor evil and was therefore allowed."

Tavi shook her head. "I don't know, and I don't want to think about it right now. Let's go eat lunch." They both stood and walked toward the house. "It'll need to be quick so I can get to the midwife house in time," Tavi said, looking again at the position of the hot sun above them.

Tullen halted as Tavi continued to walk. "You still want to train at the midwife house?" he asked.

"Why wouldn't I?" Tavi asked, stopping and turning to him.

"We accomplished more in one morning, using Meadow methods, than your midwives managed in a whole week!" Tullen said.

"Your training was very helpful," Tavi said with a voice that, while quiet, was full of tension. "That being said, the midwives are using methods they have developed over hundreds of years. You can't tell me that's worthless."

"I didn't say it was worthless! It just doesn't seem to work very well for you."

"My friends are there! We've been training together for years. I won't leave them!"

"Well, then bring them out here instead; I bet they'd appreciate being rescued from that drudgery too," Tullen retorted.

"Or perhaps you could come to the midwife house with me and see what *you've* missed," Tavi cried. "At the very least, they might be able to do something about your arrogance!"

"It's not arrogance, it's truth!" Tullen shouted.

Tavi stepped right up to Tullen and stared at him, breathing hard. He returned her stare. After several seconds, she closed her eyes. When she looked at him again, she had reined in her anger. "Are we done yelling at each other?" she asked. He gave a short nod, and she continued. "Listen, Tullen. I don't want to admit it right now, but obviously I'm learning things from you."

"I'm learning things from you and your family too," he said defensively.

That surprised Tavi. "Like what?"

Tullen's face softened into a smile. "Like the value of welcoming new people into your home, even a stranger from a different place. That's not something that would happen in the Meadow."

"I could write a list a mile long of what I think should change in Oren," Tavi said. "Including a lot of the midwife training. Be honest—couldn't you say the same about the Meadow?"

"Absolutely."

"Then maybe we should try to share the best of what we've learned with each other, instead of fighting about which place is better," Tavi said. Her voice turned harder, and she looked at Tullen pointedly. "And I don't want you to ask me again to stop training with my friends and with the midwife who gave me my blessing breath."

Tullen narrowed his eyes. "So you only want me to share my opinion if it agrees with yours."

"That's not what I said!" Angry heat flooded into Tavi's face.

"Actually, it is." Tullen smiled, but Tavi was having none of it.

"Pardon me if I don't enjoy hearing my friend disapproves of me!" she said.

Tullen's voice was calm. "I don't disapprove of *you*. I do think the way the midwives train you is stupid and ineffective." Tavi drew back and stared at him, her mouth open. "Why does it bother you so much for us to disagree on this?" he asked.

Tavi's face fell, anger replaced in an instant with sadness. "Let's go eat lunch," she said softly. "We'll talk inside." Tullen threw his hands in the air, but when Tavi walked toward the house, he followed her.

Inside, Tavi didn't say a word as she made lunch. She tried to sort her emotions as she washed a handful of carrots and prepared a plate of cheese, sausage, pickles, and biscuits. Tullen had the good sense to give her silence and space—perhaps he wasn't so simpleminded after all. When she brought the food to the table and sat across from him, she was ready to speak.

"It bothers me when we disagree," Tavi said, "because it reminds me you have another home, far away, very different from this one."

Tullen frowned in confusion. "Yet you've known that since you met me. It's never troubled you. What's the problem now?"

Tavi stared at him, trying to be patient. She couldn't expect him to understand if she didn't explain, so she took a deep breath and pushed forward. "As we've spent more time with each other, I've realized something about you and how I see you." Tavi paused. Why was this so hard to say? It didn't help that Tullen's eyebrows had risen, and he was watching her expectantly. She couldn't stop now.

"I've always seen you as a friend," Tavi continued. "And I still do, but now . . . it's more." This was silly, she needed to spit it out. "You're —you're like the gifted older brother I always wanted but never had," she blurted.

Tullen's eyebrows moved up even further. "Oh!" he said. "I thought you were heading somewhere else entirely with that. But yes, Tavi, I feel the same way! You're like my little sister. Absolutely."

Tavi gave a small smile and tried to get the conversation back on course. "Thank you. I'm glad. But I don't think you get it, Tullen. When we disagree on the right way to do something, it reminds me that your other home, this place I've never even seen, is real to you. It's full of your real family and other people you care about."

Tullen interrupted. "That's true, but I care about people here as well. You, and your family, and Narre, and Sall."

"I know that!" Tavi cried. "I mean—thank you; you're important to us too—but please let me explain." Tullen looked bewildered again, and Tavi rushed onward. "A day will come when you won't be able to jaunt off to the forest around Oren once or twice a week anymore.

Maybe your family will ask you to hunt only near the Meadow so they can see you more often. Or—you're seventeen; you're nearly an adult! Eventually you'll get married, and then you won't be able to keep coming here.

"I got upset today because I was reminded that one day you'll have to stop running back and forth. You'll have to choose where you want to be. And I'm so afraid . . ." Tavi stopped as her eyes filled with tears and her throat developed an instant knot. She tried to swallow it down. "I'm so afraid you'll choose the Meadow, and I'll lose my big brother."

Through her tears Tavi watched Tullen. He let out a breath, and said, "Tavi." He stopped, shaking his head. "I love being here. But yes, the day you're speaking of will come. The Meadow is my home. My parents live there, and my siblings. I have three grandparents still alive, and an entire community of people who care for me. I—I want to spend time here, when I can, but—" Tullen stopped and pointed toward the forest. His voice was quiet and sad as he said, "I'll always be your big brother, but the Meadow is my home."

Tears slipped out of Tavi's eyes and traced warm paths down her cheeks. "I know," she whispered. "But you're always welcome here, Tullen. For as long as you want."

Tullen's eyes didn't leave Tavi's. The food sat untouched between them. Finally he spoke. "I want to enjoy these days," he said. "I do think about how things will change, but then I turn my mind to *today*. Because our todays can be full of runs through the forest and time with friends and Misty's pickles." Tavi couldn't help a laugh, though it was combined with a sob. Tullen continued. "Can we enjoy today, Tavi?"

Tavi swallowed again and attempted a brave nod. "Yes."

Then her friend, her brother, stood, and walked around the table. "Stand up," Tullen instructed, and Tavi did so. He held his arms out, and when she walked into them, they surrounded her, one hand resting on her back and the other on her hair. She lay her head on his chest, feeling his steady heartbeat.

After a moment, Tavi put her arms around his waist, and said a word so quietly, she wasn't sure he heard it: "Today."

LATER THAT EVENING, something about her conversation with Tullen nagged at Tavi, but she couldn't place it. The next morning as she watched Tullen sprinting into the forest, toward his family, she figured it out.

Tavi had told Tullen he was always welcome at her home, but he hadn't said the same to her. He couldn't say it to her, or to any outsider. Tullen could be a guest, but never a host. And Tavi had to wonder at his devotion to a community that would refuse to accept the people he had grown to care for.

CHAPTER SEVENTEEN

I know little about Sava. I only know he is the giver of life, magic, and all that is good. I am content with this knowledge. It seems to me it would be dangerous for one person or group to claim they know all that can be known of Sava.

-*From* Savala's Collected Letters, Volume 2

CAMALYN WALKED down a busy street in Savala. It was dinner time; people were entering numerous pubs along the road for hot meals and cold ale. Her destination wasn't so indulgent.

People stared as she passed. She'd been wearing this costume for weeks now, and it stood out—but not in the way she was accustomed to. Rather than relishing the jealous glances of women and lustful leers of men she had for years accepted as her due, she was now relegated to a mere curiosity.

Camalyn walked with her head high, but in reality she wanted to run into the little boutique down the street and convince the shop-keeper to give her something—anything—to replace what she was now wearing. Her body was covered from neck to ankles with a form-less, black robe. It didn't even have a waistline. Black wool gloves covered her hands. Thank goodness autumn had arrived with its cool air; at least the clothing was weather-appropriate.

Camalyn's feet were shod in sturdy, black leather boots. They were the most comfortable shoes she'd worn in years, but they were also supremely ugly. She knew no one was looking at her shoes though. The stares were directed at her head. A heavy, black scarf covered her hair, and one end wrapped around her lower face as a veil. This was what marked Camalyn as a Karite.

At last she reached the small Karite temple. As much as Camalyn hated this place, there was a sense of relief when she entered and was surrounded by other women attired just as she was. The men even looked similar. Instead of robes, they wore black trousers and tunics, but they wore the same gloves, boots, and headscarf as the women did. They looked ridiculous, and it was impossible to tell if they were good-looking, or even to tell them apart. Children were there too, and all but the youngest were dressed the same as their parents.

"Camalyn!" Green eyes crinkled above a veil as a woman approached and gave her a warm hug.

Camalyn forced herself to return the hug but briefly panicked. Was this Lora or Endoria? She always got them confused; they were both middle-aged, plump, and annoyingly cheerful. So she settled on, "Hello, it's so good to see you!"

Camalyn made her way through the tiny foyer of the temple and into the meeting room, which held just eight long pews. She headed for her regular spot—fourth row, right side, on the center aisle. As Camalyn sat, she allowed herself a small shake of the head. She didn't believe in Sava, didn't really care about Kari or Savala, didn't expect to go to either Senniet or Kovus when she died. How had she gotten to the point where she had a *regular spot* in a Karite temple?

That was a silly question; how she'd gotten here was clear. She'd followed Konner's instructions, all of which made perfect sense, as annoying as that was. He wanted her on the Cormina Council, and despite her initial hesitation, Camalyn loved the idea. It would give her a prestige she had never thought she would attain. But if she were to be voted onto the council, she needed a way to hide her gray magic. It was one thing to conceal the gray glow around her mouth from shopkeepers when they were in the thrall of her silver-tongued speech; it would be another thing entirely to ensure that entire groups of people didn't pick up on the evidence of her gray gift.

Camalyn wished it was as easy for her as it was for Ash. He simply wore gloves. Aldin's solution was even more straightforward; he just had to keep his shoes on. In public, Sella only used her magic under the cover of night so no one would notice the dark shine in her eyes. But Camalyn, Konner insisted, needed a veil. So she had traded her gorgeous hats (she hadn't even worn the peacock one!) for this heavy, thick scarf. She wanted to strangle Konner with it.

She had to admit, however, it was a good plan. With Camalyn's speech gift, she could convince others that the religion of Cormina needed reform—and that would be her platform as she ran for council. So Konner had been coaching Camalyn on how to play the part of a devoted Karite, newly widowed, who had just moved to town to live with an elderly aunt.

An aging Karite shepherd ambled to the front of the room and stood, her stooped body still, until everyone in the room was quiet. She read from a small book of ancient Savani poetry, her voice shaking but clear.

Camalyn tuned out the shepherd; she had read every bit of Savani poetry, proverbs, and prophecy twice in recent weeks. She had also spent countless hours scouring any books Konner could find on the Karite sect of the Savani faith. Karites worshiped Sava as the only true god as did all Savani faithful. But the Karite devotion to Kari, whom they called the First Midwife, nearly qualified as worship. They even prayed to her.

According to tradition, Kari had given birth to a son, over a millennium ago. It had been a difficult birth, the baby finally emerging face-up. When he had failed to take a breath after his birth, Kari had breathed into him. He had been filled not only with life, but also with a golden glow in his chest followed by his hands. His mother had named him Savala, in honor of Sava, whom she credited with saving his life and filling him with the mysterious light.

Later Kari had become a midwife and, through various circumstances, she had learned the connection between a child's position at birth and the ability to receive magic through a blessing breath.

Savala had become a great healer, and in later generations, he was known as the First Shepherd of the Savani faith. Many faithful Savanites honored Savala, but Karites instead focused on his mother. Through Kari, magic, which had been wild and unstable, had been tamed—as much as something unexplainable and variable could be tamed.

Sava based gifting on a baby's position at birth. The arbitrary nature of this, Karites claimed, proved that the All-Knowing One cared not one mite about a person's physical appearance, wealth, status, or even talent. Therefore, true believers should place no value on those things. They asserted this was Kari's most vital message.

Karites, therefore, wore ugly clothes and veils to take the focus off their looks. They were instructed to work not to gain status, but only to provide for their needs. If any of them were rich, they hid it well. Nightly services at the temple were unencumbered by music or entertaining speakers. In fact, Karites scoffed at mainstream Savani celebrations, which they said were mere performances to highlight talent.

Camalyn scanned the room, hiding her disdain for these adherents of such a boring religion. But Konner had explained that many people —maybe even most—craved the concrete, unshakable certainty that came with radical beliefs. They wanted to be told what to do. And if that was what people desired, the Grays would offer it to them, through Camalyn.

The shepherd (whom Camalyn imagined looked hideous under that veil) finished her long poetry reading. "We are now open to words from Sava, spoken through the humble mouths of those present," she concluded, as she always did, before taking her seat in the first pew.

This part of the service was the lengthiest, and Camalyn had twice fallen asleep during it. Any worshiper who wished could approach the front to share wisdom. When someone's words sounded self-serving (or even too polished), a member of the audience would stand and ask, "Are you trapped by the trappings?" Being "trapped by the trappings" of life was the worst thing a Karite could do, and each speaker so accused left the stage, head bowed. Camalyn loved when this happened; it was more interesting than anything else in the long service.

But tonight, Camalyn would speak. Her head held low, she stood and walked to the front. She had practiced this, first with Konner and then with the whole group, more times than she could count. She was ready.

Camalyn looked all around the room, but she did not smile. For this speech, she would suppress her usual charm. "I have met some of you," she said, in a voice just loud enough to be heard, "and others I have not. My name does not matter, but if I may help you in any way, you may address me by the name of Camalyn." This last sentence was a stock Karite introduction.

Camalyn pressed her lips together, and she forced her eyes to stay calm as the pain of gray magic entered her mouth. Her next words would not be the ones usually heard in this place, and only her gift would make that acceptable—she hoped.

"I have heard Sava speak," Camalyn began, "through his servant Kari." Normally this sentence would be greeted with a "trapped by the trappings" interruption, but instead every eye was glued to Camalyn. Her gift was working, but she would speak only the words she had so thoroughly rehearsed. These people would remember what she said, even when they were no longer under the influence of her gift. They must remember her only as a humble Karite.

"I have waited for weeks to speak with you," she said, again bowing her head. "I am nothing apart from my service to Sava and my allegiance to Kari. I have not desired to be their mouthpiece, and I beg your leave to confess to you this sin: I tried to forget the words Kari told me. I tried to forget, for I dreaded being seen as anything more than a servant.

"Yet I could not forget, for when Sava himself speaks, through the First Midwife, those words are branded onto our hearts. Finally I knew I must obey the call I received. I beg your forgiveness for taking so long to do so. I am ready now to share Sava's words with you, though my wicked heart wishes anyone else could do this in my stead."

Camalyn's magic burned as it lent power and conviction to her words. She allowed her voice to grow louder. "This is what Sava says, through Kari: 'My people, the Karites, are complacent. They must speak loudly so the world will know the truth.' "

Again, Camalyn studied the crowd. It was silent. Camalyn brought her voice lower again. "This message came at night," Camalyn said, "and Kari herself stood before me. She left behind the peace of Senniet to enter our world again and share this message. Blessed be the First Midwife."

"Blessed be the First Midwife," the people repeated.

"Before she returned to her eternal home," Camalyn continued, "Kari told me she would send me a dream. As soon as I closed my eyes, I entered a deep sleep. In this sleep, I saw the Cormina Council. I saw—" She urged her voice to crack. "I saw myself, in my veil, standing around the table with the other councillors. I was sharing Kari's truths with the council and with the gallery, and they in turn shared these truths with the rest of Cormina."

Camalyn shook her head, taking several shaky breaths. She met the gazes of her listeners, and she willed her eyes to look grieved. "I hesitate to share my weakness with you, but honesty compels me. I do not think I can obey Kari. I cannot attempt to raise myself to the status she is asking of me. Sava must find a different servant."

Still holding onto her gift, Camalyn covered her eyes with her hands, hunched her shoulders, and sobbed as she walked back to her seat. She could produce no real tears, an incompetence that infuriated Konner, but Camalyn knew her gift would lend credence to her display. She sat and composed herself and waited.

It took a full two minutes, but at last a middle-aged man with dark, bushy eyebrows approached the front. He spoke in a strong voice: "You must obey. We all must."

His message was short, but it was the start of a flood. Speaker after speaker approached the front. Some expressed sorrow that in their desire not to draw attention, they had failed to tell others of their faith. Others expressed their great gratitude to Kari for visiting one of the faithful and setting them on the right path. And each of them at some point turned to Camalyn, and each of them had the same message: She must obey Sava and Kari by running for council.

By the time Camalyn left the temple late that night, fifty adults had committed to sharing religious truth with the world and to doing whatever they could to elect her as the first-ever Karite member of the Cormina Council.

When she walked into Konner's house, Camalyn ripped off her veil and enthusiastically recounted her story to the other Grays. She then became the only Karite in all of Savala to get thoroughly drunk that night—or at least the only one to do so unencumbered by religious self-loathing.

CHAPTER EIGHTEEN

Illness is illness, whether it is the body or the mind that is broken.

-*From* Midwifery: A Manual for Practical and Karian Midwives *by Ellea Kariana*

"TODAY WE ARE SETTING up for the autumn festival," Ellea announced to the awakened students. "I expect each of you to use your gifts in a practical way as we work."

She left the room, and most of the students followed. Tavi, however, stayed where she was. "Wait!" she hissed to Sall and Narre. They stopped walking. "Isn't she going to give us more instructions than that?"

"She didn't last year," Sall said.

"You can do this, Tavi," Narre said, giving her friend an encouraging smile before leading the way outside.

In the yard and the street beyond, midwives and community volunteers were setting up tables, props for various magical acts, children's games, and a stage.

Narre had been helping repair the schoolhouse after what people were calling "Tavi's Earthquake." This had given Narre a working knowledge of construction, and she headed straight for the half-built stage, where she offered to use her gift to bind boards together without nails.

Tavi glanced at Sall, then swiveled her head to stare at him when she realized his scalp was glowing. He gave her a big grin that told her his gift activation had not been accidental. Sall said, "Tavi, I can sense your fear about this new task. I have full confidence in you." She glared at him, and he laughed, his magic dissipating. "See? I just helped at the autumn festival by supporting one of the volunteers."

Tavi shoved him. "Go help with the stage," she said.

Scanning the work area, Tavi found another golden glow. It came from Rolki, a speech-blessed girl who would soon graduate from school and from magical training. The term "speech-blessed" was a misnomer in Rolki's case; her gift was in her mouth, but it had nothing to do with speech. With her magical breath, Rolki created strong winds. Tavi laughed as the girl blew tablecloths out of a midwife's arms. The midwife did not find it funny, and she sent the young prankster to pick up the scattered cloths.

Tavi didn't see any of the other students using their gifts, though they were helping where needed. She supposed they had hours to find a way to use their magic. Yet she couldn't seem to move from her place in the yard.

It had been nearly two months since the incident at the school, and Tavi had learned to activate her gifts consistently. It was especially easy if she was hungry for pickles at the time. Yet she had trouble isolating any one gift. It was a frustrating limitation. When her magic had awakened, Tavi had been able to release all but her touch gift. And on the day of the earthquake, she had sent all her magic into her feet.

Yet since then, when Tavi activated her gifts, it was all or nothing. When she did occasionally divert her magic to one area, the gift faded immediately afterward. It was infuriating; she needed to isolate gifts to minimize distraction. Tavi had recently given Sall permission to examine her emotions when her gifts were active, and he had confirmed the truth Tavi had been avoiding: as soon as she tried to isolate one gift, she was filled with anxiety. She was afraid of causing another disaster like she had at the schoolhouse.

A stern voice from behind her interrupted Tavi's reverie. "Tavi, why aren't you helping?"

Tavi knew the voice but did not turn to greet Pala. The midwife approached Tavi, then stood in front of her. And then something happened that Tavi had not expected. The older woman's expression switched in an instant, from firm to compassionate. "Dear girl," Pala said, "what's wrong?"

Tavi's mouth dropped open. Was this the strict lecturer who had once told the Dreamers, "Boredom is good for the soul"? Pala's face broke into a gentle smile. "Let's have a seat," she said, leading Tavi to a bench under a nearby tree. "You were standing there as if you were watching the world burn," Pala said. "What's on your mind?"

It tumbled out of Tavi's mouth—her inability to isolate her gifts and the accompanying anxiety and fear. "I don't know how to get past it," Tavi said. "I'm not sure I even want to. I don't want to cause another disaster."

Pala's expression returned to its customary firmness. "You may be exceptional, Tavi, but even you cannot destroy the world with your magic."

A relieved breath exited Tavi's lungs. Somehow those words helped.

Pala wasn't done. "And of course you want to get past this. Can you imagine a greater tragedy than being blessed with gifts you are incapable of using? Now, stand up." Pala stood, and Tavi followed suit.

Pala said, "I have been reading Maizum's *Treatise on Magic*, which was written just a few centuries after Savala lived." She narrowed her eyes. "You already look bored. I'll keep this short, I promise." A laugh burst out of Tavi's mouth, and she could have sworn the midwife was holding back a smile. "What do you think is the source of magic?" Pala asked.

"Sava is," Tavi replied. "Was that a trick question?"

Now Pala did smile. "Good answer, but I mean the physical source. Where in your body is magic stored when it is not being used?"

"I don't know."

"Nobody knows for sure, but many believe magic is stored in the chest, as that is always where the glow begins after a blessing breath." Tavi nodded, and Pala continued. "In ancient times, sun-blessed students were instructed to connect with the physical path of their magic, from the chest to the area of gifting. Let's apply this to you."

Pala pointed. "See that scaffolding they're trying to put up around the stage? They have no idea how it fits together, and they could use your mind gift right about now. Can you start by activating all your gifts?"

Tavi closed her eyes, pictured Misty's pickles, and felt warmth enter her whole body.

"Very good," Pala said. "Now keep your eyes closed, and place your hand on your chest." When Tavi had done so, Pala continued. "As you inhale, imagine your chest drawing all the magic away from your feet."

Tavi tried it, and she laughed as she felt her feet losing their telltale warmth. It was working! When Pala spoke again, Tavi could hear the smile in her voice. "As you exhale, imagine your chest sending magic only into your head."

Pala continued to guide Tavi. On every inhalation, the midwife told her to draw magic from one region into her chest, and on every exhalation, Tavi pictured the magic flowing from her chest to her mind. Sometimes it took multiple inhalations to release magic from an area, but gradually, Tavi felt her gifts migrating away from every area except her head. At last, the only place she could perceive the comforting warmth was her scalp. She opened her eyes to see Pala's face filled with a wide smile.

"Excellent," the midwife said. "It won't always take that long, and eventually, it will be second nature. Likely you'll also learn to only activate one area at a time. But this experiment proves something important: ancient advice still holds credence today." She gestured to the stage. "Now go help with that mess!"

Tavi ran to the scaffolding. With her mind gift active, she perceived how the wooden legs and platforms fit together. She guided the team, and the job was soon done.

Afterward, Tavi turned to find Narre watching with her mouth stuck in a huge grin. Narre grabbed her cousin, squeezing her tight. "I knew you could do it!" she said.

Tavi laughed, returning the hug. "And no earthquakes! Or whatever disaster my head could have caused."

By the time they were dismissed, Tavi had used her hearing gift to relay messages from the midwife house to workers at the end of the street and her scent gift to determine where a misplaced bucket of paint had been left. None of it was big, but she could not stop smiling.

And every time she heard Pala's stern voice giving someone directions, Tavi laughed. She knew Pala's secret: A dove's heart hid within the woman's hawkish exterior.

THE AUTUMN BREEZE was growing more insistent when Sall, Tavi, and Narre walked toward home. It was already dusk; the students had stayed late to complete the festival setup. They reached Narre's house first, and soon after, Sall told Tavi goodbye before turning onto the street leading to his house. It had been a good afternoon, full of hard work and magic. The following day's autumn festival would be even better.

With every step, however, Sall's contentment and excitement were replaced with muted, anxious anticipation of what awaited him at home. As always, his pace slowed as he drew closer.

Sall took several deep, slow breaths. When he rounded the last bend, he saw his younger brothers sitting in front of the small house, one of them stripping a branch of its bark and the other reading a book. Sall forced a smile to his lips. "Let's get inside," he said, "It'll be dark soon." His brothers groaned but didn't argue. They grabbed their school satchels; Sall realized they hadn't even entered the house since school had ended hours before. Sall had eaten dinner at the midwife house, but his brothers would be hungry.

When they stepped into the kitchen, Sall's eyebrows rose. Their small, tin bathtub sat in the center of the room, filled with murky water. His mother had bathed today. That was a good sign.

Sall lit a lantern and gave his brothers instructions on what food they could eat. He then used a bowl to scoop water out of the tub, repeatedly dumping it out the open kitchen window, until the tub itself was light enough for him to drag through the door and empty in the yard. When he had finished, he made his way through the small sitting room, down the short hallway, and into his mother's bedroom.

At a glance, Sall saw that his hope, sparked by the sight of the tub, had been premature. His mother was lying on her side in bed, her eyes dull. She hadn't even dressed after her bath, and the sheet didn't entirely cover her. Sall knew he should be embarrassed, but that feeling had disappeared years ago.

"Let's get you dressed, Mother," Sall said. He picked up her nightgown from the floor. It wasn't clean; he would need to send out the laundry tomorrow. Sall's father sent them enough money to hire out tasks such as laundry and sewing. But the man didn't seem to realize that what Sall's brothers needed was a father, not a patron.

Sall's mother slowly sat up in bed and allowed her son to slip her nightgown over her thin arms and hollow chest. She cooperated as he pulled it over her hips, and then she lay back down.

"How are you, Mother?" Sall asked.

"See for yourself," she said, as he had known she would.

Sall sighed and allowed his mind gift to activate. It was always easy around his mother. The magic was close at hand when someone he cared about felt things deeply, and his mother felt things more deeply than anyone else he knew.

The emotions that flooded Sall were the same ones he sensed from his mother daily, but they still smothered him. Most obvious was her sadness—a dense, immovable rock of darkness, on which grew damp lichens of hopelessness, muffled anger, and shame.

This had been his mother's existence since shortly after his father had left eight years earlier. Sall's brothers had no patience for it; they insisted their mother could go back to her life if only she would make the right choices. She could get up, get dressed, and even return to her job as a practical midwife, they said.

Sall had agreed with his brothers until his gift had awakened. That day he had learned in an instant that his mother's melancholy was as real as the sagging mattress on which she lay and heavier than the full bathtub she rarely used.

With an effort, Sall forced his gift to depart. He felt the customary shard of guilt—his mother was left suffering while he embraced relief.

Sall placed his hand on his mother's. She did not grip his hand, but neither did she pull away. He ventured, "I emptied the tub." There was a pause of several seconds, before he said, "A bath. Good for you, Mother." That felt awkward, but he didn't expect a response, anyway. "I'd like to bring a healer here next week, to see you."

"No."

Just one word, but Sall knew it wouldn't change, so he didn't argue. "I'll get you some food," he said, and he left the room.

CHAPTER NINETEEN

I tire of the monarchy. I have heard of ancient civilizations in which leaders were voted into office. Dare I hope we return to such a system? If everyone has a voice, surely the leaders they choose will be inclined to act rightly.

-*From* Savala's Collected Letters, Volume 1

"I MANAGED TWELVE." Tavi narrowed her eyes at Tullen. "Good luck beating that."

Sall and Narre arrived, sitting on the blanket Tavi and Tullen had spread on the grass. "What's the competition?" Narre asked.

"I told Tullen that at the autumn festival, at least half the dishes contain squash," Tavi explained. "He challenged me to see who could get the highest number of squash dishes on their plate."

Sall asked, "What does the winner get?"

Tavi and Tullen looked at each other thoughtfully, and Tullen shrugged. "I guess the winner gets tired of squash."

Tavi laughed. "Count yours!"

Tullen had used a napkin to cover his plate. With a flourish, he removed the cloth, and he was greeted with laughter. His whole plate was covered with tiny dollops of food, crammed together, a multicolored mishmash. Tavi groaned and waited as he counted. "Twenty-seven!" he concluded.

"Are you sure those all contain squash?" Sall challenged.

"I've never seen half these foods," Tullen admitted. "I did a lot of guessing."

After a few minutes of careful analysis, including two heated arguments about whether foods contained pumpkin or sweet potato, the final count was twenty squash dishes on Tullen's plate. He raised his fists in victory, and they all ate.

This was the first time Tullen had come into town with his friends. Tavi had insisted he could not miss the autumn festival, and he had agreed. The two of them, along with Narre and Sall, had spent all morning marveling at the acts of magic on the street, and Tullen's enthusiasm had not waned when the feast began. He had even offered to run and fetch some antlerfruit as his contribution, but the idea had been roundly vetoed by Tavi, Sall, and Narre.

"I have news," Tavi said when they had finished eating. She pulled a letter out of her pocket and handed it to Narre.

Narre spent a moment scanning the letter, and her face brightened. "You're coming back to school!"

Tavi beamed. "After this week's break! The headmaster met with Ellea, and they have deemed me an acceptable risk."

Tavi had never thought she would miss going to school, but her forced absence had dragged on for six weeks, and she was antsy. Training with Tullen was a useful distraction, but he wasn't always in town. And Narre and Sall always seemed to have stories about their experiences at school. Tavi was ready to feel like part of the community again.

Turning to Tullen, Tavi frowned. "I'll miss our morning sessions," she told him. "But it's still light out when I get home from midwife training. Can we train then?"

"Absolutely." Tullen smiled. "And, Tavi, Ellea is right. You've worked hard, and you've gained a great deal of control."

Tavi smiled. "Well, I'm no Narre, but I'm trying."

Something caught her eye, and Tavi squinted across the lawn. "Is that Mayor Nolin walking with my father?" she asked.

"Appears to be," Sall said.

Tullen's eyebrows raised. "Do you know the mayor, Tavi?"

Tavi's nose scrunched in disgust. "Sort of," she said. "Remember his antics on my first day of training at the midwife house?"

"And two years ago, he dragged Tavi in front of a crowd at this very festival," Narre said.

Mayor Nolin and Tavi's father Jevva walked past the midwife house together, disappearing behind it. Tavi stared hard at the building. "I wish my magic allowed me to see through walls," she said.

"Why don't you listen to them with your hearing gift?" Narre asked.

Tavi's eyes widened, and she wondered why she hadn't thought of it. "I should!" she said. "Except . . . I would have to start by activating all my gifts. I don't want to make a scene."

Still watching the doors, Tavi said, "Tullen, do you think I should—"

Tullen's sharp "Shh!" cut her off, and when Tavi looked at him, she saw that his ears were glowing, and his face was full of the same concentration she saw when he was tracking an animal. Tavi grinned. She, Sall, and Narre stayed quiet, letting Tullen focus on listening to the conversation in the parish hall.

After a couple of minutes, however, Tullen released his magic with a quick shake of his head. "I honed in on their voices," he said, "but I couldn't understand anything. My magic was blocked."

" 'Blocked' is the Meadow term for 'resistance,' " Tavi explained.

Sall raised his eyebrows. "Apparently Sava respects privacy and wants us to do the same."

Gifts always met resistance when used unacceptably. This was a universal truth, though the line between "acceptable" and "unacceptable" was blurry and difficult to predict. At times, resistance seemed to be tied to the gifted person's motives; in other instances, resistance prevented unintended negative consequences. And every sun-blessed individual accumulated stories of times their magic had encountered no resistance despite results that, on the surface, appeared undesirable —Tavi's earthquake, for instance.

Entire library shelves were covered in magical theory books attempting to quantify what constituted "unacceptable," and who or what the power was behind these moral judgments. Other shelves were full of magical theology books claiming only Sava could explain the reasoning behind every instance of resistance and that it was folly for scholars to analyze it.

Tavi's father and the mayor reappeared after several minutes. In front of the midwife house, they shook hands, and then they both looked toward Tavi, smiling. Tavi shuddered as Mayor Nolin walked toward his waiting carriage.

"I'm dying to know what they were talking about!" Narre said.

Tavi shook her head. "The more I think about it, the happier I am I don't know. I wish my father would stop speaking to the mayor at all."

They spent a few minutes speculating, but they reached no conclusions. Tavi assured her friends she would update them if she heard anything else. She was relieved when their focus shifted to the dessert tables.

WHEN THE SUN was low in the sky, the festival ended. Narre left in her family's carriage, and Tavi walked home with her parents, siblings, and Tullen. Tavi's family didn't have a carriage—there were too many of them to fit in just one, and Oren was small enough that they could walk wherever they needed to go. Sall walked with them until they reached the turnoff to his house.

Once home, Mey put on a tea kettle, and everyone gathered in the sitting room to enjoy the warmth of the fireplace. Tavi and Tullen claimed the settee and chatted about Tullen's impressions of Oren's residents.

After just a few minutes, however, Jevva stood. "Tavi, I'd like to talk to you in my study," he said.

Tavi raised her eyebrows at Tullen. She wasn't close to her father and almost never entered his study. She wanted to say no, but she knew his invitation had been a polite demand rather than a request. Standing, she followed Jevva through the house and into his study.

They both sat, Tavi on a couch and her father in an armchair.

"I had a good conversation with Mayor Nolin today," Jevva began. "He's an exceptional man."

"I saw you with him," Tavi acknowledged, choosing not to address her father's second statement.

"He thinks very highly of you," Jevva said.

Tavi frowned. "He doesn't know me, Papa."

"The mayor has watched you grow into a fine, gifted young lady," Jevva said with a smile. "He feels honored that our town is home to someone whom Sava has blessed with so many gifts."

"Well." Tavi realized she had nothing more to say, and she looked down at her hands, wishing she had something to do with them.

The reason Tavi had never connected with her father was simple. She felt that every time he looked at her, he saw only her gifts. Tavi tried her best not to care, but she couldn't quite manage indifference.

As a small child, Tavi had often been told by Jevva, "Sava has made you special, and you need to act like it." *Acting like it*, Tavi had learned, meant not acting like a child. Her father had wanted her to be unfailingly polite, kind, and reverent—at age four.

As Tavi grew older, each time she approached her father to complain about something, such as an injustice at school or a disagreement with a sibling, Jevva's response was, "Sava has given you many gifts—be content."

And now that Tavi's gifts had awakened, her father often asked her how training was going. If she didn't seem enthusiastic enough or wasn't progressing quickly enough, he admonished her, "Make sure you are being a wise manager of what Sava has given you."

So when Jevva told Tavi that the mayor approved of her due to her gifting, she wasn't surprised. It was the only approval she got from her father too.

Jevva leaned forward, and Tavi felt herself pressing further back into her seat in response. Her father switched to what his family called his "shepherd voice," a warm tone coating his pedantic message.

"When Sava gives us gifts," Jevva pronounced, "magical or otherwise, he pairs each gift with the responsibility to serve him and others. Serving is our highest calling and our highest privilege." He paused and waited for a response. Tavi nodded; she was hesitant to do so, but she didn't disagree with anything her father was saying.

Jevva smiled. "Tavi, Sava's gifts to you have been generous indeed, and the time has come for you to take the next step by lending your assistance to someone else." Tavi's gaze was wary, but her father's smile did not falter as he continued. "Mayor Nolin gave me some very exciting news today. He desires to better serve the communities in our area, by becoming a member of the Cormina Council."

Again, a pause, and this time, Tavi ventured a question to which she wasn't sure she wanted an answer. "What does that have to do with me?"

Jevva continued with that warm voice Tavi didn't trust, but now it was tinged with condescension. "I know you are still young," he said, "and you may not realize how much influence you can have on the people around you due to the surfeit of gifts with which you have been entrusted. Mayor Nolin has asked for your assistance as he campaigns for the council."

"I don't understand. How would I help him?"

Tavi's father's smile grew wider. "By going with him to his campaign events and telling the people you support him! The recommendation of an all-blessed young lady will carry great weight as the mayor seeks to gain the trust of the people. You can even demonstrate your gifts, to lend credence to your words."

Tavi looked at her father in horror. "You want me to travel around with the mayor and tell people to vote for him?"

Jevva chuckled. "Well, not by yourself! We'll send Misty with you, to avoid any hint of impropriety."

Arms crossed, Tavi shook her head firmly and said, "Papa, I wasn't even thinking of the impropriety of it, though you're right—it would be highly awkward. The biggest problem is that I can't tell people they should vote for him when I wouldn't vote for him myself, even if I was old enough to vote!"

Any hint of a smile fled Jevva's face. "Why would you say that?" he asked. "Mayor Nolin is our friend!"

"He's not my friend!" Tavi protested. "He stares at me, even more than most people do. And now I know why. He's been planning for years to use me as a campaign prop!"

"Don't be absurd!" Jevva said. "Mayor Nolin provided plumbing to our family for free because he cares about us. You are not to be a stubborn little girl! We will support him in this. You will speak up for him!"

Tavi fought to keep her temper down; if she let her father infuriate her, she would feel he had won. So she took a deep breath, clasped her hands together so tightly they hurt, and looked in her father's eyes as she spoke. "Go ahead," she said. "Send me to campaign events with him. Put me onstage. I won't fight you on this. But once there, I will do what you have always told me to do. I will tell the truth. And I'm sure it won't have the effect the mayor is hoping for."

Then Tavi did something she had never done before. Without waiting for her father's dismissal, she stood, turned her back on him, and exited the room.

CHAPTER TWENTY

Angry words can be cruel,
But not as cruel as angry silence.

-From Proverbs of Savala

WHEN TAVI LEFT her father's study, she didn't go back to the sitting room. Instead she stopped at her bedroom to grab a blanket, then walked out the back door. It was dark, so she rounded the house and sat on the front steps, which were dimly lit by the lantern and firelight shining through the front window. She could hear chattering and laughter in the room, and she pulled the blanket over her ears like a hood, muting the cheerful sounds.

Tavi was furious—not just with her father, but with herself. She wanted to brush off her father's words. He had looked in her eyes and called her a "stubborn little girl." And try as she might, she couldn't not care about it.

She was fourteen, and everyone called her a "young lady," but when she sat in front of her father and saw, once again, that she could not please him, Tavi felt like a child. She wanted to lay on the ground and throw a tantrum, to scream and kick and cry.

Her father. How could he? When he spoke, whether it was to his family at the dinner table or to parishioners at monthly meetings, he so often shared true wisdom. Despite her difficulties relating to him personally, Tavi had always been inspired by him. She wanted to live a life full of honesty and kindness and goodness, thanks to her father's words. And tonight, this same man had told her to sell her integrity for the cost of plumbing pipes.

Had she really spoken those defiant words—and then turned her back on him and left? Tavi covered her face with her hands and felt the warmth of shame on her cheeks. She had never before treated her father that way. Perhaps she should go back to him and apologize.

Yes. Yes, that's what she would do. Tavi stood, then promptly sat again. She knew what the result of an apology would be. Her father would reconcile with her—as long as she approached him with a true change of heart, which would mean agreeing to campaign for the mayor.

As much as her refusal sickened her—for her stomach was sour and knotted now—Tavi could not take that step. She didn't know where her current course of resistance would take her. She did know if she went along with her father's demands, she would lose part of herself. So she continued to sit.

THE FIRE BLAZED, warming the entire sitting room. Jevva had returned alone several minutes earlier, and Tullen had assumed Tavi was getting tea or perhaps visiting the privy. But she still hadn't come back, and he was relieved when Misty asked, "Where's Tavi?"

"I don't know," Jevva replied.

Misty stood. "I'll go check."

Jevva's voice was loud and firm. "You will do no such thing. I hope she is alone somewhere, allowing Sava to convict her of her rebellious spirit."

The other members of the family exchanged glances. Tullen looked around and, seeing that none of them were stirring, he stood. He would not ask Jevva's permission. He avoided the man's eyes and left the room, relieved when no one tried to stop him.

Tullen checked the kitchen first, then knocked on Tavi's bedroom door. Next he exited through the kitchen into the yard, walked around the house, and found Tavi on the front steps. When she saw him, she scooted over, and he sat beside her.

"What happened?" he asked.

Tavi stared straight ahead. "Nothing."

Tullen almost laughed at the absurdity of that statement, but instead, he said, "Well, if you won't talk, I will." He told her about the confrontation between Jevva and Misty, and concluded, "So what happened?"

Tavi sighed and related the conversation with her father. Tullen grew louder and louder in his responses as her story continued. "Campaign for him?" "*Demonstrate* your gifts?" "*In exchange for plumbing?*"

On that last outburst, Tavi shushed him. "They'll hear you!"

"I don't care if they hear me!" Tullen said, but he lowered his voice. "I can't believe the hypocrisy! Do you want me to talk to him for you?"

"Please don't," Tavi replied. "He's very angry, and I'm afraid he'll just send you home. That's the last thing I need."

Tullen nodded. "I understand." He did understand Tavi's request, but he did not understand her father, and he was surprised by the ire that rose in him. He growled, "I think I'm just as angry as you are now, but I'll hold my tongue so you can finish."

Tavi quickly recounted her defiant response to her father, and her less-than-polite exit. "What do you think?" she asked.

What did he think? He thought her father was an unmitigated idiot who did not see his daughter's strength of character and who was willing to trade Tavi's love for the loyalty of a politician. He thought Tavi was strong, and once again he admired her instincts. He turned toward her and was faced with hunched shoulders and a bowed head.

Tullen waited until Tavi's eyes rose to meet his. "I have a great many thoughts," he said, and the anger had left his voice. "But the one you need to hear is this: If you are at all questioning your response, don't. Your words and your actions were entirely appropriate."

Tavi sighed, but her eyes didn't leave his. "Are you sure?"

"Absolutely certain."

She smiled, just a bit. "Thanks," she whispered.

They continued to talk, and Tullen even elicited a few laughs from Tavi. He hoped she was feeling lighter by the time Misty opened the door and told them everyone was going to bed. Tullen gave her shoulder a quick squeeze before they both stood and entered the house.

WHEN TAVI WENT to bed that night, she was certain she had made the right choice. But in the coming weeks, she doubted herself again and again.

Her father didn't rebuke her. He didn't ignore her. Instead, he treated her as a casual acquaintance, and Tavi was convinced this was the worst option he could have chosen.

With studied politeness, Jevva greeted her each day with, "Good morning" and "Good evening." At dinner, his comments to her were limited to, "Pass the bread, please. Thank you." His eyes were cold, and if he cared for her at all, Tavi couldn't detect it.

The day after the confrontation, Tavi told Misty about it, and together, they told their mother. Mey's face filled with disappointment, but she did not reprimand her daughter. Tavi was encouraged by her mother's promise to talk to her father, and she was certain Mey followed through, but nothing changed. Tavi did not involve her mother any further, but she often caught Mey watching her and Jevva with sad, weary eyes.

When she told the story to Sall and Narre, and they both offered to confront her father, Tavi laughed out loud. She was glad her friends were willing to defend her, but she again refused. If Jevva wouldn't listen to his wife, he certainly wouldn't listen to his daughter's friends.

As autumn came to a close, Tavi adjusted—both to her resumed school schedule, and to the distance between her and her father. Each time she heard updates on the mayor's campaign trips, she felt an undefined anxiety. Nearly every day, she repeated to herself the words she had heard from Tullen: "Your actions were entirely appropriate."

But a cruel truth burrowed deep inside Tavi: Sometimes it felt terrible to do what was right.

CHAPTER TWENTY-ONE

For the first time, my mother is training a midwife apprentice who is gifted with magic. My mother, of course, is the one who gave the girl her blessing breath eighteen years ago. I cannot tell you how excited we were a fortnight ago, when the girl breathed into an infant born facing upward, and the glow of magic entered the babe. What joy to know that when my mother is gone, her tradition will continue!

We dream of a day when every city and town has at least one magical midwife, someone who can spread Sava's gifts to children. There are so few of us who are gifted, and the world will benefit if there are more.

-From Savala's Collected Letters, Volume 1

"Ouch!" Camalyn yelped as the carriage rolled over roads that grew rockier by the minute. The passengers inside were being tossed around like dice in a cup.

"Almost there," Konner assured them.

Ash forced himself not to frown at Camalyn, who had complained the whole way. Instead he smiled and said, "It will be worth the wait."

The five Grays were crammed into Konner's carriage, which, while luxurious, was not suited to so many passengers, nor to rural roads. They had been traveling for an hour, being thrown into one another and shivering from cold.

Konner was true to his word; after five more minutes of jostling, the carriage turned onto a long drive with minimal rocks and ruts. Camalyn wasn't the only one to breathe a sigh of relief as the ride became relatively smooth.

After a few turns of the road, a rambling, one-story farmhouse came into view. Past it were a large barn, a stable, and other outbuildings. None of it was new, but it boasted a fresh coat of paint, and the grounds were well kept. Ash couldn't hold back a proud smile when he saw it.

The driver brought the carriage to a stop in front of the house before opening the door and assisting the occupants out of the vehicle.

Sella looked around, her face unimpressed. "What is this place?"

Konner smiled. "It's our new headquarters." He turned to Ash. "Show them the inside."

Ash faced the small group and gestured to the house with a flourish. "I will be your guide today," he said with a broad smile. "I think you'll like your new home."

And he was right—they were impressed. Even Sella couldn't hide her admiration as Ash led them through the house, pointing out its features in every room. The early winter chill wasn't present inside; instead, hot air blew through vents, warming their chilled hands and red noses. Everything was new, from the glossy wooden floors to each room's hanging lamps, which boasted cut-glass chimneys and used a new fuel called paraffin. There were hot and cold water taps in two bathrooms, in addition to flushing toilets and large tubs. Off the kitchen were servants' quarters. Only at the most spacious bedroom did Ash's narrative falter. He couldn't see a place like this without imagining how much Riami would have loved to share it with him.

Inside the kitchen, one of Konner's servants was cooking something that smelled delicious. When Ash finished explaining the modern design of the stove, Aldin commented, "You know a lot about this place."

"That's because for the last three months, I have been overseeing its renovation."

Multiple questions were thrown at him at once. "This was all done in three months?" "What about your job at the healing house?"

Ash held up his hands to quiet the team. "Yes, three months." He grinned at Konner. "It's amazing how quickly things can happen with a nearly unlimited budget. As for my job at the healing house—"

Konner interrupted. "Let's go to the sitting room, and we'll talk about that."

They made their way to comfortable seating in the front room. Only Konner remained standing. "I hope you feel at home here," he began. Ash was pleased to see some measure of agreement on each of the surrounding faces.

Konner continued, "My home has been an adequate base of operations. However, it is very public, and questions are arising regarding my long-term guests." Ash and the others had claimed to be Konner's relatives. He didn't seem to regularly welcome houseguests of any kind, so it wasn't surprising to hear that people were questioning this.

"I knew we needed a different headquarters," Konner said. "Several months ago, I began searching for a place that was spacious, private, and close to town. When I found this old farm, I snatched it up.

"Around the same time, Ash approached me with his own concerns. His contact at the healing house had begun doubting his motives and questioning why he was unwilling to provide end-of-life relief to patients who were not gifted.

"We could not continue to grow our group through the avenue we had established. We stopped adding additional members. Ash resigned from the healing house and began work on the project here."

"So our group won't grow larger than it is now?" Sella asked, her candid tone making her misgivings clear.

Konner held up a finger. "I didn't say that. I have a plan. But first, let's make our way to the barn. I would like you to see what we have arranged there."

Even Ash didn't know the answer to Sella's question, and it was just one more example of Konner's unwillingness to trust him. He attempted to keep his expression neutral, but he felt a familiar, growing anger. Ash had facilitated murder (even if they appeased themselves by calling it "mercy killing") to grow this group—not to mention the sacrifice he himself had made in discovering gray magic. What else could he do to prove his loyalty? With a shake of the head, he followed the rest of the group through the kitchen and out the back door.

They hurried to the barn, shivering in the early winter wind. Konner stopped at the doors. "Ash," he said, "would you like to do the honors?"

Ash couldn't repress an excited smile as he slid open the barn doors and entered the space, where hanging lanterns were already lit. As the rest of the Grays entered, there were gratifying gasps of approval. It did not look like a barn. The floors were polished wood, just as in the house, and the room contained comfortable, quality furniture, scattered throughout. There was even a small kitchen area with a dining table.

"This is our training space," Ash pronounced. He gestured to the far wall of the barn. It was covered in narrow panels, installed side-by-side, each covered in a different material—brick, stone, wallpaper, wood, tapestry, logs, and drapery. "Aldin, you can practice your wall-walking there." Ash laughed at Aldin's hoot of glee. The young man ran across the space, took a moment to activate his gift, and sprinted up the log panel.

"Camalyn," Ash continued, "you now have a Corner Rostrum where you may develop and rehearse your speeches." Camalyn walked to a corner near the door, where a simple wooden platform was set up. Off to the side sat a heavy streetlamp, a yellow glass globe surrounding its gas light.

For weeks, Camalyn had been giving speeches at Corner Rostrums just like this one. During election season, any candidate could speak to the public from such a platform, marked by a yellow streetlamp. The candidate was guaranteed not to be interrupted by authorities. (Some candidates received plenty of rude interruptions from crowds, but Camalyn never had that problem.)

Camalyn stood on the platform with a wide smile. "It's just like the real thing!" she gushed. "Except the lamp is too short."

Ash laughed. "Nothing but the best for our next councillor—and this lamp is short enough for you to light without a ladder."

Turning to Sella, Ash said, "Come with me." He led her to a table on which sat boxes, cartons, jars, pots, and bags. They were made of various materials: wood, porcelain, leather, metal, and more. Taking the lid off an aluminum box, Ash showed Sella the empty interior. "Ask someone else to put an object in one of these," he said, "and you can hone your sight magic skills. One container can even be put inside of, or in front of, another, allowing you to practice looking through multiple materials."

"You forget I can't see through metal," Sella said.

Ash raised his eyebrow. "I didn't forget. I thought you might like to keep trying."

Sella shrugged, but Ash thought he could see determination in the set of her mouth.

Konner's voice rang through the large space. "Come to the center of the room, please."

The four practitioners of gray magic all gathered in front of the banker, who was standing in an open floor space in the middle of the room. "Ash did an excellent job with this space; would you concur?" Konner asked. There were murmurs of agreement, and Ash accepted the praise with a wide smile.

"In this training arena, you will continue to develop your skills in gray magic," Konner said. "My most important requirement is this: Be creative. This is not midwife magic school." There were quiet chuckles; all the Grays had been through at least some of the traditional, tedious training. "You can use your gifts in any ways you wish, as long as you don't cause serious harm to one another," Konner continued. "Compete. Challenge one another for power and prestige. Connect with the warrior of old who dwells within you."

Konner smiled. "One more thing. I will teach you to fight. Would anyone like to assist me in a brief demonstration?"

Ash took an unconscious step back; he had no desire to repeat his first encounter with Konner. He could still feel that brick wall scouring his face. Aldin, however, stepped forward with a naïve grin. He was several inches taller than Konner and brimmed with confidence.

"Hit me," Konner said. Aldin raised his eyebrows and moved his hand as if to slap the banker. Konner batted the hand away. "With a fist!" he insisted.

Aldin swung his fist hard, and a moment later, he was on the floor. Ash wasn't even sure what had happened; Konner had somehow grabbed Aldin's arm and flipped him as if he weighed nothing. After a brief pause, Sella applauded, and she was joined by Ash, Camalyn, and, from the floor, Aldin.

Konner reached out a hand and helped Aldin stand. In a rare moment of informality, the banker rubbed his hands together and said, "That was fun." He then schooled his face into a serious expression and looked in the eyes of each of the four practitioners of gray magic.

"I doubt you comprehend how difficult the journey ahead will be," he said in a low voice. "Ash will be king, and alongside him, we will lead the world to a place of strength again. But that will not happen without our willingness to fight. We will assault the assumptions of our foolish culture. We will combat traditional magic. And, when necessary, we will physically battle those who try to stop us. This room is where we will train and fight and learn. This room is where we will prepare."

Ash was the first to speak when Konner closed his mouth. "We need more people."

With a firm nod, Konner agreed, "The five of us are the foundation, but the Grays must grow larger. We will do so once spring arrives. We will travel to other cities and towns, for if our influence is to extend beyond Savala, our members must come from beyond Savala.

"One of your primary goals in the coming months is to become skilled in the art of persuasion. We will take turns traveling in pairs, and we will seek strong, gifted individuals who already see that our world is broken. In other words, you will find people like yourselves. You will show them a better way, and they will join us. We will become broader, deeper, and stronger as we grow."

155

Konner stopped talking but made eye contact with each person in the room. Ash saw the others leaning in, waiting to hear what the banker would say. "Ash will tell you the story of a very strong girl," Konner said. "This girl may have greater powers than we have yet seen. She could be a myth, but we hope she is not. When you travel, you will seek information on her."

He paused before speaking again. "In the meantime, we will continue to work to ensure that Camalyn is elected. She will influence Cormina from the top." He smiled. "The veiled councillor will rip the veils off her colleagues. She will expose the deceit and manipulation rooted deeply in that august legislative body. That will set the stage for a new leader—a new king—to arise."

The air felt full with solemnity and possibility until Aldin turned to Ash and said in a whisper loud enough for everyone to overhear, "I'm going to spend your entire coronation dancing upside-down on the ceiling." He broke into uncontrollable laughter. Ash didn't want to join him, but ultimately he couldn't hold back, and he guffawed along with the young wall-walker.

CHAPTER TWENTY-TWO

Before my gift awakened, I hoped to develop the ability to heal. I think many touch-blessed children harbor this desire; we want to follow in Savala's footsteps.

Instead, I was given the gift of spreading peace through my hands. Each time I use my magic to comfort a laboring mother, I thank Sava for giving me this gift. I would have it no other way.

-*From* Midwife Memoirs *by Ellea Kariana*

TAVI, Sall, and Narre sat in their favorite clearing under the winter sun. It was a little cold for a picnic, but they wanted to enjoy the outdoors while they could. The first snow of winter would normally have come by this time, and it would surely not delay much longer. Huddled close together on a blanket, the friends ate bread with jam and discussed that afternoon's training.

Sall's exposition of a particular magical theory was interrupted by a voice calling through the trees, "Hello-o-o!"

"Didn't Tullen just go home last night?" Narre asked.

"Yes," Tavi confirmed, as confused as her cousin. But sure enough, Tullen made his way through the trees and entered the clearing. "What are you doing back so soon?" Tavi asked.

"Well, I'm happy to turn around and run back home if you'd prefer," Tullen replied.

Tavi laughed. "You know that's not what I meant!"

Tullen leaned his bow against a tree. As he took multiple packs off his shoulders and back, he said, "I have a confession to make. I've been keeping a secret from all of you."

"What is it?" Narre asked.

"I've been trying to work out the details with the Meadow elders and my parents, and also with Tavi's mother," Tullen said. "It's now official."

He stopped talking, crossing his arms with a challenging grin. It only took a few seconds for Narre to blurt, "Tell us, you big oaf!"

Tullen's grin grew even wider. "I'm staying here," he said, "for the whole winter."

Tavi's mouth dropped open, and she leapt up to wrap her arms around Tullen's neck. He barely uncrossed his own arms in time to catch her around the waist, and with a laugh, he swung her in a circle before placing her feet back on the ground.

Tavi was laughing too. "That's the best news you could have brought us!" she exclaimed. "How did you manage it? I want to hear everything!"

"I'd better have a seat, then!" Tullen found a spot on the blanket, and Tavi contained her excitement and followed suit.

"I only have about half a year before turning eighteen," Tullen said. "In the Meadow, this is a time when young men and women are given more freedom. I suppose it's a test of sorts—to see how well we do when we're treated like adults. But we're still expected to contribute to the community. So several months ago when I first asked them about staying this winter—"

"You've been working on this for months?" Narre interjected. She was shushed by Tavi, and Tullen continued.

"I have! The elders told me if I wanted to leave for an entire season,

I would need to make sure I provided plenty of food for the community in advance. I have been focusing on extra hunting, and I've prepared a great quantity of dried, salted, and smoked meat. It's even more than the game and fish I usually bring in during the winter, so the elders approved of my trip.

"When I was here earlier this week," Tullen continued, "I spoke with Tavi's mother. She graciously agreed that I can stay here, as long as I take on my share of the household responsibilities. I've been told I'll become an expert at chopping wood." He grimaced—Tavi knew that was his least favorite chore. He leaned toward her and confided, "I'm hoping to make myself useful by fishing all winter instead."

Tavi couldn't get the grin off her face. "This will be fantastic!" she said.

"We'll have a lot of fun," Tullen agreed.

"I don't know if it'll be fun; I'm just glad I'll have someone to help me shovel snow off the chicken coop!" Tavi said, earning herself a shove from Tullen.

"I was listening for you all as I ran," Tullen said. "Did I hear you discussing your training?"

"Yes," Sall confirmed. "In fact, I'd like to know your views on receptive and effective gifts."

"I've never heard of them," Tullen replied.

"Receptive gifts allow the bearer to receive something," Sall explained. "For instance, I receive emotions from those around me. Effective gifts, on the other hand, effect change. Narre's abilities to break and bind are effective gifts."

Tullen was nodding. "We talk about that in the Meadow too; your words are just fancier," he said with a smile. "We call them 'gifts that take' and 'gifts that give.'"

Narre said, "The midwives told us that sometimes people discover that their gift is both receptive and effective, even after years of thinking it was one or the other."

"We've all been experimenting with our own gifts, but with no luck," Sall said.

"We encourage people in the Meadow to experiment with gifts as well," Tullen replied. "The extent of my hearing magic is the extra sensitivity of my ears—you'd say that gift is receptive. When the magic in my feet first awakened, it merely allowed me to run quickly. Later I discovered I could also sense barriers in my path, such as rocks and roots. So my stride gift is both effective and receptive."

"Tavi, your stride gift is both, too!" Narre said. "But your feet's effective skills are more . . . dramatic."

Tavi groaned as the others laughed. "Obviously I discovered that one by accident," she said, "but I'd like to know if any of my other gifts have another side to them."

"You said you've been experimenting," Tullen said. "How?"

"The midwives tell us to activate our gifts, then breathe deeply and relax," Sall said.

Tavi wasn't surprised when Tullen balked. "Breathe and relax—is that their solution for everything?"

"Not everything," Narre said, "but it can be very helpful for some people."

"Don't get him started," Tavi said. "He has very strong opinions on midwife training, though he's never been to a day of our classes." She turned to Tullen. "Let me guess, you have a better way?"

He responded with a smile. "I do! And since you asked, let's start with you. Name one of your gifted areas—but not your feet."

"My hands," Tavi replied.

"Your hands," Tullen confirmed. "First, a bit of education in case the midwives don't know everything. If a gift includes both receptive and effective abilities, those abilities are usually related, or they work together in some way. Think about the gift in your hands. You can feel blood flowing."

"I can also detect a broken bone, and sometimes I can even tell that someone has pain in a particular area," Tavi interjected. "I discovered that last week in practicum."

Tullen looked impressed. "Very good; maybe those midwives are helping you, just a bit!" Seeing Tavi's look of exasperation, he continued. "Since your receptive gift relates to physiology, your effective gift —if you have one—will likely allow you to heal people."

Tavi beamed. "I've always wanted that gift!"

"We don't know if you have it," Tullen said, "but if you do, I bet you won't discover it by laying on the ground and taking lots of deep breaths."

"So how am I supposed to figure it out?" Tavi asked.

"What helps you activate your gifts?" Tullen asked.

"You know the answer—it's desire."

"Doesn't it make sense, then, for your other magical skills to be tied to desire as well?" Tavi nodded. Tullen reached into his pack and pulled out a small knife in a leather sheath.

Eyes wide, Narre asked, "What are you going to do with that?"

"We're going to follow in Savala's footsteps," Tullen said. "Remember the story of his awakening? He accidentally healed himself after he stepped on a thorn, and then he cut his own arm open, to see if he could heal it too."

"I don't think it's a good idea for Tavi to cut her arm open," Sall said. "It may get infected."

Tullen replied, "I wouldn't make her cut her own arm—I'll cut mine instead. And I'm not worried about infection; I keep the inside of my knife sheath coated in tora root paste."

"Tora root prevents infection?" Tavi asked.

"Meadow secret," Tullen said. "I'll probably get thrown out of the community if they find out I told you." He was smiling as he pulled the knife out of its sheath.

Tavi covered her eyes. "I can't watch this!" She kept her hands up for several seconds. "Is it done yet?"

"Not even close," Sall said.

Tavi peeked through her fingers and saw Tullen touching the skin of his forearm with the knife. "Cutting oneself on purpose is a lot harder than it sounds," he said, taking and releasing a deep breath.

"Just keep breathing like that; the midwives say it will help you relax," Narre teased.

"Very funny," Tullen said—and then, with a small flick of his wrist, it was done.

Tavi covered her eyes again. "I saw you do it! I didn't want to see you doing it!"

"Well, I'm bleeding now, so let's see if you can do something about it," Tullen said. "Uncover your eyes."

Tavi pulled her hands down. She drew back when she saw blood running out of the small cut in Tullen's arm. "I don't do too well with blood," she said.

Tullen's eyes widened. "You're telling me this now?"

"Does it hurt?" Tavi asked.

"It does—more than I thought it would," Tullen admitted. "Come on, Tavi, let's try this."

Hesitantly, Tavi moved right in front of Tullen. "What do I do?" she asked.

"You'll have to touch it," he replied. Her eyes widened.

"It's the same blood you feel when your gift is active," Sall said. "It's just on the outside now, instead of the inside."

"I'm not sure that helps," Tavi said.

"First you need to activate your touch gift," Tullen said. "I wish that had occurred to me earlier. Can you do it quickly, Tavi?"

Without speaking, Tavi closed her eyes, held out her hands and pictured a cold, juicy pickle. Warmth flooded her hands, and she opened her eyes, beaming.

"You're getting good at that!" Tullen said. "Only your touch gift is active, right?"

Tavi nodded. "I've been practicing!" She had only in the previous fortnight learned to activate one gift at a time. It didn't always work, but she was glad it was cooperating this time.

"All right," Tullen said. "Reach out one hand, and put it on the cut."

Tavi fought her gag reflex as she complied, her fingers touching split skin and warm blood.

Tullen gasped the moment her hand connected to his skin. "Sava, that hurts," he said. "Let's keep moving on this. Look in my eyes, Tavi, if that makes it easier." She lifted her eyes to him, and he said, "I think it may help you first to focus on what your gift is telling you. What do you feel?"

"I feel your blood pumping under the skin, as it always does," Tavi said. "It's flowing rapidly right now."

Tullen's eyes narrowed. "That's because it hurts. A lot. Keep going; what else do you feel?"

162

"I feel the cut—well, of course I feel it, but differently than I would without my gift." Tavi paused, trying to find the right words. "I can feel the shape of the cut's edges very precisely. I also feel the blood getting thicker, starting to clot."

"Good," Tullen said. "Now close your eyes. I want you to be aware that you're trying to heal the cut, but then focus on something you desire. Just like you do when you activate your gifts."

Tavi did as instructed. Eyes closed, she pulled up a mental picture of the cut closing. Then she thought of pickles. It didn't work. Her attention was riveted by the textures of broken skin and sticky blood under her fingertips, and she had no desire for pickles. Or for any other food. Possibly ever again. Taking a deep breath to calm herself, Tavi forced her mind to picture the cut healing. What else did she desire?

Her awareness shifted to the blood flowing deeper in Tullen's arm —warm, carrying life throughout his body. Life—yes, he was full of life, overflowing with humor and intelligence and magic. And he would be here with her all winter.

But winter wouldn't last forever. Tavi imagined Tullen running back to the Meadow, sprinting through the green forest of spring. How long could her friend keep living between two worlds before he had to choose one?

Stay, her mind begged. *Please stay.*

A small gasp escaped Tavi's mouth as she felt a dramatically warmer beam of magic enter her hands. The two puzzle pieces of flesh moved under her touch, reaching toward each other. She felt another jolt of magic, of power, as the broken skin reconnected at the outer edges of the cut, then continued sealing toward the middle. Tavi's eyes remained closed, but she knew the moment the healing was complete. Her gifted fingers detected blood flowing through tiny, repaired vessels, covered by unmarred skin.

When Tavi opened her eyes, she was greeted with three joyful smiles. Elation filled her for a moment until she looked down at her hand. She stood and stumbled toward the edge of the clearing, barely making it to the trees before she stopped, leaned over, and vomited.

When she was done, her friends were standing nearby, staring at her, their faces concerned.

"Are you all right?" Narre asked.

Tavi swallowed the gorge that still fought to rise. She held her hand out as far away from her as she could. "There's still *blood* on my fingers," she managed to say.

She could have sworn Tullen was holding back a laugh as he pulled out a handkerchief and wiped her hand clean.

CHAPTER TWENTY-THREE

My most fervent wish is to return to you, my love. But my work is not yet done here. Everywhere I go, people need the gift of healing that I offer. They need to hear the truth of Sava's power. If I do not heal them, if I do not share the truth with them, who will? Please tell me you will wait for me.

-*From* Savala's Collected Letters, Volume 1

"FINALLY!" Tavi breathed as she exited her house and began the walk toward school.

The season's first snowstorm had come later than usual, but it had led to the worst winter Tavi could remember. School and training had been canceled more often than not, and she was thrilled that the roads were again passable so she could get out of the house.

Both Seph and Ista were in bed with bad head colds, and Tavi walked alone. She left early, hoping to catch Narre at home so they could walk together.

Not long after she passed the turnoff to Sall's house, Tavi saw his brothers meandering down the street. She ran to catch up. "Where's Sall?" she asked.

Berroll, his youngest brother, shrugged. "He left early. He's been doing that lately."

"Thanks, Berr." Tavi passed the boys and continued her brisk walk down the road. When she reached Narre's house, she knocked.

The door opened, and Jilla smiled. "Hi, Tavi!" she said.

"Hi, Aunt Jilla," Tavi replied. "Is Narre here? I thought I'd walk to school with her."

"Sall came by a couple of minutes ago, and they're walking together," Jilla said. "You can walk with Elim and Gillun, if you'd like—I think they're about to leave."

"That's all right," Tavi said with a smile. "I'll try to catch up with Narre and Sall." She waved and returned to the street, walking even faster.

Tavi had nearly given up hope of catching up to her friends when she rounded a bend and saw them ahead. She kept up her pace and closed the gap.

When she was close enough to have a better view, Tavi's eyes widened. Were they—? Yes, yes, they were. She was quite sure of it. She sped up a little more, and Narre must have heard her, because she looked back—and dropped Sall's hand. Sall's hand!

Tavi barely had time to soak in this new information before she caught up to her friends, who had stopped to wait for her. She blurted, "You were holding hands!" and regretted it when Sall's face turned red, and Narre let out a nervous giggle.

Then it was quiet for several seconds before Tavi said, "I guess we should walk?" at the same time that Narre said, "I'm glad the storm is over."

Another awkward silence descended.

Sall spoke up. "We should talk about this."

Narre nodded. "Yes, but let's keep going."

Their boots crunched on the slushy road as they resumed their walk. Sall cleared his throat. "Well, the secret is out," he said.

Tavi frowned, not liking the word "secret." She asked, "How long have you been . . . uh . . . holding hands?"

"Just a few weeks," Narre said.

Tavi nodded and willed her mouth into a smile. "I think it's great!" she said.

Narre stopped, turned to Tavi, and grabbed her hand. "Really?" Narre asked. "Do you think it's great, really? We didn't tell you because we didn't want it to be . . . strange. But if you think it's great, that would make me so happy."

Tavi's misgivings about the secret fled, and this time her smile was genuine. She pulled Narre into a tight hug. "Really, Narre. It's great!"

They walked in silence, but this time it was more comfortable. In another minute, the school was in sight. Narre turned to Sall. "Why don't you go put our satchels in the classroom?" she asked.

"Sure, I'll do that once we get there," Sall said.

Narre looked pointedly at him. "I want to talk to Tavi alone."

Sall's eyebrows jumped up. "Oh! Why didn't you say so?" He let out a small laugh and took Narre's proffered satchel. "See you there," he said, speeding up his pace.

Narre and Tavi slowed. When Sall was too far to hear them, Narre said, "I'm sorry I didn't tell you." She talked faster, the words pouring out. "It caught me by surprise, but all we've done is hold hands, and I haven't even been alone with you since this started, so there was never a good time to talk about it."

"I understand," Tavi said. "It just caught me off guard."

Narre smiled. "I think it's perfect. You have Tullen, and I have Sall."

Tavi's eyebrows drew together. "What do you mean, *I have Tullen?*"

Narre faltered. "Well, you . . . you have Tullen."

"Sure, in the same way I 'have you' or I 'have Sall,' " Tavi said. "Tullen's my friend."

Narre turned toward Tavi and with a little smile, said, "Are you sure that's all he is?"

"Yes!" Tavi exclaimed. "Well, he's also like my brother—that's all!"

"Your brother." Narre was skeptical.

"We've even talked about it," Tavi said. "He's like my gifted older brother. I'm like his little sister."

Narre shook her head and laughed. "All I know is, when he came and told us he was staying for the whole winter, and you jumped up and hugged him, he looked very happy. A lot happier than I'd expect a brother to look."

"I think you're seeing what you want to see," Tavi said. "It's obvious he'd never look at me that way. He's three years older than me! And look at me—well, you know."

Now it was Narre's turn to be confused. "No, I don't know. What?"

Tavi gestured to her figure that was still short and rail-thin. When she had finally begun to develop, she had been so excited, but she hadn't grown much. Tavi was sure she would always be stuck with small breasts and skinny hips. She looked enviously at her cousin, who, at age thirteen, was occasionally mistaken for an adult. Tavi said, "I still look like a little girl. Or maybe even a little boy."

"You do not look like a little boy! Or a little girl!" Narre protested. "You're adorable!"

Tavi laughed in disbelief. "Oh, that's exactly what every boy wants, an adorable girl!"

"I meant it as a good thing!" Narre said. They were entering the schoolyard, and she lowered her voice and led Tavi under a tree, where they continued to talk. "I've always been a little jealous of how tiny you are!" Narre admitted. "Think of all the women in Oren who are married! There are plenty of men out there who like women who are fat or skinny or tall or short or anything else. Who's to say Tullen doesn't like adorable, tiny women?"

Tavi couldn't help but laugh. "We're getting away from the real point," she said. "I don't like Tullen! Well, I like him—but as a friend or a brother. It doesn't matter what kind of girl he's attracted to, because I have never looked at him that way. I have far too much to think about with trying to control my gifts. I don't need to think about boys right now!" When she heard Narre's laughter, Tavi said, "This isn't a joke! Do you believe me?"

Narre stopped laughing and looked in Tavi's eyes. "I do believe you. Or at least I believe you believe yourself."

Tavi shook her head at the absurdity of her cousin's words.

As Tavi, Narre, and Sall walked home from training that afternoon, it began to snow. They huddled into their coats and complained, hoping they weren't facing another all-out blizzard.

Tavi made it home and found Tullen splitting logs on a stump behind the house. "Almost done," he said when she approached. He finished the log he was working on, set the axe against the stump, and ran his coat sleeve across his forehead, which was sweaty despite the cold.

"Guess you couldn't avoid that axe all winter, could you?" Tavi asked.

"It wasn't for lack of trying," he replied with a chuckle. He brushed snow off his shirt. "Let's get inside."

"I don't want to go inside yet," Tavi contended. "I'm afraid we'll be stuck there for the rest of the week. It's only snowing a little right now."

"That's true," Tullen said. After a moment of thought, his mouth broke into a wide grin. "How about a run?" he asked.

Tavi didn't even answer; she simply dashed forward, jumped onto Tullen's back, and shrieked when he almost didn't catch her in time. They hadn't run together in weeks, and she had missed it.

With two breaths, Tullen's gift was active. His feet churned at a speed that still astonished Tavi, and she couldn't hold back her laughter as they headed into the forest, and she again felt like she was flying.

Once the initial thrill had passed, Tavi settled into a place of contained joy. "I have a secret," she told Tullen.

"Well, you'd better share it!" Tullen replied. It always amazed Tavi how effortless these runs were for him. He wasn't even short of breath.

"Today I saw something." Tavi paused, enjoying the building suspense. Tullen did not take the bait, so she continued. "Sall and Narre were holding hands."

Tullen's response was immediate. "Well, it's about time!"

"What? You expected this?"

"They've looked at each other with doe eyes ever since I met them!" Tullen said. "Surely you've noticed?"

"I hadn't noticed anything!" Tavi insisted.

"They'll be good for each other. How do you feel about it?"

"I think it's wonderful; I was just surprised," Tavi replied. "And I wish they'd told me earlier."

"I'm sure they had good reasons to keep it quiet."

The run continued, and a peaceful silence settled between them. After a few minutes, Tullen said, "It's getting dark, and the snow is coming down heavier. We'd best head home." Tavi sighed, but she knew he was right.

As they drew closer to the house, Tavi asked, "What about you? Do you have someone special at home?"

"Oh sure, I have my parents, and my siblings—"

"I mean a girl!" Tavi interrupted.

The rumble of his laughter resonated from his back into her chest, and she smiled. "I knew what you meant," Tullen said. "There's nobody special waiting for me back home. Do you think I'd be spending all winter here if there were?"

"I suppose not," Tavi replied.

"You don't have any big, romantic secret of your own, do you?" Tullen asked.

"No, though Narre's determined I should be as happy as she is," Tavi said with a laugh. "I'm far too busy trying to control my gifts; I don't need to think about boys."

"I'm guessing that will eventually change," Tullen laughed.

They reached the house. Tullen set Tavi down, and they sat on a bench that took up the whole of the tiny, covered back porch. The over-hang was so small that large snowflakes landed on their boots. Tavi pulled her legs up onto the bench, hugging her knees to her chest. They were both a little wet from the snow, and it was cold, but she wasn't ready to go inside yet.

Jevva's booming voice floated through the window, and Tullen turned to Tavi. "How are you doing with your father?"

Tavi shrugged. "He ignores me."

"Tavi, I know how he treats you; I see it every day. How are *you* doing?"

A shiver went through Tavi, and she hugged herself more tightly. "I keep thinking if I'd done what he told me to do, things would be fine between us," she said. "But then I always remind myself of what you told me—that my actions that night were entirely appropriate."

"You tell yourself what I told you?" When Tavi nodded, Tullen pressed his lips together and looked at her.

"What?" Tavi asked.

"You didn't need me to confirm that you were right," Tullen said. "You already knew it."

"But I didn't—" Tavi began.

"You did," Tullen interrupted. "That's why you made the decision." He stood with a smile. "I'm turning into a snowman," he said. "Ready to go in?"

"You go ahead; I'll stay here for a few minutes," Tavi replied. Tullen nodded and left.

She pondered the conversation. Tullen was right. She had stood up to her father, knowing it was the only choice that would allow her to live with herself. She had even decided on her own not to apologize to him. Why hadn't that been enough to give her peace?

Enough. That word stuck in her head. She wasn't enough. Her own decisions weren't enough, not without someone else affirming them. Her gifts weren't controlled enough. And she wasn't enough physically, either; she had made that clear in her conversation with Narre.

Only—what if she was enough? And even if she wasn't sure if it was true, what if she told herself it was?

She tried it, a barely audible breath: *"I am enough."*

Tavi's mind filled with images and memories that denied her words: the earthquake, her childlike body, and Reba's rejection. These thoughts threatened to drown out the words she had whispered. So she spoke again, a little louder this time. "I am enough."

Tavi realized she was glowing softly, just a smidge of warmth filling her from head to toe. It was as if magic itself had heard her words and was whispering, *"Yes."*

She inhaled, shivering when the frosty air encountered the warmth of her body and its magic. When the glow subsided, Tavi entered the house and closed the door against the coming storm.

CHAPTER TWENTY-FOUR

The line between confidence and pride
Is as fine as spider silk
And just as sticky.

-*From* Proverbs of Savala

"WHAT ABOUT THIS?" Tavi held up a dress. It was bright yellow with enormous, puffed sleeves and a bow on the front that was so large, it extended beyond the width of the waist. The skirt was flounced with black lace accents.

Tullen examined it thoughtfully. "It's a little casual but might work well for laundry day," he concluded.

Tavi burst out laughing and put the dress back on its rack. Their small general store had added a "Ladies' Fashion Corner," but Tavi didn't know where they were sourcing the clothing. Each piece was dreadfully ugly.

"We'd better get what we came for," Tavi said. Winter storms had again kept them home, this time for a full week. Their stock of staples was running low, and this was the first day the weather had allowed them to walk into Oren. Tullen pulled Mey's list out of his pocket, and they walked around the store, picking up flour, salt, lamp oil, and more.

At the register, Tullen pointed to the glass jars behind the counter. "We'd also like one bag of ulora root candy, please."

"That's not on the list!" Tavi said.

Tullen held the paper out to Tavi, and there it was, in her mother's neat script: *1 bag of ulora root candy*. Tavi grinned, mouth already watering. "Did you put her up to that?"

Tullen just smiled and shrugged. They paid and placed their items in the bags they had brought. Once their gloves were on, they exited the store into the slushy street and turned to walk home.

Ahead was a small café. The owner was kneeling before an iron bench next to the door, swiping snow off the seat. "Hello, Mr. Sinno," Tavi greeted him as she and Tullen passed.

"Hello," he responded. He followed his greeting with a shout of pain.

Tavi and Tullen turned and rushed back. Mr. Sinno was holding one hand tightly in the other. "Knew I should have worn gloves," he said.

"What happened?" Tavi asked.

"Just cut myself on this bench," the man replied. "The snow and ice must have weighed it down so much that one of the welds came loose."

Tavi gave Tullen a hesitant look, and he smiled and nodded at her. "Mr. Sinno," Tavi said, "I'd like to heal it, if you'll let me."

His eyebrows rose. "You can heal now?"

"I just learned," Tavi said. In the previous weeks since healing Tullen, Tavi had practiced her skills a few times when her family members had small injuries. She had found that scrapes were difficult to heal and bruises impossible, though she hoped that would change with time. But the one thing she knew she could do was heal a cut.

"I'd appreciate that," Mr. Sinno replied, holding out his hand.

Tavi nearly vomited as she took her gloves off. The cut was ragged and bled freely. She looked away and brought magic into her hands by contemplating how much she desired the warmth and dry roads of summer.

When she touched the cut, Tavi's stomach flipped. But she forced herself to think not of blood, but again of her desire for summer. She urged healing magic to enter her hands and felt a satisfying rush of heat. This cut was not as clean as Tullen's had been, and it took more time and effort to heal it. But Tavi could feel her magic working, slowly knitting together the edges of the laceration. Soon the skin was again unmarred.

Movement down the street caught Tavi's eye as she pulled her hand away. She gasped—Ellea was entering the general store, two doors down. Tavi quickly put her gloves back on, realizing too late that the blood on her fingers was now inside her glove.

"Youngest healer I've ever had," Mr. Sinno said. "Thank you, Tavi. It's good as new!"

Eyes still on the general store, Tavi acknowledged Mr. Sinno with a nod before turning again toward her house.

"Let's go," she hissed to Tullen.

"What's wrong?" Tullen asked. "You look like you've seen a ghost."

"Not a ghost," Tavi said, resisting the urge to look behind her for the head midwife. "Just Ellea."

"Why don't you want to see Ellea?"

Tavi didn't answer.

"Tavi? Why?"

With a sigh, Tavi confessed, "She doesn't know I can heal."

"Why wouldn't you want her to know that? Plenty of midwives can heal."

Her answer was again delayed. At last, Tavi admitted, "It's because you're the one who helped me discover my healing gift. And you don't do things in the way Ellea does them."

Tavi was surprised when Tullen's mouth rose in a half-smile. "It sounds like she's as skeptical of my training as I am of hers," he said.

"It's not funny!" Tavi insisted. "I've learned plenty from both of you!"

"One of these days you'll need to tell her."

"But not today," Tavi said. In the silence that followed, she tried to discern why that response didn't feel right. Didn't it make sense for her to keep her healing gift secret? It would hurt Ellea to know one of her students had been training with a Meadow Dweller. Tavi didn't want to hurt the mentor she cared for.

But deep down, Tavi knew that wasn't her biggest concern. In reality, she was afraid Ellea would be disappointed in her. She wanted Ellea to approve of her.

I am enough. The words came unbidden to Tavi's mind. Did she really prefer unearned favor over honesty? If Ellea was disappointed in her, would Tavi be able to live with that? She chewed on those thoughts for several minutes before stopping altogether in the middle of the road. Tullen turned to her, eyebrows raised.

"I need to go talk to Ellea," Tavi said. "And I need to go alone."

Tullen didn't ask any questions. He just gave her a smile and a nod, and he again walked toward home.

Watching him leave was harder than Tavi had expected, but this was a conversation she needed to have on her own. She turned toward town.

"TODAY MR. SINNO CUT HIS HAND," Tavi said. She was sitting in Ellea's office, an untouched cup of tea in front of her.

"Is he all right?" Ellea asked.

"He is," Tavi said, "because I healed him."

Ellea smiled broadly. "That's wonderful! I know you've hoped to develop a healing gift."

Tavi took a deep breath. "I've known I could heal for a few weeks now," she said. Noting Ellea's surprise, she continued, "Tullen helped me discover it."

Ellea slowly put down her teacup. She was no longer smiling. "And how did that happen?" she asked.

Tavi told her mentor that Tullen had been training her ever since the incident at school. She explained how they'd found that the key to Tavi's gift activation was desire. Ellea's eyes betrayed mild amusement when Tavi told her about Misty's pickles. Then Tavi described the day when Tullen had helped her discover that desire was the key to her ability to heal as well.

Ellea did not immediately respond. When she did, it was with a grave expression and a serious tone. "Tullen has been influencing you from the beginning," she observed. Tavi nodded. "That concerns me," Ellea said.

"Why?"

"We've discussed this, Tavi. The training given by midwives has been developed for many years. When we teach you to relax and breathe deeply to activate your gifts, it is because that method has been found to be effective and safe. All our training is designed to keep you on the right path."

"Do you think I'm on the wrong path?" Tavi asked.

"Perhaps not yet," Ellea conceded. "But I have heard stories of the Meadow for years. Their traditions are different than ours. They claim to worship Sava, but they do not even have parish halls. They allow no visitors to their community, which makes me wonder what they are hiding. And as you have stated, they do have informal magical training, but that very informality is treacherous. While we midwives teach you time-proven ways to grow in your magical abilities, they encourage experimentation and instinct. No one knows what the results will be when magic is handled in such a way. Don't you see the danger, Tavi?"

Tavi's first instinct was to humbly agree so she could escape Ellea's office. An apology was on the tip of her tongue, but she pressed her lips closed to keep the words from escaping. She had come here to be honest. Pretending to agree wouldn't help either of them.

Her heart pounding, Tavi said, "My magic is different. You know that as well as I do. I need to experiment. I need to learn to use my instincts. Some of what you and the other midwives have taught me has been very useful. But it doesn't always work for me.

"Maybe if I gave it enough time, I could use deep breathing to activate my magic and discover new gifts. But I don't have time! I awakened later than everyone else, and I have six gifted areas to master, not one. Tullen is helping me learn to use my gifts. Because of that, today I healed someone. That feels right."

Ellea sat quietly for a long moment, and Tavi's heart broke seeing the sadness in the midwife's eyes. At last, Ellea spoke. "It is because you are different—and because I care about you—that I want so badly to protect you. There will be people who want to use you because of your many gifts. I want you to be able to stand against them. When you graduate from our training, I want you to have a good foundation, built on knowledge and truth."

Tears filled Tavi's eyes. "I will—I already do. You've given me that. And Tullen has too." After a pause, she asked, "When a mother is having a difficult birth, do you always follow a textbook? Or do you experiment to do whatever it takes keep her and the baby healthy?"

Ellea did not answer, but Tavi could see the midwife considering the question. Finally, Ellea said, "I appreciate you coming to talk to me, Tavi. Thank you for your honesty."

"You're welcome." There did not seem to be anything else to say. Tavi left the office, feeling she had gained strength, but had perhaps lost a friend.

CHAPTER TWENTY-FIVE

The first time I assisted with the birth of a sun-blessed child, I nearly forgot the words of the blessing, and I could barely breathe deeply enough to give the child my breath. But once I completed my task and saw light fill the baby's chest, then travel into his ears, I wept just as freely as his mother. In that moment, I felt a deep connection to Kari, our First Midwife. And I have felt close to her ever since.

-*From* Midwife Memoirs *by Ellea Kariana*

"CAMALYN, my level of respect for you has risen tenfold," Ash said. "This scarf is horrendous. It's hot, itchy and uncomfortable. I can't believe you've been wearing one of these several times a week."

Camalyn looked around the barn where Konner, Ash, Sella, and Aldin were all dressed in Karite black. "You all look so . . . devout," she said, and she lost herself in laughter.

Konner's eyebrows rose beneath his headscarf. "I'm quite sure Camalyn the Karite would not display so little control," he chided her. "Calm yourself. It's time to go."

The rest of the Grays made their way past Konner toward the waiting carriage outside. As he followed them out, he allowed himself the brief indulgence of self-congratulation. When he had met Ash over a year and a half earlier, Konner had been obsessed with magic, specifically his own, unclaimed birthright.

Now as he trained, led, and inspired these four Grays, he rarely thought about the gifting of which he had been robbed. Perhaps magic had never been his calling. Despite the impressive gifts of the Grays, Konner knew that with his strategic mind and ability to influence, he was more powerful than all of them. They knew it too; he saw it in their respectful gazes and heard it in their submissive words.

They entered the carriage and began the long drive toward Savala. Konner hoped that tonight they would rejoice that Camalyn had been elected to the Cormina Council. However, if the election did not go their way, he would switch to another strategy. As long as he was at the helm, they would succeed.

"I'm taking this off," Aldin said, unwinding the heavy scarf.

"Keep it on," Konner instructed firmly. "You need to be used to wearing it, so it looks natural." Aldin replaced the scarf.

Camalyn's eyes above her veil were amused. "All these months of dressing up and going to the temple have been worth it, just to see the rest of you looking like insane ascetics," she said.

Konner's eyebrows lifted again. "Let's hope you have more reason than that to find it worthwhile."

When they at last arrived in Savala, Konner's driver parked in an alley. All but Camalyn stood to exit. Camalyn pulled her scarf off her mouth, grinned, and blew the others a kiss. Sella, Aldin, Konner, and Ash left the carriage and made their way to the street. They walked about a block, then stood on a corner having a quiet conversation.

Five minutes later, Camalyn strode toward them, hands clasped demurely in front of her, eyes watching the street at her feet. After a moment of consultation with one another, the rest of the Grays approached her. She stopped and acknowledged them with humble nods before continuing to walk—followed now by four disciples.

As Konner had hoped, their group caught the attention of other Karites who were scattered throughout the crowd. A good number of them rushed to join the procession once they realized who was leading it.

Konner tried to keep his smile from reaching his eyes as he walked among the black-robed faithful. Since Camalyn had begun campaigning, the number of Karites in the city had grown exponentially. Even the oversized robe could not completely hide her shapely figure. She was easily recognized and readily followed.

Camalyn's message to the people of Savala was simple. She bemoaned the lack of true religious commitment in Cormina and invited others to join the Karites, who promised to help them know Sava in a deeper way than they ever had. In order to know Sava deeply, converts were asked to commit to a stringent set of Karite rules. As Konner had predicted, most of the new followers had embraced these standards, hopeful that Sava would hold up his end of the deal and bless their lives with deeper meaning.

Religious converts were easily turned into voters—hopefully enough of them. The fickle new followers would eventually find Camalyn's platitudes stale, and at that time she would adjust her message as necessary.

The walk to the Karite temple was half a mile long, and by the time Camalyn had reached it, forty people were following her. That didn't surprise Konner.

What astonished him was the great crowd waiting outside the temple. There were at least four hundred people there, many of them in dark-black Karite robes. Seasoned Karites usually wore robes that had faded to gray. Oft-worn, oft-washed robes were the closest thing to a sign of prestige among Karites. The dark robes all around were a visual reminder of how many had recently converted.

Camalyn looked behind her, and her eyes found Konner's. She bowed her head to him, but he saw a sparkle in those eyes. She had resisted this plan at first, but now she reveled in the influence she had built.

A young girl, perhaps six years old, approached Camalyn. "Will you talk to us, Cam'lyn?" she asked.

Camalyn shook her head. "I am humbled and honored that you

would ask," she said. "However, I prefer to wait quietly for the election results, as everyone else is doing."

But a woman standing nearby encouraged Camalyn to speak. The man next to her concurred, and others in the immediate vicinity begged Camalyn to talk to the crowd. Konner wondered if the little girl had somehow been placed there by his speech-blessed young candidate. Or did the people love Camalyn that much?

Soon a group physically ushered Camalyn up the steps of the temple. When she arrived on the top step and faced the people, they quieted. Camalyn made eye contact with individuals throughout the crowd. Konner knew she was likely pressing her lips together, summoning her gray magic.

Several older Karites stood at the edges of the crowd, and as Camalyn prepared to speak, Konner watched them. Above their veils, their eyes looked skeptical and angry, brows knit together. Their arms were crossed, and they stood apart from many of the new believers. Camalyn had told the Grays about these temple elders. Many of them were resisting her dynamic message. They were uncomfortable with how quickly their temple attendance was growing, and they did not trust the new converts' true commitment. However, it was impossible for them to publicly come against someone who was spreading the Karite message more effectively than anyone had in generations.

After at least a minute of looking at the crowd, Camalyn spoke. "Friends," she began, "I am unworthy of so very much. Unworthy of life itself. Unworthy of the favor of Sava. Unworthy of a position on the Cormina Council. And unworthy of speaking to you."

As the message of tedious humility continued, Konner's eyes remained on the Karite elders. At Camalyn's first phrase, their dispositions changed. Crossed arms dropped, foreheads smoothed, and every eye was on the young woman speaking on the steps. Some of the elders even moved forward. They not only listened; they loved what they heard. Would they question it later? Undoubtedly. But for now, they were in her thrall.

Konner had practiced resisting Camalyn's gifted speech, and his knowledge of her magic also made it easier not to fall under her sway. Even so, he was nearly drawn in along with the rest of the crowd. And to think her gift had been wasted on ridiculous shopping expeditions before this!

Camalyn began to speak of the Karite robes and veils. "Why must we look different?" she asked. "Because we are set apart! We are the true followers of Sava and the true disciples of Kari. Many of you are new to the Karite faith. I know you are being asked by friends and loved ones, 'Why will you not join us in drinking sweet wine? Why will you not celebrate our holidays? Why will you not wear our clothing and our cosmetics?'

"Your answer is simple. 'I do not need these shallow pleasures. I have found a much higher joy, the joy of worshiping Sava through his servant Kari.' And then you may say to your loved ones, 'Join me. Join me in living a true life. A life of wholeness, unencumbered by the self-indulgence that strips away true contentment.' "

Camalyn's attention was arrested by something in the crowd to her right, and Konner stood on his toes, struggling to see what it was. After several seconds, a man approached the steps, holding a paper which was folded and sealed with a large daub of red wax. Camalyn gestured for him to come up the steps, and he complied. They held a brief, whispered conversation, at the end of which Camalyn held her hands high in the air.

"My fellow pilgrims on this journey of truth," Camalyn said, her voice filled with soft joy, "I am pleased to introduce you to Mr. Denno, who is a clerk with the Cormina Election Commission." A murmur of excitement arose, but when Camalyn held her hands up to the crowd, they became silent.

Camalyn spoke again, "As you may have guessed, Mr. Denno has brought us the election results. However, I have news which is far more important and which brings me great joy. Mr. Denno has been standing at the back of this crowd, listening—and he wishes to become a Karite himself! Blessed be the First Midwife!"

"Blessed be the First Midwife!" the crowd cried.

"Mr. Denno, our friend Junati will speak with you about the Karite faith," Camalyn said. A tall elder stepped forward. He beckoned to the election clerk, who gave the paper to Camalyn and made his way down the steps. Camalyn continued, "And I would like to ask Retta if she will honor all of us by reading the election results." Retta, the oldest elder, climbed the stairs with Camalyn's help.

Konner smiled. By involving the elders in such prominent ways, Camalyn was keeping them on her side for the time being. She had more strategic ability than he had realized.

Retta reached the top step, and Camalyn handed the sealed paper to the fragile, old woman. The crowd was as silent as a large group could be. As Retta broke open the seal, Konner realized he was holding his hands in tight fists. He released them, his fingernails leaving irritated imprints on his palms. Although Konner had told himself this election wasn't crucial, he knew how much they had invested in it. He hoped it had been enough.

Retta's voice was high-pitched and shaky, but traveled well across the quiet crowd. "Final Results in the Election for Savala's Three Cormina Councillor Places," she read at a painfully slow speed. "Councillor positions will be given to the three residents of Savala District who received the highest number of votes. First, Aron Stimmit." This was no surprise; Stimmit had won every council election for over two decades.

"Second," Retta said, "Barria Yanno." Yanno was the one who had taken the seat Konner had wanted; she was weak but just uncontroversial enough to keep her office.

Perhaps Retta had learned to manipulate crowds in her many years speaking to fellow Karites, for she paused an obscenely long time before reading the third winner's name. Six more candidates were considered to be in the running, and Camalyn had announced her candidacy later than the other five. In addition, all of the others were sun-blessed. Konner knew how important that was to the citizenry, and they did not know of Camalyn's gift. Had her platform of religious reform, shared through magical speech, been enough? Konner exchanged brief glances with Ash, Aldin, and Sella. They appeared as tense as he felt.

At last Retta took a trembling breath and announced, "Third, Camalyn Hunt."

The crowd was quiet. This was the strangest election result announcement Konner had ever heard. The Karites, not given to exuberant displays of approval, did not seem to know how to respond to the good news.

But Ash, Sava bless him, was committed to the role he was playing. He called in a loud voice, "Blessed be the First Midwife!"

A sense of relief and excitement filled the crowd. As one, they repeated the words. "Blessed be the First Midwife!"

On the stage, Camalyn's hands were held out toward the people, and her head was bowed low, the picture of a humble servant.

Konner would have been willing to bet she was hiding a gleeful smile.

BACK AT THE FARM, heavy veils and robes lay discarded on the barn floor, and all five Grays lounged at the table, enjoying their drinks of choice. They hadn't stayed long at the temple, Konner having insisted that they should leave the people wanting more of Camalyn. But he had another reason for bringing them back here—they needed to talk.

"It's spring," Konner said. He was greeted with confused looks; this wasn't news to anyone. Konner laughed. All eyes on him, he held up his brandy snifter.

"Next week," he said, swirling the amber liquid in his glass, "our first traveling team will depart. It is time for our numbers to grow."

The celebratory mood seemed to double in a moment. Glasses clinked, toasts were made, and the Grays reveled in the future they were creating.

CHAPTER TWENTY-SIX

Everywhere I go, people tell me stories they have heard about healings I have performed. Nearly every tale centers on someone who has been pulled back from certain death. At such times I urge them not to discount the value of minor healings. When I heal a small scratch, boil, or abrasion, the person I touch experiences Sava's love. That may be just as profound as a saved life.

-*From* Savala's Collected Letters, Volume 2

"Ow!"

First Tavi felt pain; then she heard the laughter of a classroom full of trainees. Ellea's lecture on early magical history had lulled Tavi to sleep, and someone had roused her with a sharp pinch. Narre's sheepish grin exposed her as the culprit. The burn of a blush took over Tavi's face and neck. Things were already tense between her and Ellea; the last thing she needed to be doing was falling asleep during the midwife's lectures.

"Is everything all right, Tavi?" Ellea asked.

"Yes," Tavi murmured.

Ellea let out a small chuckle before continuing her lecture.

Tavi wished they could do away with lectures in spring—or at least have them on the lawn. Even Ellea was boring when lovely weather and soft grass waited outside.

Five more minutes into the lecture, Tavi was again fighting a losing battle with her sagging eyelids. She was relieved when the classroom door opened, jolting her back to attention. When she looked behind her to see who had entered, her relief flew out the window into the cool spring air.

Mayor Briggun Nolin stood in the doorway. His hair, usually combed to perfection, was in disarray. "Pardon me," he began, not sounding apologetic at all, "but I must have a word with Tavina Malin."

Tavi's eyes widened, and she stared at Ellea, trying to send a message through that gaze—*I don't want to talk to that awful man!*

Ellea, however, was looking at the mayor. The request had obviously surprised her, but she responded, "Of course," before shifting her eyes to Tavi. She must have seen the distress in her student, because Ellea amended, "Mayor Nolin, please make it quick; this is an important lecture, and Tavi should not be gone for long."

Tavi gave Ellea a nod of gratitude before standing and walking toward the door. Mayor Nolin stood in the hallway waiting for her, and the wrath on his face did not bode well. Tavi closed the door and faced him.

Mayor Nolin held out a piece of paper, creamy white with the remnants of a red wax seal adhered to it. He was gripping it so tightly that his hand shook, and he advanced a step closer to Tavi to thrust the paper in her face. She stepped back in response.

"Do you know what this is?" the mayor asked through a snarling mouth, his bright teeth shining. Tavi barely had time to shake her head before he continued, "This message contains the election results."

Again he stepped closer, and again Tavi backed away, this time bumping against the hallway wall, across from the classroom door.

The mayor thrust the paper at Tavi's face. "You'll notice my name is not listed!"

Tavi looked down at the paper inches from her eyes and read the name of Modun Slead, written in fine calligraphy. Councillor Slead was not popular, but voters had found him more palatable than the other options—including Briggun Nolin.

The mayor was standing so close, too close, his angry eyes locked on Tavi. He expected a response. "I see that," Tavi said.

"You *see* that?" The response burst out of Mayor Nolin's mouth, and Tavi was assaulted by hot breath that smelled of liquor.

Tavi realized she was hunched over, cowering. Well, that was about to stop. She was strong enough to stand up to this little man who found it acceptable to bully a young girl. Tavi straightened and met the mayor's gaze. Inside, she trembled with disgust and fear, but she was determined not to show it.

"I would have won had you campaigned with me!" Mayor Nolin's voice rose in volume. "I installed plumbing in your family's home! When your gifts awakened, I spoke with the midwife—that one teaching right now—and told her to give you the best education possible! This is the gratitude you show? You selfish child!"

While the mayor was speaking, the door to the classroom behind him had opened. Mayor Nolin took no notice, but Tavi saw Narre standing there with fire in her eyes. Tavi held out her hand to deter Narre's involvement, but she appreciated her cousin for continuing to stand watch.

"Mayor Nolin." Tavi's voice was stronger than she had expected, and it built her confidence. "If you need to remove the plumbing from our home, that's fine. But I won't ask people to vote for someone like you. Ever."

Her response further infuriated Mayor Nolin. He crumpled the paper and threw it down the hall with an angry grunt. Immediately, he pulled his hand back, looked at it, and put his finger in his mouth.

"Paper cut?" Tavi asked.

The mayor slammed both his hands on the wall to either side of Tavi. She responded with a sharp gasp but stood her ground.

"You're not only an ingrate; you're stupid! I would have helped you as much as you helped me!" Mayor Nolin shouted, small flecks of spittle hitting Tavi's face.

Tavi saw Narre's wide eyes, and she knew her cousin was about to come to the rescue. But Tavi wanted to fight this battle herself. She would use one of her mother's tactics, developed to perfection over decades of parenting. Whenever Tavi exploded with anger, Mey's response was calm and quiet. It took the wind out of Tavi's sails.

"Mayor Nolin," Tavi said, her voice low and calm, but firm and not the least bit sweet, "move your hands."

The mayor's eyes widened. He pulled his hands away and folded his arms across his chest.

Tavi's next instinct caught her by surprise, but she didn't resist it. "Let me see that paper cut," she instructed the mayor.

"What?" he asked, baffled.

"The paper cut," Tavi said. "Let me see it, please."

She couldn't believe he complied. But he did, and in seconds, Tavi summoned healing magic into her hands and mended the tiny cut. She was getting good at this. When she pulled her hands away and looked back at Mayor Nolin's face, she saw confusion rather than anger. He was speechless—and that didn't happen often.

Tavi shifted her shoulders back, lifted her chin, and spoke. "That is what my magic is for," she informed the mayor. "Sava gives us magic so we can do good things with it, not favors for dishonest mayors." Perhaps it wasn't worded perfectly, but it would have to do. Tavi strode past Mayor Nolin, gave Narre a grin, and entered the classroom.

Narre, however, wasn't ready to return to class. She shouted into the hallway, "If you were depending on a fourteen-year-old to get you elected, you probably didn't deserve the position in the first place!"

The sound of the door slamming reverberated through the classroom, but a moment later it opened again. Narre's voice was even louder this time. "Maybe next time you're running for office, you can tell the story of how the great Tavina healed your paper cut!"

This time, when her classmates broke into laughter, Tavi joined them.

CHAPTER TWENTY-SEVEN

Many people assume sun-blessed students have fewer troubles than ordinary adolescents. This is, of course, preposterous. These are still young men and women, navigating the waters of pre-adulthood. They struggle to understand life and its utter lack of fairness. Magic provides no protection against disappointment.

-*From* Training Sun-Blessed Students *by Ellea Kariana*

SPRING CONTINUED to offer Oren the gift of delightfully mild weather, as if she wanted to erase the memory of Old Man Winter's aggression. Tavi marveled at the town's general atmosphere of cheer and optimism. Even Mayor Nolin's scowls and her father's disregard didn't bother her too much.

Tullen had returned home after the new year celebration at the beginning of spring, and he was again visiting a few days at a time. He still trained Tavi often and sometimes took her on short hunts. When Narre and Sall came over, the four of them spent beautiful afternoons together, exploring the forest and their magic.

At the end of spring, Narre celebrated her fourteenth birthday. The next day, she pulled Tavi to a quiet corner of the schoolyard and confided that Sall's gift to her had been a kiss—their first.

"Finally!" Tavi exclaimed. Anticipation of The First Kiss had consumed Narre for weeks. Unsure if Sall's delay had been due to an overabundance of shyness or self-control, Narre had been unwilling to initiate a kiss. That meant Tavi had been subject to innumerable conversations on the topic.

"What was it like?" Tavi asked.

Narre took a moment to think about that. "Nice . . . and kind of clumsy," she concluded.

Tavi laughed. "I'm sure it'll get better." That was all the advice she had; she had no kissing experience of her own—except kissing her mother goodnight, and surely that didn't count.

Spring exited gracefully when summer arrived. Sunny weather was interspersed with occasional showers. Tullen celebrated his eighteenth birthday in the Meadow. A few days later when he visited Oren, Tavi and Misty surprised him with a celebratory dinner they had prepared, complete with roasted antlerfruit. Sall and Narre were in attendance, along with Tavi's family, except her father. Tullen couldn't stop smiling.

Tavi's fifteenth birthday was several weeks later, during the summer break from school. Tullen planned his weekly trip accordingly, and the four of them spent the day roaming the forest, playing games, and drinking great quantities of fresh lemonade. It was perfect.

As summer dragged on, both school and training felt like drudgery. The classrooms were hot despite open windows, and each day Tavi counted the hours until she could go home. She hoped each day to find Tullen waiting, but an entire week went by without him coming. Tavi felt concern, but she knew he occasionally needed to delay a trip.

When the next week of school passed without Tullen's arrival, Tavi was truly worried. But as she and Misty began their weekend with a late breakfast, Tullen appeared in the open kitchen doorway.

"Tullen!" Tavi cried, standing up and greeting him with a hug. "Where have you been?"

His smile was wobbly. "I couldn't make it until today."

"There are plenty of biscuits," Misty said. "Have a seat."

Tullen complied, and as they ate, Tavi and Misty updated him on various minor happenings he'd missed. After a few minutes, Tavi observed, "You're quiet today."

Again, that uneasy grin. "I have a lot on my mind." He looked toward the door. "Can we go into the forest, Tavi?"

Tavi looked at the unfinished biscuit on his plate, and her eyebrows furrowed. "Sure," she agreed. Tullen stood and hurried outside, leaving his plate on the table instead of taking it to the sink. And right then, Tavi knew.

They walked silently to the place they called "our clearing," and Tullen gestured for Tavi to sit. She remained standing.

"You're leaving," Tavi stated.

Tullen's eyes met hers. "Yes," he replied.

Weary in the thick summer air, Tavi sat where she was. Tullen sat across from her. "Why?" she asked.

Tullen let out a long sigh. "I'm an adult, and more is expected of me," he said. "The elders want me closer to home. They want me to hunt more, and 'participate in Meadow society.' That's how they worded it. And . . ." He stopped, shaking his head and looking down.

"And what?" Her voice was quiet, tight.

"It's not important."

"But it is."

He met her gaze again. "They have . . . other concerns."

Tavi let the silence linger before prompting, "Tullen."

"It's not important," he repeated.

"They're concerned about us, aren't they?" she asked. "All your friends who have the audacity not to be Meadow Dwellers."

Tullen closed his eyes briefly and nodded. "The elders believe I've been too influenced by—the outside world."

Tavi wanted to laugh or cry at the stupidity of that, but she didn't have the energy. Instead she watched Tullen. His shoulders were broad, and his feet were big, but he was still gangly. Sitting with his legs folded, he looked like a boy trying to fill up a man's body, trying to fit into a man's life. His normal confidence was depleted, and in his hunched shoulders, Tavi thought she saw the struggle he must have had during the previous days.

"Do you agree with the elders?" Tavi asked.

Eyes cast down again, Tullen took a deep breath, but it had a hitch in it. He tried again, with the same result. Finally, he spoke one word, in a shaky voice. "No." Two more of those labored breaths, and five more words. "But my family is there."

Tavi nodded, though it required unexpected effort to do so. "It's your home," she said.

Tullen looked at her with shining eyes. "It's my home," he agreed.

Then he was crying, with hoarse sobs she hadn't ever heard from him, and shaking shoulders. And as he had done for her, on a day so long ago they had surely been mere children, Tavi sat next to Tullen, put her arm around him, and let him cry into her shoulder.

There were more words, but nothing new was said. Tullen gave Tavi a hand-drawn map showing two routes to the Meadow. "For emergencies," he said. Tavi placed it in her pocket and kept her hand over it.

At last, they stood. Tullen's eyes were puffy, and Tavi wished she had given him the same gift of tears he had given her. But she had known this would come—she had known, and she was allowing the reality of it to settle into the grooves of expectation she had carved into her heart.

"I must go back," Tullen said. "They didn't want me to come, but— I had to. Now I must go."

Tavi nodded. "I know you have to go." She referenced more than his immediate exit, and she hoped he understood.

She opened her arms, and he walked into them. He rested his chin on top of her head, and she pressed her ear against his heart. They stood there a long time, and when Tavi pulled back, it hadn't been long enough.

But Tullen gave a little wave, and with a smile that nearly reached his eyes, he breathed, "Goodbye, Tavi of the Town."

And he was gone.

CHAPTER TWENTY-EIGHT

The Cormina Council is necessary. But I find myself asking, is it a necessary good or a necessary evil?

-*From* Small-Town Cormina: A Midwife's Reflections *by Ellea Kariana*

"He won't be happy to see me," Konner said.

Camalyn's eyes slid his way. "You've said that at least three times since we got in this carriage."

"I simply want you to be prepared," Konner insisted. "He and I are not on good terms."

"It's not as if he'd send me home after he invited me here," Camalyn replied.

Konner dropped the subject. "Put on your scarf. We're almost there."

A groan exited Camalyn's mouth as she wrapped the heavy scarf around her head and the lower half of her face. Moments later, the carriage came to a stop in front of a grand house. A waiting servant opened the carriage door and helped Camalyn out. When he saw her companion, he raised his eyebrows in polite disdain. Konner stepped out and gave Camalyn a pointed look. *Even the servant knows I'm not welcome here.*

Konner had been glad to hear Camalyn had been invited to a councillor's house—the second such recent invitation she'd received—and that she had finagled an additional invitation for her "good friend." But when she had told Konner that the hospitable councillor was Mola Ronson, the banker's enthusiasm had cooled.

For years, Konner had kept a close eye on the council, gathering useful information about its members. He knew, of course, who was in debt, but also which members were cheating on their spouses or lying to their business partners. And he knew who relied on illicit substances to cope—such as Mola Ronson, who battled an addiction to lijani powder. Perhaps "battled" wasn't the correct word. Lijani had won this fight, and Mola was just trying to ensure his secret did not escape. He kept his hair long to conceal his telltale red ears.

A year earlier, Konner had seen Ronson on the street. Because of the positions each held, they knew each other by sight and had stopped to shake hands. Konner had taken the opportunity to lean in close and murmur, "Really, Ronson, lijani? That stuff will kill you."

And then Konner had discovered that Mola was at that moment under the influence of "that stuff." The esteemed councillor was not a pleasant addict. His whole face had turned purple, and he had spent the next five minutes screaming against the injustice of Konner's lies. Since then, the politician had not only avoided the banker; he had actively spoken against him in private.

Konner had good reason to believe this meeting would not go well. But the servant was waiting at the open door, so Konner smiled and followed Camalyn inside.

Ronson spied Konner and turned to Camalyn with a frown. "This is the friend you mentioned?"

"Yes, this is my good friend, Konner Burrell. Have the two of you met?"

DINNER WAS DELICIOUS AND AWKWARD, full of conversations started by Camalyn and continued by no one. She had unwrapped her scarf from the bottom half of her face—Karites were allowed this luxury while eating in private residences. Throughout the meal, Ronson alternated between glaring at Konner and ogling Camalyn. Konner wanted to laugh out loud at the man's continual shifts in mood. *It seems he wants to take a bite of both of us.*

After eating, Ronson crossed his arms and fixed his gaze on Konner. The banker smiled and said, "I hear you have the finest collection of tobacco in Savala." He reached into his suit jacket's inner pocket and pulled out a pipe. *Your move.*

Ronson flushed and stood more quickly than was necessary, his chair legs squeaking as they slid backward. He was angry, but he was still a gentleman, and he would not turn away a guest. "Shall we retire to my study for drinks?" he asked, directing the question to Camalyn. She beamed at him before standing and wrapping her scarf, leaving only her eyes visible.

In the study, Ronson poured brandy for himself and Konner, Camalyn having declined his offer. They sat in comfortable chairs, and Ronson handed Konner a bag of tobacco, not bringing out his own pipe. Konner smelled the product. It was unimpressive, and he sat it on the table next to him, leaving his pipe in his pocket.

"Camalyn has something to show you," Konner said. Both men turned to Camalyn, whose tense eyes betrayed the pain associated with her gray magic. Konner gave her a nod, and she unwrapped her scarf.

Ronson gaped at Camalyn. Pointing at her mouth, which was surrounded by a storm of gray light, he asked, "What is that?"

Camalyn pointed at the tobacco next to Konner and asked, "Is it good quality?"

"Average at best."

Camalyn instructed Ronson, "Bring your guest your best bag of tobacco so he can fill his pipe."

Ronson walked to his tobacco cabinet, opened it, and stood on a stool. He reached to the back of the top shelf, retrieved a small bag, and brought it to Konner, before sitting.

The room was quiet. Konner packed his pipe, lit it, and took several puffs. He nodded his approval.

As soon as Camalyn released her magic with a sigh, Ronson sat up straight, taut as a bowstring. He looked at the bag of tobacco, then back at Camalyn, who had not replaced her scarf. "Why was your magic gray?"

Konner answered, "Because gray is now the color of power."

"I don't know what that means." All the man's pride and spite were gone.

So Konner told him. He was careful; this presentation must differ from those he had given to the other Grays. He did not address the council's inefficacies; that might put the man on the defensive. Instead, he wove together tales of ancient epics and bold ideas for the future, at every turn hinting at how Mola Ronson might be part of that vision.

Ronson was mind-blessed. With his gift active, he could see the weaknesses of others' arguments. However, he often encountered resistance, which was taken as Sava's cue that Ronson was attempting to argue on the wrong side—however right it appeared to be. He had gained the trust of the other councillors; they knew his magic was a flawless indicator of which way they should lean in a legislative dilemma. With Ronson's resistance gone, he would be empowered to argue effectively for any side. Konner painted this picture for the man.

Ronson's curiosity was escalating to desire. Konner could see it. But the man had questions; they were burning in his eyes. So Konner silenced himself and puffed on his pipe while he waited.

"I wasn't surprised to see that you are speech-blessed," Ronson told Camalyn. "I'm certainly not the only one of our colleagues who has guessed it." Konner glanced at Camalyn; her expression was neutral. They had known her persuasive powers were likely to be questioned by her fellow councillors. Ronson's attention shifted to Konner. "And what you say is certainly intriguing. I am not sure, however, if I believe it. I would not have expected Camalyn to encounter resistance when she compelled me to give you good tobacco. It was the hospitable thing to do. All I've seen at this point is that her magic looks different, not that it operates differently."

Konner smiled. "I'm sure we can come up with a better demonstration if you will give us leave to discuss this briefly?"

Ronson nodded, and Konner stood, beckoning Camalyn to follow him. They walked behind Ronson's desk and engaged in a brief, whispered conversation. At the end of it, Camalyn pursed her lips and activated her magic.

Camalyn approached Ronson. In her hand was a long, pointed letter opener, retrieved from the man's desk. "Mola," Camalyn said, "take this." When he had done so, she instructed, "Hold the point of the letter opener against the large blood vessel in your neck. Use your fingers to find your pulse first if you need to." Camalyn's calm tone belied her words. When Ronson had obeyed, she said, "Push it into your neck. Gradually push harder, and don't stop unless I tell you to."

As calmly as if he were pouring tea or reading the newspaper, Mola Ronson pressed the pointed metal into his skin, increasing the pressure a bit at a time. It was not sharp enough to easily cut him, and Konner resisted the urge to wince as he watched the man's skin stretching inward, further and further. At last, the metal broke the skin, and Ronson's eyes widened at the pain, but he continued pushing.

"Stop." Camalyn's voice was not loud, but the effect was immediate. Ronson held the tool where it was. A bead of blood made its way down his neck. "Remove the letter opener." When he did so, his neck bled freely, and Konner handed his own handkerchief to the man. Camalyn instructed him to press the cloth against his neck.

A moment later, Camalyn's mouth lost its gray light, and Ronson shook his head to break his stupor. Based on his previous interactions with the man, Konner expected him to explode in rage. But Ronson merely looked at both of them and said, "I'm convinced. And I'm interested."

So Konner told him more. He explained the violent catalyst necessary for a gray awakening. Mola Ronson was a power-hungry lijani addict, and Konner guessed the man had lost most respect for conventional morality years before. So when he concluded with, "Will you join us?" he was surprised with the councillor's response.

"Absolutely not."

Camalyn's jaw dropped. "But, Mola, you could use gray magic to convince the council to go whatever direction you believe is best. You could forget about the resistance that holds you back. Imagine if you and I were a team. You would see the weaknesses in arguments, and I would—"

Ronson cut her off. "It's not that. I agree, gray magic is . . . it's incredible. I want it. But throughout my career, I have made many decisions of which I am not proud. I must draw the line somewhere. I will not murder."

Konner spoke. "We can find someone who is already dying. It will be a mercy to bring them to Senniet sooner."

"No."

"I felt the same way, Mola," Camalyn said. "But I knew I was ending a life that had already lost all joy. It was hard, but it was worth it."

"No."

"Ronson," Konner said, "Think of what we could do together."

"I will help you if I can," Ronson said. "You're right—our nation is weak, and we need to do something differently. Whatever I can do to be your advocate, let me know. But I cannot kill. Call me naïve, but I still believe in Kovus, and I don't want to go there when I die."

Konner and Camalyn shared a long look. They both turned back to Ronson, and Konner said in a low voice, "There is one thing you can do to help us."

Camalyn again activated her magic. She pulled a cloth out of one pocket and a bottle out of the other. In a moment, the lid was off, and she poured the liquid liberally onto the cloth. She handed the cloth to Ronson.

Tears filled Camalyn's eyes as she said, "Mola, I want you to hold that cloth up to your mouth and nose. Breathe deeply into it." A moment later, she gave further instructions. "Cover your mouth and nose better—that's very good. Deep breaths, as if you're smelling a flower. Very good, Mola. I know you're sleepy. Don't fight it. You deserve a nice rest. Very good."

ON HIS WAY OUT, Konner told a servant, "Camalyn will be staying with

Councillor Ronson for a bit. They desire privacy." The servant nodded. Camalyn would ensure Ronson stayed asleep, and the servant would ensure they were not disturbed.

Konner instructed his carriage driver to make one stop before going home. He spent a quarter hour at that destination before he was again on his way. Once he arrived at his estate, the nighttime hours dragged by. At last, the clock struck two, and he exited out the back door into the black night.

Ronson's house was only a mile from Konner's. He made it there on foot in under twenty minutes, arriving at the back yard through an alley gate that Camalyn, Sava bless her, had unlocked.

Councillor Remina Birge was waiting for him. Konner smiled and nodded. Her responding smile was uncomfortable, but determined. They made their way into the house through the unlocked kitchen door.

Camalyn had been invited to dine with Birge a few days earlier, and she had brought Konner with her to the dinner. Neither had been surprised when Birge, whose hearing gift allowed her to detect lies, had accused Camalyn of not being a true Karite. (Konner had, however, been surprised when this confrontation had happened after the soup course, before the main course had even been served. It was rather crass.) Camalyn had admitted to the deception.

Birge's gift would be invaluable to the Grays, and after dinner, Konner and Camalyn had spoken with the woman about their plans. She had not hesitated, insisting she wanted to be part of it. Lying was a universal trait, Birge said. And she had long believed magical resistance to be pointless. Despite being prevented from using their gifts improperly, councillors continued to be self-absorbed and power-hungry. If magic was freed of its restrictions, she said, at least people would be less hypocritical.

And Birge was a pragmatist. She had no problem with ending the life of someone who was dying anyway. However, when Konner had stopped at her house three days later and told her of Mola Ronson's refusal to be part of their vision, he had been nervous. Would Birge refuse to take Mola's last breath? But she had proven herself to be made of tougher stock than Konner had guessed. Did she want to take the life of her fellow councillor? No. But did she see the need to ensure that Ronson did not share what he knew about the Grays? Unequivocally yes.

Konner and Birge crept through Mola Ronson's dark house. Camalyn was waiting in the study, sitting next to Ronson, whose head still lolled in sleep. Konner sniffed the air and lit his pipe with the strongest-smelling tobacco he could find in Ronson's cabinet, hoping to cover the ether odor with a more pleasant scent. The open window would help too.

Birge's task only took a few minutes. Her whole body shook as she pinched Ronson's nose and took his final breath. She then pressed her hand on his mouth and waited. Despite the trembling, she held her position until they were sure the man was gone.

Camalyn had sprinkled lijani powder all around Ronson, also dipping his fingers in it. When he was dead, Camalyn put the powder on his nose, using her fingers to coat his nostrils with it.

Remina Birge gasped, pressing both hands against her chest. Moments later, gray light traveled to her head, and she moved her hands there, closing her eyes against the pain. "It will be worth it," Konner said.

When Birge's gray awakening had abated, she and Konner left. Camalyn would depart soon thereafter, making enough noise to wake a servant. She would tell them that Ronson was enjoying "a little powder." When someone found the man dead in the morning, everyone would agree it had only been a matter of time before his addiction got the better of him.

In the alley, Birge turned to Konner. "I didn't ask. How many of us are there?"

"You and Camalyn are the first two councillors," Konner said, "And there are three others."

Birge's expression grew cold. "Tell me there will be more than five of us."

"We're working on it." Konner's voice was firm. "We will bring on more councillors. And I have a team who is traveling as we speak. We have high hopes for the talent we may discover in rural areas. There will be more Grays, Remina. Very soon."

CHAPTER TWENTY-NINE

The students I train treat me with such respect. They seem unaware of how little I know about magic, even after all this time.

-*From* Savala's Collected Letters, Volume 2

TAVI YANKED the kitchen door open. "What do you need?" she demanded. When the visitors on the porch gave no reply, she snapped, "I don't know why you had to bang on the door like that."

Sall said, "You didn't answer when we knocked politely."

"Where's your family, anyway?" Narre asked.

"They left to spend the afternoon with the Terelsons," Tavi explained. "I didn't want to go."

"We're coming in," Narre said, pushing past Tavi into the kitchen. Sall followed her, and they sat at the table. With a sigh, Tavi pulled out a chair and joined them.

"So, he's gone," Narre said, her voice gentler than it had been before. Tavi wasn't surprised they knew. That morning had been the monthly gathering at the parish house, and Tavi hadn't attended. Her family must have told Narre why. "How are you doing?" Narre asked.

"I'm fine."

That response earned her skeptical looks from both her friends. Sall pointed at his head. "May I?"

Tavi didn't have the energy to argue, so she shrugged and said, "Sure."

After a deep breath, Sall's magic activated, and his scalp began to shine, creating a golden halo around his head. He kept his eyes on Tavi for a moment before releasing his magic. "I'm sorry," he said with a sad smile.

"Me too," Narre agreed. Tavi was surprised to see tears in her cousin's eyes.

"I suppose there's no use pretending I'm all right," Tavi sighed. She looked between Sall and Narre. "Why do I keep driving away the people I care about the most?"

Sall didn't appear surprised at the question; he already knew every one of Tavi's varied emotions, including her stinging sense of rejection. But Narre's eyes widened. "You haven't driven anyone away!" she insisted.

"First Reba, and then my father, and now Tullen." Tavi felt tears enter her eyes, but she held them at bay. "I'm surprised the two of you are still here."

"Reba stopped being friends with all of us," Sall pointed out. "You didn't cause that. As for your father, he chose not to accept your decision about the mayor. Again, it's not your fault."

"And Tullen?" Tavi wasn't sure she wanted to hear the answer, but now the question was out there.

"The Meadow is his home," Narre said.

Tavi remembered saying that very thing to Tullen the day before. But after a night of little sleep, it didn't feel like a good enough explanation anymore.

"You're not just sad—you're angry, too," Sall pointed out.

Tavi slammed both hands on the table. "Of course I'm angry! He was my best friend, and he left! I can't believe he would do that to me!

I want to break something!" She slammed her hands down again, causing her palms to sting.

Narre's lips tilted up in a small grin. "I have an idea," she said. "Tavi, put on your shoes, and leave a note for your parents. We're going to my house."

Narre held up a small board, grasping it tightly in both hands. They were standing in front of the workshop her father kept in his back yard. "Hit it, Tavi," she instructed.

"I'll hurt my hand!" Tavi protested.

"You won't. I promise. Just hit it."

Tavi noted the glow that had filled Narre's hands, and she nodded in understanding. She pulled her fist back and slammed it into the wood.

As promised, it didn't hurt. Narre's touch gift broke the board as soon as Tavi's knuckles hit it. The resulting *snap* was highly satisfying, and while Tavi still felt simmering anger in her chest, her mouth insisted on smiling. "Again," she said.

This time, Narre propped a larger piece of lumber in between two sawhorses. She kept her hands on it, and when Tavi's fist connected with it, the wood shattered into thousands of tiny pieces. A small chuckle escaped Tavi's throat.

They continued to experiment with various types of wood. Tavi reveled in the feeling of smashing things to pieces and in the gratifying sound of the wood cracking.

Each time, Narre surprised Tavi with the method she used to break the wood. One board was transformed into hundreds of tiny cubes when Tavi hit it. Another broke into small chips, with the exception of a large "T" that thudded onto the ground. Narre picked it up and handed it to Tavi. "That can stand for 'Tavi' or 'Tullen,' whichever makes you happier," she said. That time, she was rewarded with a genuine laugh from Tavi and a tight hug.

Narre said, "I don't think I can use any more wood. Later on I'll need to bind some pieces together so my father can use them." When Sall leaned over and whispered something to her, she smiled and said, "Let's try it!"

Narre ran off, and when she returned a minute later, she was struggling to carry a large rock. She placed it on the ground in front of Tavi. Her glowing hand resting on its side, she said, "Kick it."

Tavi raised her eyebrows but said, "All right." She backed up a dozen steps then took a running start, kicking at the rock with all her might.

When the toe of Tavi's boot hit the rock, it exploded. Fine dust shot away backwards, Narre having diverted the debris so it didn't slam into them.

Tavi couldn't stop laughing. "You just . . . made a rock . . . explode!" she gasped. When she caught her breath, she turned to Narre. "Let's do that again!"

After several more pulverized rocks, they decided they'd had enough for one day. They moved to the back porch where they drank water and enjoyed the summer sun.

Sall turned to Tavi. "Better?" he asked.

She nodded, absentmindedly tracing the wooden T with one hand. "That's exactly what I needed." She smiled, but as the thrill of kicking and hitting wore off, she felt the sadness returning. She sat quietly, sipping her drink. Finally, she broke the silence. "I miss him."

Narre reached over and took Tavi's hand. "I know."

THE NEXT AFTERNOON, Tavi walked to the midwife house with Narre and Sall for their afternoon training. Their schedule would start with an hour in the practicum room. Upstairs, they checked a list posted in the hall to see what skills they were required to practice.

"Blindfolded again?" Sall groaned. For the past several practicum sessions, he had been instructed to put on a blindfold before attempting to discern someone's emotions. Sall entered the room to seek students who would allow him to practice on them.

Narre checked the list and grinned. "Metal and rock!" she

exclaimed. Having gained a fair amount of competence in binding fabric to wood, she was at last moving on to binding smooth metal to rough rock. She had been looking forward to this.

Tavi's eyebrows furrowed when she checked the list. Next to her name, it simply read, "See Ellea." She glanced in the room and saw the midwife waiting for her in the back.

Tavi approached Ellea nervously. It had been over half a year since their conversation about Tavi's healing ability. While she was glad she had told Ellea the truth, she had felt a wall between them ever since.

When she approached and saw the warm smile on Ellea's face, Tavi's anxiety was tempered with relief. "It's been some time since I've observed you in practicum," the midwife said. "Will you please activate one of your gifts for me? Your choice."

Tavi closed her eyes, about to dream up the juiciest pickle she could, but she was suddenly hesitant. Her eyes opened, and she asked, "How do you want me to activate it? Your way or . . . mine?" She had almost said, "Your way or Tullen's?" and was glad she had caught herself.

"Whichever you prefer," Ellea said.

Tavi nodded, again closing her eyes. *Ears—pickle.* It was that simple. At the same moment her mouth watered with the desire for a pickle, her ears filled with warmth.

Ellea was still smiling. "Very good. You can release it now."

Tavi let her magic go. She looked directly at Ellea and said, "I did that by thinking of pickles." Ellea only nodded, so Tavi continued. "I've tried over and over to activate my gifts by breathing and relaxing. It works every once in a while, but I usually just find myself getting frustrated. Ellea, my gifts are tied to desire. I don't think there's any way to change that. Plus, I've been learning to trust my magical instincts, and I'm feeling more confident. I can activate my gifts faster than ever before, even one at a time. I know I'm not always doing it in the way you want—"

Tavi realized Ellea's hand was up, and she wondered how long the midwife had been trying to halt her monologue. She pressed her lips together, feeling her cheeks burning even warmer than her ears had.

The smile on Ellea's face was gentle. It was the smile Tavi had always loved receiving. "You're not in trouble," Ellea said.

"I'm not?" Tavi whispered.

"No," Ellea said. "I didn't realize our previous conversation had bothered you so deeply. I'm sorry it took this long for me to follow up with you."

"It's all right."

"I burned my finger on the kettle today," Ellea said. "Do you think you could heal it for me?" She held out a finger that sported a small section of shiny, red skin. It hadn't even blistered.

"I haven't healed a burn yet, but I think I could do it," Tavi replied. She closed her eyes, and in several seconds, her magic was in her hands. She took hold of Ellea's fingertip, her gift detecting which skin was healthy and which was burned. Just for some variety, Tavi thought about ulora root candy instead of pickles. Her diagnostic gift was joined by healing magic, and she could feel the skin of Ellea's finger changing. She wasn't sure how to heal a burn, and she hoped her gift knew what to do. A few seconds later, she removed her fingers.

"Perfect," Ellea said, holding up the finger, which held no trace of the burn. "You may release your magic if you'd like." When Tavi had done so, Ellea looked in her eyes. "I'm proud of you."

"You are?"

"I am." Ellea sighed. "When you told me you were learning magic from another teacher, I was frightened. But I've had months to think about that and to wonder why that was my reaction. I'm still frightened, Tavi. But you said it yourself, you are different. Perhaps you need training I can't give you. I'm glad you have Tullen to help you, and I'm hoping you'll teach me some of what he's taught you—if you can be patient with an old woman who is set in her ways."

"I don't have Tullen to help me anymore," Tavi said.

"Why not?"

"The elders at the Meadow told him he has to stay there now."

Ellea shook her head and snapped, "I'm not a bit surprised. I've always thought they were—" Then her eyes caught Tavi's, and she stopped. She beckoned her student toward the door. Tavi followed, and once they were in the hallway, Ellea opened her arms. As soon as

Tavi stepped into the embrace, she surrendered to the tears she had been avoiding since Tullen's departure.

Tavi felt a wave of peace enter her through Ellea's touch-blessed hands. The midwife murmured, "It will be all right."

And Tavi believed her.

CHAPTER THIRTY

I need your counsel, and I beg you to reply quickly. Sava has brought me here, yet my heart calls me home. What is to be done? I fear the one I love will not wait any longer. Please advise me, my friend. I cannot find the answer, no matter how I try.

-*From* Savala's Collected Letters, Volume 1

TULLEN WOKE, and it took a moment to figure out where he was. He had been dreaming of Oren, and first he thought he'd woken in Tavi's house. But, no—instead of cotton bedding, he lay on animal skins, a perk of being one of the Meadow's hunters. And on the bed across the room slept his brother Tona. Yes, he was home.

Home. The word wasn't as inviting as it had once been. But Tullen didn't want to think of that right now. He had made his choice.

Tullen walked into the small sitting room. His mother was gone; she liked to start her weaving early in the summer. But his father Kley was there, spreading fresh butter on a slice of bread. Meals were served in the Meadow's large meeting hall, but some families preferred to eat light fare at home for breakfast. "Morning," Kley said, offering the bread to Tullen.

"It's all right, I'll get my own."

"Don't be silly. I can cut another." His father pushed the bread into Tullen's hand.

"Thanks."

Kley smiled. "It's always good to have you home."

Tullen ate, considering the two previous days, which had been his weekly leisure days. On the first, Tullen had run to Oren to say goodbye to Tavi, and on the second, he had stayed home, ruminating. He was ready to get back to hunting. He needed to return to his routines and work toward a goal. And if his mind insisted on thinking about what he had lost, he would share those thoughts with only the trees and animals.

"I think I'll go west today," he told his father. "I'll stay close to home, of course. I'm hoping to get a deer."

Kley looked up. "Son, the elders are placing you on a different duty for now."

Tullen waited for more information. When it didn't come, he asked, "What sort of duty?" He was certain he wouldn't like the answer.

"Tower watch."

Gritting his teeth, Tullen stared at the man in front of him.

"Be patient, Tullen." His father's eyes held compassion. "They want you to get a different perspective."

"This was Aba's idea, wasn't it?" Aba was the oldest elder. She was a writer, and even her punishments were poetic. A "different perspective" indeed—from the top of a five-story tower.

"I believe she had something to do with it," Kley said. "Handle it with humility, and you'll be back to hunting in no time."

Tullen's only response was a grunt.

TULLEN COULD LOOK for animals all day and not get bored. Watching people all day was a different story. The tower was right next to the Meadow gate, and Tullen's duties were twofold: Call down to the gate guards if any strangers approached, and keep an eye on the community inside the walls. As Tullen watched throughout the morning, nothing of consequence happened below. He observed only the routines of a typical day.

People worked, scattering to their jobs throughout the Meadow or outside the walls. Even children worked on assigned chores, and at a set time, they switched from manual labor to mental labor, learning academic skills from adults and older adolescents. There were breaks, during which adults shared tea and conversation, and children played games. A little before noon, people began to drift toward the meeting hall for lunch.

It was boring. And it was beautiful.

As tedious as it was to watch from above, Tullen was reminded of why he loved the Meadow. He loved the feeling of true community. Children not only had parents; they were guided by dozens of "aunts and uncles" too. The people took care of each other; no one went without food or shelter. And he loved the values of hard work and carefree play. After all, hard work wasn't so hard when everyone was encouraged to serve within their strengths.

Until you anger the elders. Then you're required to work in a boring job until you're back to being a humble, devoted Meadow Dweller.

The punishment wouldn't have bothered Tullen so much if he'd actually done something wrong. But all he'd done was make friends in Oren. Good friends. Good *people*. And when he had been told he was needed at the Meadow, he'd taken less than half a day to run to Oren and say goodbye. For that, he was now a prisoner—and his cell was a guard tower, of all things.

Tullen's thoughts were interrupted by footsteps on the stairs below him. Perhaps it was Aba, coming to tell him he could hunt again. He pulled open the trap door at the bottom of the guard tower.

It wasn't Aba. Tullen was greeted by a mass of dark, curly hair, an upturned, smiling face, and two hands carrying a plate of food and a cup of water.

"Jenevy!" Tullen greeted her. "Is that for me?"

"Of course!" Jenevy reached the top of the steep steps and entered the small tower.

Tullen took the food, set it down, and gave her a hug. Of his dozens of "sisters," Jenevy had always been one of his favorites. "You could have sent the food up the pulley porter!" he said, referring to the small box used to send messages and items between the ground and the tower.

"And missed the opportunity to see this view?" Jenevy walked to the railing at the side of the tower, looking over miles of trees.

Tullen tucked into the food. After he'd eaten several bites of meat pie, he asked, "Anything new with you?"

Jenevy laughed. "Nothing with me. The most interesting topic in the Meadow right now is you!"

"Me?"

"Half the community thought you wouldn't return when you ran off two days ago," Jenevy said.

Tullen took a bite and chewed slowly. When he had swallowed, he said, "But my family is here."

Jenevy glanced back at him, her forehead furrowed, before turning back to her view. "I didn't think you'd come back," she admitted.

Tullen watched Jenevy's back. At first glance, she appeared to be relaxing, enjoying the vista. But her hands held the railing with a too-tight grip, and her shoulders were square and tense. "I didn't want to leave my family, Jenevy," Tullen said.

She turned around, and now her gaze didn't shy away. "Your family—do you mean there or here?" she asked. When he didn't answer, she gave him a tight smile. "I'm teaching an afternoon mathematics lesson," she said. "I'd better go."

Tullen watched her climb down the stairs. What was that look she'd given him before she'd gone? Jenevy was eighteen, just as he was. She was likely hoping to marry and raise a family in the Meadow.

A couple of years earlier, when they had been old enough to consider adult things but not old enough to take on adult responsibilities, Tullen had entertained casual daydreams about building a life with Jenevy. At some point—he wasn't sure when—that dream had dissolved into the past, joining other discarded desires such as finding gold buried in the forest.

But now Tullen was back in the Meadow to stay. He needed to be thinking about his future, just as Jenevy was. She was beautiful, and they had always enjoyed spending time together. When Jenevy had turned toward the stairs, Tullen's instinct had been to hug her good-bye, as he would have done in the past. What, he asked himself, had stopped him?

Tullen walked back to the railing. This time, he wasn't watching the Meadow. His gaze meandered south, in the direction of a certain small town on the edge of the forest. He stood there a long time, sharing his thoughts with only the wind.

CHAPTER THIRTY-ONE

Sand looks like water
To one who is thirsty enough.

-*From* Proverbs of Savala

REBA MINNALEN SAT ON A BARSTOOL, watching the few people eating dinner at the Oren Inn and Pub. Several autumn leaves had blown in the room, and she knew she should sweep before it got too busy, but she didn't want to. When she had been hired as a barmaid, Reba had been ecstatic. By the end of her first shift, she had realized just how dull her new job was.

Her father had been more than happy for her to work. She suspected that his enthusiasm was due to her dismal grades at school and her lack of progress in developing her gift. He seemed relieved that she had found something she could do, and it didn't hurt that she was earning a few chips.

The week before, Reba had approached the pub owner with her best flirtatious smile. "My sight gift will be such an asset," she told him. "From across the room, I can see when drinks need to be refilled." She did not mention that when she tried to activate her gift, she was only successful about half the time. He had probably hired her more for her magical figure than her magical eyes, anyway.

Nem, the most regular of the regulars, was already in his seat. Every night, he came early and left late, slowly spending his substantial inheritance on alcohol. At least he tipped well—when he was sober enough to think of it. "Reba!" he called, his late-afternoon voice not yet slurred. "Come on over, sweetie."

Reba pasted on that flirtatious smile again, though she hated wasting her looks on Nem. She swayed her hips just enough as she approached his table. "Ready for another?" she asked.

Nem held up his glass, which was still half full. "Nah, just wanted to say hello," he said. He reached out, and Reba shifted away before his hand could "say hello" to her backside.

Shaking her index finger at him, Reba gave him a look of mock rebuke, pouting her full lips. "Don't be naughty!" she said, and she winked and turned. As soon as she was no longer facing Nem, Reba allowed her face to reflect her disgust.

The pub began to fill over the next hour. It was a nice enough place, and most of its patrons this time of night weren't drunks like Nem; they were individuals and families who wanted a hearty meal. Reba kept busy taking orders, serving food and drinks, and charming the customers.

The stairs at the back of the pub creaked, and Reba looked up to see two young men making their way down from the rooms on the second floor. Now this was interesting. The younger one was a little thin for her taste, but he had a fantastic smile she'd like to see directed toward her. And his friend—once Reba looked at him, she couldn't look away. He appeared a few years older than the skinny one, and she admired his thick hair, white teeth, and broad shoulders.

"Is that for us?" A voice asked.

Reba nearly dropped the food she was holding, and she uttered an embarrassed, "Pardon me!" She set down three full plates, one for the woman who had spoken and the other two for her husband and young son.

Reba then made her way to the bottom of the stairs where the two men waited. "You can take whatever table you like!" she said. Then she leaned in and gestured toward the family she had just served. "You might want to sit far from them; that kid throws food." She winked and was rewarded with two handsome smiles.

After serving one more table, Reba approached the two men. They ordered beer and beef stew. She served them, and with her best smile in place, asked, "Did the two of you arrive in town today?"

"Sure did," the older one said. He was polite but didn't seem inclined to give more information than that. Reba headed back to the bar.

There was a temporary lull in responsibilities, so she tried to activate her sight gift. It was difficult in the loud atmosphere of this place, but she took several deep breaths as she had been taught. She allowed her vision to relax and let out a happy sigh when she felt warmth enter her eyes and the surrounding skin. Examining all the glasses across the room, Reba noticed just one empty—Nem's. She released her magic with a frustrated huff of air and headed to his table to offer a refill. His answer, of course, was yes.

With that taken care of, Reba swayed her way back to the table where the two men sat. "Gentlemen, how is the stew?" she asked.

"Best we've had on the road!" the younger man said.

"I'm so glad to hear it!" Reba replied. She was about to turn around when the other man spoke.

"You're sight-blessed!" he said with a warm smile.

Delighted, Reba confirmed, "I am! It helps me better serve my customers; I can see when they need a refill." She glanced down at their glasses. "Speaking of which, neither of you have taken more than a sip!"

The older one laughed. "I'm savoring it," he said. "My name is Jay." He held out a gloved hand.

"I'm Reba; it's a pleasure to meet you." She reached out with her palm down, inviting a kiss on her hand. Jay didn't take the bait; he shook her hand, then let it go.

"I'm Vinn," the younger man said, and Reba shook his hand too.

"What brings you to Oren?" Reba asked. But just then, she was interrupted by the booming voice of Gerval, the owner.

"Reba," he called from behind the bar. "Two new customers!"

With a coy grin, Reba said, "Let's talk in a bit." She spoke to the new patrons, brought them their ale, and checked on the rest of the tables.

Once everyone was settled, Reba walked back to Jay and Vinn. She was prepared to coax them into conversation, but it wasn't necessary.

"We're scholars," Jay said with a grin that didn't look scholarly to Reba. "We're working for the monks at the monastery west of Savala, in the mountains—have you heard of it?"

Reba didn't know much about the monastery, but she gushed, "Oh, yes, I've heard that's a beautiful place!"

"It is," Jay confirmed. "Actually, we'd love to talk to you! We are traveling around Cormina, speaking with those who are gifted. The monks want to know more about how sun-blessed people throughout the land use their gifts."

They wanted to talk to her about being sun-blessed? Reba was rarely given attention for her gifts; all the honor seemed to be saved for her peers. She gave the men a wide smile. "I would love to help in your studies, however I can!"

Vinn spoke up. "And will you also introduce us to your gifted friends? The more Blessed we meet, the better."

Again, they were interrupted by Gerval. "Reba!" he called. When she looked his way, he gestured to an empty table that needed to be cleaned. Reba excused herself and did the job as quickly as she could.

By the time she had refilled more drinks, served dinner to a family of six, and again dodged Nem's eager hands, Reba was surprised that Jay and Vinn were still nursing their drinks and their stew. She sauntered back to them. "What were we discussing?" she asked with a laugh.

"Your friends," Vinn said. "I'm sure you know others who are gifted?"

"Oh, of course," Reba said. "They're so arrogant, though. It's surprising in such a little town, but most of the Blessed here think very highly of themselves. I doubt any of them would want to talk."

"We'll start with you," Jay said, "and you can tell us about others. The monks are eager to know what gifts are represented in the rural areas."

"Sure!" Reba said. Out of the corner of her eye, she saw Gerval watching her, hands on his meaty hips. She put on an embarrassed smile for his sake, excused herself, and tended to the rest of the customers.

Gradually, those eating dinner finished and settled up. There was always a lull between dinner time and the late-night drinking rush. Jay and Vinn, however, seemed content to stay at their table. They switched to hot tea, saying they needed focused minds for their research.

When Reba walked by the bar, Gerval instructed, "Grab yourself some stew before the drunks get here." She gave him a genuine smile this time; she was hungry.

Once she had a steaming bowl, Reba headed toward an open table in the corner. Vinn looked up and asked, "Care to join us, Reba?" Jay pulled out a chair for her, and Reba happily changed direction and sat with them.

After a couple of minutes of small talk, Jay looked at her seriously.

"Reba," he said, "I have a question for you. It's a sensitive topic, but something tells me you're brave enough to discuss it. The monks are interested in magical resistance. When Sava doesn't allow you to use your magic, how do you react? It must be frustrating."

Reba nodded with an aggravated sigh. "It's so upsetting!" she said. Her voice lowered. "See that man over there?" She pointed her head toward Nem. "If I bring him refills all night, he's more likely to tip me well. My gift helps me keep a close eye on him. But after he's had a few, I can't use my magic to see into his glass anymore!"

Jay and Vinn laughed. "Apparently Sava is a teetotaler," Vinn said.

"Not at all!" Jay asserted. "She said the gift works at the beginning of the night. That tells me that, as long as it's in moderation, Sava himself loves beer!"

"It may seem funny to you," Reba protested, "but with what that man puts me through, I expect him to tip me! I'm simply asking my magic to help with that!"

Both men's faces became somber. "Others have told us that too," Vinn said. "It's almost as if magical resistance is . . ." He paused, as if searching for the right words.

"Is pointless," Jay finished for him. "Sava trusts us by giving us gifts. Don't you think he should trust us to use them properly?"

Reba's eyes widened. "I've been thinking the same thing for the longest time—but I've never heard anyone willing to say it out loud! Wait, did you say 'us'? Are you gifted too?"

Jay looked embarrassed. "I didn't mean to give that away," he said. "We get too much attention if we display our gifts when we travel, but you seem trustworthy, and I don't mind you knowing I am touch-blessed."

"And I'm stride-blessed," Vinn admitted.

"I can't tell you how wonderful it is to meet others who aren't satisfied with how magic works!" Reba enthused.

"Reba, how was your stew?" Gerval's voice was tinged with impatience; he was already back to work polishing glasses behind the bar.

"Delicious, thanks!" Reba responded. She looked at Jay and Vinn with good-natured chagrin as she stood.

"I hope we can talk more," Vinn said. "Maybe tomorrow morning when things are slow here?"

"Oh, I'd love that, but I can't in the morning," Reba replied. "I have school."

Both sets of eyebrows rose. "You're still in school?" Jay asked.

"Just for a few more months," Reba lied. "I turned eighteen recently." She never told her customers she was only fifteen, and she looked at least three years older.

Jay smiled. "What time do you work in the afternoon?"

"If you get here around four, it'll probably just be me and Nem," Reba said. "I should be able to talk then!"

"We'll be here!" Vinn said.

Jay stood, and Vinn followed suit. "I think we'll go upstairs to get some rest," Jay said. "Travel is always tiring!"

Reba admired Jay's broad shoulders and slim waist again, and she gave the men a flirty smirk. "Sleep well, boys!"

They retired to their rooms, and Reba set to work cleaning tables.

For once, she worked vigorously. Perhaps she didn't have a gift that made her light up like a bonfire, as Tavi did, or magical hands that could break things in two, like Narre. But she was important, with her sight gift. She'd always known it, and Jay and Vinn saw it too.

Reba scrubbed the tables, counting the hours until she could talk to them again.

CHAPTER THIRTY-TWO

When a small town experiences crime, people are shocked. "I expect that in a big city," they say, "but not here!"

I have lived in a large city, and I have lived in a small town. Human hearts are just as unreliable in one as the other.

-From Small-Town Cormina: A Midwife's Reflections *by Ellea Kariana*

"MOTHER SAID you need to help me weed the garden." Misty was entirely too chipper, and Tavi grimaced. "Come on, it's beautiful outside," Misty insisted.

Tavi stood and put down her book. Maybe weeding wouldn't be too bad; she couldn't seem to focus on the story she was trying to read, anyway.

Misty led her sister to a corner of the garden where one of their mother's squash hybrids was growing. They both sat, and Tavi dug her fingers into the cool soil, reaching for the roots of a small weed.

"I have an extra spade if that's easier," Misty offered.

Tavi shook her head. "If I'm going to be in the garden, I'm going to get my hands dirty."

They worked silently. It felt good to be outside; Tavi had been spending too much time cooped up in her room. The morning sun wasn't yet high in the sky, and cool autumn breezes tickled the nape of Tavi's neck. Each weed she pulled gave her an odd satisfaction.

After several minutes, Misty asked, "How are you doing?"

Misty had been asking that question often in the weeks since Tullen's departure. Many days, Tavi didn't want to talk about it. But with her hands in the soil and the genuine love she heard in her sister's voice, something shifted in Tavi. She filled her lungs with a deep breath, let it out, and admitted, "I'm still sad."

Misty lifted her head, and her eyes were glistening. "I'm sorry, Tavi," she said.

"I think he was the best friend I've ever had," Tavi said. "He made me...better."

"Better at your magic?"

Tavi shook her head and continued to work on a stubborn weed. "Well, he did help me a lot with magic. But he also—he helped me be better at . . . being me."

"That might be the sweetest thing I've ever heard," Misty said.

Tavi wasn't done. "But I've been thinking a lot," she said. "And as much as I hate the thought of never seeing him again, a lot of other people help me in the same way he did—including you." Her throat caught as she looked at her sister. "You're still here, and Sall and Narre, and Mama, and the midwives. I think I'll be all right."

Misty was smiling now, that look of joy she wore every time Tavi made her proud. "When did you get so grown up?" Misty asked.

Tavi groaned. "Most days I still feel like a child."

"Half the time, I do too," Misty admitted. They both laughed.

After pulling several more weeds, Misty said, "I don't think I ever told you about the time my heart was broken."

Tavi insisted, "He was just my friend, Misty."

"Oh, don't get your hackles up," Misty said. "You can get your heart broken when you lose a friend, you know." Tavi's shoulders slumped, and Misty asked, "Can I tell you my story?"

When Tavi nodded, Misty put down her spade. "I was a little older than you," she began, "just sixteen. There was a boy I'd liked for years —Clem. One day at school I finally had the courage to talk to him, and I couldn't believe when we hit it off. We'd eat lunch together, and he'd walk me home every day, even though he lived in the opposite direction."

"He sounds nice," Tavi said. "What happened?"

"We spent a lot of time together for several months," Misty replied. "He was the first boy I held hands with, and my first kiss. He made me happy. And then one day, it all stopped. He barely even looked at me. No more lunches, no more walking home together."

Tavi frowned. "Why?"

"I don't know." Misty shook her head. "I still ask myself that. I thought he'd come talk to me about it, but he never did, and the more time that passed, the sillier I would have felt asking him what happened. It just—ended."

"And your heart was broken?"

"Into tiny little pieces," Misty said with a sad smile. "I cried every day for weeks." She reached out a dirty hand and placed it on Tavi's knee. "It does get easier."

Tavi had never thought much about Misty's romantic life. She wanted to know more. "Was there ever anybody after Clem?" she asked.

Misty shrugged. "A few boys, here and there, but nothing serious. And it's been years since there's been anyone at all."

"Why?"

The simple question seemed to make Misty sad. "I'm not sure," she said. "I think I got scared by how sad I was after things ended with Clem, and eventually the opportunities weren't there anymore."

Tavi wasn't sure how to respond to that. She shifted her attention back to the weeds, and Misty followed suit.

After a few minutes, they turned to innocuous topics such as their mother's plans for the garden. There was another lull in the conversation, and Tavi heard what she thought were galloping hooves on the dirt road. She lay down her spade and craned her neck, and sure enough, a dust cloud was making its way toward their home.

"Someone's in a hurry," Tavi commented.

Misty had taken notice too. "They sure are," she agreed.

The horse and rider slowed as they passed the garden, and then they turned into the yard. Tavi raised her eyebrows, and as the rider got down and rushed to the front door, she said, "It's Mr. Minnalen!" Why would Reba's father be here, and in such a hurry? She continued to weed, but after a few minutes, she couldn't stand the suspense. She stood and strode toward the house.

"You can't weed while you're walking!" Misty called.

"I'll be back," Tavi assured her. She walked across the large garden to the house and entered through the kitchen. Runan Minnalen was there, pacing behind the table. Tavi's mother stood on the other side of the table, her face filled with worry.

"What's wrong?" Tavi asked.

Mey looked at Mr. Minnalen hesitantly, but he took no notice of her or of Tavi. For several seconds, Tavi waited, until she lost her patience and took a few steps so she was standing directly in front of where Reba's father was pacing. She repeated herself, more loudly. "What's wrong?"

Mr. Minnalen's eyebrows rose as if he had just noticed Tavi's arrival. He stopped pacing and stared at Tavi, his eyes filled with horror. After several seconds he spoke. "Reba is gone," he said.

"Gone? What do you mean?" Tavi asked.

But that seemed to be all Mr. Minnalen could say. Mey gestured to the table. "Have a seat, Tavi, and I'll get you a snack." Tavi started to comply, but Mey said, "Goodness, please wash your hands first."

Tavi looked down; she had forgotten about the dark soil staining her hands. She walked to the sink and turned on the tap—how quickly they had become used to running water in this house. When she finished, she sat. Mey had already placed bread and cheese on the table for her, and Tavi quietly thanked her.

Mey spoke to Tavi in a calm voice. "Last night Reba left the house, telling her father she was going to stay with Iris." Iris was one of Reba's newer friends. "When Mr. Minnalen went to Iris' house this morning, Iris knew nothing about Reba coming. Mr. Minnalen has been riding to all Reba's friends' homes to see if any of them know anything." Tavi started a bit at the word "friends," but she let it go. Mey continued, "I've sent Seph to go get your father in town, so he can help look for Reba."

Tavi looked again to Mr. Minnalen. "That's terrible!" she said, and she meant it. Reba hadn't proven to be a good friend, but Tavi didn't want anything to happen to her.

Mr. Minnalen pulled a crumpled paper out of his pocket. "She left a note," he said. "When she wasn't at Iris', I thought perhaps she'd changed her mind and stayed home last night. I checked her room and found this." Mr. Minnalen handed the note to Mey, then pulled a handkerchief out of another pocket, using it to dab at his glistening face. He resumed his pacing.

Mey scanned the note then handed it to Tavi. It said,

Dear Papa,

I'm with trusted people, and I am safe. Please don't worry about me. I'll send word when I can.

–Reba

Tavi's eyebrows furrowed. How honorable could these "trusted people" be, if they would ask Reba to leave without even telling her father?

"Pardon me," Mey said. "I'm going to send Ista to gather a couple of neighbors. We need as many people looking as we can get." She exited the kitchen.

Tavi sat helplessly for several seconds. The back door opened, and Sall walked in. "Hi, Tavi, I—" He saw Reba's father and stopped in surprise. "Mr. Minnalen, I'm glad I found you here," he said. "Where's Reba?"

Mr. Minnalen showed no sign of hearing the question, and Sall looked at Tavi in confusion. Tavi explained, "Reba is gone, Sall. She left last night and didn't return. Mr. Minnalen found a note. She said she left with people she trusts."

Sall's face went white, and he pulled out a chair, almost falling as he sat. "No," he breathed.

Tavi placed her hand on Sall's arm. "Sall, we're going to do whatever we can to find her," she said.

He said nothing, but just sat shaking his head. Tavi demanded, "Tell me what's wrong, Sall! You're scaring me!"

That snapped him out of his stupor, and his eyes met Tavi's. "I went to see Narre this morning. Her mother . . . she said last night Reba came over. Narre left with her to stay the night at her house. But when I went to Reba's, nobody was there. And if Reba is gone . . ." He stopped talking, his eyes filling with tears and his hands covering his mouth.

Tavi's eyes widened, and she couldn't get enough air. She took deep, gulping breaths, and her ears filled with the ocean sound of her own blood, pumping urgently. Mey reentered the kitchen then, and when she saw Tavi, she sat in the chair next to her, her hand clamping on her daughter's shoulder. "What is it?" she asked.

Tavi could barely talk, but she forced the words out, half sobbing. "Narre is gone too, Mama. She's gone."

CHAPTER THIRTY-THREE

My dear, your letter has done nothing less than tear my heart in two. I have been away for too long. I see that now. Please write again. At one word from you, I will cross the world to come back to your side.

-*From* Savala's Collected Letters, Volume 1

TAVI AND SALL sat on the bench on her tiny back porch. Their tears had stopped, and Tavi wondered if Sall felt as exhausted as she did. Lunchtime had come and gone, but they weren't hungry.

"Where are they?" Tavi asked, frustration in every word. Sall didn't respond. Tavi huffed, stood, and walked around to the front of the house. She looked down the road, saw nothing, and returned to the bench.

As soon as Tavi had told her mother that Narre was missing, Mey had departed to tell Shem and Jilla, Narre's parents. Meanwhile, Jevva had returned home. Shem had driven his carriage to Tavi's house to pick up Jevva, Runan Minnalen, and two men from nearby homes.

Together they had traveled into Oren, hoping to discover something about Narre and Reba's disappearance.

Tavi wanted to look for the two girls, but Jevva had insisted she stay home. Mey was still with Narre's mother Jilla. Despite her father's instructions, Tavi couldn't stomach the thought of continuing to wait while others searched. Turning to Sall, she said, "I think we should search the forest."

Sall didn't look up as he responded, "Reba would never go into the forest."

It was true; Reba had always hated the forest—the bugs, the tripping hazards, and how easy it was to get lost. "But maybe someone forced her to go there," Tavi pointed out.

"If that's the case, they're so far away now, we'd never find them," Sall said.

Tavi snapped, "Look at me, Sall!" When he lifted his head and met her gaze, she demanded, "What are we supposed to do?"

Sall almost never lost his temper, but now his eyes blazed with anger, and he shouted, "I don't know!"

Tavi closed her eyes briefly, and when she opened them, she had calmed. "We have to find her," she said. He nodded, expression helpless, before turning to stare at the trees.

Tavi heard voices, and she stood again, rounding the house to see who it was. Mey, Jilla, and Narre's brothers were walking toward the front door.

"Mama!" Tavi said. "Did you hear anything?"

"No." Mey looked nearly as distraught as Jilla. "We're going to walk to as many houses as we can, to see if anyone knows anything."

"Oh, good!" Tavi said. "I'll come with you."

Mey shook her head. "I'm sorry, Tavi, you can't go. We need you, Sall, Ista, and Elim to watch Gillun."

Tavi eyed Narre's youngest brother. "You want us to stay here? Gillun doesn't need four people watching him!"

"I know," Mey agreed, "but Jilla and I feel this search should be carried out by adults."

"But Narre is one of my best friends!" Tavi said.

"Tavi, every moment we stay here talking about this is a moment we aren't searching," Mey said sharply. "Where are Misty, Jona, and Seph? They'll come with us."

Knowing that arguing would be futile, Tavi replied, "They're in the house." She beckoned to Elim and Gillun to follow her to the back yard.

Long hours passed. Tavi played marbles with Gillun and even convinced Sall to join in. However, they were both too anxious to play for long. They sat, watching Gillun explore. When Ista and Elim realized how dismal the mood was in the yard, they waited inside.

As the sun was setting, Tavi's parents and siblings returned. When Tavi heard them, she rushed to meet them, followed by Sall.

"Did you find her?" Tavi asked.

Mey shook her head sadly. "Come inside; we'll put out food and talk while we eat."

Tavi nodded, but once in the kitchen, she bombarded her mother with questions. By the time cold chicken, bread, apples, and cheese were placed on the table, she knew some of the basic facts.

Despite searching all over town, they had not found Reba or Narre, or anyone who knew where the girls were. The best information they had gathered was from the owner of the pub where Reba worked. According to him, for the past three days, Reba had engaged in several conversations with two men who claimed to be scholars. The men had left town the previous night, which was also the last time Reba and Narre had been seen.

Armed with this lead, Reba's and Narre's fathers had gone to the small office of safety to speak with the officer on duty, Les Andisis. He already knew of the missing girls, and one of his colleagues had begun canvassing neighborhoods near the girls' homes. However, when Officer Andisis had heard about the two men, his concern had mounted.

At this point of Mey's explanation, dinner was ready. Tavi tapped her foot as Jevva prayed to thank Sava for his provision and to ask that the girls be kept safe. Mey then continued, "Officer Andisis has heard of girls being taken from other towns and being brought to Tinawe."

Tavi and Sall were both leaning forward, plates untouched. "Tinawe?" Sall asked. "Why?"

"For . . ." Mey looked to Jevva for help, but he only raised his eyebrows. With a small sigh, she turned her attention back to Tavi and Sall. "For illicit purposes," she said. "They are brought there to . . . give services to men."

"What?" Tavi blurted, panic rising in her chest. If Narre had been taken for that purpose—it was unthinkable! For many years, anyone who facilitated prostitution in Cormina had been punished harshly. Meanwhile, men and women who had been forced or lured into such a life were, when discovered, protected and provided for by local governments and parishes. She was horrified to hear that, despite all this, the trade was flourishing in Tinawe, one of the largest cities in the nation.

Sall's voice was quieter than Tavi's, but the intensity could have cut through steel. "What will be done to get them back?" he demanded.

Jevva answered him. "First thing in the morning, Shem and Mr. Minnalen will go to Tinawe. Officer Andisis will go with them."

"Father," Tavi said, "I need to go too. My gifts—"

"No." Jevva's answer was firm and immediate.

"Uncle Shem and Mr. Minnalen aren't gifted," she retorted. "Is Officer Andisis?"

"He is hearing-blessed," Jevva replied.

"Oh, I'm sure that will be very helpful for rescuing two young girls in a large city," Tavi snapped.

"That's enough, Tavi," Mey said sternly. The room was quiet. Tavi glared at her father, and he returned her stare dispassionately before shifting his attention to his dinner.

Sall broke the silence. "Thank you for all your assistance," he said. "I need to go home now, if you'll please excuse me."

"You haven't eaten a thing!" Mey said.

"I'm fine," Sall replied.

Mey gave him a small smile. "We will be praying."

Sall nodded and made his way out of the kitchen. Without asking to be excused, Tavi stood and followed him. Once the front door closed behind them, she said, "Sall, does it bother you that those three men will have almost no magical assistance in trying to find Narre?"

"Yes," he replied, his gaze not leaving hers. His breaths came quickly.

Tears filled Tavi's eyes. "I don't know what to do."

"Tavi, I don't either!" Sall snapped. "Do you have any idea how much I want to fix this right now?" He shook his head. "I have to go home. But come to my house in the morning before school. Maybe one of us will have an answer by then."

Tavi nodded, though she couldn't stomach the thought of going to school without knowing where Narre was. Sall turned to go, but she rushed to him and gave him a tight hug. He returned the embrace, and she felt his chest convulse with a sob. He pulled away and walked briskly toward the street.

Tavi opened the front door, stepped inside, and gasped. She ran back through the door and caught up to Sall.

"My scent gift!" she exclaimed. "Sall, I can track her."

His face filled with sudden hope. "Will it work?"

"I don't know; I've barely even practiced with that gift. But we have to try. Do you have any clothing of Narre's?"

"I have—I have a sock," Sall admitted, and if the light hadn't been so dim, Tavi knew she would have seen his blush. "She was barefoot at my house once, and I kept one of her socks."

Tavi couldn't help it; she laughed. "Oh, Sall, I had no idea you were so . . . a sock?" When Sall's face screwed up in further embarrassment, she assured him, "It's very sweet. And odd. Bring it tomorrow, all right?"

Sall nodded. "See you tomorrow."

Tavi found it almost impossible to sleep, and when she did finally succumb to her exhaustion, she dreamed of Narre, tied up, being transported in a dark wagon to a dirty brothel in Tinawe. She sat up, heart pounding, on the verge of tears. An hour later she again fell asleep, but the dreams proved even worse.

At dawn, Tavi gave up on sleep and dragged her body out of bed, trying not to wake her sisters. She was sore all over, doubtless due to her utter lack of relaxation the previous day and all night long. She got ready and impatiently waited until her normal departure time. Finally, she left the house and strode briskly toward Sall's.

From down the street, Tavi saw him waiting in his front yard. A modicum of relief hit her; at least she was not going to be alone today. As she drew closer, Tavi saw that Sall was gingerly holding out a sock, grasped between two fingers. Despite her nerves, Tavi suppressed a laugh at the sight.

"I wanted to touch it as little as possible," Sall explained. "I didn't want too much of my scent on it."

Tavi nodded. "Let me see it," she said. He handed it to her. "Are your brothers gone?" she asked.

"They left for school already," he replied.

"Good." Tavi lifted her eyes from the sock to Sall. "You realize we're skipping school, right?"

His face looked a little sick at the thought; his behavior and grades were among the best in their class. But he nodded in slow agreement.

"Let's go to Narre's," Tavi said.

They walked nearly to their friend's house, stopping under a dense group of trees in a neighbor's large yard.

"No time like the present," Tavi said nervously. She had heard of scent-blessed investigators tracking criminals, but it wasn't a common occurrence. She had no idea if her barely developed scent gift was up to the task. But she closed her eyes, shifted her attention to her nose, and then focused on her single greatest desire—to see Narre safely home.

A burst of magic flooded Tavi's nose, so much warmth it was almost uncomfortable.

"Wow," Sall said.

Tavi opened her eyes. "What?"

"It's very bright," he said, staring at her nose.

"Apparently strong desire equals strong magic," Tavi said. She brought the sock up to her nose. She inhaled deeply, then lost herself in a coughing fit. She had never enjoyed the strong odors that came with her scent gift, and the pungent sock overwhelmed her.

When the coughing stopped, Tavi said, "Sall, let me smell your hands."

He raised an inquisitive eyebrow, but complied. After a brief sniff of his palms, Tavi again smelled the sock—this time with a shallower inhale. "Good," she said. "I can tell the difference between your scent and hers."

Sall nodded in understanding. "What's next?" he asked.

Tavi took a moment to think. "Her scent will be all along this road, because she walks one direction to school and another direction to my house. Let me see if I can pick it up at all."

Tavi experimented, with input from Sall. First, they discovered that she needed to leave the sock behind so it didn't interfere with picking up Narre's scent on the road. They threw the sock into a small pond behind Narre's neighbor's home. Tavi was confident she would not forget the scent.

At the road, Tavi took another deep breath—and there it was. It wasn't the strong odor of stale sweat; it was the underlying scent that had permeated the sock, the scent that *was* Narre. Though Tavi had never tried to isolate Narre's scent in the past, it was somehow completely familiar to her once she picked it up. It wasn't a bad smell or a good one; but it was entirely unique. It brought tears to her eyes. When she told Sall of her success, he swallowed and blinked hard, nodding his approval.

They didn't spend long on Narre's street; Sall was nervous that Jilla would see them and send them to school. Once Tavi knew she had the scent, they walked west and turned south on a road that would meet up with the main western road out of town, toward Tinawe. Almost as soon as they turned south, however, Tavi frowned.

"I've lost it," she said. "I don't smell Narre here at all."

"Are you certain?" Sall pressed. "You have to be certain!"

Tavi knelt on the dirt road, her nose an inch from it. She crawled the whole width of the road, twice.

"I'm sure," she said.

"What if she went somewhere else first?" Sall asked. "Maybe they took a different route."

That was a good point. Tavi released her magic, and she and Sall walked until they'd reached the westbound road out of Oren that would lead them to Tinawe. Reactivating her gift, Tavi tried to pick up Narre's scent there, but she could not.

"There are two more main roads out of Oren," Sall pointed out, turning to continue walking before he'd even finished speaking. Tavi followed him, and they made their way to the road that led south out of the city. Narre's scent was nowhere to be found.

Frustration was thick in the air as they made their way toward the main road that headed east out of Oren. The road was several feet away when Tavi again activated her gift. As soon as magic flooded her nose and she inhaled, Tavi's eyes snapped open, and she cried, "I smell her!"

Sall rushed to her side. "You do?'

Tavi led him to the road, and they walked down it. "Yes, yes, she was definitely here," Tavi said. "I don't even have to get on my knees; she was here."

Sall stopped, and when Tavi noticed, she turned to him. His expression was crestfallen. "That means her father went the wrong way," he stated.

Tavi felt her magic dissipate as the truth of his statement sank in. Not only had the search party gone the wrong way; they had gone the opposite way. She closed her eyes in frustration, but her vision filled with the previous night's dreams—Narre screaming, Narre crying, Narre in pain. And this time, there was no one coming to get her.

Tavi's eyes snapped open again, and she forced herself to think of their next steps. After a moment, she squared her shoulders, stared at Sall, and spoke with a conviction she didn't quite feel yet.

"We're going to find her."

CHAPTER THIRTY-FOUR

*I love all the students in my training programs. I remember each of them by
name. Yet I have always held a special fondness for those whose births I
attended. When I look at a young man or woman who received their breath of
blessing from my lungs, I want nothing more than to protect them. And often,
I cannot.*

-From Midwife Memoirs *by Ellea Kariana*

"WHAT DO YOU MEAN BY, 'WE'?" Sall asked.

"We," Tavi replied. "You and I are going to find Narre. And Reba
too, of course."

"I can't."

"You can't? Why not?"

Clearly flustered, Sall said, "I can't. I can't leave."

"Sall, you love Narre!" Tavi exclaimed. "Or I'm assuming you do!
Do you love her?"

"Yes!"

"Then come with me!"

"I can't!" Sall repeated. Tavi stared. He insisted, "Narre will understand! She knows—she'll understand!"

"Her life may be in danger, Sall! What exactly will she understand?" Tavi demanded.

Sall froze. After several seconds, he said, more quietly, "She will. We have talked about . . . many things. She will understand, Tavi."

Tavi shook her head. "I have no idea what you're talking about, but I don't have time to argue with you. If you're not coming, I'm going alone." She strode down the street.

Sall followed her, and neither of them spoke. Tavi reflected on her words. Could she do this alone? Travel on roads she'd never stepped foot on, using a gift she hardly knew how to use, to find two girls whose location was unknown? She believed Narre's life was at risk; did she really have the skills and bravery to rush into such a situation?

Those three words returned to her mind: *I am enough.*

And with that, the doubts were gone. She *knew.* Tavi knew Narre had gone down that eastbound road. She knew if her friend was not found soon, she might not be found at all. She knew no one was better suited to find Narre than the all-blessed girl who loved her.

Scratch that. The all-blessed *woman* who loved her. Tavi might only be fifteen, but she had to think of herself as a woman if she was to go on this journey alone.

Urging her shoulders back and tilting her chin up, Tavi walked even faster, the cool autumn breeze not quite keeping up with the perspiration she was producing. Her heart felt ready to burst with grief and worry and, yes, confidence.

The midwife house was on the road they were traveling. They had barely passed it when they heard a voice. "Tavi! Sall!" Turning, they saw Ellea coming down the steps of the house.

Sall and Tavi exchanged a glance. They should be at school, and before too long it would be time for them to come back here for their afternoon training. Yet they had just passed the midwife house, and it was obvious they weren't walking from their school. They hesitantly strode toward Ellea and met her in the yard.

But the head midwife had not called to them to chide them. Her eyes were wide and expectant. "Have you heard anything about Narre and Reba?" she asked.

Tavi let out a frustrated sigh. "No," she said. "But we discovered something. Their fathers left for Tinawe this morning, but they went the wrong way. Narre left town on the eastbound road."

"How do you know this?" Ellea asked.

Tavi explained how she had used her scent gift to track Narre.

Ellea's face showed surprise. "Using a scent gift to track is difficult."

"I know what I smelled," Tavi insisted. "There was no question."

"Oh, dear girl, I'm not doubting you." Ellea's face softened with a smile. "I have every confidence in your gifts. Now I assume you're heading to the office of safety to pass along this information?"

Tavi and Sall looked at each other. Again, Tavi was the one to speak. "I don't think they'd believe me," she said. "And, really, they're not handling the investigation well at all."

Ellea's expression was wary. "What are you planning to do?" she asked.

Again, the two trainees shared a glance. This time, they stayed quiet.

"Are you planning to search for them yourselves?" Ellea asked.

More silence. Sall broke it. "I'm not," he said.

"But you are?" Ellea asked Tavi. She was answered with a nod. "Tavi, you can't go." Ellea was firm. "You aren't ready for this. You have done well developing your gifts, but you don't know what you'll encounter. You're only fifteen; your parents will never allow you to leave!" Tavi's expression must have held guilt, because realization filled Ellea's voice. "You're not going to tell them."

Tavi said, "Ellea, I have to find my friend."

"No!" Tears filled the midwife's eyes. "Someone needs to find her," Ellea said. "Someone—but not you. Tavi, it's so dangerous. You aren't ready."

Tavi felt her resolve quavering, but she shored it up with words. "I'm the best person to search for them."

Ellea reached out and grasped Tavi's arm. The older woman's hand glowed golden, and Tavi felt more peace than she had experienced since the previous morning. "Promise me you will talk to your parents about this first," Ellea said softly.

Tavi nodded. "I will."

"Promise me."

Tavi forced herself not to look away. "I promise."

The midwife smiled though she still looked worried. She grasped Sall's shoulder with her other glowing hand. Tavi looked at her friend, and his face, too, softened with peace.

"Sava bless you both—and Sava bless Reba and Narre," Ellea said.

"Sava bless you," Tavi and Sall replied.

Ellea let go of them and of her magic. Sall and Tavi turned and continued down the road.

When they were out of earshot, Sall said, "You'll tell your parents?" Tavi gave him a look of hesitant guilt, and he said, "You lied."

Tavi again felt tears filling her eyes. She was so tired of crying. "I didn't want to lie," she said, "but I have to do this."

Sall turned his head to her. "I understand. And, Tavi?" He paused, and when he spoke again, his voice was strained. "Thank you."

When they reached the turnoff to Sall's house, they both stopped.

"Please search for them with me," Tavi pleaded.

Sall's head dropped. "I can't."

"If you change your mind, be at my house early in the morning," Tavi said. "As if you're picking me up for school."

Sall hugged her. "Bring her home," he said, choking on the words. He let her go and turned down the path to his house.

As Tavi continued walking, she felt as if her head would burst from all the anxious thoughts it held. What had happened to her confidence? Oh, that's right—Ellea had happened.

Tavi loved Ellea. She respected the midwife who had given her the gift of a blessing breath and who had poured such wisdom and care into her. Tavi also trusted Ellea. That trust was mutual, and now Tavi had broken it.

Guilt filled her chest, pressing against her ribs as if it wanted to escape. She wished it would. As the guilt scoured her insides, doubt bombarded her mind. What if Ellea was right? Tavi was fifteen; what was she thinking, planning to walk along a scent trail to find her friend who was in danger?

Tavi hit her temple with her palm as if to force out the confusion. It didn't work. "You aren't ready," Ellea had said. Tavi wanted to be furious with her mentor, but she was too full of worry, shame, and self-doubt. She had no room for anger.

Her house was in view, but Tavi wasn't ready to see Misty or her mother. She walked past a neighbor's house and entered the forest. In a few minutes, she had reached her favorite clearing—"our clearing," as she still thought of it, even though the other half of "our" was gone for good.

Tavi sat in the dry, cool grass. She was tired of thinking and grieving and imagining terrible things. Magic—she wanted magic, needed the peace it offered, just for a few minutes. Closing her eyes, she held her hands in front of her, loosely weaving her fingers together. She took a deep breath and released it fully. What did she desire?

All Tavi could think of was how overwhelmed she was, how old and tired she felt. Her magic would never come if that was her focus. *What do I desire?*

She desired security, encouragement, and relaxation. She desired to be carefree, to enjoy life.

She desired Tullen.

At that thought, Tavi's eyes popped open in surprise. She saw her hands, folded together, and she wished that instead, her fingers were intertwined with Tullen's, that he was sitting with her instead of thirty miles away.

That's your brother you're thinking about, Tavi chided herself. She pulled her hands apart and shook them as if to rid herself of the unwelcome longing invading her consciousness.

It was chilly. She wrapped her arms around herself, closed her eyes again, and focused on her hands. Touch magic; that's what she needed. Tavi pictured a pickle, sour and juicy and salty. Just a hint of sweetness.

Her magic did not come. Food didn't sound good, not even Misty's pickles. Tavi pulled her arms tighter around herself, warding against the chill.

But it wasn't her own arms she wanted to feel. Tavi couldn't stop thinking about Tullen, how his arms, wiry and strong, had felt around her when they'd said goodbye. And because she wanted the comfort of magic, and this seemed to be the only thing her muddled mind was willing to desire, she gave in.

Tavi leapt into her imagination. Tullen's warm arms were holding her. His strong heartbeat pulsed against her cheek, and his chin rested on her head.

Soothing magic filled Tavi's hands, and she pressed them against the center of her chest. She could sense the blood entering her heart, then pumping out to the rest of her body, over and over in steady repetition. She tried to focus on this rhythm of life, to allow it to ground and calm her. But her thoughts insisted on returning to the man who could not be more than a friend, who could not even be that now.

Tavi tried to recall his face, every aspect of it. She found that she wasn't sure whether his eyelashes were long or short, and the shape of his nose escaped her. But his lips—those she could picture in perfect detail. A little thin, but wide, and always ready to broaden further into a smile. She could see the "V" at the center of his top lip, and the small mole that barely intruded on the edge of his bottom lip. For Sava's sake, when had she memorized his lips?

Tavi's hands moved to her warm cheeks. With her gift, she detected blood flooding innumerable tiny vessels near the surface of her skin. Blushing even when no one was around to see her. Narre would laugh.

Narre. Tavi pulled her hands off her cheeks, clenched them as tightly as she could, then flung her fingers open, shoving every drop of magic out of her. What was wrong with her, thinking about a romance that couldn't even happen, when her friend was in danger, and she could do something about that?

Her magical reprieve had offered one benefit. It had driven out the overwhelming confusion. Tavi's mind was clear again—well, mostly clear, though a little befuddled after the turn her thoughts had taken when she'd called on her magic. But it was clear enough to tell her that yes, she must find her friend.

Tavi might or might not be enough for this task; she might be making the worst mistake of her life; but she was sure of one thing: if she did not go, and something happened to her cousin, she would never recover from her regret.

AS SHE WALKED to her house, Tavi reflected on the promise she'd made —the lie she had told—in front of the midwife house. Talking to her father was out of the question, whatever Ellea thought. And while her mother might respond more kindly, she still wouldn't allow Tavi to go. But could she leave home without telling anyone? She pondered this question and continued to walk.

When Tavi entered the kitchen, Misty was kneading bread, and she looked up sharply. "Why aren't you in school?"

Tavi ignored the question. "Where's Mama?" she asked.

"She's with Aunt Jilla," Misty answered. "Why are you home?"

With her mother gone, Tavi knew what she needed to do. She would divulge her plans to her sister. Misty might insist on tattling, but if she did, Tavi could leave town before her sister had time to track down their mother.

Tavi got right to the point, explaining her scent-based tracking and sharing what she and Sall had discovered. She took a deep breath and said, "I'm going to go find her, Misty."

When she heard Tavi's declaration, Misty pulled out a chair with a floured hand, and sat. Tavi followed suit.

"This is a bad idea," Misty said.

"Her life may be in danger, and I'm the best person to find her," Tavi stated.

"I agree with you on that. But you're fifteen. Mother and Father will never allow it."

Tavi remained calm, rational. "You're the one who said just yesterday that I've grown up. Besides, I'm not planning on telling Mama or Papa." She eyed her sister, trying to gauge Misty's reaction to that statement.

Misty's face was hard. "You are not traveling alone to who-knows-where."

"Yes," Tavi replied. "I am."

"No, you're not. I'm going with you."

Tavi's mouth dropped open. That wasn't the response she'd expected. Her voice softened. "You'll come with me?"

Misty nodded and smiled. "It's probably still a bad idea," she said. "But I understand why you need to go. And I've taken care of you since you were a baby; I'm not going to stop now."

Tavi stepped out of her chair and hugged her sister tight. Misty's voice spoke into her ear. "We have to tell Mother."

Pulling away, Tavi protested, "She won't let us go!"

"You forget, I'm an adult. I can go wherever I want. And I'm willing to take you with me even if Mother disapproves."

Misty appeared distinctly uncomfortable with her defiant words, but she did not change them. Taking her sister's hand, Tavi said, "Thank you."

They packed food that wouldn't spoil on the road, trying to keep their bags light. Cheese, sausage, and dried fruit were their staples. When they moved to their room to pack a change of clothes each, they heard their mother enter the house. The two sisters gave each other nervous glances before walking to the kitchen.

They explained their plan and the reasoning behind it. Mey's first response was silence. She looked between the faces of her daughters, back and forth.

Finally Tavi spoke. "Please say something, Mother."

"Wait here a moment," Mey said. She left Tavi and Misty sitting at the kitchen table, looking worriedly at each other.

Mey returned, holding a leather pouch that was closed with a drawstring. She placed it in her eldest daughter's hand, and Misty's eyes widened. With fumbling fingers, Misty loosened the top of the pouch and put her hand inside. The contents jingled. "Mother, this is a lot of money," she said softly.

"When I sell my produce, I save one chip out of every ten," Mey explained. She grabbed Misty's hand with her left, and Tavi's with her right, and her voice took on an urgent tone. "I don't want you starving or dying of cold or being taken advantage of," she said. "Stay in good inns. Get help from kind people. Eat enough to give you energy to keep walking. I want you to find those girls."

"Mama—thank you." Tavi knew her quiet words were inadequate.

But Mey wasn't done. "We'll go to Shem and Jilla's before your father gets home," she said. "They have a pack horse, and I know they'll let you use it. This afternoon we'll get everything ready; tomorrow, after your father goes to the parish hall, you can pick up the horse and leave."

"A pack horse—that's a good idea!" Misty said.

Despite the worry in her face, their mother chuckled. "Were you really planning to carry all the food and water you'll need, plus everything else?"

Tavi looked at Misty with wide eyes. She was quite sure her sister's thoughts mirrored her own—they hadn't even considered their need for water.

When she felt a tight squeeze on her hand, Tavi looked back at her mother. Mey's eyes had filled with tears, but the lines of her face were firm. "Come home." Her words were a demand, not a request. "I've watched what Jilla is going through, and I—" Her voice caught, and she swallowed hard. "I am not willing to lose my oldest and my youngest. Come home."

Tavi nodded, trying to hold back her own tears. In the end, she didn't succeed, and emotion overtook her sister and her mother too. Three wet handkerchiefs and six swollen eyes later, they at last stood to make preparations.

CHAPTER THIRTY-FIVE

Act, before it is too late.
And if you think it is too late,
Act anyway.

-*From* Proverbs of Savala

SALL DIDN'T GO to school—again. Until the previous day, he had never missed school unless he was sick, or when his mother was having a particularly bad day, or when one of his brothers was sick. On second thought, that meant he'd missed school quite a bit, but never like this, simply choosing not to attend. Today his brothers had also refused to go, and he hadn't even fought them on it. Now he was sitting in front of his house, on the cool ground, staring at nothing.

He had grown accustomed to sensing the overwhelming emotions of others, but now, it was Sall's own feelings that attacked him with staggering intensity. Deep shame topped the list. Tavi was right to expect him to go with her, but every time Sall reexamined his decision, he considered his mother, lying in that bed, dying a slow death of the mind. He thought of his brothers, who had proven their inability to eat well or go to school regularly without Sall's guidance. He needed to be with Tavi, who must be hours down the road by now, but even more he was needed here.

Underneath the shame was a bone-filling anxiety. Where was Narre? Dared he hope she was even now on her way home? Or had they hurt her; had they . . . no, he would not even let himself consider the worst possibilities. Yet those unacknowledged thoughts percolated below the rest.

The sun warmed him, and Sall realized it was straight overhead. With an effort, he stood. He was home at lunchtime; he might as well try to get his mother to eat.

There was leftover ham in the ice cellar and stale bread in the kitchen. Sall made four sandwiches. After calling his brothers in from outside, he took a plate to his mother.

She refused the food. And today, of all days, Sall couldn't take it. He grasped her chin and attempted to pull it down. Her teeth locked, and he yelled in her face. "Mother, you need to eat!" Her eyes grew wide, but her mouth was immovable.

Sall continued to try to pry open his mother's mouth until his thumb slipped, and his nail took a small chunk of skin out of her chin. He cursed and pulled away, watching the fissure bead with blood. Still his mother kept her mouth closed.

"This is unacceptable!" Sall bellowed. "You don't want to live; why am I trying to force it?" His customary patience was miles away, farther than Narre, wherever she was. Sall let the words come that he'd wanted to say for so long—the words he didn't believe but did feel. "You are a coward, Mother! You are a coward who refuses to take the risk of living! You claim to love us, but you treat us with contempt! You care nothing about your family! Nothing, Mother! Nothing!"

Sall stopped, finding that raising his voice took too much energy. Exhaustion weighed him down, due to two nights of little sleep. He sat on the edge of the bed and looked at his mother. Tears were streaming down both her cheeks—and yet her mouth was still closed, lips firmly pressed together, as if she feared that opening her mouth might invite a bite of ham sandwich. Seeing the absurdity of it all, Sall let a humorless laugh escape his chest.

Then he saw his brothers standing at the door. Berroll, who was twelve, stared at his crying mother, his eyes wide. Lorn, just a year older than Berr, smirked at Sall. Doubtless he loved seeing his brother lose control.

"I'm bringing a healer tomorrow." Sall's voice was quieter now, but loud enough for all three of them to hear. His mother's head shook adamantly.

"Fine," Sall said. He stood. "I can't do this any longer." He left the room, exited the house, and walked all the way to the street. He had no idea what to do next, so he sat next to the road.

After an hour of quiet, an idea occurred to him. It was something he would not have considered before this horrendous week had begun, but now he was ready to act on it. Sall returned to the house, told his brothers they were going on a walk, and turned on his heel, heading back to the street. Whether due to boredom or curiosity, Berr and Lorn soon followed.

MEY WOVE a lattice of crust atop an apple pie in a halfhearted attempt to get her mind off the absence of Tavi and Misty. She was nearly done when there was a knock at the front door. After wiping her hands on her apron, and then using the same cloth to brush away a tear she discovered on her cheek, she made her way to the door and found Sall waiting on the porch.

"Sall! Come in," Mey said. The poor boy looked even thinner than usual, and his eyes were haunted.

"I came with Lorn and Berr," Sall said, "but I sent them behind the house because I need to speak with you alone. Is that all right?"

"Of course," Mey said. She ushered Sall to a chair in the sitting room. "Can I get you some tea?"

"No, thank you."

"How are you doing with Narre gone?" Mey asked, sitting across from Sall.

He shook his head. "Not well—but that's not what I'm here to discuss." Mey lifted her eyebrows, and he continued. "I need to tell you about my mother."

As Sall explained his mother's condition, Mey attempted to hold back her emotions. Before her husband left, Sall's mother Hilda had been Mey's friend. Mey had rarely seen her in the eight years since, and she had known Hilda must be struggling—but what Sall described was far worse than Mey would have guessed. She was struck with guilt that she had not tried harder to check in on her old friend. Any attempts she had made early on had been rebuffed, and she had let it go, not realizing that Hilda was falling deeper and deeper into despondency.

When Sall paused, Mey spoke. "I am so very sorry. Is this why you didn't go with Tavi?"

Sall hung his head. "Yes," he murmured.

"What can I do to help?" Mey asked.

After clearing his throat, Sall looked around the room, finally allowing his eyes to rest on Mey's face. She gave him a small, encouraging smile. His voice was hesitant. "That's actually why I came here —to see if you can help. I've been attempting to take care of my brothers because my mother, she can't care for us. But as Lorn and Berr get older, I'm realizing . . . well . . . I make a terrible mother." His mouth twitched into a sad half-smile.

Mey's heart, already broken multiple times during the previous two days, again cracked. She leaned forward in her seat. "Sall," she said, "I will do whatever you need me to do."

He stared at her and blurted out his request. "I want my brothers to live here, please."

Mey had hoped he would ask that, but his appeal didn't go far enough. "I would like nothing more," she said, "and you may live here too."

Sall's palms rose in protest. "Oh, no, my mother needs me. Otherwise—"

Mey's quiet, firm voice cut him off. "We will ensure that your mother is looked after," she said. Sall didn't respond, but his eyes held hers. She explained, "The parish takes care of those who are ill, along with the healing house. Perhaps you will still want to visit her, but others will arrange for her needs to be met."

"She won't allow it," Sall said. "She wants no one to know about her . . . condition. I offer to send her a healer at least once a week, and she always declines."

Mey nodded. "I'm not surprised. The healers will take things slowly, building trust with her. They have seen others in this condition many times. They will do all they can to help her, Sall."

Several more seconds of silence passed. Mey spoke again. "With only Jona, Seph, and Ista here, it feels empty." She smiled. "It will be good to have three more boys in the house."

"You're very generous," Sall said, "but I'm concerned that you feel obligated. And you're not. She's my mother, and they're my brothers."

"Use your gift to tell yourself what I'm feeling," Mey said. "Please."

Sall activated his mind gift, the gentle glow of it turning his hair into a halo. He turned his eyes to Mey, and the anxious tension on his face melted away. She knew what he was sensing—the love of a mother paired with a true desire to help in the ways she had offered. After Sall released his magic, he simply said, "Thank you."

Mey spent the afternoon helping Sall and his brothers move clothing and other necessities to her house. As the boys gathered their things, she went into Hilda's bedroom. The woman there was unrecognizable, with her dirty hair, sallow skin, and sunken frame. Mey wept, wondering how Sall had cared for his mother for so long without himself slipping into despair.

Hilda lashed out with words and ineffective fists when she saw her former friend. Mey hoped it was not too late for Hilda to be coaxed back to health. The healers would invite her to live in the healing house until she could again care for herself, but they would not force her to move if she refused. They would help as much as Hilda allowed.

As they walked to Mey's house with their last load of supplies, they met Jevva, who was coming home from work. Mey gave him a quick recap of the situation, and he agreed to speak with the healing house and the parish caregivers the following morning.

Once home, Mey asked Jevva to join her in the kitchen where she was greeted with the forgotten, unfinished apple pie. She put on a kettle of water for tea and sat at the table with her husband.

"There's something I need to tell you," Mey began, "and you won't like it." She told him of Tavi's discovery, and of the trip Misty and Tavi had begun, nine hours earlier.

As soon as Jevva heard his daughters were gone, he leapt out of his seat. Leaning over the table, propped on his hands, he shouted one word: "What?"

Mey remained seated and calmly repeated, "Misty and Tavi have left to find Narre and Reba."

Jevva's hand slammed on the table. "Tavi's rebellion has reached new heights!" he cried. "First the way she spoke to me, and now this!"

Mey's voice became hard and sharp as steel. "Please sit," she said.

Jevva complied, but his loud breathing and red face remained. "She did not even deign to ask my permission!"

That was it; Mey let her tongue loose. "I don't know why you would expect her to talk to you about anything, let alone her current pain, when you have barely acknowledged her existence in months!"

"I am her father!" Jevva roared.

"You drove her away!" Mey shouted. "If it wasn't this situation with Narre, it would have been something else! When you insisted that she do something against her conscience, you lost her! I hope it isn't forever, but you certainly haven't done anything to change it!"

Mey's breaths were as ragged as her husband's. She expected him to react with further anger, but instead, the furious lines of his face transformed into furrows of grief. For the first time in many years, she saw tears in his eyes.

One of Jevva's hands combed through his hair, then grasped the back of his neck. He spoke, his voice now quiet, nearly a moan. "I know. I know. I have hated myself every day since we spoke about the mayor, but . . . what was done was done. I did not want to approach her with regret after she had spoken to me in that way. Instead, I—oh, Sava, I have ruined things with my pride." His hands moved over his eyes as he took two long, unsteady breaths. He looked again at Mey. "I wish I could help her now."

As Mey stared at her husband, her anger shifted to sadness—for Jevva's failing and his grief; for Narre and Reba, wherever they were; for Tavi and Misty, on a quest that might end in heartbreak. Mey took the hand of the broken man in front of her. "I think there's a way you can help," she said.

CHAPTER THIRTY-SIX

I do not know why Sava chose to connect childbirth and magic. However, I do see similarities between them. Both inspire awe. Both require strength. And both often refuse to meet our idealistic expectations.

-*From* Midwifery: A Manual for Practical and Karian Midwives *by Ellea Kariana*

"ANOTHER ONE?" Tavi gaped at Misty. She received a rueful smile in response, and the two sisters stepped away from the road into a small copse of trees.

"Eat some grass, Miss Mella," Misty said, giving the old pack horse a slap on the rump.

Dry leaves crinkled as Tavi and Misty sat under a tree. "Let's see," Tavi said.

Misty took off her right boot and sock, and sure enough, a blister had formed on the bottom of her big toe. Tavi activated her touch gift, and in seconds, the blister was gone.

Once she had released her magic, Tavi commented, "All those years

I spent waiting for my gifts to awaken, just so I could hold my sister's sweaty foot." Misty laughed.

Before continuing on, they performed several tasks that had become routine. While Tavi activated her scent gift to ensure they were still on Narre's track, Misty watered Miss Mella and gave her a snack. Each girl grabbed an apple from the horse's pack saddle, and they ate them as they continued down the road.

Two days earlier when they had begun traveling, it had been rough. Neither Tavi nor Misty were used to walking for hours on end. It didn't help that Tavi's nightmares about Narre had prevented her from getting a good night's sleep before departing. Three hours into the first day, Tavi had been exhausted, and she and Misty both had blisters. A few hours later, they had reached a small town and stopped there for the night. They had made it thirteen miles, and it had felt like twice that many.

At the inn that evening, it had occurred to Tavi that she could probably heal the blisters, and with a bit of effort, she had learned to restore the skin nearly to its normal state. This skill made the second day much better, but after ten miles they were again exhausted, and Misty's knee was hurting. Tavi hadn't learned to heal aching joints, and her attempts were ineffective. After five more miles, they had stopped at a small guesthouse for the night.

Now it was their third day of travel, and it was going well. While their legs had been stiff when they'd risen that morning, they had loosened up once on the road. Tavi's blister-healing had improved in speed and effectiveness. The cool autumn air was pleasant for walking, and Tavi's worries were tempered by optimism.

"You've become quick at activating your gifts," Misty commented. "I don't know if you can explain it to someone who isn't sun-blessed, but what do you do to make your magic work when you're ready for it?"

Tavi was happy to describe the process to her sister, explaining the connection between desire and gift activation. "When I first discovered this, I was thinking about how much I wanted one of your pickles!" she said with a laugh.

"My pickles?" Misty laughed too. "I'll admit they're very good pickles, but I never thought they were magical! Is that still what you think about?"

"Sometimes," Tavi said.

"What else works besides pickles?" Misty asked.

"Oh, I just think about whatever I want at the moment," Tavi hedged. She was relieved when Misty didn't inquire further. Ever since her solitary time three days earlier, Tavi had found that the surest way to send magic directly where she wanted it was to think of Tullen. But she wasn't sure she wanted the teasing that would come if she admitted that. Or would she receive pity rather than teasing? Either way, she preferred to keep her feelings to herself.

They walked for a while in silence, and Tavi's thoughts drifted again toward Narre and Reba. Nausea invaded her stomach, and a scene from a recent dream flashed into her mind—Narre crying with large, hulking men standing above her.

Tavi shook her head. The more she worried, the slower she walked, and that didn't help her friends a bit. She shifted her thoughts, imagining instead what it might be like when she found Narre and Reba.

Tavi expected the reunion with Narre to be full of relief and joy. Finding Reba, however, might be different. Tavi wondered if her old friend would even be glad to see them. And if she was indeed ready to go home, would the trip be awkward? For many months, the two hadn't held a conversation longer than a few sentences. Tavi pondered how she wanted Reba to react. Perhaps she was being too optimistic, but she hoped that after the rescue, their old friendship would be salvaged and repaired.

It was mid-afternoon when Tavi noticed a mile marker on the road. "We've gone sixteen miles today!" she exclaimed. Soon after that, a small town became visible on the horizon, and they were relieved to find the Four Points Inn, which was clean and welcoming.

Once Miss Mella was settled in a stable, Tavi and Misty rented a room. After freshening up, they walked down to the dining room and ordered a hearty dinner. Every evening Tavi was amazed at how hungry she was after the day's travel.

As they ate and again bemoaned Tavi's difficulty in healing aching joints, Misty held up a finger to stop her sister from talking. When Tavi grew quiet, she heard it too. Raindrops on the roof.

Tavi left the windowless dining room and rushed to the inn's sitting room, which had two windows. Sure enough, large drops of rain were spotting the glass. She dashed out the front door, and as she did so, the rain began to pour, soaking her almost immediately. Within a minute, she reached an intersection of two roads—the one they had been traveling, and another that went north and south. Tavi's scent gift was active seconds later, but all she could smell was rain and soil. Narre's scent had washed away.

"WHAT DO you really think of Mama's sweet potato sandwiches?" Tavi asked.

Misty's answer was immediate. "I can barely force them down." Her eyes grew wide, and she covered her gaping mouth with a hand.

The girls had arranged to bring their food to their room so Tavi could change into dry clothes. There they had discussed what course of action they should take, with Tavi's scent gift useless. They had determined that she would need to use her speech gift to ask questions of those who might have seen the missing girls and the two men who were suspected of taking them.

Tavi had rarely practiced her speech gift. Now they both sat on the bed while Tavi compelled her sister to answer her questions. As she asked questions that Misty might normally have refused to answer, she *almost* felt guilty at how much fun she was having.

After answering several more questions with more honesty and less tact than she would ever have willfully chosen, Misty said, "I think your speech gift works just fine."

Tavi laughed and released her magic. "My biggest concern is that my mouth will be glowing. Whoever I'm talking to will know I'm using magic."

Misty pondered that. "I don't think it will matter. They'll answer you regardless. Later they might be angry that they succumbed to your gift, but by then you'll have answers."

Tavi yawned. Looking out the window, she said, "The rain's stopped. Hopefully we can get some information tomorrow morning and then get back on the road. Let's go to bed."

THE NEXT MORNING, Tavi and Misty went downstairs for breakfast. The inn was owned by an older couple, and the wife was both cook and server. She approached Tavi and Misty to take their order.

After ordering a large breakfast, Misty introduced herself and chatted with the woman, who was polite but not particularly friendly. When she left for the kitchen, Misty whispered, "You should activate your gift when she brings our food."

Twenty minutes later, the woman exited the kitchen holding two plates heaped with eggs, bacon, toast, and chunky applesauce. Tavi saw her coming and was suddenly anxious. Usually she liked to close her eyes when activating her gift, but she was afraid that would seem odd, so she simply looked down. Tavi thought about how much she wanted to eat, but when the breakfast she desired was placed in front of her, it broke her concentration.

Misty rescued the moment by turning to the woman and gushing about the meal. "How do you make your applesauce? It looks divine!"

As the woman shared her applesauce secrets, Tavi again bowed her head. Now that she had food, she could close her eyes as if giving thanks to Sava. In a moment, her mouth was warm with magic. She urged more of it into her mouth, wanting to be sure it was effective.

"I have a question," Tavi said when Misty's conversation with the owner had died down. "We know a group who was traveling this way; they would have been here about three days ago. It was two men and two young women." She described the two men based on what the owner of the Oren pub had told her and Misty on their way out of town, and then she described Reba and Narre. An arrow of anxiety entered Tavi's throat as she asked the all-important question: "Did you see them?"

The woman answered readily. "Two men came through here,

looking as you described, a few days back. They stopped for food but did not stay. There were not any girls with them."

No girls. Tavi's breath left her lungs. But she held onto her gift and managed to say, "Please tell us everything you remember about the men."

It took little time for the woman to disclose all she recalled. The men had driven an enclosed wagon, which they had tied to the furthest post from the inn. One of them had come in, ordered food that would keep well on the road, and left. Soon after, the second man had entered and asked if he could purchase a pillow. While this request was strange, he had offered eight chips for it, far more than a new pillow would cost. The owner had sold it to him. The wagon had then left.

"How much food did they purchase?" Tavi asked.

The woman replied, "Enough to feed the two of them for four or five days, at least."

"And did you see which road they took on their way out?" It was a crucial question, and Tavi's heart beat faster as she asked it.

"They went north," the woman responded.

Relief filled Tavi—they knew which direction to go. "Thank you," she said with a nod. Misty echoed the statement, and as the woman left, Tavi released her magic. The woman turned back, giving the sisters a suspicious look, but she entered the kitchen without talking to them any further.

Tavi and Misty packed their things after breakfast. They settled up with the woman's husband on their way out. Once they had paid, he gave Tavi a stern look. "My wife tells me you are speech-blessed," he said. "What was the purpose of using your gift as you conversed with her?"

Tavi used the excuse she and Misty had already discussed. "My gift activates when I'm hungry," she said. "It helps me choose my words wisely. I'm sorry if it made your wife uncomfortable." She forced herself to smile. The owner accepted the response, but he looked skeptical. Tavi and Misty exited, picked up Miss Mella from the stables, and made their way to the northbound road.

CHAPTER THIRTY-SEVEN

I would give up all my possessions and even my magic to see you once more. Why will you not answer me?

-*From* Savala's Collected Letters, Volume 1

THE DIRT ROAD was covered in a thin layer of mud, thanks to the rain. Tavi and Misty realized their skirts were getting dirty and would soon grow heavy with mud, so they tied the hems of their dresses into loose knots above their knees, leaving just their shin-length slips hanging down. Doubtless it looked ridiculous, but they didn't care.

Walking in the mud didn't seem so bad at first, but after an hour, the sisters were already feeling tired. They stopped for a rest, groaning at their dirty shoes and Miss Mella's muddy hooves. After cleaning her up and wiping the soles of their boots on tree trunks, they continued walking.

"No blisters yet today?" Tavi asked.

"No," Misty said. "I wore two pairs of socks, and it seems to be helping."

"Good." Tavi looked up at the sky, which was still dreary. She hoped it didn't rain on them. Her mind turned to Narre. Had she stayed dry in the rain? Was she warm? At this thought, Tavi shivered, flipping up the collar of her coat. It was the first day they'd needed coats; the storm had ushered in cooler weather.

They stopped at the top of a hill for an early lunch. The grass off the road was still wet, so Misty doubled a blanket before setting out a small picnic on it. When they tried sitting, the dampness soaked through onto their skirts and legs. "Guess if you can eat standing up, we can too, Miss Mella," Misty said as she and Tavi stood, both groaning as if their joints had aged decades in the previous three days.

Tavi ate dry bread and sausage in silence. She was already tired of their travel food. If she felt like this on day four, what would it be like in a week or a month? So much of this trip was unknown—how long they would be gone, the weather, where they would stay each night, and, above all, Narre and Reba's location, situation, and safety. The uncertainty irritated Tavi, like an insect bite that wouldn't stop itching.

Without speaking, she and Misty prepared to resume their trek. They wrapped up their food and repacked it on Miss Mella's strong back. The sisters trudged to the road, and Tavi turned Miss Mella north. Before they could take two steps, however, Misty grabbed Tavi's arm. "What's that?" she asked, pointing down the slope they had ascended before lunch.

Tavi squinted and saw what Misty was pointing at. It appeared to be another traveler, coming their way. "Let's get going," Tavi said. "I don't want company right now."

Misty didn't move. "Doesn't it seem like they're traveling quickly?" she asked. "Could it be an animal?"

Looking more closely, Tavi's lip curled in confusion. "You're right; whoever it is, they're fast," she agreed. "But I don't think a wild animal would be using the road."

They continued to watch, and a moment later, Tavi gasped. She thrust the pack horse's lead into her sister's hand before sprinting down the hill. The gap closed quickly thanks to the other traveler's speed.

Tavi was soon forced to slow to a walk due to sobs she couldn't repress. When she was close enough to see details, she cried even harder—it wasn't one person, but two. She halted, her emotion choking her, as the other two travelers covered the last few feet.

Tullen stopped, his grin threatening to break his cheeks. Sall jumped off his back, brushing himself off and adjusting the small pack he carried. In another moment, strong arms were around Tavi. She felt her feet leave the ground, and she barely got her arms around Tullen's neck before she was spinning, spinning, spinning across the road, her legs flying behind her, Tullen's gifted feet moving at impossible speeds.

When the movement stopped and she was back on the ground, Tavi realized her cries had turned to laughter. Tullen's voice joined hers, their mirth loud and uncontrollable. After the constant worry and grief of the past several days, it was as if something hard and dark had broken open in Tavi. All was not well, not even close, but for that moment, she could smile.

In time, Tavi and Tullen both caught their breath. "Apparently you're glad to see each other," Sall said. "Shall we walk up the hill to Misty?"

Tullen's arm went around Tavi's shoulders, and he squeezed (in a very brotherly manner, she reflected ruefully.) Sall then accepted Tavi's warm hug, and the three of them walked toward Misty. Tullen smirked at Tavi. "I admire your bold wardrobe choice," he said, his eyes on her tied-up skirt.

Tavi shrugged. "When you're a world traveler, you do what's necessary."

As they walked up the hill, Tullen and Sall refused to answer Tavi's questions. "Let's wait until we're all together," Sall insisted. Tavi didn't complain. She basked in the moment and the closeness of her friends.

As they neared Misty, her sardonic voice reached them. "Sure, Tavi, I'd love to hold onto Miss Mella for you while you race down the hill!"

Tavi laughed. "Thank you, Misty!"

In another minute, Misty was exchanging hugs with Tullen and Sall. Questions flew from both sides. Misty broke in. "Hold on," she said. "We've got hours to walk and talk. Why don't we update you on our journey so far, and then you can tell us how you both came to be here?"

They all agreed, though Tavi was reluctant to wait for answers. She and Misty described their trip so far. As they shared what they had learned from the woman at the inn, they were all reminded of the reason for their travel, and the celebratory atmosphere waned.

"We're going to find her," Misty said. She looked at Sall, who nodded.

Tavi had so many questions. She could tell Sall might not be ready to talk yet, so she turned to Tullen. "How did you even know to come? And how did you find us?"

"I'll take the second question first," Tullen said. "We knew you'd gone east, and we hoped you'd stayed on the main road. That took us to the Four Points Inn, but the owners refused to tell us whether or not you'd been there."

"In other words, we wouldn't have found out anything without your speech gift," Misty told Tavi with a proud smile.

Tullen continued, "Thankfully, another guest heard our questions and told us you had just left this morning. We set off to find you. Since I was carrying Sall, we made good time. We tried the eastbound road first. When we'd gone far enough to be quite sure you weren't there, we returned to the inn. By then, I needed to rest; my magic was almost depleted. We ate, then tried the northbound road. And here you are."

That brought a small smile to Tavi's face. "Tullen, how did you even know to come? And Sall, why did you change your mind?"

"Sall, why don't you go first?" Tullen suggested.

Sall nodded slowly. "There is something you need to know about my family," he said. "I wish I'd told you a long time ago, Tavi." He went on to tell them about his mother, with just enough detail to convey the seriousness of her condition.

"Oh, Sall," Tavi said. "I had no idea. I just thought—oh, never mind."

"It's all right, you can say it," Sall said.

"I thought your mother wasn't very welcoming," she admitted. "You never invited us in, so . . . I'm sorry. I should have asked you why."

"I wouldn't have told you," Sall said. "I finally told Narre every-thing, just a few weeks ago." He looked away, swallowing, before he continued, his voice strained. "I wanted so badly to come with you, Tavi. I've spent so long caring for my mother and my brothers, I saw no way to leave them."

Misty asked, "What changed?"

Sall explained his desperation, and his decision to talk to Mey. Both Tavi and Misty smiled and nodded as they heard about their mother's response. Mey had always opened her home and her heart to those in need. Sall then related the argument he'd overheard between Mey and Jevva.

"When your father expressed a desire to help, your mother retrieved a paper from your room, Tavi," he said. "It was a map to the Meadow." At this, Tavi and Tullen shared a smile. Sall continued, "She told him that Tullen might be willing to catch up with you and help with the search. I asked if I could come along, and the next morning, your father and I left for the Meadow. We took Shem and Jilla's last horse and took turns riding. It seemed wise to use the long route, so we could travel on roads instead of through the forest. It took two days, but we made it there."

"And you were allowed into the Meadow?" Tavi asked.

"We were turned away at the gate," Sall said. His voice grew angry. "Emphatically turned away, even though we explained the importance of our visit. But Tullen saw us from the guard tower, and he came into the forest to find us a few minutes later."

"And you came," Tavi said to Tullen, unexpected emotion dense in her voice.

"I came," he said, his eyes meeting hers.

"Why were you in the guard tower?" she asked.

He laughed and shook his head. "I was supposed to be getting a new perspective on things."

"What about our father?" Misty asked. "Where is he?"

"He took the horse back to Oren," Sall said. "We knew we could go much faster if Tullen could run, and he couldn't carry me and your father at the same time."

There was a pause. Tavi was grateful to hear her father had wanted to assist his daughters, but she couldn't help the hurt she felt. She wished he had come with Tullen and Sall. Finally she voiced her question. "Are there any—other reasons our father didn't come?"

Sall's eyes met hers, and she saw compassion there. "He wanted to come. But he didn't think his body could handle days or weeks of walking." Tavi nodded; her father's knees were weak. "Also," Sall added hesitantly, "he wasn't sure you'd want to see him."

Tavi's heart sank. When Misty took her hand and squeezed it, Tavi didn't let go. She and her father would have a lot to talk about when she got home. But for the first time in many weeks, she wanted that conversation.

"We appreciate you both coming," Misty said. "I think we're in good shape now, with all the gifts the three of you have. Not to mention my astonishing intelligence and personality."

That elicited smiles from everyone. They continued to walk and talk, the miles passing more easily for Tavi than they had on any of the previous days. Even the gloomy skies seemed somehow full of hope. As they conversed, however, Tavi did not ask the one question that pressed on her more acutely than any of the others. *Tullen, why did you come?*

For some reason, the question scared her. It would have to wait.

CHAPTER THIRTY-EIGHT

When you fail, try again and again,
That your perseverance may be rewarded.
Nonetheless, you may continue to fail—
Such is life.

-*From* Proverbs of Savala

TAVI LOOKED AROUND THE TABLE. There was Misty, the sister she could always count on; Sall, her smart, kind friend; and Tullen, who had come back.

And at that moment, she didn't like any of them.

What was more, she was convinced they felt the same way toward her. Hours before, they had arrived in Benton, a small city. Eager to find information on the two men and the missing girls, they had begun visiting inns and taverns. The venture had been almost pointless, and now they were hungry, sweaty, and frustrated.

Tavi was nearly ready to renounce magic. Using her speech gift to question one person after another, only to be told they hadn't seen the described travelers, had been infuriating.

After numerous failures, they had found an innkeeper who had seen the two men. He had even heard a female voice coming from the enclosed wagon. Upon hearing that, Sall had looked as if he might attack the man to find out more information. Tullen had kept Sall in check as Tavi had continued to ask questions, ultimately learning that the man had no idea what direction the travelers had gone.

Dinner arrived, and once they had eaten enough to sate their ravenous hunger, they discussed their plans for the next day. The best option, they concluded, would be to split up so they could talk to more people. If Tullen, Misty, or Sall met someone who seemed to know something but was hesitant to talk, Tavi could visit that person later, speech gift at the ready.

Tavi again examined her tablemates. Now that she was no longer hungry, she found the three of them . . . tolerable. It would take a good night's sleep to get her back to the point where she liked them again.

"No one wants to talk to me except to ask why such a young girl is in a public house by herself," Tavi seethed when she met her friends for lunch the next day. "Before I can even activate my gift, the entire room is offering to help me find my parents."

As planned, the four travelers had gone different directions all morning. At lunch, they had no further leads.

"We should have thought of that," Misty told Tavi. "Fifteen isn't too young to walk around town alone, but you look at least two years younger than that." At this, she received a pronounced glare from Tavi. "It's all right, you'll be grateful for that in another fifteen years or so."

Tavi raised an eyebrow. "That makes me feel so much better."

Ever the optimist, Tullen said, "This means meeting for lunch was the best thing we could have done. We'll make a small adjustment to our plan. Tavi and Misty, why don't the two of you stay together this afternoon?" Misty agreed with the suggestion, and Tavi reluctantly conceded. *So much for being enough,* she thought.

Tavi's mood turned around, however, when she saw the immediate difference in how she was treated when she was with Misty. In the locations they visited that afternoon, fellow patrons greeted them with amiable smiles. No one offered to find Tavi's parents.

At the first three pubs, the sisters learned nothing more than who had the best tea (the second location), and who had the cleanest toilet (the third). When they did find someone who could help them, it happened more naturally than either of them would have expected.

They were at their fourth pub of the afternoon, and they both ordered tea. They were the only customers in the room. As they sat at the bar, Tavi grasped Misty's arm and squeezed. It must have been harder than she'd intended, because Misty squealed—but she followed Tavi's eyes to the barmaid behind the counter. Her eyebrows rose.

The young woman had cut a loaf of bread in half, and she was examining the two pieces from every angle, her head glowing as golden as an autumn sunset.

"Talk to her," Tavi whispered.

Misty turned to the barmaid. "Excuse me."

The woman put down her knife, released her magic with a small shake of her head, and approached Tavi and Misty. "Can I get you something else?" she asked, her voice eager and friendly.

"No, though the tea is delicious," Misty said. "I simply wanted to ask about your mind gift. I'd love to hear about it."

With an open smile, the woman said, "Oh, sure! I'm Brindi." She extended a hand first to Misty, then to Tavi, who both introduced themselves.

Brindi pulled a stool up on her side of the bar, her eyes bright with enthusiasm as she talked. "I have a mind gift," she said, "but of course you know that! My gift allows me to see and understand details in a way I normally can't."

"How were you using it with the bread?" Misty asked.

"I have a little secret," Brindi said, her voice lowering. "By this time next year, this pub will have the very best bread in Benton—possibly in all of Cormina." Tavi and Misty both smiled, and Brindi gave a little laugh. "I've discovered that if I activate my magic before examining the bread, I notice so many things I wouldn't have understood before. I see details in the texture of the crust and crumb, and how they have changed from the previous loaf, and—oh, I'm going to bore you, but suffice to say that within a couple of minutes, I know that bread more closely than I know my own mother. I keep thorough records," she said, pulling out a notebook and flipping through pages covered in pencil notes and diagrams, "so I can determine what's working and what isn't."

Misty was leaning forward, soaking in every word that Brindi said. Tavi feared that her sister's passion for bread-baking was overriding their true goal. "How long have you cultivated your starter?" Misty asked, and that led to a detailed discussion of hydration levels, rise times, and baking temperatures.

After several minutes, Tavi decided it was time to steer the conversation back on track. "What a wonderful use of your gift!" she said.

"It's probably silly, but it makes me happy," Brindi replied. "I'd love for you to try the bread!" Tavi and Misty eagerly agreed. As she spread butter on two slices of bread, Brindi continued talking. "It's funny, this is the second time this week that someone from out of town has come through, wanting to know more about my gift! A scholar came in a few days ago, and he had questions too."

Tavi and Misty exchanged eager glances. "What did he want to know?" Tavi asked.

And that was all it took. Brindi told them of the handsome young man who had entered her pub a few days before, asking her all about her mind gift.

"Was he gifted?" Misty asked.

"I don't know," Brindi responded. "But he had a very interesting story. He said he was traveling with another friend. They're both studying magic for some monks that live in the Savala Mountains. He asked me how I feel when my gift doesn't work. Apparently they're studying magical resistance. Well, these days, I don't encounter much resistance—I guess Sava likes bread as much as I do."

Tavi forced herself to laugh, but the story about monks reeked of deception. She knew about the monastery outside Savala; her sister Tess was a monk there. It wasn't a scholarly monastery; it was contemplative, focused on prayer. The monks were extremely private; Tavi didn't see any reason they'd send out traveling representatives.

Brindi continued, "I told the man I think it's good for Sava to place limits on magic. He kept asking me questions though. He seemed to want me to admit that I get angry when my magic doesn't activate—but I don't."

"I've never heard of traveling magical scholars!" Misty said. "Did you talk about other things too?"

"He told me my bread was the best he'd had in months." She grinned, and Tavi and Misty nodded in agreement. "And he was very interested in our Blessed community here in Benton. He wanted to know about who the most gifted people are, especially young people like me. And then he asked whether any of our Blessed are old or close to death. He wanted to know names, and where he might find them. I suppose he has a lot of research to do!"

"A handsome man who's also a scholar," Misty said, a faraway look in her eyes. "I'd love to meet him myself!" She winked at Brindi. "What was his name?"

Brindi giggled. "It was Jay—but I have to admit, if he comes back, I may give you some competition for him! He was far more interesting than the men in Benton!"

Misty's eyes were so glazed with romance, she almost fooled Tavi. "I don't suppose you know what direction he went?" Misty asked dreamily.

Brindi shrugged. "I'm sorry, I didn't even see him leave. I turned around, and he was gone. He'd left money on the countertop for his meal. He tipped well!"

Misty tipped well too, and she and Tavi said their goodbyes. Finally, a few pieces of the puzzle were in place—and this time, Tavi hadn't needed to use her magic once.

WHEN TAVI and Misty arrived at the inn where they had all planned to meet for lunch, Sall and Tullen were waiting in front of the building.

"We're going, *now*," Sall said, and he stepped into the street and began walking.

"What's this about?" Tavi asked Tullen. "I'm hungry."

"Sall will explain on the way," he said. "It's important."

As they walked, Sall told them that he had, on a whim, visited the city's midwife house. In many towns and cities, the midwife house served as the center of the town's magical community, and he hoped they might know something useful.

When the midwife had heard Sall's story, she'd told him a story of her own. A few days earlier, one of her magical students had met a man claiming to be a scholar. He'd visited her father's butcher shop and asked her several questions about gifted residents in Benton. She'd reported the conversation to the midwives, one of whom had confirmed what Tavi already knew: The monks outside Savala would not have sent out traveling researchers.

Later, the student had delivered an order of sausages to the supposed scholar at the Three Horse Inn where he was staying. She'd confronted him with the lie he'd told. He had brushed it off, and she hadn't pressed. But as she had left, she had heard him say, "Let's get out of here" to an unseen fellow traveler.

Sall led them all to the Three Horse Inn. The owner immediately resisted when Sall approached him with questions. Tavi glanced at Tullen, activated her speech gift, and took over the conversation, asking about two men who may have arrived in an enclosed wagon.

"Sure, they looked like city boys," the owner said, his gruff voice emanating through a nest of gray whiskers. "They told me they wanted to sleep right inside that big wagon of theirs, and they asked if they could keep it in my barn." He pointed to a large barn across a small field. "I demanded a hefty advance payment, and they obliged. I left them alone after that. They're long gone now."

"Let's go look in the barn," Tavi said.

"No need for that," the man replied.

Tavi's frustration rose. Her speech gift only compelled answers, not action. If they could get in the barn, they might find some clue as to the direction the men had gone. When Tavi pushed, however, the owner did not budge. Finally she gave up, asking, "Did you see any girls with them, about my age—or a little older?"

"Just the two men."

Tavi shoved aside the mental image of Narre, cooped up in an enclosed wagon for days on end. "Do you remember anything at all about them?"

"They stayed out of my way; I stayed out of theirs. I remember nothing in particular."

"When did they leave?"

With dirty fingernails, he scratched his balding head. "I reckon it was four days ago." His visitors sighed; their unsuccessful investigative work in this cursed town had resulted in the gap widening between them and the people they sought.

Tavi's magic was extra-warm against her lips as she asked the crucial question. "And where did they go from here?"

The answer came readily. "I have no idea. I didn't see them leave."

Four pairs of shoulders fell. Tavi's magic fled her body, along with her hope. She and her fellow searchers began the trek back to their inn.

Their speed was perhaps half what it had been on the way there, every step weighed down with dejection. Even Tullen's customary confidence had been stifled.

They were quiet for the first half of the walk. Sall had picked up a handful of small rocks and was throwing them as far as he could into the fields on the south side of the road. Finally, he spoke. "We can't give up."

He was met with responses of, "We won't," and "Of course not," but there was little enthusiasm behind the words.

"We should go to Savala," Sall declared.

"But those men aren't really scholars, and they've probably never been to that monastery," Tavi protested. "We have no idea if they're going to Savala."

"I know," Sall acknowledged. "But think about where we came from and where we are now. Of all the large cities within traveling distance, Savala seems to be their most likely destination."

"How do you know they're in a large city?" Misty asked.

Sall threw another rock, hitting the side of a barn this time. "It's the most reasonable conclusion. It's a lot easier to hide people in a crowded city than a small town."

Or they could be hidden in the middle of nowhere. Tavi left the thought unspoken. As difficult as searching in Savala sounded, scouring large stretches of nearly uninhabited land would be impossible.

"I think we've dried up our leads in this town," Tullen said. "Let's travel toward Savala tomorrow and see if we can pick up their trail again."

CHAPTER THIRTY-NINE

I came close to being married once. And through the years, I have dreamt of what it would be like to love and be loved completely. But I have observed many families, and I have come to realize how rare that gift is—deep, unconditional love. Marriage is not rare, but this type of love is. It is difficult not to think back on the one I cared for, wondering if he could have given me that.

-From Midwife Memoirs *by Ellea Kariana*

"TAVI! WAKE UP." Tavi's dream was interrupted by urgent words and a hand on her shoulder, which she shook off with a groan. "Wake up!" the voice insisted.

Tavi opened her eyes. In the thick blackness of the room, she couldn't see who was standing next to her, but as she became more alert, she recognized Misty's voice.

And then she heard something louder—thunder. Tavi sat up, alert, and made her way to the small window in their room, bumping into Misty and a chair along the way. The street outside was invisible until nearby lightning lent it false daylight for a split second. As the sisters stood at the window, large raindrops began to tap it in a slow cadence. This escalated into rain so heavy it shook the glass.

There was another tap, this time at the door. Misty made her way there and, upon opening it, found Sall and Tullen. Stepping aside, Misty let them in.

Tullen placed a lit lantern on the room's tiny desk, and the four would-be travelers sat on the two beds. Tavi was the first to speak. "I hope this storm passes quickly like the last one did."

"If it doesn't, we'll need to wait for the roads to dry somewhat before we leave," Tullen said. "The good news is, if our lying scholars are in the path of the storm, they'll be in the same boat."

"That's a poor metaphor; a boat would probably be the best mode of transportation at the moment," Sall pointed out.

The storm showed no signs of letting up. The thunder increased in volume, and the rain struck with such force that Tavi worried the window would break. No one seemed inclined to sleep, so they sat or reclined on the bed, talking quietly.

The day before, their discouragement had prevented them from fully thinking through their travel plans. They began to discuss how Tullen's gifted feet might assist their pace. After half an hour contemplating various options, they decided to pay the inn's owner to board their horse. They would leave town on foot to avoid the extra attention that came with Tullen's gift. Once out of sight, Tullen would take one person on his back. After several miles, he'd drop off that traveler and go back for another.

Tullen's gifted running pace was several times faster than any of them could walk. Even though he would have to take them all separately, they would save time. Perhaps more importantly, they would save energy. Tullen's gift allowed him to run for about two hours. At the end of that time, he wouldn't be sore; his magic would simply be depleted. Thankfully, it only took about half an hour of rest for his gift to return.

With a plan in place that might allow them to close the gap between themselves and Narre, the mood in the room took a positive turn. Misty, however, expressed concern that Tullen wouldn't be able to carry her. To prove it, he activated his stride gift, and she got on his back. Once there, she was so nervous that she nearly strangled him. Tullen was forced to toss her on a bed so he could breathe. Misty giggled, and the others followed suit. They tried to stifle their merriment to avoid waking any fellow guests who hadn't already been disturbed by the thunder, but the attempt backfired. They gave in, roaring with laughter, releasing the tension of the previous day.

The rain was heavy for two hours—long enough to make the roads too muddy for travel. When the downpour shifted to something gentler and quieter, Sall and Tullen returned to their room. The four of them slept late into the morning.

NONE of them would have chosen a day indoors, but the muddy roads made it the only viable option. They did their best to stay busy, trying to distract themselves from their helpless situation.

Sall taught them a complicated card game. He was the only one whose strategy was effective, but they all made valiant attempts. Next, Tullen showed them the Meadow's most popular poker game. They gambled with dried beans the cook gave them. Misty ended up with most of the beans, and Tavi was sure her older sister would never let her forget it.

The inn's owner, who lived in a small house steps away from his place of business, surprised them by bringing out several books from his personal library. They each chose one, and when Tullen's book ended up being the only one worth their time, he entertained them by reading several chapters aloud, complete with ridiculous character voices.

As Tullen read, Tavi watched Sall. His eyes were far away; she knew he must be thinking of Narre. She understood; she too had found it difficult to keep her mind at peace during the quiet activity of the day.

At dinner, they ate thick lamb stew, a meal that seemed made for a chilly, dreary day. The rain had stopped completely, so after dinner, the four of them made their way to the large, covered back porch, where several lanterns were lit. Most of the other guests had gathered there; it seemed everyone was eager to spend time outside after being cooped up in a stuffy inn.

Tullen and Sall sat on a bench, leaving two wooden rocking chairs for Misty and Tavi. They all wore coats to ward against the cold. After an hour, the chef had pity on all the guests and brought hot tea to the porch.

The conversation often steered toward Narre and Reba—where they might be, whether they were safe. But this line of discussion always resulted in frustration because of how little they knew, and Tavi felt a sense of guilty relief every time someone changed the subject.

As the evening wore on, all the other guests went inside to their warm rooms. After sleeping so late, however, Tavi and her friends weren't ready to go to bed. The chef brought more tea, and a reflective silence fell.

So much about this trip felt wrong to Tavi. She had never dreamed that her first time traveling so far from home would involve coercing information out of strangers, hoping to find one of her closest friends. Tavi's eyes were drawn to Tullen, who was gazing out at the dark yard beyond the porch. Having him here felt right and good. She wondered how long it would be before he returned home to the Meadow. She attempted to force the intrusive thought away, but it settled in her chest, a slight ache.

Out of the corner of her eye, Tavi noticed Misty watching her with a small smile. Turning to Sall, Misty said, "I'm ready for some of that pumpkin bread, how about you?" The chef had left the bread in the dining room for anyone who wanted it, but Sall and Misty had been the only ones in their group who had expressed any interest.

"Sure," Sall said, appearing relieved to be drawn out of his thoughtful state. A moment later, Tavi and Tullen were alone on the porch. Tavi gave him a smile, and as she did so, she shivered with the cold.

"Stay there—I'll be right back," Tullen promised. A couple of minutes later, he returned with a quilt. He put it around his shoulders, sat back on the bench, and said, "Get over here; you're freezing."

Tavi was content to sit on the other end of the bench, wrapping the edge of the quilt around her. But Tullen scooted over, placed his arm around her shoulder, and pulled her close. Tavi was suddenly warm, and she sighed, letting herself relax into Tullen's side.

They sat that way for several perfect minutes, Tavi silently reflecting that she might never go to bed. Her mind wandered, eventually settling again on Narre, and she was surprised to find tears escaping her eyes. She wiped them away.

Tullen sat up, examining her face in the lamplight. "What is it?" When she didn't answer, he murmured, "Is it Narre?"

Tavi nodded, and Tullen wiped a fresh tear off her cheek. "It must have been so hard for you these past days," he said, his voice barely loud enough for her to decipher his words.

Again, Tavi nodded. Tullen settled back on the bench, nudging her head so it leaned on his shoulder. "I'm glad you're here," she whispered.

She didn't know if he'd heard her until, several seconds later, he answered, "Me too."

Their short exchange had brought the question back to Tavi's mind: Why had he come? Once the question was there, she couldn't rid herself of it. Tavi sat up, holding the quilt around her shoulders but turning her body to face Tullen. His eyebrows rose in an unspoken question. *Just ask,* she admonished herself. *You're staring at him, and it's getting awkward.* So she let the words slip out. "Why did you come back?"

Tullen sat up straighter, turning just as Tavi had, his eyes not leaving hers. "When I received the message from Sall and your father, I was already packing my things—I had planned to return to Oren the next day."

That wasn't what Tavi had expected. She didn't respond with words, but apparently her surprise was written on her face, because the quiet rumble of a laugh escaped from Tullen's chest. "I was coming back," he confirmed.

"Why?" It wasn't much more than a whisper, and Tavi was surprised she had the breath for even that one word.

Tullen inhaled deeply, then sighed the air out, his eyes sliding to the side, his face thoughtful. When he again looked at Tavi, there was an intensity to his gaze. "After I returned to the Meadow—that day I said goodbye to you—everything was different. I saw my home in another light." Tullen shook his head. "I could talk about this for hours, and I'm sure we will, but it came down to one thing. I realized how much I hated being told to choose between the people I care for. And then it occurred to me: nobody in Oren was asking me to choose. Only the Meadow would require that.

"I thought about it for weeks. Eventually I knew I had made the wrong decision. Not that choosing the Meadow was wrong. Choosing at all was wrong. By choosing, I was supporting the Meadow's unwillingness to welcome new people and new ideas. But I don't agree with that. Last week I did what I should have done in the first place. I told the elders I would not choose between the Meadow and the outside world."

"What did they say?" Tavi breathed.

"They said if I left, I would not be allowed to return."

"Oh, Tullen. Your family!"

His eyes glistened in the lantern light, and Tavi knew hers did as well. "I know," he said. "I spoke with my parents and a few others. I think they understand."

"But you'll never see them again?"

Tullen's mouth tightened, and she saw the muscles in his jaw clench before he spoke again. "I will try," he said. "I refuse to choose, Tavi. I will do what I can to visit my family, and if I am turned away every time, that will be the choice of the elders. I hope that eventually, they will change their minds—or be replaced by others who will open their eyes to look beyond the walls of the Meadow."

Tavi reached out her arms, giving Tullen a tight hug. "I'm so sorry."

"Thank you." He let her go, pulling back to see her face. "Tavi . . ." he started. He looked toward a nearby lantern as if trying to find words there. After several long seconds, he turned to her again. "What I told you is true, but—that's not all."

"What do you mean?"

His voice was quiet and earnest. "Tavi, I missed you."

She felt a sudden need to blink several times, and her mouth moved without any words coming out. Feeling like a fool, she asked, "You missed me, and Sall, and Narre? And my family?"

He laughed, and it was full of kindness. "No, Tavi. I missed *you*."

Clarification—she needed clarification. "Like a sister, you mean?"

That small laugh again. "It's been a long time since I thought of you as a sister." He let go of the quilt, which fell off his shoulders, and his hand reached out and tentatively touched the side of her face.

Tavi's heart pounded so urgently; she was sure Tullen could see the pulse in her neck, her temple, even her lips. Then his hand found hers, pulling it off the quilt it was holding. When the covering fell to the bench, Tavi found she didn't need it. Tullen held her hand, turning it to face upward, and traced it with the fingertip of his other hand—each of her fingers, and her palm. She shivered, and it had nothing to do with the cold air. Then their palms were together, and his fingers wove in between hers, and they both closed their hands at the same time.

A sudden rush of warm magic flooded every bit of Tavi, head to hand to toe, fueled by a desire entirely different from any she had felt before. Tullen let out a delighted laugh. Tavi was struck with messages from every gift at once. Unwilling to be distracted by them, she directed the magic into only her hands. It flowed where she instructed it. Her touch magic drew in the sensation of Tullen's heartbeat, strong and fast. Tavi's mouth spread wide in a joyful smile.

Then Tullen was holding her other hand, and he pressed his lips to her glowing palm. There was that shiver again. Next his hand was on her hair, her cheek, running down the length of her arm, back to her hand. His eyes found her face and stayed there.

After a moment, Tavi asked, "My speech gift isn't active, is it?"

"No."

"Oh—you keep looking at my lips."

And again he laughed. "I can't stop looking at them," he said. "They're beautiful. You're beautiful."

Tavi's first instinct was to argue, to give him a line about looking like a nine-year-old boy. Instead, she allowed herself to smile. "You too."

It wasn't the most eloquent response, but Tullen must not have minded at all because he touched her lips, first with his fingertips, and then with his own lips.

She melted into the kiss. It felt natural and good, full of life and youth, more perfect than anything had a right to be. Her hand still clasped his, and her magic absorbed the pulse of both of their hearts, racing to see whose could beat the fastest.

When the kiss ended, he rested his forehead on hers. "My glow bug," he whispered. And she kissed him again.

CHAPTER FORTY

While some labors progress in a predictable way that gladdens the hearts of midwives and mothers, many do not fit established patterns. A woman's pains may for a time become further apart rather than closer together, or shorter rather than longer.

An unpredictable labor is discouraging for the mother. She will need your assurances that even when the road is full of switchbacks and stones, it still leads to the promised destination.

-From Midwifery: A Manual for Practical and Karian Midwives *by Ellea Kariana*

"TAVI AND I KISSED LAST NIGHT."

Tullen's words received reactions as varied as his tablemates. Sall's eyebrows rose. Misty laughed and clapped, giving a brief hug to Tavi, whose face was red as an apple. Tullen, meanwhile, winked at Tavi and continued eating his eggs.

278

"I can't believe you said that," Tavi said, her head shaking, hands held to her hot cheeks.

"What?" Tullen asked, his wide eyes conveying confusion that Tavi didn't trust for an instant. "Why would you want to hide that?" After a moment, he gave Tavi an apologetic smile, but his eyes were sparkling. He took her hand under the table. "Sorry," he said, sounding anything but.

"Let me guess, in the Meadow, all of this is spoken of openly," Misty said. Hearing Tullen's affirmative grunt, she murmured to Tavi, "You can take the boy out of the Meadow, but you can't take the Meadow out of the boy." Seeing Tavi's continued consternation, Misty gave her a kind smile. "It's all right, it's not as if it's a surprise."

Tavi tried to resist, but her mouth rebelliously broke into a grin. She interlaced her fingers with Tullen's and didn't let go until she discovered that using a fork with her left hand was impossible, and she reluctantly reclaimed her right hand.

"I, for one, had no idea," Sall said. "But I'm happy for you." He held up a forkful of breakfast potatoes, as if toasting his two friends. His smile, however, had a touch of sadness to it, and Tavi knew who he was thinking of.

The sun was out, but the roads were a mess of sticky mud, so they spent one more day at the inn, playing games, reading, and waiting for their travels to resume. Their patience wore thin, and they were relieved when the clouds were held at bay by a bright sun.

The next morning, they checked out of the inn, told Miss Mella goodbye, and walked through the town. Each of them carried a small bag of supplies. They headed east again, taking the road that led to Savala.

After half an hour of walking, they were far enough from Benton to avoid most curious eyes. Tullen first took Sall on his back, running ten miles. When he returned to Tavi and Misty less than three quarters of an hour later, they had walked two miles on their own. Tullen picked up Misty, carried her to meet Sall, and then came back for Tavi.

He greeted her with a mischievous smirk and a kiss that made her glad she didn't have to walk on her wobbly legs. She hopped on his back, and they raced down the road. Tullen was even faster on roads than he was in the forest, and Tavi laughed aloud when he got up to his top speed. Twice, they stopped for quick kisses, and though it didn't make their trip noticeably longer, Misty gave them a knowing smile when they arrived.

As Tullen had used his gift for nearly two hours, they rested for half an hour, letting his magic replenish. Sitting in dry grass next to the road, they basked in the bright sun.

After the break, Sall again jumped on Tullen's back. Tavi and Misty were surprised when Tullen returned just a quarter of an hour later. "There's a small town a few miles from here," he told them. He carried first Misty and then Tavi to meet Sall, and they began to walk the last half mile into the town.

As she usually did, Tavi had kept an eye on the mile markers. "We've gone almost twenty miles today, and it's not even lunchtime!" They soon found an inn where they paid a few quads to freshen up in the well-appointed bathroom. Once done, they had an early lunch in the attached pub.

Luck was on their side. A girl who appeared to be several years younger than Tavi and Sall served their lunch. At first she was hesitant to answer questions about visitors to their establishment, but once Tavi activated her gift, the girl was eager to gossip. She told them all about the handsome man who, several days earlier, had driven up in an enclosed wagon. He had come inside to eat and to order food for the road.

The girl's description included no new information. She turned to help another customer but then came back to the table. "I almost forgot!" she said. "He tried to pay with a bank note—can you imagine? Of course we told him we only take chips and quads, no big-city bank notes."

Speech gift still activated, Tavi asked, "Which bank?"

"Savala Bank and Trust," she answered. "I remember it because it sounded very trustworthy, but my pa told me it doesn't matter what bank it is; we won't take their notes. He also told me the word 'Trust' means something different when it's in a bank name."

"What a good memory you have!" Misty said. The girl smiled and returned to the kitchen.

A few minutes later, their entire table was subjected to glares from a man that Tavi guessed was the girl's father—and the pub's owner. It seemed he didn't take to curious customers any more kindly than he took to bank notes. They rushed through the rest of their meal and left the pub.

At the town's only other inn, they didn't receive further information on the people they sought, but they found out that the next town was fifty miles away, too far to travel in one afternoon. They settled in for the night, rather than traveling farther and sleeping on the road. They would start bright and early the next morning.

THEIR STRANGE MODE of travel continued, becoming routine as the days passed. Storms hit every couple of days or so, minor enough that the roads were still passable, but with enough rain to wash away Narre's scent. Tavi was aggravated by this, and by the number of inns, pubs, taverns, and shops they visited without gleaning any new information other than confirming that the men had been seen.

Tullen's stride gift didn't save as much time as they had hoped. While it helped them travel more quickly, most days they still only visited one town. They used their extra time to properly canvas each community, searching for more information.

The days ran together. In a small town that looked like every other small town, an innkeeper told them two men with an enclosed wagon had left the town three days earlier. He said they had stayed overnight at the inn's carriage house.

The inn's owner readily answered Misty's questions with no need for Tavi to use her speech gift. However, he didn't seem to know much. He gave them keys to their rooms, and they walked up the stairs. As they did so, they heard a woman enter the lobby, most likely the owner's wife. He began updating her on his conversation with Misty.

Tavi activated her hearing gift as she continued toward her room.

Glancing at Tullen, she saw he had done the same. This time it seemed Sava wanted them to overhear; they encountered no resistance.

"Of course I remember them," Tavi heard the woman say. "Odd men, wanting to stay in their wagon when we have perfectly comfortable rooms here."

"It seems our new guests are related to them. They need to find them to pass along an important message," the owner said. "Do you remember anything they said?"

The woman's voice was clear as crystal to Tavi's glowing ears. "Yes—I overheard them when I walked to the carriage house to bring them dinner," she said. "They were arguing about whether they should go to a farmhouse, or some other person's house. I think it was Kale's house, or—no, that wasn't it. Konner's house? Yes, that was it. The younger one said they should go to Konner's house, and the older one insisted on the farmhouse. It seemed they'd never stop arguing, so I finally left. I brought them dinner an hour later."

Tavi's eyebrows raised, and she searched for a slip of paper while she listened to the rest of the conversation, which consisted of the woman saying that, no, they shouldn't pass on this information to their new guests, who might be lying to them. Tavi laughed at this; the woman was astute. Finding a pencil in her pocket and a scrap of paper on the desk, Tavi wrote,

FARMHOUSE

KONNER'S HOUSE

She and Tullen repeated the overheard conversation to Misty and Sall. It wasn't a lot to go on, but it was more than they'd had before. They exchanged quiet words of relief and celebration.

THREE DAYS LATER, they reached small foothills at the south end of a mountain range that spread north for countless miles. After thrilling, magically assisted runs up and down the hills, they stood at the top of

a rise. Before them was a city far more vast than any of them had seen or imagined—a city that likely boasted dozens or hundreds of nearby farmhouses, and far too many men named Konner.

Filled with apprehension, Narre's four friends walked toward Savala.

CHAPTER FORTY-ONE

Whether our paths be right or wrong,
We all leave tracks for those behind us.

-*From* Proverbs of Savala

"It's so tall," Misty said.

Tavi, Misty, Sall, and Tullen stood across the street from the three-story Savala Bank and Trust. It was in fact significantly smaller than some of the edifices in the city. But none of the buildings in Oren or the Meadow had more than two stories. Ever since their arrival the previous day, all four travelers had been in awe at the size of the structures, the streets, and indeed the city itself. Even with a map, they still had trouble navigating the crowded, often-meandering roads.

The desk clerk at their small hotel (small by Savalan standards, but larger than any inn they'd seen prior to entering the city) had sold them the map and given them an address for the bank. They had fought their way through morning crowds, arriving at the correct street and number—where stood a haberdashery, rather than a bank.

The woman behind the desk of the small shop had condescendingly informed them the bank was on East Central Street, rather than West. After walking four miles, they had at last arrived in front of the bank.

"We should go in," Tullen said.

"We don't even know what we're looking for." Sall's voice was low and tense.

"Anything useful," Tavi said. "Anything at all. Stick to the plan. The worst they can do is throw us out."

"Or kill us and let our bodies rot in the vault," Tullen said cheerfully. No one laughed.

With a pessimistic huff, Sall stepped into the street, and his friends followed, carefully avoiding carriages, horses, horse droppings, and pedestrians. The bank's oak doors looked even larger up close, soaring several feet taller than Tullen and Sall. Tullen opened the heavy door and held it for the others, following them in.

The outside of the bank had been impressive, but the inside was even more striking. Marble floors, polished to a perfect sheen, stretched across the large lobby. Columns supported the ceiling, which stood three stories tall near the doors. Beautiful artwork decorated the bright-white, plastered walls.

Four tellers waited behind a gleaming wooden countertop trimmed in brass. Misty and Sall approached the teller on the far right while Tavi and Tullen meandered toward a large painting on the left wall.

The painting was beautiful. It depicted Savala kneeling before his mother Kari, holding up his glowing hands with a look of awe on his face. There was a bloody axe next to Savala, and his trousers were torn, with blood on the edges of the fabric. The skin under the tear, however, was smooth and unmarred. The artist had taken license; *Savala's Collected Letters* never mentioned him healing himself of an axe injury, nor did any of the histories. Tavi didn't care though; the image was inspiring and exquisitely painted.

Tullen's arm came around Tavi's back, lightly resting on her shoulder. The touch jolted her back to the moment, and as she continued to gaze at the painting, she remembered to listen for Misty and Sall.

"It's been such a difficult time, I'm sure you understand," Misty was saying. "First our mother, and then our father—now I'm all that

285

my brother has left!" The teller murmured what might have been bland words of comfort, and Misty continued. "I know our parents had money deposited here, and we need to withdraw it."

Tavi picked up a few words of the teller's response, including "sorry," "letter," "judge," and "certificate."

Misty's voice grew louder. "I don't have any of that yet! I need money to get all of those things; that's why I'm coming to you! How do you expect me to get those things if you don't give me the money?" She only let the clerk get in a few words, before she wailed, "You don't understand how difficult this is! My mother and father, both dead, within three weeks of each other! I'm coming to you for help!"

As Misty's pleas and cries continued, Tavi followed Tullen's gaze to the three other tellers. Each of them watched Misty's emotional collapse with great interest. Tullen quietly steered Tavi further down the left wall.

The tellers sat in what was essentially a large box within the lobby. The edges of the long, tall countertop behind which they sat ended in walls that extended to the back of the room. Only someone with a key could cross from the lobby into the tellers' seating area, or approach the vault behind them. While the vault was secure, apparently no one was too concerned about customers taking the stairs at the back left corner of the room. They were only blocked off by a golden rope.

Once Tullen and Tavi were out of the tellers' sight lines, they ran quickly and quietly up the stairs. As Tavi had said earlier, they didn't know what to look for. They dreamed of finding a list of the bank's customers. Perhaps they would find mention of someone named Konner. Seeing the size of the bank, however, Tavi was losing hope in the practicality of that plan. Surely they wouldn't come across a long list of customers, sitting on an empty desk. Still, they had so few leads; they had no choice but to make the best of this one.

At the second floor, Tavi and Tullen encountered a long hallway with doors along either side. They walked down it with as little noise as possible. The first door on the right led to a large room, extending the whole length of the hallway. Several clerks sat inside. Some of their desks were mounded with papers; others were neat as a pin; but all the employees appeared hard at work. None looked up as Tavi and Tullen passed.

On the left, they passed three doors. Each had a nameplate reading "Lending Officer," with a name below. Only the second door was open, and the man inside looked up with a hopeful smile. Tullen gave him a nod in return, but he and Tavi continued walking.

Last, they came to a room on the left. The sign on the closed door read, "FILES." Tavi gave a nervous gasp when Tullen tried the handle. However, the room was empty, save for a few tables and a long wall of polished wooden file cabinets along its length. Tullen closed the door. "I'll take the left, you take the right," he whispered. Tavi nodded and did as he'd asked.

They began looking through the drawers. "Each of these has a different address on it—no names," Tavi said after glancing through all three drawers in the cabinet.

"Hmm. Those may be properties that the bank has issued loans for," Tullen said. "Mine is full of names; why don't you come over to this side? We'll see if we can spot the name 'Konner' anywhere."

Tavi agreed, and she and Tullen looked through the first two cabinets. Each drawer contained dozens of files, and it was slow work.

Several minutes later, they had found nothing useful. Tavi grabbed Tullen's arm, putting one finger over her lips. He stilled, and they both listened. It took only a moment to confirm that footsteps were approaching.

Tullen's eyes widened; then his expression shifted to determination. "Trust me," he said. With one hand he pushed the file drawers closed, and with the other, he pulled Tavi to him by the waist.

When she realized he was about to kiss her, she quickly adapted, standing on tiptoes to reach him, and pressing her lips to his. They pulled apart when the door opened and a thin, middle-aged woman with a severe face stepped in.

Tavi didn't have to feign embarrassment. "Oh, I'm so sorry," she said, stepping back.

Tullen laughed nervously. "We were looking for the privy—I think we went the wrong way."

It came as a shock when the woman's pinched face broke into a mischievous smile. "I went the wrong way a few times when I was your age too," she said. "The privy is on the first floor."

Tullen grinned at the woman as they passed. In the hallway, he leaned his head toward Tavi's and whispered, "I'm glad you were the one that came upstairs with me. If it had been Misty or Sall, I'm not sure how they would have reacted when I kissed them." Tavi barely kept herself from bursting into laughter. When they reached the stairs, she turned to go down, but Tullen grasped her hand, pointing up.

"You really want to risk being caught again?" Tavi asked, her voice low.

"Turned out pretty good last time," Tullen responded with a grin. When Tavi didn't budge, he grew serious. "We're here, and we can't leave without seeing if there's something useful up there. We'll try to make it fast."

Tavi knew he was right. She shoved down her nerves, and they trotted up the stairs as quietly as they could.

At the top, they approached the first door, which was closed. The nameplate read, "QUINT RAWLEY, Vice President." Tavi gave Tullen a panicked look. The executive offices!

Tullen's ears started to glow, and he pointed at them, then at Tavi's. She shook her head in confusion, and he pointed more urgently to her ears. Seeing his meaning, she activated her magic, sending it into her ears only. Then she heard Tullen. He was whispering incredibly softly, barely more than a breath, but her gifted ears picked it up.

"I have an idea," he said. "You can walk down the hall and see if there's anything useful. If someone stops you, enter their office and distract them as best you can. Then I'll give it a try and see if I can go farther."

"Let's try it," Tavi breathed. "Give me a moment to think of a story." They both released their magic, and several seconds later, Tavi began walking, trying to look confident.

She didn't get far. The second office door, belonging to Vice President Sessar Kehl, was open, and Mr. Kehl stood as she tried to pass. "Can I help you?" She turned and entered his office.

"I'm so glad you asked," she said in an excited, shrill voice. "I'm writing an essay on this building, and—oh my, you have the loveliest view from your office!" She was at his window by then, placing one palm on the glass, and pointing out with the other.

Just as Tavi had hoped, the stuffy man turned to look at her. "Did someone give you permission to come up?" he asked.

"Oh no, but I was sure you wouldn't mind," Tavi said. She leaned closer to the window and pressed her nose to it, doing her best to act even younger than she appeared to be. "I can see so far from here!" she said with a giggle. She pointed out several buildings, making inane statements like, "The red brick is so nice!"

She had the executive's full attention. He placed his hand on her shoulder. "You must leave!" he said. "The tellers can give you whatever information you need on the building, but this office is no place for a school girl."

Tavi pulled her face away but didn't leave the window. "Do you know how old this building is?" she asked. Sessar Kehl's patience had expired, however, and he grasped both her shoulders and walked her to the door.

"Don't come up those stairs again," he commanded.

Tavi laughed, making it as carefree as she could manage, and headed toward the stairs. Kehl was watching her, and she had no choice but to walk down.

Relief filled Tavi when she reached the bottom and found Tullen waiting for her. "I activated my hearing gift again," he whispered, "and it sounds like Misty and Sall are outside."

The two walked across the lobby, attracting no attention from the tellers. Once they were outside the bank, they gave a unison sigh of relief.

"There!" Tullen said, pointing down the street. Sall and Misty were waiting for them beside a tall street light. As they walked, Tullen said, "I found something."

"You did? What?"

"I'll tell all of you together."

As soon as the four of them met again, they walked toward the hotel. Tullen said, "Tavi and I walked through the second and third floors. There wasn't anything useful—until I saw the last door on the third floor." He stopped talking, continuing to walk, not looking at any of his companions.

"If you don't tell us soon, I may kill you in your sleep," Sall said. Tavi raised her eyebrows; her friend's tension had gone through the roof since they'd arrived in Savala.

"Noted," Tullen replied dryly. "The last office belonged to the president of the bank—*Konner* Burrell."

CHAPTER FORTY-TWO

It seems you do not understand. When I first found you, I also found myself.

-*From* Savala's Collected Letters, Volume 1

"THAT WILL BE SEVENTY-TWO CHIPS, three quads."

Tavi tried not to appear as shocked as she felt. Misty had no such qualms. "Seventy-two and three?" she exclaimed. "Why, in Tinawe, I could get this for forty—and the hat would be higher-quality." Misty had never been to Tinawe.

The shopkeeper looked taken aback, but she conceded, "I could possibly go down to sixty-eight, but no lower. I won't even make a profit at that price." Misty huffed, and after another minute of bargaining, she paid sixty-one chips, two quads. The shopkeeper wrapped and boxed it all, and Misty and Tavi left the store.

Back at their hotel, Tavi tried on her new dress, which laced up the back, allowing Misty to fit it well on her small frame. To the dress, Tavi added the hat and stockings Misty had purchased, and she completed the look with heeled boots. All but the stockings were secondhand; the shop specialized in selling items that wealthy women had barely worn. Brand new clothing had proven to be prohibitively expensive.

The previous evening, Tavi and Misty had returned to East Central Street, waiting at a tea parlor across from the Savala Bank and Trust. When bank employees had begun leaving for the day, Tavi had spotted the woman who had caught her and Tullen. Thanks to Misty's friendly ways and Tavi's speech gift, the woman had readily told them where the bank's president lived. "It's on Silverstone Avenue—just look for the largest home. He'll probably be there; he rarely comes into the office these days."

When Tavi, Misty, Tullen, and Sall had found Silverstone Avenue the next morning, they had gawked at the home that must belong to Konner Burrell. It was stately and enormous. To Tavi, it looked like a cross between a castle and a spacious hotel. A safety officer patrolling the street had walked toward them, and rather than risk a confrontation, they had left. Later when they'd tried again, a different officer had been on patrol. He had run after them, demanding to know their business. Their excuse about sightseeing had not been well-received.

At lunch, Sall had been the one to suggest that one of them should get clothes that would draw less attention than their traveling garb, which had seen better days. Now, as Tavi looked at herself in the long mirror in her hotel room, she wasn't sure she'd succeeded in drawing less attention to herself.

The dress was a rich, dark red, the color of fine wine, and Misty had laced it uncomfortably tight. The skirt flowed beautifully from her hips, and Tavi could quickly get used to the extra height from the boots. Then there was the hat. It was constructed of gorgeous felt, the same shade as the dress, with cream-colored silk flowers all along the band. Misty had put Tavi's hair up in a twist, and she had pinned the hat at a stylish angle toward the back of her sister's head.

Tavi couldn't believe what she was seeing. She looked—and felt—like a woman.

When she heard a knock at the door and Tullen's muffled voice from behind it calling, "Let's see!" Tavi turned and walked to the window, suddenly self-conscious. Misty opened the door.

"Why does it lace up like a shoe?" Sall's reaction wasn't quite what

Tavi had expected, but it put her at ease. She laughed and turned around to find Tullen still standing in the doorway, staring at her with an unreadable expression.

"What?" she asked, her discomfort returning.

A smile started at the edges of Tullen's lips, hitting his eyes before it grew wider. By the time he had crossed the room to her, it was a face-filling grin. "Wow," he said.

She looked down at herself, smiling. "I like it too."

Tullen ran his fingers lightly down the soft fabric on her back, from her shoulder to her waist. He shook his head and spoke again. "Wow."

"You've found yourself an eloquent one, Tavi," Misty said. "Let's go."

By THE TIME they neared Konner's house again, Tavi had been forced to stop twice to heal her blisters, though that did nothing to relieve her cramped toes. How did women wear these cruel, heeled boots all the time? Perhaps they were wealthy and went everywhere in carriages, rather than on foot.

I stick out like a sore thumb, Tavi thought as she glanced at her three companions in their drab, worn clothing. She missed her thick, comfortable, woolen dress and her sturdy boots.

They sauntered down a road that ran parallel to Silverstone Avenue. This street was not as luxurious, and, more importantly, was devoid of nosy safety officers. Misty, Sall, and Tullen found a narrow alley where they could wait in the shadows. Across the street from it, another alley led to Silverstone Avenue.

In the dim alley, Tullen activated his hearing gift. He wore a knit cap over his ears, and it suppressed the golden glow. "I'll be listening for Narre's and Reba's voices, and for yours," Tullen told Tavi. "If you need anything, just tell me—I'll get there as quickly as I can."

Tavi nodded. She wished the hat perched on the back of her head was more practical. Not only were her exposed ears cold; she also couldn't activate her own hearing gift without attracting attention. But she pasted on a brave smile, turned to Sall, and said, "We'll find her."

Tavi squeezed both Tullen's and Misty's hands before walking through the dirty alley, across the cobblestone street, through the second alley, and onto Silverstone Avenue.

Sure enough, a safety officer was patrolling. He was on the other side of the street and facing the other way, however, so Tavi turned onto the raised sidewalk. She put on the most confident air she could manage, her back straight and chin tilted upward. *I reside in one of these homes, and I am taking my midday constitutional,* she told herself. It didn't take long for the safety officer to turn and see her, but the only acknowledgement he gave her was brief tip of his hat. Tavi responded with a slight nod before again turning her eyes straight ahead.

She only dared a short glance at Konner Burrell's mansion as she passed it on the opposite side of the road. When she reached the end of the street, Tavi crossed it and turned toward the banker's house. As she approached, she was relieved to see that the safety officer was several houses away, again with his back toward her. Tavi opened the iron gate at the front of the property, cringing as it squeaked. She closed the gate behind her and stepped into a beautiful, decorative garden. She walked down a curving, stone-paved path, through tall hedges, toward the house.

The dress Tavi was wearing felt even tighter, and she looked down, surprised to see that her pounding heartbeat was only barely visible from the outside. She forced herself not to slow down, quickly reaching the front door. Before she could convince herself not to, she knocked.

Nothing happened. After a full minute, Tavi looked toward the windows. They were all covered. Could it be that no one was home? Didn't a house like this have servants? She fidgeted with her hat band, and her attention was drawn back to her sore feet. She had a ridiculous urge to sit on the front steps and take off her shoes. This impractical thought caused her to smile, which was her state when the door opened.

A maid stood there, breathing heavily. "So sorry, ma'am, I barely heard the knock from the back of the house, and the other staff said I was imagining things." She returned Tavi's smile and pointed at a black button, set in filigreed brass, mounted on the stone next to the door. "Next time, push the doorbell. It will ring in four different rooms. Now—how can I help you?"

As the woman spoke, Tavi activated her speech gift. By the time the maid was done speaking, Tavi could feel magic rushing into her mouth and the surrounding skin. The maid's eyes were drawn to the glow.

The best way to distract someone from paying attention to her speech gift was to give them a question to answer, so Tavi didn't delay. "Is this Konner Burrell's house?" she asked.

"Yes ma'am." The words were accompanied by several swift head nods.

Tavi needed to determine whether they had found the correct Konner. "My colleague has a delivery for him, but it is to be sent to the farmhouse, and I've misplaced the address. Can you please send me in the right direction?"

"Of course; I work there every other week," the woman began, and Tavi's heart leapt at the answer. The maid pointed west. "You'll head that way—"

Her instructions were cut off when a tall, solid bear of a woman, also wearing servant garb, approached from the side, grasped the maid's shoulders, and pulled her from the doorway. Before Tavi could even think of what to say, the glowering woman swung the door closed with a resounding slam.

Tavi spoke softly, knowing Tullen was listening. "In case you couldn't hear that, the door was just slammed in my face." She turned around, trying to think what her options might be. The greenery blocked her view of most of the street—and also kept the safety officer from seeing what had just happened.

Tavi walked down the path, following it around two curves, through the tall hedges. That put her out of sight of the first floor windows where she guessed the stern servant was watching her. Let the woman think she was leaving. Instead of taking the path all the way to the gate, however, Tavi ducked behind a hedge. Once there, she breathed deeply, drawing magic from her mouth into her chest. On her exhale, she pushed the magic into her ears.

Tavi spent a minute listening for Narre and Reba. Tears pricked her eyes when she didn't hear either of them. Well, she'd have to see if there was anyone else worth hearing. First, she attempted to pick up the voice of the maid who had opened the door. After several seconds, she heard just three words. "I know, but—"

The maid was interrupted by a harsh, deep voice, likely from the woman who had slammed the door. "I don't want to hear excuses," she began.

Tavi shifted her attention, listening for any other voices in the area. Before this trip, she had been working on discerning what direction voices were coming from. She picked up a few conversations but determined they were from surrounding homes. Then she heard a male voice that seemed a little closer. It seemed to be coming from somewhere behind the house. "I instructed you to have her saddled and ready half an hour ago," the voice barked. "It's a long ride to the farmhouse." Tavi gasped—*the farmhouse.*

"Nearly ready, sir," a different voice replied, this one rough and humble.

Tavi moved, creeping through rows of hedges. "Someone is about to go to a farmhouse on a horse," Tavi whispered, "I think it's Konner Burrell. Tullen, you have to follow him. I'll try to see what direction he goes so you can catch up to him." Tavi listened just long enough to hear Tullen's confirmation; then she again shifted her focus to the men behind the house. They, however, were silent.

Moving from plant to plant, Tavi made her way to the side of the house, staying hidden as much as she could—which wasn't as much as she would have liked. As luck would have it, she only saw one servant, a young gardener. He was napping against the side of a fountain, and he didn't stir as Tavi continued to move through the grounds.

Finally she rounded the house, shocked at how long it had taken. Why did anyone need a home this big? She reached the back yard, which was far larger than she would have expected in the middle of Savala. In addition to a garden full of gorgeous plants, she saw a small stable and a carriage house.

Soon Tavi spotted a middle-aged man, of below-average height but above-average fitness, exiting the stable. His sturdy arms, clad in a beautiful blue coat, were crossed, the picture of impatience. A few minutes later, he was followed by an old man leading a chestnut stallion. It was the most beautiful horse Tavi had ever seen—all sleek muscles; its mane, tail, and coat brushed to a sheen. It wore a saddle that Tavi guessed was worth several times more than Miss Mella herself.

Without a word, the blue-coated man mounted the horse. He rode it through the grounds and along the opposite side of the house from where Tavi was hiding. Tavi crept back the way she'd come. By the time she neared the path leading to the gate, she heard the clip-clop of hooves trotting on cobblestones. Giving up on any semblance of stealth, she released her hearing gift, rushed to the gate, threw it open, and looked down the street.

"He's going west, Tullen!" she said, giving him a brief description of man and horse. "Follow him! Try not to let him see you, but don't worry about hiding from anyone else. He's reached the end of the street—he turned north! Go!"

Tavi realized she was still standing at the open gate, apparently talking to herself, and the safety officer had taken notice of her. She gave a smile of true embarrassment before walking across the sidewalk and to the street. She navigated the cobblestones with some difficulty in her heeled boots, but she kept her head high even when she wobbled. The officer did not follow her, and she gave a sigh of relief.

TAVI SIPPED her third cup of tea, waiting for Tullen to return. She conversed with Misty and Sall, but couldn't stop looking toward the door of the tea house. Sooner than she'd expected, Tullen walked in— and she could tell from his expression he didn't bear good news.

"He made so many turns, it was as if he was afraid of being followed," Tullen said. "I was trying to stay far enough back that he wouldn't spot me, but eventually I lost him. I kept running, going down as many streets as I could, but he was gone." He finished talking, and then he glowered at Tavi. "Why in Sava's name are you smiling?"

"On my way back here," she replied, "I walked along Silverstone Avenue where the horse had just been. I picked up her scent. We can track the horse—and that means we can track the man, too." She grinned at Tullen again. "Let's run."

His face transformed from frustration to excitement. He grasped her hand and pulled her toward the door. "Let's fly."

It turned out that "flying" through the city, while trying to track a horse on streets where hundreds of horses passed daily, was impossible. Every minute or so, Tavi requested that they stop to double-check the scent. Nearly as frequently, Tullen had to slow or halt altogether due to curious onlookers in their path. Savalans might have occasionally seen gifted young men running faster than any horse, but they certainly weren't used to seeing such a man carrying a red-clad, golden-nosed passenger.

After twenty minutes of this, both Tavi and Tullen were grouchy, and they agreed that walking through the city would be far more practical. Tavi was already feeling her grasp on her scent gift slipping, so she released her magic, only activating it every few minutes or when they reached the end of a street. She repeatedly lost the scent and had to backtrack to find where the man on the horse had turned. Having planned to travel at unbelievable speed, their plodding pace was infuriating.

After half an hour, Tavi insisted they stop at a cobbler who handed over a pair of sturdy walking boots in exchange for the shoes she had just purchased. The new pair was ten times more comfortable, and probably worth half as much as the fashionable boots Tavi had been wearing.

Two hours after they'd begun, they reached the western edge of the city where the well-kept cobblestone road they traversed turned to dirt. Buildings and pedestrians were at last spread out. They walked a few dozen feet down the road, and Tullen asked, "Still on the right track?"

Tavi activated her magic, giving a tired smile when she picked up the horse's distinct scent. "We are," she confirmed.

"My legs are so tired, the only thing that will help is to run," Tullen said with a grin.

Tavi laughed. "Thank goodness. Let's go."

It felt like freedom itself to travel at the speed of a sparrow, especially after hours at a snail's pace. Soon they reached open road with few buildings and fewer cross streets, and Tavi let out a whoop of joy. The cool breeze tickled her ears, then took the hat right off her head. They both laughed, and Tullen skidded to a stop and went back for it.

Tracking the horse was far easier than it had been in the city. Each time they approached a turnoff, Tavi activated her gift to check which direction the horse had gone. Twice, they followed new roads. Just fifteen minutes after they'd started running, they found themselves on a narrow drive leading off the main road. Tullen set Tavi down, and they moved into the thick trees next to the drive. Staying in the wooded area, they followed the curving course of the rutted road.

The trees soon ended, the drive continuing through a few acres of fallow fields. They stopped, and beyond the fields, they saw several buildings—including a large farmhouse.

Suddenly Tavi lurched forward as if she meant to break into a run. Tullen caught her arm before she could leave the trees.

"Wait!" he demanded. "I want to go too, but we can't run in without a plan; it's not safe." Those words broke through Tavi's determination, and she turned toward Tullen. She pulled up the edge of his hat and saw he had activated his hearing gift, just as she had.

"You hear her too, don't you?" she asked, her voice desperate. "It's Narre."

CHAPTER FORTY-THREE

I have noticed that magical students often go through phases when they take far too many risks. Their age lends itself to overconfidence, and magic exacerbates this natural condition.

-*From* Training Sun-Blessed Students *by Ellea Kariana*

"I HAVE A GIFT FOR YOU," Misty said. With a grin, she held up a pair of pants.

"What are those for?" Tavi asked.

"They're for you!" Misty held up another pair. "These are for me. I purchased them when you were gone yesterday. If we're to go on a rescue mission, we can't be tripped up by skirts."

Tavi smiled. "Ellea would be proud."

The afternoon before, as Tavi and Tullen had stood in the woods within view of the farmhouse, Tullen had insisted they wait until the next day to attempt a rescue of Narre. Sall and Misty should be with them, and they should all have input on their plan, he had said.

Tavi had known he was right, but leaving that property, with Narre so close, had been torturous. Back at the hotel, they had spent the entire evening examining various scenarios and planning as much as they could.

Tavi pulled the pants on. Misty had done a pretty good job on the fit; they were a little long and were cut for a boy's body, but it was nothing that couldn't be fixed by rolled cuffs and a belt. They paired their pants with long-sleeved shirts, which Misty had also purchased.

When Tavi looked at herself in the mirror, she laughed out loud. Maybe she did look like a nine-year-old boy now, but she loved it. She kicked her leg as high as she could, relishing the freedom.

When the sisters entered the room next door, Tullen and Sall both broke into uncontrollable laughter. Misty and Tavi spun around, resulting in enthusiastic applause.

"What do you think?" Tavi asked when the room quieted.

"If anyone can pull it off, you can," Tullen said with a grin.

Sall studied them. "It's practical."

Misty sat on the one chair in the room, her legs stretched out in front of her. "I don't think I'm ever going to want to take them off," she gushed.

A few minutes later, they had purchased travel-friendly food from the dining room, and they took to the streets. They were all surprised by how little attention the sisters drew in their unconventional clothes. It took a lot to shock city folk.

Getting out of the city required a walk of several miles. Once they reached the outskirts, Tullen activated his stride gift and carried one of them at a time, just as he had done on earlier travel days. Soon they were all sneaking through the woods toward the farmhouse, following the path as Tavi and Tullen had done the day before.

They stayed in the woods, circling around the cleared portion of the property. When they reached a spot close to the back of the farmhouse, providing a good view of most of the property's buildings, they advanced further into the woods. They could no longer see the house, but the first step of their plan involved listening rather than watching. They found a small open space to sit, and when they were settled, both Tavi and Tullen activated their hearing gifts.

Tullen was the first to hear anything. "Men are talking, near the front of the house," he whispered.

Tavi shifted the direction of her listening, and, sure enough, her glowing ears soon found two male voices.

"I'll talk to her," a man said. There was a pause, and Tullen repeated what he had heard to Sall and Misty. Sall's body was so taut, Tavi thought it would break. He clearly hated having to hear this secondhand.

Moments later, the same man spoke again. "Narre, we're going to do some grappling in the barn," he said.

Tavi's ears filled with the beautiful sound of Narre's voice. "I'll stay here," she said firmly. "I told you, I don't want to train with you."

"I'm sorry, you have to come." The man's voice wasn't unkind. "Aldin's coming too, and you know we need to keep you near us."

"You could always tie me up again." Narre's voice was cold and angry.

"We didn't enjoy doing that, and we don't want to do it again." The man was losing patience. "Come on." The conversation ended.

They had tied her up. Tavi struggled to speak past the lump of anger and grief that filled her throat. She and Tullen looked at each other, and she shook her head, unable to speak. He repeated the brief conversation to Misty and Sall.

Tavi had expected Sall to rage when he heard it, but instead, he placed his face in his hands, his shoulders shaking. Misty sat with him, murmuring words of comfort.

After another minute, Tavi again heard the men speaking. They discussed the grappling they'd be doing, and within moments, most of the conversation consisted of short fighting instructions and frequent grunts.

After several minutes of this, Tavi turned to Tullen. "Let's take shifts," she suggested. This was part of their plan, to avoid either of their hearing gifts waning. He agreed to take the first shift, and Tavi released her magic.

During the next few hours, Tavi and Tullen listened but gleaned little useful information. The men encouraged Narre to learn fighting skills from them and also to practice her own gifts. She refused on both counts. After the three of them had returned to the house for a quiet lunch, they went back to the barn for more "practice," the nature of which was unclear. Tavi heard one of the men say, "Time for some wall walking," but she couldn't determine what he meant by it.

As mid-afternoon approached, Tullen, who was again on listening duty, turned to Tavi, excitement in his eyes. "One of the maids is about to carry laundry to the clothesline," he said. "Can you use your speech gift to get information from her?"

Fear and exhilaration filled Tavi in equal quantities. She crept through the trees until she could see the house. She waited there until the maid hanging up clothes came close to her, and then Tavi activated her speech gift, took a calming breath, and stepped out of the woods.

The maid started when she saw Tavi. Not willing to waste time on small talk, Tavi got right to the point. "When Narre arrived, was another girl with her?"

"Only for one night," the woman answered. "She left the next morning with Sella."

"What is Sella's last name?"

"I don't know."

"Why is Narre here?"

"They want her to join them," the maid said. "I try not to listen too much when they're talking. They value their privacy."

"Join them? In what?"

The woman was clearly scared, but she answered, Tavi's magic compelling her. "Gray magic," she said.

Tavi narrowed her eyes. "What's that?"

"I don't rightly know."

"Where does Narre sleep?"

"In the little room at the center of the house. It's small; I reckon it used to be a storage closet."

"Does someone sleep in there with her?" Tavi asked.

"Ash does," the woman replied.

At that bit of information, Tavi went off-script, asking a question she needed the answer to, though she feared it. "Does this 'Ash' hurt her? Or force her to—do anything?"

The maid shook her head firmly. "Oh no, Ash is a gentleman. He just stays with her to make sure she doesn't leave."

"Narre is our friend, and she was taken here against her will." Tavi's voice turned angry. "You may not know this, but they tied her up. Please—will you help us free her?" This was the riskiest part of their conversation; Tavi could compel the woman to answer her questions, but not to do as she asked.

The maid's answer was instant. "Oh no, I would lose my job. I need this job." She looked back toward the house. "I'm sorry about your friend; but—I should go."

"I understand," Tavi said. "Please, can you help us at all? Maybe—make sure the back door is unlocked tonight?"

The woman took a moment to think about that before nodding sharply. "I'll try." She picked up her empty basket and rushed toward the house.

Nothing else happened until later when Tavi and her companions were eating a cold, quiet dinner. Tavi, who was on listening duty, spoke up. "Konner just arrived." She listened more and added, "He said hello, and then he must have gone to a room by himself."

Aldin and Ash talked little after dinner, and Narre barely said two words. Two hours after dark, they all went to bed, and it was another hour before the maids finished their cleaning and turned in.

At a time they estimated as midnight, Tavi and her friends agreed they should implement their rescue plan. Only Tullen and Tavi would go inside the house. Sall had been vehement in his opposition to this decision, but the others had insisted that Tavi's and Tullen's gifts were best suited to a rescue. Misty and Sall would travel to a meeting spot they'd all scouted earlier in the day, two miles away and off the beaten path.

All four of them grasped hands in a circle. "Sava bless you," Misty whispered. They all repeated the blessing. Misty and Sall then gathered the group's supplies, stood, and began making their way slowly through the forest.

As they'd agreed to do, Tavi and Tullen waited in place, giving their friends time to get away. Tullen sat against a tree, and she curled up next to him. His arm came around her shoulders, pulling her even closer. With her head resting on Tullen's chest and his hand lazily drawing shapes on her upper arm, Tavi tried to relax. But all she could think about was Narre's closeness, and the minutes dragged on, made slower by her anxiety.

At last, Tullen murmured that it was time to go. They both stood and activated their hearing gifts. Tavi grasped Tullen's hand, and they made their way through the trees.

Walking through the dark was difficult. They navigated by touch, traversing first the woods, then the yard, and finally, the home's back porch.

The porch planks squeaked, and Tavi held her breath, as if that would help. But they reached the back door without apparent detection. They paused for a moment; Tavi knew Tullen was activating his stride gift, just in case they needed to escape quickly. He tried the latch, and Tavi allowed herself a smile when the door opened.

The room they entered was warm. "There's a stove," Tullen said. Tavi knew he had spoken so quietly that no one but she could hear. They both wore knit caps, covering their glowing ears.

Navigating by touch, they made their way along the left wall of the kitchen, soon exiting into a narrow hallway. After several steps, they turned right into another hallway.

An archway was on the right and a door on the left. Narre wouldn't be through the archway; she would be in a closed room. They turned to try the door.

They had agreed that Tavi would activate her sight, scent, and speech gifts any time they needed light. She did so, and with her face aglow, Tavi stood close to the door, acting as a lantern. Tullen's hands were steadier than hers, and he pressed the latch and swung the door open. Inside, they could make out a sink, toilet, and tub. They sighed, and Tavi released all but her hearing gift.

Continuing down the hall, they soon found themselves at a door that felt solid and had a fancy, metal handle. It had to be the front door. They turned and reached the original hall they'd encountered, turning right. Almost immediately, they found another door. It too was closed.

Tavi activated her facial gifts again and took a sharp breath when she saw the glint of a brass bell, tied tightly to a nail protruding from the door. There was a second bell above it, another on the left, and a fourth tied to the door handle. Tavi's heart galloped; this had to be Narre's room. Surely the bells were there to notify the house's other occupants if the door was opened. Furthermore, the room seemed to be near the center of the house, just as the maid had described.

"How do we get those off?" Tullen's murmur reached Tavi's ears.

Tavi held up a hand, asking him to wait. In two breaths, she had moved some of her active magic to her mind. She examined one knot and smiled. In a bare whisper, she said, "Hold the clapper. I'll untie it." Tullen's skeptical expression was clear even in the dim, magical glow, but Tavi pointed to her head, and he nodded in understanding. He pinched the bell's small clapper, holding it tightly.

Tavi had never learned to tie more than a square knot, but this complex knot made sense to her. She knew, with the perfect instinct of her mind magic, how to thread the end back through the loops, under, then over, then under again, at every step loosening rather than tightening, until the bell was held by a simple string. With steady hands, Tullen removed the bell, kneeling to set it silently on the floor next to the door.

They repeated this process three times, the last being the most difficult, as it required Tavi to be on Tullen's back to be tall enough. By the end, they were both sweating, but Tullen put Tavi down, and they smiled at the four silent bells in a row on the floor.

Tullen pointed at the latch and looked at Tavi inquiringly. She let go of her mind magic then nodded. He reached out his hand and slowly opened the door.

Tavi's face illuminated the room. Her heart leapt into her throat when she saw a man sleeping in a bed directly in front of the open door. It must be Ash. She tiptoed past him and stifled a sob when she saw Narre, sleeping in a small bed at the back of the room.

Tavi shook her cousin's shoulder. Narre pulled away, not quite waking. When Tavi shook her again, she woke. A gasp escaped Narre's mouth when she saw who was in front of her, glowing golden. Tavi put a finger over her own mouth.

"Tavi," Narre whispered.

Tavi shook her head harder, tapping her own lips insistently with her index finger, and Narre closed her mouth, her eyes wide. Her head swiveled to look at Ash. Tavi followed her friend's gaze. The man was still unmoving on his bed.

Tavi beckoned to her friend. Narre showed admirable self-control as she sat up gradually, not making a sound. Just as cautiously, she pulled two quilts off her legs, gathering them on the foot of the bed.

Next, Narre turned so her legs hung off the mattress. She slid to the edge of the bed. Both her feet met the wood floor, and she took Tavi's outstretched hands and stood. She and her friend shared a smile before navigating around Ash's bed. Tavi gestured to the door, stepping aside, letting Narre go first.

Tullen waited outside the room. Narre walked through the door toward him. Tavi was just two steps behind—and then everything went wrong.

A hand grabbed Tavi's fingers, clamping down like a vise. She cried out and could see her horror mirrored on Narre's face, even as Tullen grasped Narre and pulled her down the hallway.

Then Ash wrenched Tavi away from the door so violently that she felt something snap in her middle finger. Immediate agony engulfed her hand, a pain so overwhelming that the rest of her body went numb. Ash let go of her and took a few steps down the hall, but he immediately returned. Through her pain, a single thought entered Tavi's mind: *They got away.* Tullen's stride gift had been active; he must have picked up Narre and run.

Ash grasped Tavi's shoulders and pushed her into a seated position on his bed, but his eyes were so full of panic, she doubted he truly saw her. "Don't move," he said. "I'm only going into the hallway." He exited and closed the door. "Aldin! Konner!" he bellowed. He continued to call their names, over and over.

If Tavi could have breathed, she would have screamed, but her throat seemed to have frozen with the shock of the pain in her finger. All she could do was hold her breath, her mouth open wide. She had to heal her finger.

The desire for relief was so strong that as soon as Tavi beckoned to her magic, it rushed in, a violent wave of hot, healing magic. With her left hand, she grasped the middle finger of her right, but that light touch felt like the pressure of a burning brick. Now her breaths came all at once, fast and deep, and she barely avoided a scream. Tavi forced herself to apply enough pressure to determine what was wrong.

Knowledge of the injury rushed into Tavi through her touch gift. One of the bones in her finger had broken all the way through. She couldn't hold back the sobs as she sent magic into the area, far more than it needed. She had never healed a bone, but it was even easier than a cut, the two pieces drawing back together without any pesky blood. The relief was immediate, though her crying continued. Tavi flexed and released her hands, letting go of her magic before Ash could return. He mustn't know she was gifted.

The healing had taken less than a minute. Footsteps approached, and Tavi heard the three men discussing what had happened. One set of feet ran off, and then two men entered the room, their faces all pale light and dark shadows in the glow of the lantern the younger man held.

They gazed down at her, and Tavi wanted to be strong, but all she could do was meet their gazes as she wept in discouragement and fear.

CHAPTER FORTY-FOUR

Believe someone is entirely good,
And you will be disappointed.
Believe someone is entirely evil,
And you will be surprised.

-From Proverbs of Savala

"Who are you?" Ash asked.

Tavi took several deep breaths, stalling her cries.

Ash again asked, "Who are you?"

Tavi lifted her chin and spit out an answer. "Narre's friend."

"Well, I could have guessed that much," he said. He stared at Tavi, and she forced herself not to look away. "I'd like to sit down; can you please move to Narre's bed?" he asked. Tavi complied, and both men sat on Ash's bed, facing her.

"Listen, I'm Ash; this is Aldin. You can talk to us. We're not going to hurt you." Without thinking, Tavi rubbed the finger he had broken, and the movement caught his attention. "Wait—did I hurt you?" he asked. She let go of the finger and shook her head. "Please," he said, "what's your name?"

"I'd rather not say," Tavi replied.

Aldin asked, "Are you sun-blessed?" Tavi shook her head, and he sighed in consternation, turning to Ash. "We exchanged someone with an amazing touch gift for her?"

Ash's eyes narrowed. "When I caught you, your face was glowing." She didn't respond, and he turned to Aldin. "It was so fast; I'm not sure what I saw. But I think she has sight and speech gifts."

Tavi felt the corner of her mouth turn barely upward. If they only knew. She forced her face back to stoicism.

Ash leaned forward, his expression serious. "Listen, I'm not ready to go back to sleep. And you can't be in here alone without bells on the door. Do you want to come have some coffee or tea with us, or do you want me to put the bells back up, and you can sleep?" He gave her a small smile.

Tavi gawked at him, stunned at his friendliness. "You kidnapped my friend, and now me."

Ash looked down at his hands. "There's a lot you don't know," he said. "We'll talk about that later. For now—a drink, or sleep?"

Tavi considered it. Every instinct told her to stay far away from this man who had hurt both her and Narre. Yet what could she do to escape if she were here, at the center of the house, behind a door guarded by those bells? If she displayed trust—counterfeit though it would be—they might be inspired to give her more freedom. And that could help her escape.

"I'll have tea," Tavi said.

"Good," Ash replied. "Let's go to the sitting room. Aldin will get us our drinks." Aldin raised his eyebrows at this but didn't argue. Ash pointed at Tavi's feet, still covered in dirty boots. "And would you mind taking those off? These floors are new. Plus, it's warm in here."

Ash was right; it was warm. Tavi unlaced her boots and pulled them off, followed by her socks, coat, and hat. She padded along the wooden floor, following Ash to the sitting room.

Once seated, Tavi refused to answer questions about who she was. In turn, Ash withheld information about Reba and about why they'd been holding Narre. The two of them came to a conversational stale-mate, and when Aldin returned with the drinks, he and Ash talked quietly with each other.

Tavi watched them. She kept her expression smooth, but her heart-beat wouldn't slow down. These were the two men who had taken Narre, then tied her up. They appeared normal, yet minutes before Ash had been so violent as to break Tavi's finger.

Tavi gritted her teeth against her fear. She picked up her teacup and used Nydine's breathing exercises until she could hold the cup without her hand shaking. If she was going to get out of this place—and she must get out—she would need a clear mind.

First, she had to try to contact Tullen. He might be listening with his hearing gift. Tavi brought her teacup to her mouth and took a sip of the hot liquid. With the cup still held near her mouth, she tilted her head down. She hoped the cup was providing enough cover, but she wasn't confident of it. Oh, well—no risk, no reward. The men didn't seem to be paying her any attention, anyway.

"Tullen," Tavi breathed, the minimal sound swallowed by Aldin's voice and the crackling of the fire. "I'm fine," she continued. "I'm looking for a way to escape." She paused, risking a short glance toward the men, who were still wrapped up in conversation. One more sentence, that's all she would risk. "I wish I was with you," she sighed.

And just like that, desire hit her, entering her heart like a knife, spreading throughout her whole body. And desire turned into magic.

Tavi tried to repress it, but it was too late. She sat up straight, feeling the magic from the crown of her head to the soles of her bare feet. Both men looked up at once. Aldin gasped, and Ash stood so quickly that his chair rocked on two legs before falling on its side.

In a moment, Ash had crossed the room. He stopped several feet away from Tavi. His gaze traveled across her glowing face, then over the rest of her. The magic even shone through her light-colored clothes. Ash's eyes met hers, and he spoke one word, realization filling his voice. "Tavi."

She blinked and gasped. He knew her name. Tavi wasn't sure why that fact frightened her so much. She had to get out of this house. While the men stared at her, she took a minute to listen to the areas surrounding the farmhouse, but she couldn't find any voices. She would have to try later.

Tavi took a deep breath, filling her lungs with air, drawing most of her magic back into her chest—all but her stride gift, which she kept in place. She felt immediate relief as most of her magical senses were muffled. With an exhale, she sent every drop of magic from her chest into her feet.

Tavi had felt small creatures in the ground a moment ago—moles, perhaps. Now that her feet were flooded with magic, she sensed much more. The soil was populated with ants, earthworms, and termites, each organism moving with purpose.

Extending her magical senses deeper, Tavi felt for the weak spots between deep rocks, the places where the earth nearly begged to split apart. She would give the ground what it wanted; she would break it, destroying the house with it, and perhaps in the chaos she caused, she could escape.

Tavi thought of Tullen, Misty, Sall, and Narre, of her desire to be with them again, and she sent her magic into the deep rocks and the cracks between them.

Or she tried to. As soon as Tavi's magic attempted to change the earth under her feet, it encountered the unmistakable barrier of *resistance.* Clearly what she was attempting would cause harm, and Sava was putting a stop to it. She stared at her feet, pressing them into the ground, pushing her magic as hard as she could. But the resistance she encountered was like sand on a fire; not only was her magic prevented from spreading into the earth; she could also feel her power dissipating more quickly the more she tried to force it.

In moments, Tavi's magic was gone. She huffed in frustration, and, looking up at Ash, she saw fascination written on every plane of his face.

"You tried to shake the earth," he said, "and you couldn't." Seeing Tavi's surprise, he smiled. "For years I heard stories about you, Tavi. I didn't even know if the tales were true. And then we met Reba. Do you know how many hours I was on the road with her—and do you realize how much she loves to talk?" He grinned, asking, "Is the schoolhouse in Oren repaired now?"

Tavi would have been embarrassed at that question, had she not been fixated on what he had said first. Just like Tullen, Ash had heard stories about her for years. How many people knew about her? And what did they want from her?

The front door opened, and Konner entered the sitting room—without Narre or Tullen. "Aldin, care for my horse," he instructed, holding out his lantern. Aldin took it and exited. Konner's eyes found Tavi. "Is something amusing you?" he asked.

She didn't even try to wipe the smile off her face. "I guess you didn't find them," she said.

Konner raised an eyebrow and walked toward the fire.

"Konner," Ash said, "this is Tavi."

The banker's eyes widened. "This is her?" he asked. Ash nodded. Konner approached Tavi, a slow smile filling his face. "How wonderful," he said. "I'm Konner Burrell." He didn't offer her a hand; it was as if he knew she'd refuse it. Pulling a chair near Tavi, he gestured to Ash to do the same. "Let's talk," he said, sitting.

These men knew who Tavi was, and they were glad she was there. This realization injected fear back into her veins. Tavi didn't want to talk. But Ash was determined, righting his fallen chair and dragging it closer to hers.

"You're not the only one who gets frustrated when you encounter magical resistance," Ash said. "We all do. Wouldn't you want to have full control over your magic if you could?"

Tavi shook her head, trying to regain the small measure of peace she had found before her gifts had activated. She met Ash's eyes. "Resistance or not, I trust Sava."

Ash nodded, a smirk tugging at his lips, as if he was willing to accept the answer but did not believe it. He said, "Magic fills your entire body in a way no one else has ever experienced. Yes, you have magic in all the typical areas. But when magic floods you—as it just did—it doesn't just fill those areas. You also have it here." He touched his chest. "And here." His arm stretched to pat his back. "And here, and here," he added, hands touching his arms and legs, "and everywhere else." He pointed down and up the length of his body. "Have you ever asked yourself what good all that magic is? Is it there for effect? Because a glowing girl is fascinating to see?"

Tavi's breaths were coming more quickly, but this time it wasn't due to fear. *Of course I've wondered why. Of course I've asked myself these questions.* Tavi kept her expression as disinterested as she could, but she was desperate for Ash to continue.

When he spoke again, he was quiet, and Tavi had to lean forward to hear him. "Tavi, I don't think you were meant to simply have a greater number of gifts than the rest of us," he said, his voice as warm as his smile. "I think you were meant to do magic in an utterly unique way—to discover a power no one else has known. I think that's your purpose, as the first all-blessed person."

When Tavi responded, her voice was strained, and she wasn't sure why. "I don't know what you mean."

Ash laughed. "Neither do I, not exactly. But I think you'll learn to join your gifts together, so the whole of your magic is greater than the sum of its parts. I'm no fortune-teller, Tavi. But I know this: you're fifteen. From all I've heard, you're a quick study. Whatever you become, you will be greater than you are now, most likely far greater. But if you continue to be limited by this asinine thing we call 'resistance,' you'll never be able to use your power to its fullest potential."

"But resistance is part of magic," Tavi protested, fully engaged in the conversation despite herself. "There's no way to change that."

Tavi followed Ash's gaze to Konner, who was smiling. He gave Ash a brief nod.

Ash stood. "Aldin," he said, "a little grappling, if you please?" Tavi turned to see Aldin standing against a wall; she had not even noticed him reentering the room.

"In here?" Aldin asked.

Ash nodded. They moved to the middle of the room. Ash pushed a table away, making a space barely big enough to fight in. Tavi watched intently. The men began by shaking hands. But Ash didn't let go. Aldin looked down at his own hand, trying unsuccessfully to pull it away. Ash's hands both began to glow the gray of a storm cloud, and Tavi's breath caught in her throat.

In less than a moment, Ash forcibly spun Aldin around. The young man's arm was pinned behind him by one of Ash's gray hands, and his neck was squeezed by the other.

The movement was so quick that Tavi's gasp didn't even begin until the action was done. Ash gazed seriously at her.

"Resistance should have stopped me from doing that," Ash said. "Or from doing this." He twisted Aldin's arm back and forth at high speed, and the younger man let out a real groan.

Tavi couldn't keep the horror off her face. "Stop," she heard herself beg.

Ash let go, releasing both his magic and his friend. The men shook hands again before returning to their seats.

Ash's smile was back. "You may not have the desire to fight someone," he said. Looking at Aldin, he added, "Thanks for being a good sport, by the way." Aldin nodded cheerfully. His attention back on Tavi, Ash continued, "But if you learn to do magic our way, you can use it however you need to, free from archaic constraints. Free from resistance."

For an hour, they discussed gray magic. Tavi was overwhelmed with horror, fear, and enthrallment in equal measures. She had already been afraid of these men. Now she knew two of them had magic unencumbered by resistance, magic that could be used to harm. It was a terrible thought.

Yet Tavi couldn't stop listening and asking questions. She found it impossible to grasp the magnitude of gray magic, of what it would mean to her and to the world. It was as if she were trying to breathe on top of a mountain, the thin air never quite filling her lungs. She was fascinated and frightened, curious and cautious.

Many of Ash's answers, however, were evasive. He talked about how it felt to use gray magic (calling it "uncomfortable," which Tavi sensed might be an understatement) and about its limitations (none, beyond each bearer's constraints of strength, tolerance, and control.) However, he refused to say how one gained gray magic or how many people already had such capabilities.

When the clock on the mantel read half past three, the room filled with the sound of snoring. Aldin was draped across a chair, fast asleep. Ash laughed and suggested they go to bed.

Konner, who had closely observed the conversation without being part of it, stood. "Ash," he said, "I'd like both you and Aldin to stay in the bedroom with our guest. One of you should always be awake, keeping an eye on her." He turned to Tavi. "In time, we hope your stay with us becomes a willing one," he said. "Until then, please don't attempt to escape or use your magic."

He took a step closer to her and spoke quietly. "Aldin told me a story I think you should hear. On the way out of Oren, your friend Narre attempted to use her gift to break the sides of the wagon. Ash and Aldin tied her hands to her ankles. Had she tried to use magic to break the ropes, she would have also broken her ankles. After that, she was very cooperative."

Tavi drew back, tears filling her eyes. She looked at Ash and Aldin in disgust.

Ash's expression was as angry as it had been when he'd discovered Narre's escape. He growled, "Konner, this isn't necessary."

Konner didn't even look at Ash. His eyes still on Tavi, he said, "My point is, these are good men, and the last thing they want to do is hurt you. Don't give them reason to do so."

Tavi tried to blink away her tears, tried to regulate her breathing. But her cheeks were soon wet, and a single sob escaped her mouth. She turned around, rushing toward the bedroom, knowing Ash and Aldin would be close behind.

She didn't think she would be able to sleep, not after everything she had experienced that day. But perhaps it was because of all that had happened that Tavi found herself bone-weary as soon as she lay down. Within minutes, she fell asleep to the sound of tinkling bells being attached to the door.

CHAPTER FORTY-FIVE

The first time I met another person with gifted hands, I assumed she would be a healer. I was astonished when she instead used her hands to redirect a river. Sava's creativity has astounded me countless times since.

-*From* Savala's Collected Letters, Volume 2

TAVI WOKE WITH THE SUN, faced by a very sleepy Ash. "Hope you got some sleep," he said, his voice gravelly.

Her first thought was of this man, tying Narre's hands to her ankles. Tavi wasn't interested in small talk with him. "I need to go to the bathroom," she said. *And you need to go straight to Kovus.*

"It's this way."

Ash led Tavi to the kitchen, where two maids were cooking break-fast. "Tisra, please accompany Tavi to the bathroom," Ash instructed. "You know the rules."

The maid, who was not the one who had left the door unlocked for Tavi, led the way out of the kitchen, Tavi following. When they arrived at the bathroom, Tisra walked in first, stepping to the side to give Tavi room to enter.

"Are you planning to stay here with me?" Tavi asked.

Tisra nodded. "I apologize."

"Can you at least turn around?"

"Only for a moment." Tisra turned to face the door.

As Tavi used the toilet, she activated her hearing magic. "I'm in the farmhouse, and I'm fine," she breathed, the hissing and tapping of her consonants sounding loud in the tiled bathroom.

"What was that?" Tisra asked.

"Just talking to myself." Tavi listened for a moment, but she didn't hear her friends.

Tisra warned, "I'm about to turn around."

Tavi tensed her jaw, tight enough to feel it in her ears. When she released the tension, her magic dissipated too—just as Tisra turned toward her. The maid's eyes narrowed as if she had seen something suspicious. Tavi smiled innocently, flushed the toilet, and washed her hands.

Tisra led Tavi to the dining room, where Ash and Aldin sat. A hot breakfast waited. Tavi wasn't hungry, but she ate well, determined to keep her strength up. As they finished eating, Konner entered the dining room. Tavi immediately felt her entire body tighten. After Konner's delight in sharing the story of Narre being tied up, Tavi felt disgusted by him.

"I'll be in Savala observing the council meeting this morning," Konner said. "I would like to check up on a few of the councillors." His eyes found Tavi's. "You'll let Ash and Aldin know if you need anything, won't you, Tavi?" She gave a tight nod.

When Konner left, Tavi's body again relaxed. She looked toward the two men at the table and found Ash's eyes on her. "You're afraid of him," he observed. Tavi did not reply.

"Smart girl," Aldin mumbled, his mouth full of a biscuit.

Ash ignored that. "Why aren't you afraid of us?" he asked Tavi. She shrugged. She did fear them, but she was working hard not to show it.

Aldin said, "Your friend Narre was afraid, especially at first."

Tavi gave them both a look of disdain. "Perhaps that's because you stole her from her hometown and brought her here against her will."

"We didn't hurt her, and we don't want to hurt you either," Aldin said.

And Tavi believed him. But she also believed they would hurt her if they must. And that frightened her terribly—these two men were genuinely friendly, yet would resort to violence because they believed so strongly in their cause. She glanced at Ash's hands, which, when filled with gray magic, could surely break one of her bones or snap her neck before she even had time to react. Not that Tavi had the skills to fight back even if she could see an attack coming. She held back a shudder.

These were men whose actions would quickly become unpredictable if they had reason to fear her. So she would remain submissive until she was ready to act.

AFTER BREAKFAST, Ash and Aldin guided Tavi out the kitchen door to the nearby barn.

From the outside, the only thing eye-catching about the building was its wavy metal roof. Tavi had never seen its like. Inside, the barn held few reminders of its original purpose. It was heated, just like the house. Sun streamed through small windows, and Ash lit several hanging lanterns for more light. Tavi's mouth dropped when she saw the polished wood floor, the indoor Corner Rostrum, and the various tools and pieces of equipment she guessed were meant to help them learn to do magic, fight, or both.

"It's like a practicum room," she said. "Sort of."

Ash laughed. "I trained with midwives in my hometown for several years. Trust me, this is far more practical than their practicum!"

"Practicum was the most boring part of my training," Aldin said.

"You mean the training you went to for all of three months?" Ash asked.

Aldin grinned, unabashed. "If it had been more interesting, I would have gone for longer. And not skipped half my classes."

"Well, no sense having a place like this if we don't use it," Ash said. "Want to start with some grappling, Aldin?" Upon Aldin's ready agreement, Ash turned to Tavi. "Can we teach you some too?" He glanced at her pants. "You're dressed for it."

There was no way Tavi would put herself in the hands of these men in such a literal way. She pasted on a polite smile. "Why don't you just explain what you're doing, and I'll observe?" she suggested.

"All right," Ash said. "We won't use our gifts; that way you can see how the skills work without magic muddying things up."

The men fought, frequently slowing to show Tavi the mechanics of various holds, kicks, punches, and blocks. It was nerve-wracking, imagining them using that violence against her. Yet it was also more interesting than she would have expected. They even demonstrated throws, telling Tavi she could learn to throw someone much larger than herself. That intrigued her, but she tried not to let her face betray her interest.

As they fought, the windows darkened, storm clouds pushing into view. During a brief break, Ash lit more hanging lanterns. Raindrops slammed loudly into the metal roof. Tavi wondered how close her friends were and if they had any shelter. Ash and Aldin continued to fight, raising their voices over the rain as they explained their movements to her.

After an hour of grappling, both men were so covered in sweat, they looked almost as if they'd been caught outside in the storm. Aldin suggested a rest.

"You two sit for a spell," Ash said, raising his voice over the rain. "I need to use the facilities; I'll be right back." He exited the barn and jogged through the rain toward the house.

This was it. Tavi was in a large barn with only one captor, and he didn't strike her as the most cautious of sorts. She turned to Aldin with a smile. "I know you're tired, but I want to see your magic," she said, nearly yelling to be heard.

Aldin took the bait. "I bet you've never seen anything like it," he boasted, jumping to his feet and running across the barn floor. Tavi couldn't see a glow anywhere on his body. But when he reached the end of the room, he kept going—vertically, up a panel of brick on the barn's back wall.

Tavi's hand covered her open mouth. Aldin was right—she had seen nothing like this. He must be stride-blessed, but uniquely so. She laughed aloud before she remembered her true goal. But though Aldin was across the room, he was watching her. She didn't know if she could get away quickly enough to avoid him catching her. She needed a way to distract him.

"You think that's amazing?" Aldin shouted. "Wait 'til you see this." A moment later, he was on the ceiling, sauntering upside down as if he hadn't a care in the world, somehow hiding whatever discomfort his gray magic caused him. Tavi shoved down her astonishment and forced herself to focus on her escape. Aldin quickly reached the center of the room, near where Tavi stood.

"You're right—I'm amazed!" Tavi called. She pointed to the panels on the far wall. "Can you walk on all those surfaces? Even the logs?"

"Of course!" And Aldin did exactly what she wanted him to do— he turned his back to her, swaggering back across the ceiling. "I've been practicing daily . . ."

He continued talking, but Tavi was already on the move. She sprinted, focused and desperate, the rain drowning out the sound of her footsteps. In moments she had exited the front of the barn, leaving the sliding door open behind her. She barely noticed the rain as her legs churned, her pants making running easier than it had ever been before.

Once outside, Tavi turned left. She rounded the corner of the building, crouching low as she ran past the side windows, nearly slipping in a patch of slick mud. If she could make it behind the barn, she would be out of Aldin's sight when he exited the building, which would certainly happen soon. To her left, through the windows, she heard him calling, "Tavi?"

But Tavi had reached the corner. She turned left, now hidden by the back wall of the barn, and again she heard Aldin's voice. "Tavi!" he roared, and she was sure he was now outside. Her only hope was to make it to the woods, a hundred yards ahead of her. Even if he saw her, she was confident she could lose him among the trees. Never had

Tavi so desperately wanted the gift of speed that Tullen had, but she willed her legs to travel faster. She blinked against the driving rain entering her eyes and focused on the tree line.

A sound entered Tavi's ear, a rhythmic percussion, distinct from the rain. She risked a glance to the left. At the same time that her ears identified that terrible, natural drumbeat, she saw its source. Galloping toward her at top speed was a majestic chestnut stallion, ridden by Konner Burrell.

CHAPTER FORTY-SIX

I have taught countless lessons on power, tolerance, and control. Yet the more students I train, the more I am convinced that confidence is just as important as any of these other magical traits.

-*From* Training Sun-Blessed Students *by Ellea Kariana*

TAVI KEPT RUNNING, running, *running*, but she could not compete with the pure speed of the strong beast that Konner Burrell rode, and the gap was closing quickly.

The woods were still thirty feet away when Konner halted his horse halfway between Tavi and the trees. He stayed mounted. Tavi stopped and looked behind her but didn't see Aldin; he must not know yet what direction she'd gone.

"I thought you'd gone to Savala," Tavi called above the incessant barrage of rain. They were the first words that came to her mind. She didn't care what the answer was; she simply wanted him to talk rather than riding closer to her.

"I turned around; I couldn't stop thinking about the all-blessed girl," he said. "You can't leave so soon, Tavi. You haven't even shown us your gifts yet."

Tavi didn't answer; she was too busy filling her mind with desire for her friends and filling her feet with magic. It was invisible behind the thick leather of her boots, but she felt it there, from her toes to her heels.

"Where were you going, Tavi?" Konner's voice held no kindness as he watched her from the height of his horse.

She knew he thought he had her trapped; she couldn't outrun four strong legs that had been bred to race. But her magic was warm and strong, and when she sent it into the earth, it rushed willingly between the cracks deep beneath her feet.

The horse started, backing up as the ground shook. Tavi saw her problem though. She was shaking the earth directly underneath her and would likely hurt only herself—or again encounter resistance.

Konner's face filled with amusement. "Not very smart to start an earthquake underneath yourself," he said, laughing. He looked past Tavi. "Over here!" he called, his voice cutting through the rain.

Tavi turned and saw Ash and Aldin approaching from the direction of the house. Ash's hands were colored the same gray as the low clouds, and filled with the same lightning. Tavi's breath caught in her chest as she wondered what the man planned to do. She couldn't let Ash get close to her. A thought filled her mind. *Perhaps my magic can be sent in other directions too.*

Tavi pivoted, one foot facing Konner and the other facing the two younger men. She pushed her gift into the earth, powering it with every drop of desire that filled her, desire for friendship, love, and justice. Her magic was eager and malleable as she pushed it not directly underneath her, but into the ground in front of Konner and also in front of Ash and Aldin.

With a groan that drowned out the rain, two huge cracks formed between Tavi and the men. She continued to propel the magic in both directions, laughing as they all, even the horse, screamed. She widened the cracks into ravines, too broad to jump over, and again she pivoted, and created two more ravines. Tavi was standing on a rough square of stable ground, bordered on all four sides by crevasses. The cracks continued to shake and widen, until she called on her magic to halt, and the ground stilled.

Joy filled Tavi as she stood on her island of earth, safe from the three men who watched her with helpless eyes. She lifted her arms from her sides, tilting her hands and then her face toward the sky, welcoming the rain that continued to fall on her. Then Tavi released the barrier corralling her magic, allowing it to flow from her feet into the rest of her body. It was suddenly so easy. Her whole form was an empty vessel, eagerly accepting the flow of power that filled it. Strong, vibrant, golden light shone from her body, cutting through the gray rain, and she again laughed aloud.

Movement caught Tavi's eye, and she turned to her right. Aldin was rushing toward the ravine nearest him. It was at least fifteen feet wide, and Tavi's magic could sense that the bottom of it was dozens of feet below. But when Aldin reached the crevasse, he did not stop. He bent gravity and walked down its side.

Tavi gasped and rushed to the ravine. She attempted to send magic there, to widen it further, but she encountered immediate resistance. This man was not meant to be put in danger, and an animal roar of frustration came out of Tavi's mouth as she watched Aldin pick his way through the miniature mountains and valleys of the ravine's sides. Konner's deep laugh reverberated through the air.

Not wanting her magic to dissipate, Tavi did not push against the resistance. Instead she forced herself to take a deep breath, thinking through her options—but she seemed to have none. Aldin's progress was rapid. He would reach her, and the men would find a way to get Tavi across the crevasse. And then they would hurt her, worse than they had hurt Narre. Tavi felt panic invade her chest.

Then a voice reached her—a young, strong voice that matched none of the enemies who now surrounded her, a voice traveling on the currents of magic filling her ears. "I'm coming, Tavi. I can see you, and I'm coming."

Tavi didn't allow her joy to show itself in a smile, but she stood straight, gazing all around her, unflinchingly returning the stares of Ash and Konner. A moment later, a figure exited the forest, running so fast he was a blur. Konner and Ash both bolted toward him, but Tullen easily outran them.

He approached the ravine at an unbelievable speed, and he wasn't slowing. He wasn't slowing! Tavi heard herself scream his name. "Tullen!"

Then he was there, and he still didn't stop; instead he leapt, a jump so far it was as if he flew across that great crack in the earth that Tavi had created. He barely made it, and for a terrible moment, Tavi knew he would plummet into the ground. But he landed hard at the edge of her island, rolling past her, skidding to a stop mere inches from the opposite ravine.

Tavi wanted to collapse or cry, but instead, she held back her emotions, unwilling to let any of her magic slip away. She ran to the balled-up figure lying on the muddy ground, and when she saw his face filling with something halfway between a grimace and a smile, she said in a voice of quiet fury, "What was that?"

Tullen pushed himself to his feet. "That was an experiment," he said, rotating his shoulders, wrists, and ankles. "I'm glad it worked."

Tavi shook her head and was horrified to find a smile growing on her face. "You are crazy," she said, "and remarkable. And remarkably crazy."

Tullen grinned, then stepped close to her. "We've got to get you out of here, and fast. They'll find a way to get across these cracks."

"One of them is walking down the side of that one," Tavi told him softly, inclining her head to where Aldin was. They both walked there, and Tavi was horrified to see that Aldin had reached the bottom of the ravine and was on his way back up. He was still quite deep, the sides of the crack too close together for him to stand upright, but he was slowly crawling toward the top.

Tullen's eyes widened, and he shook his head, as if to force himself to focus on something besides the gravity-bending young man. "I need to carry you, and we'll have to jump for it," he said.

"You barely made it across when you were at top speed. There's no way you can leap that distance when you don't have the space to accelerate."

"We don't have a choice," Tullen insisted.

"Wait," Tavi said, putting her hand on his chest. She could feel his tension when he covered her hand with his, but he didn't argue. Tavi closed her eyes.

Ash's words from the day before flooded into her mind. And once again, an idea filled her head, unlike anything she had tried before, as if it came from Sava himself.

Tavi stepped around Tullen, toward the edge of the ravine in front of them. Ash was to her right, Konner to her left, and both watched her intently. Tavi widened her stance, and once again, her magic was eager to rush into the earth. Two more chasms formed, starting at the far edge of the one in front of them, both lengthening all the way into the trees and beyond. In between them was a strip of solid land, a pathway for their escape—if they could get across the crevasse at their feet.

Konner's voice was urgent and lacked his usual control. "Aldin!" he cried. "Hurry! She's—doing something! Hurry!"

"I'm going as quickly as I can!" Aldin's reply was far too clear; he must be near the top.

Tavi didn't have time to ponder, delay, or doubt. Ash had suggested that she could use her gifts together, combining them in powerful ways. Tavi's feet could move the earth, and her hands could heal, and her mind could see how things were formed. She stood at the edge of the chasm in front of her, between the two new cracks that extended away from her. Her mind magic saw the two great shards of earth that had cracked apart, and she knew how they must knit together, how the puzzle pieces fit. Placing both palms on the ground, she joined the healing power of her hands to the earth-moving power of her feet. She sent cascades of pure magic into the ground, moving it. Healing it. Just like the cut Tullen had given himself in the forest, the ravine in front of Tavi mended itself—more slowly than she wanted, but it was working. *It was working.*

Tullen's cry cut into Tavi's magical reverie. "He's at the top!"

Tavi swiveled her head and saw Aldin, who was climbing over the final barrier of earth that protruded from the edge of the ravine. The crack in front of her was not fully closed, not entirely stable, but she hoped it was enough. It would have to be.

"Let's go!" she cried, and in another second, Aldin was rushing toward them, but Tullen had already scooped her up, holding her in a way that felt just as unstable as the earth beneath them. The gifting in his feet led them safely over the remaining cracks of the not-quite-healed crevasse, and then they were speeding toward the forest on solid ground, pursued by Konner's screams and by Aldin who, despite his breathless sprint, grew further away with every second.

CHAPTER FORTY-SEVEN

This will be my last letter. My love, I pray that you live a life full of joy. I wish I could be part of it.

-*From* Savala's Collected Letters, Volume 1

WHEN THEY WERE out of immediate danger, Tullen stopped briefly so that Tavi could move to his back. Her body found its customary, comfortable position as Tullen continued to speed through the trees of the forest, putting distance between them and the Grays.

Five minutes into their run, Tullen finally spoke. "Are you all right?"

Tavi smiled, amazed at how relaxed she could feel when traveling at this speed. She kissed Tullen's neck. "Couldn't be better. And by the way, thank you."

"For what?"

"For saving me."

Tullen laughed. "I didn't save you, Tavi. You saved yourself. All I did was provide transportation."

Another minute of peaceful silence passed, during which it occurred to Tavi that the rain had stopped. She lifted her head from its position on Tullen's shoulder, and she realized they were traveling south, rather than east toward Savala. "Where are we going?" she asked.

"We'll be taking a different route home," Tullen told her. "It would be too easy for Konner and his men to track us if we returned the same way we came. We won't be able to pick up our things from the hotel— including your red dress." He sounded a little disappointed about that.

After a moment, a thought struck Tavi. "But, wait—" she began.

Tullen interrupted, "Don't worry, Tavi. We'll send someone else to pick up Miss Mella once we're safely home."

"That's not it. We can't go home yet. We've got to find Reba." Tullen was silent. "Tullen, we have to find her," Tavi repeated.

An uncustomary hesitation filled Tullen's words. "We need to talk about that—but if it's all right, I'd like Narre to be the one to explain," he said. Tavi didn't like that answer, but she let it stand.

A few minutes later, Tullen slowed to a stop. He let Tavi down, and she looked at him questioningly. "Almost there," he said. His hands moved wet hair out of her face. "Narre is excited to see you," he said. "And I'm probably terribly selfish to stop before we get there, but—" He paused, and swallowed before continuing. "I'm so very glad you're safe."

Then he was holding her to him in a grip so tight it almost hurt, but she melted into it. Her ear pressed against his chest, and her thoughts matched the rhythm of his heartbeat. *I'm home. I'm home. I'm home.* Tavi gently pulled away and smiled up at him. "Should we go?"

He nodded, but instead of letting him lead her away, she found herself touching his face, his arms, the shirt that stretched across his shoulders. She tilted her face toward his, and when he kissed her, magic filled her. She grew suddenly warm, and she couldn't tell if it was from the glow of her gift or from Tullen's tight hold on her and the pounding rush of blood through her body.

Tullen pulled back and took a deep breath. "If I don't stop . . . then I won't stop," he said. He smiled, and the open desire in his face took Tavi's breath away. At that moment she loved the gifts the Meadow had given him—his frankness, his lack of shame, and his respect. He laced his fingers in hers and led her through the trees toward their friends.

Tavi's reunion with Narre was full of tears, wet hugs, and laughter. It was loud and joyful, and Tavi somehow knew Tullen had chosen this meeting place, a clearing surrounded by miles of trees, for that very reason.

When emotions had calmed, Tavi confirmed that her cousin was healthy and whole. Narre assured Tavi that she hadn't even been cold for long after her rescue. Tullen's stride gift had quickly gotten her to Misty, who had brought extra boots and clothing.

They all sat to eat. Exhaustion hit Tavi, a byproduct of her lack of sleep, the rescue, and the amount of magic she'd used. But she turned to Narre and asked hesitantly, "Can you tell me what you know about Reba?"

Narre nodded slowly. "Reba wasn't kidnapped," she began. "She went willingly."

Tavi had known that might be true, but it still made her heart sink. "She wanted this gray magic they're peddling?"

"Yes," Narre confirmed. "When she met Ash and Aldin in Oren, they convinced her she should go with them so she could learn to use gray magic. But they also asked her about her magical friends. She told them about all of us. Not just us"—and she pointed at herself, Tavi, Sall, and Tullen—"but all the other trainees in Oren too."

Narre paused. "They wanted you, Tavi. But Reba didn't think she could convince you to leave your house, so she came to me instead." She shook her head. "I can't believe I fell for it. She had ignored me for so many months, and I was excited that she wanted to be friends again."

"It's all right, Narre," Misty said with a gentle smile. "Never be angry with yourself for trusting too much."

Narre shrugged. "What happened, happened. When we left my house, Ash and Aldin were waiting a little way down the road. They forced me into their wagon, and we left town right then." A haunted look filled her eyes.

Tavi didn't try to stop her tears. "I'm sorry." Out of the corner of her eye she saw a glow, and she turned toward Sall, whose mind magic was active. He took Narre's hand, gazing at her with a look that left Tavi feeling she was intruding on a private moment.

After a pause, Tavi asked, "Where is Reba now?"

"She left with Sella—another one of the Grays—the day after we reached the farmhouse," Narre said, confirming what the maid had told Tavi. "They were taking her to—to convert her magic to gray magic."

When Narre didn't continue, Tavi whispered, "How?"

Narre looked at Tullen. "You didn't tell her?"

"Not yet," he replied.

He took Tavi's hand, and Narre explained the process, the murder of a Blessed, and the breath Reba must steal to free her magic from Sava's restrictions.

Tavi's face contorted in horror. "Reba is going to kill someone?"

"Yes." Narre took a deep breath. "It will be someone old, who doesn't have long to live anyway, someone from one of the towns Ash and Aldin visited. The plan was for them to enter the town at night, and Reba would . . . complete the task then. They'd leave before anyone even knew they'd arrived. It's—it's likely done by now."

Tavi tried to let that sink in. She couldn't fathom it. Her childhood friend, convinced to kill so she could use her magic any time she wished. Her weak magic. Surely Reba realized that even without the possibility of resistance, she would never be strongly gifted. But whatever her reasoning, she had made her choice. And Tavi's heart broke with the finality of it.

Tavi reached into her pack. From the bottom she pulled out her wooden flute. She had brought it, hoping Reba would appreciate the token from home. Despite not playing it in nearly two years, when Tavi placed her fingers and mouth on the instrument, it felt right. She breathed in deeply, the crisp autumn air filling her lungs, and she played. It was a slow, sad melody, a simple song of loss and love.

When the last notes had faded from the air, Tavi lay down where she was, using her pack as a pillow. She slept.

TAVI WOKE FEELING REFRESHED. She had pressing questions on her mind. Sall and Narre were taking a walk, but when they returned, she said, "We need to talk about what's next."

Sall looked at her in confusion. "What's next is clear. We're going home."

"Of course we are," Tavi agreed. "But after that, I'm going to fight the Grays."

Each of Tavi's friends met her gaze. She took a deep breath. "And let me make something clear. I'm not asking you for permission. But if any of you want to join me, that would be . . . welcome." She didn't want to beg or oversell. But she also didn't want to do it alone, and her breaths became shallow as she waited for a response.

Sall's voice was the first to speak up. "Of course I'm going to help you fight them. They need to be stopped." He gave a small smile. "And next time, I want to be part of the action."

Narre took a deep breath and released it. "It's hard for me to think about ever seeing those people again," she said. "I might have to wait to give you a firm answer, but I think I'd rather do something about it than just sit in Oren, hoping they don't come back."

Misty grasped her sister's hand. "I'll do anything for you, Tavi."

They all looked at Tullen, but he had eyes only for Tavi. "I think you could do it all on your own," he said.

"I think I could too." And she meant it.

"But there's no way I'd miss out on it. I'm in, Tavi of the Town."

Tavi smiled, surprised at the intense relief that filled her. "You know," she said, "The Grays have one advantage. They have a name. We're just . . . us. We need a name too."

"The Golds," Sall said, as if he'd been waiting for the question.

The Golds. There was no need for discussion; every voice raised in enthusiastic agreement.

They quieted. As Tavi began to gather her things together, she looked at the four others in the clearing, each of whom was watching her. Sister. Cousin. Friend. And the one beside her, who was something more.

Tavi stood, swinging her pack over her shoulder. "What are we waiting for? Let's go home."

EPILOGUE

ASH STOOD next to Aldin in the middle of the barn. Their clothes were still sodden, and Aldin's were covered in a layer of mud from crawling in the ravine.

From a few feet away, Konner stared at them. Cold fury was written on every muscle of his body and every line of his face. Ash hadn't been so afraid of the man since the first day they'd met.

The banker spoke. "I am losing faith in both of you." Ash forced himself to keep his eyes on Konner, even as Aldin's head dropped. Konner continued, "You traveled for months. We've spent an astounding amount of money. I've trained you, using time I could not spare.

"And what is our result? One ridiculous girl with a weak sight gift. And two powerful young women who would have benefited our team immeasurably both slipping through our fingers."

Aldin said, "We also got Camalyn elected."

Konner's nostrils flared, and his volume rose. "I got Camalyn elected!"

The men across from him did not respond, and Konner again spoke with a cold control. "I have one task for you. I don't care if it is difficult. I don't care if it takes time. I don't care if you have excuses; I certainly don't want to hear them." He looked directly at Ash. "I don't care if you find this task unpalatable." Ash's stomach tightened, but he kept his expression blank.

"You will bring this all-blessed girl back to me." Konner's eyes bored into Ash's. "You will keep her with us, regardless of her feelings on the matter. She will become a Gray. You will ensure that all of this happens, whatever it takes."

Konner spun on his heel and took several steps toward the door. He halted but kept his back toward the two men. His voice filled the barn. "And if the two of you can't do whatever it takes, find someone who can."

A NOTE FROM BETH

Thanks for reading *Facing the Sun*! Will you take a minute to write a short review on Amazon or Goodreads? It's the best way to let me know if you'd like me to keep writing books like these—and to help others find this story.

Continue the adventure as Tavi and her friends face off against Konner, Ash, and the other Grays. Order *Facing the Gray* today.

Want to delve deeper into the life of one of the characters? Download a free deleted scene from *Facing the Sun* at BookHip.com/JQQBRH.

Okay, now that all that's done, can we chat for a minute? I want to thank you from way down in the bottom of my ice cream-loving heart for reading this, my first novel. I've wanted to write a book for so long, and I can't tell you what it means to me that you're reading these words.

I had a blast writing the Sun-Blessed Trilogy. Is there something you've always wanted to do, but you haven't gotten around to it? For me, writing a book fell into that category.

I'd like to be your cheerleader for a minute. That thing you've always wanted to do . . . I bet you can do it. Really. Just take the first step. For me, that meant titling a Word document "Brainstorm 4-22-17" and typing out book ideas.

What's your first step? Take it. You can do it, because you the step doesn't have to be perfect. *None* of the steps have to be perfect! *You are enough.*

Email me at beth@carolbethanderson.com or through my website at carolbethanderson.com. I'd love to hear from you!

And again . . . thank you for reading. You're even better than cookies and cream ice cream.

-Beth

P.S. That whole thing up there about reviewing this book, ordering the next one, and downloading a free deleted scene? Well, what are you waiting for? Do it!

PREVIEW OF FACING THE GRAY

SUN-BLESSED TRILOGY BOOK 2

RELIN: I consider myself a man of culture. Yet when my sword slices through the air and imbeds itself into one of my enemies, I feel a thrill my civilized pursuits have never offered me.

-*From* Relin: A Play in Three Acts *by Hestina Arlo*

She couldn't get enough air.

The fight had proceeded nonstop for several minutes. Her adversary was larger than her in every way: nearly a foot taller, with longer limbs, broader shoulders and bigger muscles. Her quick footwork and dodges had kept her out of his reach for long enough to make them both breathless and tired. And that was just what she'd wanted to do. If it were a matter of strength, he would prevail every time. But when they had each reached the end of their energy, determination became the greater factor. And Tavi Malin was determined.

She drew closer. Keeping her eyes on his, she snapped her foot out, kicking the inside of his knee. He wasn't expecting it, and she used the distraction to step in further, aiming a punch into his gut.

He took the punch, recovering so quickly that before she could step away, his arms were around her, gripping the back of her shirt and pulling her in to take her down. Quick as a blink, Tavi relaxed her knees, her hips dropping. An image blinked into her mind: herself as a slippery fish in his grasp. It wasn't enough; he still had her. She thrust her forearm into his chin, pushing it toward the sky.

It worked. His head snapped back, he let go of her shirt, and his arms loosened their hold. Tavi slipped out of his grip, but she wasn't fast enough to avoid his long reach. His right hand grabbed her left shoulder, squeezing tight.

Before he could pull her close again, Tavi's left hand shot up, grasping the underside of the arm that held her. In one movement, she twisted in, bringing her back against his chest. Taking advantage of her momentum, she bent at the waist and pulled his arm. His feet left the ground, and he flew over her, landing on his back in front of her with a smack and a groan.

Tavi stared at him, her only movement the rapid rise and fall of her chest. She had thrown him as if he weighed nothing. She had done it.

Cheers and laughter snapped Tavi back to reality. She approached her adversary and extended a hand.

"That'll leave a bruise," Tullen said as he grasped her hand and pulled himself up. Despite his words, he was smiling.

"I sure hope so," Tavi replied. "If you're bruised, you can't pretend it didn't happen." She didn't even try to suppress her grin. Other trainees surrounded them, congratulating Tavi and giving Tullen some good-natured ribbing.

The tenor voice of Safety Officer Les Andisis rose above the ruckus. "Sall and Stara, you're up next." Taking the cue, Tavi, Tullen, and the others stepped off the fighting mat while Sall and Stara walked to the middle of it.

With Tullen to her left and her cousin Narre to her right, Tavi watched her friend Sall, who was uncomfortable fighting, despite months of practice. He shook the hand of the trainee in front of him. Stara was the youngest magical trainee in Oren, a speech-blessed girl just eleven years old. She was of average build, but stronger than she looked. *This should be a good match*, Tavi thought.

As the fighters circled each other, Tavi felt a tap on her shoulder. She turned. Officer Andisis beckoned her.

Once they were a dozen steps away, the safety officer spoke in a low, firm voice. "You know my rule, stay away from the fancy moves. You could've hurt yourself, throwing him like that. There're plenty of other ways you could've taken him down."

Tavi's head dropped, and she tried to drum up some remorse, but it was hard. It had been the most fun she'd had in weeks. "Yes, sir," she said.

"Where'd you learn that, anyway?"

Tavi looked up and bit her lip.

"Where?"

"When Officer Lavvin was here one day, he showed us."

"Hmm. I'll have a talk with him." Officer Andisis gave her a stern look. "Don't do it again, Tavi. Beat your adversary the easiest way you can. This isn't a show. When you're in a real fight, all you'll care about is walking away safe." Tavi nodded, not breaking her eye contact with him. She caught the twitch in his eye and at the edge of his lip before he said, "Bet it felt good, though, didn't it?"

Tavi tried to keep a straight face. "Yes, sir."

He gestured toward the mat, where Sall and Stara still circled each other. "Let's watch this fight."

After the day's scheduled matches, the trainees entered the midwife house. Greeted with the cries of a woman in labor, they tiptoed up the stairs. Nydine, their meditation teacher, was waiting.

"Lay out your mats, please, and stand in position," As her students situated themselves, Nydine's face wrinkled in disgust. "An entire class of trainees who have been sweating outside for the last three quarters of an hour. I may need to talk with Ellea about the order in which she schedules our summer classes."

Despite the stuffy, malodorous room, meditation class was just what Tavi needed. By the end, her aggression had fled, and her limbs felt relaxed and loose. Afterward, all the female trainees stayed in the room to change back into their dresses.

When the Golds—Tavi, Tullen, Narre, Sall, and Misty—had returned home from Savala nine months earlier, tales from their trip had quickly spread. Tavi and Narre had both escaped after being captured by the Grays, practitioners of gray magic whose gifts were free from the moral restrictions of ordinary magic. No one knew how the Grays would use their power, but everyone agreed it was dangerous, and an undercurrent of panic had entered the town of Oren.

Ellea Kariana, Oren's head midwife and leader of the town's magical training program, had been particularly concerned. It hadn't taken long for Tavi and her friends to convince their teacher to incorporate physical fighting into the training schedule. And Ellea had declared that if the young women under her tutelage were to fight, they would wear pants, without a skirt on top.

Tavi groaned as she pulled her dress over her head, already missing the pants she had just taken off. She buttoned up Narre's dress, then allowed Narre to return the favor. "One of these days," Tavi said, "I'm going to walk out of the midwife house in my pants and wear them all the way home."

"I don't think Ellea would stop you from leaving," Narre said. "But—"

"But my father might stop me from entering the house," Tavi interjected.

"And my mother would do the same," Narre agreed. They put their pants and shirts in a dirty laundry basket before leaving the room.

Ellea was standing in the hallway. "Tavi, may I please have a word with you in my office?"

"Sure." Tavi told Narre goodbye and followed the midwife downstairs.

Once they were seated in the comfortable office, Ellea said, "I'd like to update you on what's happening in Savala."

Tavi leaned forward. "Have any of the Grays been arrested?"

Ellea frowned. "Unfortunately, no. The safety officers in Savala say they can find no evidence corroborating our story of Narre's abduction. I have a hard time believing the Grays covered their tracks so thoroughly, but there seems to be nothing else to be done on that front for now.

"However, Pala has settled into her new position as a midwife in Savala. I suspect she asked to transfer there specifically so she could learn more about the Grays. She's very concerned about them, and she's become a bit of an armchair detective."

"What has she told you?"

Ellea unfolded a letter and glanced down at it. "You mentioned visiting the house of Konner Burrell?" When Tavi nodded, Ellea continued. "Pala met a young man who works as a gardener at Mr. Burrell's house, and she employed him to work as the midwife house's errand boy a few hours each week. His name is Evitt, and he's agreed to gather information for Pala."

Tavi's face broke into a smile. "That's wonderful! What has he told her?"

"Very little so far," Ellea said. "He's only identified two of the Grays at the house: Konner and Ash. Now that he knows what to look for, we hope he'll find a way to get inside the house and gather more information."

"I hope so too," Tavi said. "Thank you for telling me this, Ellea."

The midwife gave Tavi a sad smile, covering her student's hand with her own. "I'd prefer not to share it with you, because I want you to stay safe. But your trip to Savala made it clear that I can't protect you. Your magic, Tavi—it continues to grow stronger. As much as I would like to keep you safe in Oren, I know you'll be needed in the fight against the Grays. And you'll need all the information you can get if you are to succeed."

An unexpected lump filled Tavi's throat, and she swallowed past it. "Thank you."

Ellea nodded, pulling her hand away from Tavi's. "You may tell your friends and your sister as well. I'm guessing when the time comes to confront the Grays, you'll all be together."

Tavi grinned. "I'm guessing you're right."

Ellea dismissed her, and Tavi picked up her satchel before walking to the front door. When she opened it Tullen, Sall, and Narre were waiting at the bottom of the steps.

Tavi's reaction upon seeing them was a twinge of annoyance. Well, it was more than a twinge. And it was more than annoyance. "You could have gone home without me," she snapped as she strode past her friends.

Three sets of footsteps caught up to her. "We don't like this any more than you do," Narre said. "But it's how things are for now."

A huff was Tavi's only response. The four of them walked along the dirt road for two silent minutes.

After confronting the Grays in Savala, Tavi had been relieved to return home. But her parents had been frightened that the Grays would come to Oren for her. Narre's parents had been even more panicked than Tavi's. The Grays had held Narre for weeks, and Tavi had almost expected her Uncle Shem and Aunt Jilla to lock Narre in her room forever, just to keep her safe. Instead, Narre's parents had declared their daughter could not be in public alone, and Tavi's parents had adopted the same policy. Sall lived with Tavi's family, and the rules applied to him too. However, the lack of independence didn't seem to bother Narre or Sall half as much as it did Tavi.

Tavi crossed her arms and kicked the dirt on the road as she walked, fuming over the injustice of it all. Despite fear and uncertainty, she had traveled to Savala and helped her cousin escape. The very next day, Tavi had herself escaped from the Grays by using her magic in more powerful ways than ever before. When she'd left Savala, she had felt as though she could conquer the world. And had her courage and competence earned her greater trust? No, she had instead been rewarded by the hovering of three friends who'd turned into mother hens.

Tullen was the first to speak up, and though Tavi wasn't looking at him, she could hear his smile. "Tavi, I know you'd have preferred to walk home alone, but what if someone were to attack us? We're depending on you to pick up our attackers and hurl them to the ground."

Tavi's rebellious mouth insisted on smiling at that image. She glanced at Tullen. "I might not be as easy on them as I was on you."

That broke the tension, and all four of them laughed. Tavi tried to hold onto her frustration, but it fled like a bird freed from its cage. As she took a deep breath of the mild summer air, she realized she was still smiling. *It's too nice of a day to stew over my lack of independence.*

Tavi would have loved the freedom of walking home alone, probably would have danced the whole way. But this was life, at least for now. She grasped Tullen's hand, linking her fingers in his, and they continued to walk down the dusty road.

Order *Facing the Gray* today!

ABOUT THE AUTHOR

Carol Beth Anderson is a native of Arizona and now lives in Leander, TX, outside Austin. She has a husband, two kids, a miniature schnauzer, and more fish than anyone knows what to do with. Besides writing, she loves baking sourdough bread, knitting, and eating cookies and cream ice cream.

facebook.com/carolbethanderson

twitter.com/CBethAnderson

instagram.com/CBethAnderson

ACKNOWLEDGMENTS

For decades, I said I wanted to write a book. At some point, I kind of gave up on the idea . . . but it turns out the dream wasn't dead, just dormant. One day, I decided maybe it was time. I sat down and started brainstorming, and *voila* (I think that's French for "insert about a million in-between steps), here we are!

Writing books can be a solitary pursuit, but getting to the point of publishing certainly isn't. So many people contributed to the creation of the book you're holding. Typing their names on this page isn't thanks enough, but at least it's a start!

A lot of people read portions of the book in its early phases. I called these "alpha readers." Special thanks to my mom Cathy Norris, my sister Becki Norris, and my friends Toni Wall and Kerry Ognenoff for all of their early feedback. If it wasn't for them, Tavi's birth story might have been way more graphic. Some of you would have liked that; others of you are now contemplating sending my alpha readers thank you notes! My kids Ana and Eli acted as "alpha listeners." They listened to me read the book aloud as I finished chapters. It was great fun, and I also got good feedback from their brilliant brains!

Beta readers read the completed manuscript and gave feedback that turned out to be monumentally helpful. In fact, I did two rounds of beta reading, because I made so many changes due to the feedback I got in the first round. Massive thanks go to beta readers Dick Carroll, Kim Decker, Brenda Elliott, Matthew Fleming, Charee Harrison (my "first super-fan"), Leah Hodges, Melissa Lavaty, Kathryn E. Lee, Sarah E Lentz, Sheri Mayo, my twin sister Becki Norris, Alex Pollnow, DeDe Pollnow, Renee Thompson, Jeff Shaevel, Toni Wall, and Nicole Wells.

When writing a fantasy book, it can be hard to make up a bunch of character names. So I asked my newsletter subscribers *(psst...sign up for the newsletter at carolbethanderson.com)* to submit ideas. Special thanks to the folks whose suggestions were used in the book. I'll list the name of the person who gave each suggestion, followed by the character name(s) they suggested in parentheses. Thanks to Dennis Coonrad (Zagada), Deann Flores (Jenevy), Shelia Keiser (Brindi, Quint), Jonah Kramer (Maizum), Linda Kramer (Nem), Leah Hodges (Tisra), Sheri Mayo (Sessar, Kehl), Tracy Mercer (Rawley), Monique Nadeau (Kley, Nydine, Rolki, Aba), and my aunt Dironda Thurlow (Kale). The book is more interesting thanks to these fantastic names!

Thank you to Madysun Waldrop for sending me my first ever fan art.

Thank you to Dennis Coonrad for encouraging me to create audiobooks.

Thank you to Toni Wall, for coming up with my publishing company name.

Thank you to my insightful, knowledgeable, cheerleading editor, Sonnet Fitzgerald.

Thank you to my talented, creative cover designer, Mariah Sinclair.

Thank you to my husband Jason and our kids Ana and Eli for putting up with my obsessiveness and long hours!

Thank you to the midwives at the Austin Area Birthing Center for inspiring so much of this series. You walked with me through the births of two children, showing me that *care* can be the most important part of medical care. Pregnancy and childbirth are personal, miraculous, emotional, and at times confusing and painful. You held my hand every step of the way.

Thank you to my friends who encourage me to be vulnerable, let me be me, and remind me of this truth: *I am enough.*

Thank you to God, the ultimate Creative One who shared a little ember of His creativity with me.

And you—yes, you, the one reading this—thank you! It's an honor to have your eyes on my words.

-Carol Beth Anderson
Leander, Texas, 2018

CPSIA information can be obtained
at www.ICGtesting.com
Printed in the USA
BVHW03s1514111018
529810BV00021B/40/P